"Call me whatever you wish. I am at your service, and I will be whatever and whomever you wish me to be tonight."

Isobel stared at Blackwood, melting with desire. Surely she was dreaming. She couldn't bear to look away, afraid he'd dissolve into mist.

"I shall call you Thomas," she said brightly, attempting to lighten the dangerous situation. "I once had a cat named Thomas."

He frowned. "You wish to name me for a cat? You should know that my price is far higher than a tidbit of fish tossed from your plate."

"And what would your price be, my lord?"

He leaned forward to whisper in her ear. "Your all, my lady, and nothing less."

She forced a little laugh. "If you ask me, most of the gentlemen of the *ton* live like tomcats. They sleep all day, prowl all night, and fight over females. And they are inconsiderate lovers."

He tipped his head and grinned like a cat, wide and slow. "On the contrary, sweetheart. I am a very considerate lover."

Heaven help her, she was lost.

"Prove it," she dared him.

Secrets OF A Proper Countess

LECIA CORNWALL

WITHDRAWN

AVON
An Imprint of HarperCollins*Publishers*

AVON BOOKS
An Imprint of HarperCollins*Publishers*
10 East 53rd Street
New York, New York 10022-5299

First Avon Books mass market printing: April 2011

Avon Trademark Reg. U.S. Pat. Off. and in Other Countries, Marca Registrada, Hecho en U.S.A.
HarperCollins® is a registered trademark of HarperCollins Publishers.

Printed in the U.S.A.

10 9 8 7 6 5 4 3 2 1

*To Stephen, Griffin and Olivia, and in
memory of Mary, wordsmith extraordinaire*

Secrets
OF A
Proper Countess

Chapter 1

Isobel Maitland, the Countess of Ashdown, was staring at the man like a three-penny whore. She should have been ashamed of herself, since she could not afford to be caught doing something even as mildly shocking as gazing at a handsome gentleman at a ball.

But she was standing in the shadows in the corner of Evelyn Renshaw's crowded ballroom, hidden behind the mask that covered most of her face. She felt perfectly invisible, and she was most definitely enjoying the view.

The gentleman in her sights was tall, lean, and handsome, with a trim athletic body built for every single one of the sins he was reputedly guilty of. Beneath his black half-mask, Isobel watched his eyes glitter as he spoke to the coterie of adoring females who surrounded him. He grinned, a flash of teeth and dimples deep enough to drown in, and she felt her heart flutter, then turn to stone as one of his admirers pressed her ample bosom against his arm.

In Isobel's opinion as a voyeur and a woman, his mouth was the most fascinating thing about him. She watched his lips quirk and grin and ripple as he charmed the mesmerized clutch of costumed ladies, and felt her own lips twitch in response. She couldn't hear him all the way across the room but could tell that the conversation was wicked. A lady's blush, a flutter of a fan against a hot cheek, a gape, the pucker of a painted mouth, gave everything away. The rogue just grinned at the discomfiture he was causing, one corner of that mouth turned up irresistibly.

Isobel knew exactly who the gentleman was, despite his mask, and she'd heard all the tittle-tattle about where his sinful lips had ventured, and what that firm, smirking, thoroughly masculine mouth was capable of. She'd admired him from the shadows at other social events, even imagined flirting with him, but had never dared to stare at him in such a blatant fashion before tonight. She ran her finger along the stiff lace that trimmed her mask, glad for the disguise.

Phineas Archer, the Marquess of Blackwood, was notorious, titled, wealthy, and thoroughly dangerous to a lady's sense of decorum. His illustrious family name, his grandsire's vast wealth and his status as England's most eligible bachelor, kept him acceptable to polite company despite his reputation. Blackwood's credentials made the *ton* willing to turn a blind eye to his "adventures." Especially now, with the London Season newly begun, and a fresh crop of debutantes being herded into Town to find husbands, Blackwood was in hot demand.

Still, Isobel could see that he was out of place in Evelyn's elegant ballroom. He had rough edges, despite his fine breeding and excellent tailoring. It was something dangerous in his eyes, she decided, or perhaps the way his gaze constantly scanned the room like a predator on the hunt.

Blackwood leaned in to whisper something in a lady's ear, and she swayed in response. He caught her elbow in a practiced move to keep the chit from swooning. Isobel smiled.

He was *very* good at playing the rake.

If she were the kind of woman who gambled—and she most certainly was not—she would wager that Blackwood's name topped every dreamy-eyed debutante's list of potential husbands. Of course, every matchmaking mama believed it would be *her* sweet, virginal daughter who would capture, shackle, and tame the wicked marquess at last. Realistically, the mamas, if not their starry-eyed daughters, knew that if an innocent bride failed to satisfy his wild ways, she'd at least have her husband's wealth to console her and convince her to turn a blind eye to his scandals.

From where Isobel was standing, well back in the shadows, she secretly thought it would be a great pity indeed if the devilish, elegant, carefree marquess was curbed.

She wondered if it was even possible.

Tales of his escapades made anything that appeared on the stage at Covent Garden seem dull by comparison. The gossip he created was a sinful pleasure to take with afternoon tea in London's finest drawing rooms. Isobel hung on every word, savored every story, though she feigned the same indignation and indifference as every other respectable lady, while her toes curled in her shoes.

Beneath the cerise silk of her mask, she shut her eyes and smiled, letting her deliciously wicked little thoughts have their way with her. Those shoulders, the way he moved, it was all quite—

"Have we met?"

She opened her eyes.

The Marquess of Blackwood was standing right in front of her.

Up close, he was taller, broader, more dangerously male than she'd realized. Her heart kicked into a fast trot, and a hot flush swept over her from her toes to her hairline. She looked around, but thankfully no one was looking back.

"You were staring," he added, ignoring the fact that she was too stunned to speak. His tone was playful, his voice deep and sensual. It vibrated across some tightly drawn string inside her.

She felt as if he'd caught her naked.

She stared at the curious, amused little smile on his face and the dimple in his chin. His lips curved into a deeper grin, and she knew he recognized her affliction for what it was. The knowing eyes behind his mask were fixed on her wide-open mouth, which was painted a sinful scarlet to match her costume.

She shut it with an audible snap and drew herself together.

It wasn't possible that he could have recognized her, since they had never actually met. He had never so much as *glanced* in her direction at the few social events where they were both present. As a prim and respectable widow, she was hardly his type.

There were strict rules governing her behavior, carefully noted in her husband's will, and enforced by her mother-in-law. Fortunately, Honoria despised costume balls, and was not here. Besides, while her mother-in-law might control her life, she could hardly control her thoughts, and this wasn't the first time she'd let her mind roam where her hands could not go where Blackwood was concerned.

While wicked thoughts were harmless enough, he was now standing before her, grinning, waiting for her to say something.

"I—" Isobel swallowed hard and considered. She should flee without another word, but the possibilities of remaining intrigued her. What harm could there be in flirting with the handsome rogue for a few moments before someone else caught his eye?

How long had it been since she'd seen a gleam of appreciation like that in a gentleman's eyes? Her husband had been dead for two years, and even before that— She bit her lip.

This could be her only chance to flirt, to feel pretty and admired. Who would know if she enjoyed a few brief moments basking in the warm glow of such a harmless pleasure?

Dozens of ladies flirted. Why shouldn't she? She squared

her shoulders, met his gaze, and let anonymity make her bold.

"No, we have not met, sir. But is that not the point of a masquerade ball? Enjoying the mystery of not knowing to whom you are speaking until the unmasking?"

He chuckled, a low, seductive sound that flicked a fingernail over her nerves, already stretched taut in awareness of him.

"Yet is unmasking not a most unfortunate exercise?" he replied. "At midnight, we will all congratulate each other on our clever costumes and feel naught but disappointment when Cleopatra turns out to be Lady Dalrymple, squeezed into a tight corset and wearing too much paint. Better to remain masked, I say. More tantalizing."

His eyes roamed over her, slowly taking her measure from head to toe, and she forced herself to stand perfectly still. Under her silk tunic, her nipples tightened.

"Your costume is a triumph, if I may say so, my lady. I don't think I've ever seen one like it before."

Isobel stroked the damask lapel of her long, form-fitting Turkish vest, which modestly covered the flowing silk of the undertunic and baggy harem pants from neck to calf. The movement made the tiny bells hidden along the hemlines ring softly. She felt pretty and even desirable in his company, rare emotions for her. They coursed through her veins like champagne bubbles, intoxicating her.

"Thank you, my lord, but I must point out that your own costume is rather lacking in originality."

He wore a black domino and a plain mask over regular evening dress, though he'd at least gone to the effort of strapping on a rather ornate antique sword. The weapon lay along his hip and thigh, emphasizing his height, glittering with precious stones set into the hilt and scabbard.

He bowed. "Indeed. You are quite correct, of course, but

I decided to attend this party at the last possible moment. I borrowed the mask and domino from an actress I know rather well. The sword belonged to one of my ancestors. I took it straight off the wall, strapped it on, and ordered my coach in this direction." He flashed his rogue's grin at her again. "Now I'm glad I did."

She smiled back, knowing the mask covered her blush as well as it hid her identity, and the embroidered slippers hid the way her toes curled in delight.

"I suppose I should ask you if you'd care to dance, or if you'd like a glass of lemonade, or . . ." He bowed low over her hand and lifted it to his lips, his eyes never leaving hers. " . . . perhaps a stroll in the garden?" Even to a sheltered widow like Isobel, his meaning couldn't have been clearer. She read it in the hot gaze that licked over her from behind his mask, and in the slow circles his thumb was tracing over her palm as he raised her fingers to his lips once more.

She plucked her hand from his, and let herself be more brazen still. "Sir, you must have mistaken me for someone else! If you knew anything about me at all, you'd know I much prefer champagne to lemonade, and a stroll in the gardens will not offer you any opportunities to steal a kiss. Lady Evelyn keeps her gardens extremely well lit during her parties to prevent such liberties." She saw appreciation in his eyes for her wit. It warmed every silk-clad inch of her.

He offered his arm. "Then let's find some champagne, and after that . . ." He leaned in close to her ear, letting his voice tickle, his words excite. "After that we shall see about extinguishing a few burning brands in the garden."

The whispered suggestion sent a delicious little shiver up her spine.

She should run to the shelter of Evelyn's sane and impeccably moral company, or excuse herself and flee to the ladies' withdrawing room until she was more herself. But she didn't.

Tonight she wanted to be anyone but Isobel, the frumpy widowed Countess of Ashdown, the woman no man had ever looked at the way Blackwood was looking at her now. It was dangerous, exhilarating, and impossible to resist.

She laid her hand on the fine wool of his sleeve, gave him an alluring smile meant to suggest she did this all the time, and let him lead her astray.

Chapter 2

Phineas couldn't imagine who the lady might be, or why she was standing like a sentinel in the shadowed doorway of Philip Renshaw's study.

He knew every other female in the room. In fact, he could probably identify most of them in the dark if he had to, just by touch, or scent, or taste alone.

He'd spent an hour waiting for her to move away so he could do what he came for and search the study, but she had stayed put, watching him from her corner, her gaze like a caress.

She was not the kind of woman who usually captured his interest. He liked his bedmates as notorious as himself, married, preferably, so there was no risk of permanent entanglement. In this woman, he sensed a reticence that made her irresistible.

She was a distraction he didn't need tonight, but one he couldn't ignore, since she was in his way.

He let his gaze glide over her again. Her costume was a marvel, though it was not low cut or revealing. In fact, it had a high-necked collar and a forbidding row of tiny pearl buttons that locked the tunic tight as a strongbox over the tempting swell of her breasts. It was a garment meant to deter even the most stalwart attempts to reach the flesh beneath. It made him itch to try.

It was not just the uniqueness of the costume. It was the

way the lady wore it, the way she moved like flowing water, that gave the impression that somehow she was more feminine, more alluring, than any other woman in the room.

Behind her half mask, her eyes sparkled without coyness, and didn't give away so much as a clue about her identity. Even her hair was completely covered by an embroidered cap and a veil, and he could not guess the color of it. Her painted lips were mobile, expressive, and his mouth watered to taste her, though he couldn't tell if she was beautiful or not. No, he was very certain he did not know her, but he wanted to.

Badly, and for a variety of reasons.

They stood sipping champagne in fluted crystal glasses, flirting under the guise of idle banter. It was making Phineas sweat. Still, he was a man who knew how to bide his time, and use every tool—especially idle banter—to seduce a woman. He was confident that he'd have what he wanted before the evening was over—both the charms of the luscious lady and her identity, should she prove worthy of future attentions.

"Look—Caesar is Sir John Unwin, don't you agree?" he asked.

"Indeed, but the lady dancing with him is not his wife. I know Primrose Unwin quite well," she replied tartly.

"So do I," he drawled. She shot him a quick look, and blushed and lowered her eyes again when he grinned. So she wasn't an experienced flirt. It made the situation all the more interesting. "I believe Unwin's partner is Davina St. Claire, though she probably has no idea that her Caesar is Unwin," he continued. He'd know the heart-shaped mole on Davina's lush breast anywhere, and her low-cut costume did very little to hide her charms. Unwin was drooling on the mole.

The lady by his side regarded him with delight. "Why, my lord, I do believe you know more gossip than even the best informed tea party of society tabbies!"

"Perhaps, but in my defense I also know how to keep a

secret, Lady . . . um, what should I call you, my dear?" he asked.

She tilted her head and considered, pursing her lips in a way that had him instantly aroused. "Yasmina will do, I think. It is in keeping with my disguise." She drawled the exotic name, and regarded him with a playful little smirk that he read as a dare. "And what would you like to be called, my lord?"

Phineas grinned. "I can think of any number of things. But since my disguise is minimal, I suggest you call me by my name. I am—"

She put a finger to his lips before he could reveal himself. She had to step closer to do it. So close she almost leaned against him. He tensed. He could slip a hand around her waist, open the door and take them both inside Renshaw's office in the guise of seduction. It was a ploy he'd often used before. But he could smell her perfume, light, sweet, and exotic. It shot a bolt of pure lust straight to his groin and drove every sensible thought from his brain.

"Not your real name, sir! It would spoil the illusion," she admonished. Her finger was soft, cool against his mouth, and he caught her wrist to keep it there. He flicked his tongue over the tip of the delicate digit, a light, moist, sensual caress, while his eyes held hers. He watched her mouth go slack, saw how she caught her bottom lip between white teeth. Her eyes drifted shut for a moment, and he noted the way her breasts rose and fell in heated agitation.

If one small touch could do that, one little lick—he felt his body harden in anticipation, and he swallowed a groan. He turned her hand over and touched his tongue to the pulse point at her wrist, reveling in her sharp intake of breath.

"Call me whatever you wish, my lady—Lancelot, or Tristan, or Romeo. Anything will do." His eyes burned into hers from behind his mask. "I am at your service, and I will be whatever and whomever you wish me to be tonight."

Isobel stared at him, spellbound. The room wavered and spun, and all she could see was him, all she could feel was the heat from his eyes, his body. She was melting with desire. Surely she was dreaming. She would wake up in her widow's weeds at Maitland House and realize she'd imagined the whole encounter.

She couldn't bear to look away, afraid he'd dissolve into mist and leave her shivering in the cold disappointment of reality.

Someone jostled her as they passed and broke the spell. She lowered her gaze to their joined hands, and pulled away, clasping her tingling fingertips. She drew herself up and looked him straight in the chin.

"I know," she said brightly, attempting to lighten the dangerous situation. "I shall call you Thomas. I once had a cat named Thomas. He would be quite companionable when prevailed upon, but diplomatically absented himself when he was not wanted." It was certainly a description that fit Blackwood well.

He frowned. "You wish to name me for a cat? You should know that I dislike the beasts intensely, and my price is far higher than a tidbit of fish or fowl tossed from your plate, Lady Yasmina."

Isobel picked up her champagne from the table and sipped it. Her hand shook, and the sparkling wine did little to soothe her nerves. Had she offended him? It didn't matter. This was an anonymous flirtation. She could say anything behind her mask.

She teased him with a saucy stare. "And what would your price be, my lord?"

He leaned forward to whisper in her ear. "Your all, my lady, and nothing less."

Her body throbbed. She was out of her depth. She forced

a little laugh, and strove to return to lighter repartee, where she had some control. "If you ask me, most of the gentlemen of the *ton* live like tomcats. They sleep all day, prowl all night, and fight over mice and females. Their fine fur is of great importance to them, and they are indifferent fathers and inconsiderate lovers."

He tipped his head to one side and grinned like a cat, wide and slow. She was his nervous prey, and that look offered her no quarter. "On the contrary, sweetheart. I am a very considerate lover," he purred.

Heaven help her, she was lost. Perhaps it was the champagne. Perhaps it was the disguise. Perhaps it was his heart-stopping proximity, the heat that rose from him, or the faint scents of rich soap, fine wool, and male skin. Or maybe it was her desire to feel loved, if only for a moment. What if this was her only chance?

"Prove it," she dared him.

The next moment his hand was under her elbow and he was leading her with desperate haste through the costumed throngs toward the open doors that led to the garden.

He didn't say a word, and neither did she, though she knew where he was taking her and what he intended to do when they got there. She should protest, or pull away, no, *run* away before she did something regrettable, but she went with him, down the torch-lit pathways of Lady Evelyn's elegant garden.

They reached a small Chinese pavilion by the fishpond. He let go of her only long enough to seize the nearest torches, pulling them out of the soft earth and casting them into the pond, where they expired with a hiss of protest, leaving the two of them in deep, velvety darkness.

He was beside her, unseen, his arms enfolding her, his mouth on hers, hungry and demanding. She met him kiss for kiss, sparring with his tongue as if she'd done this a thousand times, was an old hand at sexual adventures in dark gardens.

He lifted her off her feet, still kissing her, and carried her into the pavilion. It felt too good to stop, and she surrendered, pressing against the hard length of him, feeling his desire, letting it fuel her own.

A night bird gave a frightened cry as they entered, and flapped away into the night, and she gasped in surprise, sure she was caught, but he captured her indrawn breath in his mouth and laid her on the cushioned bench.

Heavens, she'd taken tea with Evelyn on this very bench only last week. Was it on Tuesday? She couldn't remember. Didn't care. He was working on the buttons of her caftan, exposing her flesh to the chill night air and the heavenly warmth of his hands on her bare skin.

He kissed her, devoured her, and her hands tangled in the fabric of his shirt, holding him to her, needing more. His mouth was so hot, so sweet, and she couldn't imagine anything more delicious than his kiss. She could not have stopped kissing him if she wanted to. She was drugged, intoxicated and bewitched.

He trailed his mouth down her throat while he opened more of the pearl buttons ahead of his questing tongue and teeth. Isobel was hard-pressed to keep up, her own fingers inexpert and shaking as she fumbled with his cravat, trying to undress him as he undressed her.

She gave up with a sigh as he opened the caftan, pushed away the filmy silk undertunic and drew her nipple into his hungry mouth. The sensation drove the last clear thoughts from Isobel's mind. She wanted him, all of him, all at once.

He might be a notorious rake who'd done this a thousand times with a thousand women, but at this moment he was her rake. All hers. She felt her power surge, heightening her desire, and she writhed beneath him, moaning and murmuring wicked things.

She let her hands roam over his back until they found the

place where his shirt met his breeches. She tugged, needing to feel his skin under her hands. She briefly wondered
where his cloak and jacket had gone, but it didn't matter. It
must be magic. She had never felt like this before, never been
so wanton, so desperate. She wanted pleasure *now*, and she
meant to have it.

Her hands found flesh, and she explored the damp silk
of his skin, the fascinating flex and play of his muscles. His
body was marvelous, male perfection. The scent of his skin
poured over her, intoxicating her far beyond anything the
champagne had done.

She pressed her mouth to his chest, trying to taste him,
hampered by his shirt. It was tangled in his breeches, and
the sword belt still fastened around his hips. The fabric was
caught on one of the ancient jewels in the hilt, resisting her.
She muttered in dismay. She felt his heart pounding under
her lips, felt the breath singing through his body as his muscles tensed in pleasure at what she was doing. She found his
nipple and bit gently, then sucked the hard pebble through the
fine linen of his shirt, hearing him gasp for breath.

Boldly, she reached beneath the waistband of his breeches
and caressed the hard muscles of his buttocks. His hips
strained against hers, his hardness pressing against her body.
It felt delicious, even through layers of clothing. She was soft
where he wasn't, yielding where he advanced. She spread her
thighs, cradling him between them, welcoming the pressure,
the pulsations of pleasure. He fumbled with the sword, cursing it, trying to unbuckle it, failing. With a grunt he shoved it
out of the way, still fastened to his hip. It banged against the
bench, adding cadence to their rhythmic movements.

Isobel was wild with wanting.

She thrust her hand between their bodies, seeking the
opening of his breeches, but the sword belt was once again
in her way. Frustrated, she had no memory of how buttons

or buckles worked, only knew that she needed to touch him, to feel him without the barrier of his clothing.

She tugged, and the buttons from his breeches clattered on the wooden floor of the pavilion.

She shoved the fabric open, past the damnable sword belt, now clasped around his naked hips, found his erection and took it in her hand, feeling the hard, hot velvet throb of him. He groaned and thrust against her palm, drawing breath through his teeth. He was suckling her breast, murmuring incoherently, his hand exploring the curves of her body, finding places she hadn't even known existed before he touched them. She arched upward, reaching for the hard, hot shadow of him as he loomed above her.

"Inside," she muttered. "Come inside me."

He kissed her mouth, smiling against her lips, as breathless as she was.

"Not yet, sweetheart," he said. He laughed softly when she whimpered and squirmed restlessly beneath him. She was on fire, desperate for release.

He returned to suckling her nipple in the most annoyingly leisurely fashion. When she moaned, wishing he'd do that forever, he switched to the other side. The night breeze cooled her heated skin, and she gasped when he took the sensitive flesh back into the heat of his incredible mouth again.

She dug her nails into his shoulders, trying to draw him to her, too far gone for words. His hand slid over her body, slipping past the ribbon ties of her loose trousers with expert ease. She writhed as his palm descended over her belly and hips with infuriating slowness to caress the curls between her thighs. Maddeningly, he paused above the place she needed him most, teasing and tormenting her. Helpless, she arched her hips and drew his mouth down to hers, biting and sucking at his tongue and lips, hearing his breath turn to grunts of suppressed desire.

Her hand found his erection again, and she explored a male body with complete abandon for the first time in her life. Slick moisture oozed from the tip, and she rolled her thumb over the head, making him pant. His fingers still hovered, merely tickling the delicate lips of her sex, caressing her with the lightest possible strokes when she needed pressure and friction.

Just as desire was becoming frustration, he touched her. His fingers found the spot where she wanted him most. She arched her back and cried out, but he was ready for that. He caught her moan in his mouth and continued to circle the wild, wet bud with his fingers, taking her beyond madness to a place of such absolute pleasure she thought she would die without it, or perhaps die *of* it. She had no idea, but she never wanted it to stop.

He plunged his fingers inside her, working her, pleasing her, until she could stand no more. She grasped the damp wrinkled linen of his shirt and sobbed for breath.

He positioned himself and drove into her as she climaxed once more, sending her soaring even higher in that instant. Her body rippled around his, drawing him in, enveloping him. She seemed to fly forever, the hard thrust of his body into hers driving her back to the heavens whenever she began to descend to the earth.

By the time he groaned and arched into her one last time, she was spent, exhausted and sated with pleasure.

Blackwood held her as they caught their breath, and caressed her gently, drawing his cloak over the disarray of their clothing, keeping the cool night air off her sweat-soaked skin. He cupped her chin and turned her head so he could kiss her gently, his movements slow and languid and delicious. She could smell her sex on his fingers, and under his expert tongue she felt desire rising again, against all odds, and she sighed and rolled her hips restlessly against his.

"I suggest we find somewhere more private for the rest of the night," he murmured in her ear, nibbling on the lobe.

Sanity hit her like cold water.

She shoved him, and he rolled off the narrow bench and crashed to the floor with a grunt of surprise, tangled and tripped up by his sword. She fumbled for the ties of her clothing and searched the dark floor for her caftan and her slippers and her mask. She cast a horrified glance at the shadowy form of him, still sitting on the floor of the pavilion, unmoving. He was baffled, no doubt, but she had to leave. If she were caught— She squeezed her eyes shut.

"Perhaps it's time we had our own unmasking," he said from the floor. "I'm Phineas Archer." She was too embarrassed, too busy fumbling with her clothes to reply. "Well? Don't you think we should be properly introduced after what just happened?" he prompted.

"No!" she gasped. "Oh, good heavens! This should *never* have happened!" She could not find her other slipper in the dark, and the clatter of the sword warned her he was getting to his feet.

Startled, she took the single slipper she had and fled in her bare feet back up the stone path as if the devil himself was on her heels. He did not call her back. She slipped into the shadows as near to the house as she dared and straightened her costume with shaking hands, her body still tingling from his lovemaking. She hastily pulled her mask into place as she entered the ballroom, and beckoned a footman to summon her coach.

Phineas listened to the retreating sound of the bells on her costume as she fled. He fumbled for his clothes, tripping only once over the damnable sword. The erotic encounter had been over too soon, but it was still early, and he had time to go inside and find what he came for. She wouldn't be guarding the door now.

He almost laughed out loud when he realized that the buttons from his breeches were gone and there was no way to close the front of his clothing. Whoever she was, she'd been one of the most passionate women he'd ever had. Unlike most of his lovers, she was ingenuous, eager to please and to be pleased. He would almost say she was a near innocent, though innocent ladies did not allow themselves to be seduced in dark gardens with two hundred people only steps away. Yet, despite the disguise, and the anonymity of the whole encounter, there was no artifice in the way she made love.

He grinned in the darkness. His mission was lost for tonight, and Lord Renshaw's secrets would remain his own for now. He wished she'd stayed a little longer. Just thinking about her had him hard again, his cock pushing hopefully through the ruined face of his breeches.

Yasmina. That's all he had, a made-up name. He shook his head, still dumbfounded, and searched the dark pavilion for his coat and his cloak. He wasn't usually so easily distracted when he had work to do, but she had been exceptionally diverting.

He found his garments easily, but the telltale buttons took a few minutes longer. A gardener or guest who found one button would hardly remark upon it. A scattering of six buttons in such a secluded spot screamed scandal. Phineas Archer was an expert at avoiding scandal.

Unless, of course, he wished to be caught.

He found the buttons and pushed them into his pocket. He pulled his cloak over his gaping breeches and turned to go, and almost tripped over something. It skittered away to hit the wall with a soft chime. He picked it up and carried it into the light. It was the lady's shoe, delicate and encrusted with pearls and embroidery, with a curled-up toe that was hung with a little bell.

Phineas tucked the souvenir into his pocket and strolled casually toward the side gate like the seasoned rake he was supposed to be, and slipped out onto Brook Street to find his coach.

Chapter 3

Phineas opened one bleary eye the next morning at the soft rustle of his valet moving around his bedroom. Burridge was holding his ruined breeches in one hand and a handful of buttons in the other. The exotic little slipper lay on the desk.

"I don't tell tales, Burridge, so don't even ask," Phineas said.

The valet grinned. "No, my lord, of course not, but I'd bet this tale would be interesting indeed."

"Never mind. I've been waiting for you to put in an appearance this morning."

The valet's eyebrows shot up into his neatly combed hairline. "My apologies, my lord, I had no idea you wanted me. Of course, any time you do, you need only ring the bell," Burridge said pointedly. He concentrated on deftly folding the ruined breeches, and Phineas knew he was hiding a smirk. Burridge probably thought he had been too drunk to even find the damned bell.

He'd spent years cultivating his image as the worst rogue in London, until even his servants believed he was. It was damned irritating at times. He played his role so expertly he hardly knew which half of his personality was the real Phineas anymore. Was he the rake, the gambler, the seducer of ladies young and old, or was he still an honorable man who just happened to handle the crown's dirty work?

Annoyed, he threw back the covers and sat up awkwardly. Burridge's eyes widened, and Phineas glared as his servant choked on a laugh, turning it into a cough.

"Just get it off, would you? It's been plaguing me for hours."

Burridge immediately came to undo the clasp that still held the sword against Phineas's hip. He fumbled for a few minutes then looked up apologetically. "I'm sorry, sir, but it appears to be stuck fast. A bit rusty, perhaps. Should we summon Mr. Crane?"

Phineas gave the belt an angry tug. The last thing he needed was his dour butler seeing him in such a state, and thinking the worst.

"No. I'll dress first, then I'll find Crane myself."

"Yes, my lord. What will you wear? Will you be going out this morning? Riding in the park, perhaps?" the valet asked as he crossed to the dressing room.

"Yes," Phineas mumbled, still fiddling with the belt. "On second thought, no. At least not until I get this damned sword off."

Half an hour later he was in the salon, dressed in fawn breeches, polished Hessians, and a crisp white linen shirt. He'd dispensed with a coat to allow his staff better access to the sword that clung to him like an eager lover who refused to be dismissed. Crane had given up after twenty minutes of undignified jiggling and tugging and suggested they send for the gardener, who arrived with an astonishing assortment of tools.

Phineas pretended to read the newspaper and tried his best to maintain his dignity while his staff knelt at his feet and worked to free him. If the ancestor who owned the sword had been present, he would have run the bastard through with it. After he'd tortured the secret of its removal out of him, of course.

A maid came in with coffee, her eyes widening at the unusual sight. Phineas watched as she set the tray down and poured, nearly overfilling the cup as she kept one eye on the activity. She sidled away at a sharp warning from Crane, only to pause near the door, her lip caught between her teeth.

"What is it?" Phineas snapped.

All eyes turned toward the girl, who bobbed a nervous curtsy. "Begging your pardon, my lord, and Mr. Crane. If I might suggest it, I think Thomas could be of assistance," she said.

Crane frowned. "The footman?"

"He had, um, special talents with locks and such before he entered service," she explained, her face reddening.

"You mean he's a picklock?" Phineas asked, and the maid blushed.

"Oh, he isn't anymore, my lord! I mean, I'm sure he still remembers a few tricks o' the trade, but he'd never ever do any such thing now, of course." She twisted her hands together. "Unless you wanted him to, and it was an order."

Crane stood. "That will do, Mary."

Phineas looked at the gardener. The man was eyeing the hatchet that lay at his feet. It was the only tool he hadn't yet tried. "Send for Thomas," Phineas said wearily, and regarded the gardener coolly. "If he fails, then you can try lopping off my leg."

When his grandfather arrived, and entered the room without being announced, Phineas was still seated in the chair, with three members of his staff kneeling at his feet, watching in fascination as Thomas the footman, former picklock, worked at the clasp of the sword belt.

"What in blazes is going on, Blackwood?" the Duke of Carrington demanded, glowering down his beaked nose at his heir. He didn't bother to say hello, and Phineas felt his gut clench, ready for another confrontation. He should have realized that no pleasure was without punishment, and Yasmina had been exactly the kind of sinful indulgence that attracted retribution.

The servants almost knocked each other over trying to rise and bow to the duke at the same time, and Crane snapped to attention. "May I announce His Grace, the Duke of Carrington?" he intoned.

"Never mind, man, I'm here already!" the duke growled.

Phineas crossed his legs casually. "Good morning, Your Grace. 'Tis only a masquerade costume gone wrong. Forgive me for not getting up."

The duke strode forward and assessed the situation. His sharp black eyes traveled over the sword, then swept up to glare at Phineas. "That's the Archer sword, you fool, not a masquerade costume! Get out of the way, all of you, before you damage it. It is a priceless family heirloom, captured at Agincourt by one of the first members of the Archer family."

Phineas had heard the tale before, of course. That Archer, who humbly shot arrows for a living, had captured a French knight in battle, and wisely kept him alive. He'd won the sword, a rich ransom, and the king's favor.

His grandfather reached for a large ruby near the hilt of the sword and pressed. The belt parted, and he caught it before it fell to the ground. The staff sighed with relief.

"Out, all of you," Carrington commanded, then turned to his grandson as they scrambled to obey. At least he waited until the door was closed, Phineas noted, before beginning his lecture.

"I suppose I should not be surprised by this. You have always treated your heritage carelessly," he began, and picked up the untouched cup of coffee and sipped. He grimaced, set it down without a word, and crossed to pull the bell. "*Hot* coffee," he ordered when the door opened almost at once. Phineas rolled his eyes. Crane had obviously been hovering, waiting for a chance to serve the duke.

"To what do I owe the rare honor of a personal visit, Your Grace?" Phineas asked. "You usually just summon me to Carrington Castle when you wish to give me a dressing-down." It was almost two years since he'd seen him last, yet his grandfather never seemed to age. He always seemed as ancient, cold, and impenetrable as the very stones of the ancestral keep, even when Phineas was a child.

Carrington's eagle eyes roamed the salon of Blackwood House, examining the heirlooms and art that decorated the walls, and stopped on the dark space on the wallpaper where the sword normally hung. He replaced it on the hooks before turning back to Phineas.

"I am here because your sister is in Town."

"Which sister, sir, Miranda or Marianne?" Phineas asked. He hadn't seen his younger sister Miranda since the duke sent her to school in Scotland, and it was months since he had a visit from his elder sister. He missed them, but circumstances forced him to stay away. They did not belong in his world, and he had not been welcome in their circle for years. He was eager for news of them, but didn't let it show.

"I'm speaking of Miranda. She's making her come-out this Season."

Phineas looked at his grandfather in surprise. "Her come-out? Surely she's too young for that. She can't be more than fourteen or fifteen at the most."

"She's eighteen!" Carrington snapped.

Phineas said nothing. How had little Miranda reached the age of eighteen without his noticing?

"Most girls come out at seventeen. I've made her wait an extra year, Blackwood, in the vain hope that you'd marry and reform before she was exposed to your disgraceful behavior. I cannot wait any longer. She is the granddaughter of a duke, and I have only one great-grandson to date. If the worst should happen to Marianne's son, and you fail in your duty to marry and get an Archer heir, it may fall to Miranda to breed the next Duke of Carrington. If I might remind you, you have a birthday of your own coming up in a few weeks. You will be thirty-two."

"I doubt you've come to wish me a happy birthday," Phineas said lightly.

He went over the long list of his most recent misdeeds in his mind. It was too soon for his grandfather to have heard about his tryst in Lady Evelyn's garden. Unless he'd spoken to Burridge on the way in, of course. He wondered how long it would be before Carrington—and all of London—knew he'd come home last night with the buttons to his breeches in his pocket.

"I've come to invite you to Miranda's debut ball," the duke said. He withdrew an envelope from his coat and tossed it on the table. Phineas picked it up and opened it, scanning the elegant engraved invitation briefly.

"Should I convey my regrets to you or Great-Aunt Augusta? I assume you do not actually wish me to attend."

"I do not," the duke confirmed. "But your sister does. Most heartily, in fact, so I've come to insist on your attendance."

"Then for Miranda's sake, I shall be there," Phineas replied stiffly.

The duke fixed him with an icy glare. "On one condition, Blackwood. I insist you curtail your whoring and gambling for the duration of Miranda's stay in London. I also expect, as I do every year, that you will avail yourself of the opportunity of being in polite company to find a suitable bride. It is past time you got an heir. If you do not, then I shall be forced to—"

"Leave every penny that's not entailed to Marianne's

son," Phineas said, completing the familiar threat. The duke scowled. They both knew it was groundless. Carrington would never destroy the wealth and power of the dukedom, no matter how much he despised Phineas. It would break four hundred years of Archer tradition.

"Don't be flippant, Blackwood. You've had your years of freedom and frivolous behavior. It is time to accept your responsibilities and think of the future. I do get the London newspapers at Carrington Castle, you know. I'm fully aware of everything you get up to."

"And I thought I was being discreet," Phineas quipped, and watched his grandfather redden dangerously. Fortunately, Crane entered with the coffee.

Phineas waited until he set the cup before Carrington. "Whisky, please, Crane," he said, and watched his butler's eyes dart to the duke for permission. "Now," he ordered, and Crane crossed the room to the decanter.

There was no point in arguing with his grandfather. Still, the situation presented a number of problems. Either White-hall or the duke was going to be very unhappy with him. He could not be rake and gentleman both. Duplicity made people suspicious, less trusting, and less talkative.

He took the tumbler of whisky Crane offered and downed it at a swallow under the duke's censorious gaze. "Another," he said.

"It's not yet ten o'clock, Blackwood," the duke said primly.

But he swallowed the second tumblerful as well. Discreet behavior was not how he did his job. This wasn't going to be easy. Or pleasant. Pleasure reminded him of the lovely Yasmina. Such encounters would be impossible if his sister was present. Still, he'd dare much to have her again, to touch her soft skin, hear that sigh, feel her nails in his flesh as he—

"Why are you grinning like that?" the duke demanded, shaking Phineas out of his erotic daydream.

"I was thinking of Miranda's debut, of course," Phineas answered.

The duke glared at him. "Well don't smile like that at her. It's most unpleasant, and I was in earnest when I said that I expect you to behave yourself while she's in Town."

Phineas got to his feet. "I'm sure someone will be providing you with regular reports of my activities once you return to Carrington Castle." He cast a pointed glance at Crane, who had the grace to blush.

The duke raised his brows at the dismissal. "I'm staying in Town. When Miranda receives an offer of marriage, I must be available. As a matter of fact, I will be staying here."

"Here?" Phineas asked, his stomach sinking. "With Great-Aunt Augusta, you mean?"

"Here," the duke replied with a thin smile. "In this house."

Chapter 4

I sobel reluctantly opened her eyes and blinked at the toast and tea that had been left on her bedside table. Both were stone cold.

She squinted at the clock on the mantel and gasped. It was nearly noon. She threw back the covers and would have shot out of bed, but every muscle in her body ached. It was a very pleasant ache, and she lay back and smiled. She felt warm, satisfied and rested, and she tried to recall the last time she had woken this late, or feeling this good, but it was something that simply had never happened before.

Blackwood!

She hadn't dreamed it. Every single caress had been gloriously real. Robert had never made her feel this way. Not even in the early days of their marriage when he still pretended to like her.

She listened for footsteps in the corridor, but the house was silent, so she burrowed back under the covers. She touched a fingertip to her mouth, marveling that she'd really dared to—she let her lips spread into a wide grin—in Evelyn's garden, for heaven's sake! She suppressed a giggle, but it bubbled out as a sigh.

Blackwood!

He'd more than lived up to his reputation, far surpassed

her wildest dreams of what it would be like to— She gasped as heat pulsed through her body, pooled in her belly, breathless at the images that flitted through her mind. His eyes, his mouth, his hands, oh, his hands! It had been a daring risk, but well worth it, she gloated. It wouldn't matter if he was discreet or not. He had no idea who she was. She grinned and stretched like a wanton cat.

Her bare foot popped out from under the covers into the cold air of her room, shocking her back to reality. What was she thinking? Her behavior had been shameful! She should never have taken a simple flirtation so far. There would be terrible consequences if Honoria found out.

Her mother-in-law would not understand that Blackwood was utterly irresistible and she had been rendered mad for one foolish instant by his smile, his eyes, his—

What had she done?

Perhaps she was just as wanton as her mother after all. With her face burning, Isobel got up and wrapped her robe around her body like protective armor, knotting the sash so tightly it nearly cut her in two. She held her breath and waited, but there were no shrieks of rage from Honoria's rooms, no pounding feet on the stairs as they came to demand an explanation for her behavior.

Not that she had one, except that it had been *Blackwood*. How could she have acted otherwise?

She gulped down a cup of cold tea to steady her nerves. She ignored the toast. She couldn't eat with her stomach in knots, her heart in a tangle, her mind and limbs mush from—

Blackwood.

She crossed to the basin to splash her face with cold water before reverie could carry her off again. It hit her like a slap, and she looked at herself in the mirror that hung above the basin. She didn't look any different. Well, her eyes were brighter, perhaps, and her cheeks rosier. Her lips looked—

well, they looked soft and plump, like she'd spent the night in a dark garden kissing someone.

Not just *someone*.

Blackwood.

She sucked her moony grin into a tight pucker and scrubbed her glowing face with a cold wet flannel.

Isobel rang the bell and waited for her maid to arrive. After a few minutes with no Sarah, she went to the wardrobe and chose a suitable dress herself, gray serge with a black edging, plainly cut and suitable for a respectable widow. Honoria had chosen it. Isobel put it on, knowing she had been anything but respectable last night.

It was over, she told herself. It would not be repeated, and the whole thing was best forgotten. She buttoned the hated half-mourning gown all the way to her chin and sighed. Such an encounter could never be truly forgotten. Tucked away perhaps, for private reflection, but who could forget *Blackwood*?

She picked up her comb, horrified to note that her hazel eyes still glowed and her cheeks shone. She pulled her russet hair into a matronly bun and practiced looking sober and sensible. Perhaps if she kept her eyes downcast and didn't meet Honoria's gaze, her mother-in-law wouldn't notice anything amiss. She shut her eyes and tried to banish Blackwood to a secret corner of her mind.

There was a knock on the door, and Isobel spun, but it was only Sarah, her maid, come at last. " 'Morning, Countess. You rang for me?"

"Yes, some time ago," Isobel replied with a smile, giving her hair a final pat with nervous fingers. A veritable forest of pins, twice as many as Sarah would have used, held her unruly curls in submission.

"I'm sorry. Her ladyship had me help count the silverware again," Sarah said. "I couldn't get away. If so much as a teaspoon goes missing . . ."

She let Sarah complain. Honoria often pressed Isobel's maid into helping with menial chores. Counting silverware was not part of the duties Sarah had been hired to perform. Nor was polishing crystal or sorting linen. Isobel had objected, carefully, but Honoria insisted if the girl was unwilling to work she should be dismissed. Isobel couldn't bear to lose Sarah.

Sarah kept her secrets.

"Never mind, Sarah, I'm dressed now. I'm going up to the nursery to see Robin," Isobel said, patting the maid's shoulder sympathetically. "We're going to feed the ducks this afternoon." She held the door as Sarah carried out the breakfast tray.

Isobel climbed the stairs to the third floor, catching herself humming. She clamped her lips shut before anyone heard her, but a thrill crept up from her toes, and she took the last few steps two at a time like a giddy girl.

Blackwood!

At the nursery door, she smoothed her gown and went in, a smile of anticipation on her face. Her five-year-old son looked up from his lunch and grinned, and for the first time since she'd left Evelyn's party, all thoughts of Blackwood vanished.

"Mama!" the Sixth Earl of Ashdown crowed with delight, and threw himself around her knees, burying his face in her skirt. Isobel didn't care that he'd been eating tarts and her gown now sported wrinkles and small jammy handprints. She ignored Nurse's offer of a napkin to wipe it away and ruffled her son's soft curls.

She sat on the floor with her child while Nurse looked on fondly. He had so little time to play. Honoria insisted that Robin spend his days learning reading, numbers, French and Latin. She wanted her grandson to go to Harrow at the earliest possible age. The fact that Isobel thought he was too

young for that didn't matter. Her husband's will left the raising of their son to his mother and brother.

Isobel had not realized how much Robert hated her until
his will was read. True, theirs had never been a warm marriage. They were wed by arrangement, with no consideration
of love, or even regard, but still it shocked her when his will
placed herself and Robin so entirely under his family's
control. If she married or even formed friendships without
Charles and Honoria's approval, she would be barred from
her son's life. Charles was given the management of her fortune, to keep her from the kind of temptations a woman rich
in her own right might fall prey to.

Robert's will insisted that his widow's behavior must be
impeccable, in keeping with the sterling reputation of the
Maitland family. If there was the faintest whiff of the kind
of scandalous behavior that Isobel's mother had engaged in,
Honoria would see that every respectable door in London
was closed to her.

While the opinions of society mattered little to Isobel, her
son was the only good thing in her life. She could not bear to
lose Robin, and so she behaved as they wished her to. Mostly.

She looked at Robin's bright face now, at the red hair that
came from her side of the family, the smile and eyes that were
all her mother's. How it must rankle when Honoria looked
at him.   •

Robin prattled on about ducks, and Isobel bit her lip,
thinking of what she'd risked for a few moments of pleasure
in Blackwood's arms. It must never, ever, happen again, even
if she had to live the rest of her life without a man's touch.

The door opened without the courtesy of a knock. Isobel,
with her back to the portal, watched as Nurse's smile fled,
and she knew who it was before even turning to look.

"Good day, Miss Kirk," Nurse said stiffly, confirming
the intruder's identity. Isobel's heart sank as she turned to

meet the disapproving glare of Honoria's paid companion.

"Lady Honoria and Lord Charles sent me to tell you that they are awaiting you in the dining room, Countess. You are fifteen minutes late for luncheon."

Jane Kirk eyed Isobel as if hoping to catch her at a greater misdeed than merely sitting on the floor of the nursery. In addition to writing Honoria's letters and reading to her from improving books, Jane was her ladyship's spy.

Jane's eyes narrowed with speculation now, and Isobel felt her skin heat, remembering she was indeed guilty this time. She wondered if there was some telltale sign that a woman had been recently bedded, and very well bedded at that. She wanted to hide, but instead she rose as gracefully as possible and returned the companion's glare.

"You have stains on your gown, Countess," Jane Kirk said coldly, and Isobel felt relief that jam was all she had noticed. "I shall inform Lady Honoria that there will be a further delay while you change your dress."

Isobel resisted the urge to smooth her gown. Jane held the door open, expecting her to obey Honoria's summons immediately. Instead, she turned to hug Robin, who had gone quiet, his smile lost at Jane's unwelcome intrusion.

Isobel kissed his cheek, and whispered in his ear. "Ask Nurse to have Cook pack up all the dry bread, and I'll meet you at the duck pond at three o'clock."

"I shall save my own bread from luncheon," Robin whispered back.

"Me too," she replied, and he smiled.

"Growing children need their food, and ducks are dirty creatures," said Jane with disapproval, leaning in to hear the private words between mother and son. Robin's smile faded once more. Isobel suppressed a sharp retort. It would only get her into trouble.

"I'll see you in the park," Isobel said, sending her son a

conspirator's grin as she left the room, ignoring Jane Kirk's sour expression.

Honoria glared at Isobel as she took her seat at the table. "Luncheon is always served precisely at one o'clock, Isobel. You are more then half an hour late. It was very inconsiderate of you to have kept Charles and myself waiting."

"I'm sorry. I was with Robin in the nursery," Isobel murmured.

Honoria's frown deepened. "You baby that boy far too much. You should limit your visits to one per week, and for a few minutes only. You fly in at the most awkward times and interrupt his lessons."

Isobel stared at the plate of soup before her. It was cream of leek, which was Charles's favorite and therefore served regularly. Isobel detested it. She let her lip curl for a moment.

"You fill the boy's head with nonsense, telling him fairy stories," Charles added, snapping his napkin in the air before laying it on his lap. "He needs more time with his tutors. His Latin is abysmal."

Isobel forced herself to swallow a mouthful of the hated soup to keep from asking her brother-in-law just how good his own Latin was. She recalled Robert telling her that Charles had been at the bottom of all his classes at school. Yet Robert had made him responsible for managing their son's affairs until he came of age. She, of course, was not permitted to know the details of how the earldom was being managed.

Resentment tasted as vile as the soup. She would order Robin a dozen new storybooks from Hatchard's the moment luncheon ended, and not a single one of them in Latin.

"Jane said she found you rolling on the floor of the nursery, your gown disheveled and filthy. She said your hair needed combing. Is this the way you believe you should appear before an impressionable child?" Honoria demanded.

Isobel bit her tongue so hard she tasted blood, but didn't argue. There was no point in making her mother-in-law angry. Especially today. She felt hot color creeping over her cheeks, and the knot of anger in her throat made swallowing more soup impossible.

"Blood will tell, I suppose," Honoria added, shooting the familiar barb at Isobel's mother.

Isobel concentrated on placing her spoon just so on the edge of her bowl before she clasped the linen napkin in her lap and twisted it, imagining it was Honoria's fat neck.

It was hardly her fault that her mother had run off with an Italian musician, abandoning her cold marriage when her daughter was only ten. She had chosen happiness and love, two things Isobel would eternally lack, thanks to Robert's will and Honoria's twisted ideas of proper behavior.

At least she had her secret tryst with Blackwood to soothe the sting of Honoria's comments today. She suppressed a smile as a tingle bubbled through her tainted blood.

Her mother-in-law was expounding on the right way to raise a boy, and Isobel stopped listening. Honoria had no right to tell anyone how to be a mother, having raised two such odious, unfeeling, self-centered sons as Robert and Charles.

She let her mind drift back to the delights of Evelyn's garden, the delicious anonymity of it all. Perhaps she truly was like her mother, and it just took a man like the notorious—

"Marquess of Blackwood," Charles said out loud, and Isobel looked up at her brother-in-law in horror. He laughed at her, his piggy eyes disappearing into pouches of sallow skin.

"Woolgathering again, were you?" He laughed. "I can imagine the blackguard's name would shock you, and rightly so." She continued to stare, and he rolled his eyes at her lack of comprehension and stabbed a finger at the newspaper beside his plate.

"It says Blackwood's youngest sister is making her debut this season. For all she's the granddaughter of the Duke of Carrington, she'll not find it easy to get a proposal from a decent gentleman, with Blackwood's name associated with her own."

"Poor girl," Honoria said. "I'm sure you understand what she will endure, Isobel, with your mother's reputation what it was. You would have faced the scorn of good society yourself, if you'd been allowed to make your debut. You should be thankful that discreet arrangements were made for you to marry quietly, to spare you such an ordeal."

Isobel gave the napkin another killing twist. No, there had been no balls, no dances, no parties in her honor, no pretty gowns, no flirting or fun of any kind. Her marriage had been a dry legal matter, made with the sense that Robert was ashamed of her, even if her dowry made him very rich.

Honoria picked up an envelope from the little silver tray by her elbow. "Look, here is our invitation to the young lady's come-out ball. It will be something to see, won't it?" She tore open the heavy cream envelope and scanned the invitation, then waved it at Charles. "The ball is only a week away! Lady Miranda's great-aunt is hosting the event, and the Duke of Carrington will be in attendance. If the duke is there, it seems likely that the Prince Regent will put in an appearance. They might have given more warning—I'll need a new gown for the occasion." She fussed with her frilled shawl, preening. Honoria fancied herself a pillar of fashion, but she chose styles meant for girls half her age. Her penchant for ruffles made her look ridiculous, and even older than her fifty-eight years.

Charles chuckled. "Well, I suppose it will be *the* event to attend this Season. I'm personally looking forward to it.

I'd like to see if the poor girl can rise above her brother's reputation. If she has a big enough dowry, I might even court her. D'you suppose Blackwood will dare to attend the ball?"

"Isn't Lord Blackwood one of England's most marriage-able men?" Isobel asked. "He is wealthy, titled, and—" And handsome, charming, and sinfully good at making a lady forget herself. She swallowed. "—and heir to a dukedom," she finished breathlessly.

Honoria snorted. "He'll never marry a truly respectable girl. None of the best families would accept a rake and a fool like him as a son-in-law. My guess is he'll have to marry a foreigner, and then he'll forever be an outsider."

"As he deserves." Charles thumped his empty wineglass down and signaled for more.

Isobel read the naked dislike in her brother-in-law's eyes and wondered how it was possible to hate a man for his rep-utation, yet consider marrying his sister. She suppressed a shudder.

Marrying Charles would be even more unpleasant than being tied to his older brother. If she got the chance, she'd warn Blackwood's young sister to run for the nearest convent rather than consider a match with Charles Maitland.

"I suppose you'd best attend as well, Isobel. The invita-tion includes you." Isobel felt her mouth twist. As Countess of Ashdown, the invitation was probably addressed to her. Honoria would not be able to go at all if she didn't attend.

"Be ready at ten o'clock. You may wear your maroon bombazine. Have your maid hang it now so the creases fall out in time. It is a dignified, sober garment, nothing to draw unwanted attention to yourself," Honoria said sternly. "I shall ask Jane to advise you on your hair."

Isobel forced a smile. "Thank you, but I'm sure Sarah will know the right style for such an event. Miss Kirk will need all her time to dress your hair, Honoria," she added, keeping her tone sweet. The barb went unnoticed.

Charles waved the folded newspaper at Isobel. "I read that Evelyn Renshaw's masquerade ball was a great success," he said.

Isobel regarded the next course of her lunch as it was placed before her. A whole trout stared up at her in dull surprise, as if it knew just what she'd been up to at that ball. She carefully placed a sliced almond over the fish's judgmental eye and toyed with the limp green beans that shared the plate.

"According to the *Times*," Charles went on, "the Prince Regent was in attendance last night, in costume, of course. Did you see him?" Isobel looked up in astonishment, and he laughed. "No, of course you wouldn't have seen him if he was in disguise! You probably spent the entire night in a corner nursing a glass of watered lemonade as usual. Anyway, it seems His Highness has been heard to say that he loves to masquerade."

Honoria gasped. "Indeed? But they are such unseemly affairs! Does he often attend such parties? How would anyone know if he was in attendance?"

Isobel couldn't resist. "How would anyone know he is not? A hostess might claim the triumph of having the prince attend her masked ball, and who would be the wiser?"

Honoria blinked at her. Charles scowled. Neither understood. Clever conversation sailed over their dull heads like clay pigeons.

"Well, anyway," Charles said, "His Highness has hinted that he would love to attend more costume balls this Season."

"How positively wicked of him!" Honoria turned to Isobel. "Well? *Did* anything scandalous occur last night?"

Isobel slid her eyes to her plate, feeling a hot blaze of shame burning up from her knees to her hairline. "At Evelyn's? Of course not. She would never allow any impropriety," she replied, her voice remarkably steady, despite the thump of her heart against her ribs. She recalled the wet heat of Blackwood's mouth on hers, the marvel of his hands on her breasts, and swallowed a sigh.

"Well, Prince Regent or not, I wouldn't be caught dead at a masquerade," Honoria said, her lips pinched in distaste. "One might be speaking to entirely the wrong sort of person and never even know!"

"But surely you might also find yourself speaking to the Prince Regent when the time comes to unmask," Isobel countered.

Honoria considered that, her eyes widening. "Oh! Yes, indeed."

"It's predicted that masquerade balls will be quite popular this Season," Charles read further. "You may find yourself attending one or two after all, Mother, if you wish to be fashionable."

"I am always fashionable," Honoria preened, patting her hair. It was newly cut in the latest short style. It did not suit her. It made her protuberant eyes bigger, her heavy jowls more pronounced. "I suppose I'll need a costume. I'll ask Jane to suggest something, just in case. Now that's settled, what are your plans this evening, Charles? There's a musicale at Lady St. John's."

"I'm going to my club," Charles said dismissively.

Isobel held her tongue. She planned to go to the theatre with Evelyn Renshaw, and did not wish to be forced to join Honoria at the St. John musicale. She had heard Lady St. John's daughter sing, and it wasn't an experience she wished to repeat.

Besides, while Honoria approved of the wealthy and virtuous Lady Renshaw as a suitable companion for her, there was every chance her mother-in-law might disapprove of the play being shown, and insist she accompany her to Lady St. John's instead.

"Please excuse me," she said before Honoria began to ask questions. "I have a fitting with my modiste this afternoon." She didn't mention her plans to meet Robin in the park afterward. If Jane had reported it, Honoria was certain to disapprove. She held her breath, but since Jane had a wrinkled gown with a jammy handprint to tattle about, it appeared she'd forgotten to mention Robin's outing.

"Choose plain garments, Isobel," Honoria warned. "You are still in mourning. Stay within the limits of your allowance. Charles will not countenance extravagance." She looked pointedly at the navy blue gown Isobel had on.

It was trimmed with a pale gray ribbon. She knew that Honoria would have preferred the ribbon to be black, but Robert had been dead for over two years, and she was sick of the half-mourning garb her mother-in-law insisted upon. Honoria had resumed wearing colors scant months after her son's death.

"I need a walking gown, some night attire—" she began, but Honoria drew in a monstrous gasp of air, like a whale coming up from the deep.

"Isobel! Such loose talk is not appropriate in front of Charles! A lady does not mention such garments!"

Honoria always needed to find fault with something. Isobel shot a glance at Charles. He let an oily glance slide over her body when his mother looked away. Isobel felt ill. "Please excuse me," she said again, rising with dignity.

After checking the hall for Jane Kirk, she raced up the stairs two at a time and tidied her hair, ready to enjoy the afternoon with her son.

Chapter 5

Phineas did what he usually did when faced with his grandfather's overbearing sense of order. He left.

Now he stood in the doorway of the club's crowded lounge in a foul mood. Adam De Courcey, Earl of Westlake, was waiting for him at a corner table with his watch in his hand. Phineas fixed his customary roguish grin on his face as he handed his hat to the concierge, but today it felt lopsided at best, a death's head grimace at worst.

"I say, Blackwood, come join us!" Arthur Philpott called, stopping him before he'd gone a dozen steps across the room. "We're making a wager as to who can drive all the way to Brighton . . ." Philpott paused dramatically and chortled at his own cleverness. " . . . blindfolded! Isn't it brilliant?"

Phineas cast a sidelong look at Westlake and saw his brother-in-law roll his eyes. He wished he could do so himself. Instead, he turned his most practiced grin on Philpott. "But who is to wear the blind, you or your horses, old man?"

He moved on as laughter erupted, leaving Philpott to decide whether the comment was an insult or a jest. It was barely noon and the four men who shared Philpott's table were well on their way to roaring drunk. He pitied the horses. By Phineas's estimation, one horse had more wit than Philpott and all his cronies together. If only heaven had seen fit to give the nags Philpott's fortune and set Philpott to pulling the silly, high-perched phaeton he drove as if he were per-petually blindfolded.

"Blackwood! It's good to see you," Lord Bridges said as Phineas passed his table. "I hear your sister is making her debut. You'll make my introduction, I hope? I intend to take a bride this year . . ." Phineas paused, his teeth clenched to keep his devil-may-care smirk from slipping. The old roué said that every spring, but this year Miranda would be in his path. Bridges waggled his eyebrows, his jowls shaking as he rubbed his hands together. "Is she pretty? Hardly matters with the kind of dowry she's got, but it can't hurt, eh?"

Phineas resisted the temptation to ram the man's yellow teeth down his throat. "I'd be delighted to introduce you, old chap. A toothless girl with a wooden leg needs all the help she can get," he managed to quip, and walked away.

Bridges was old enough to be Miranda's father, and therefore his own father too. He paused, tempted to turn and point that out, but caught Adam's impatient stare and kept walking. Damn Bridges. His reputation for gambling and whoring was worse than his own. Miranda deserved better. Much better.

The way the day was going, and in his present black mood, it was hard to keep playing the rake. He knew the wicked pre-dilections of every gentleman in the room. They drank, gam-bled, and held the whores they bedded in higher esteem than the ladies they courted and married. He couldn't imagine sweet, innocent, bright-eyed Miranda consigned to a husband of that ilk. He scanned the room and realized there wasn't a man present to whom he'd willingly entrust his sister.

Except Adam, of course, he thought as he approached his brother-in-law's table. The Earl of Westlake was happily married to Phineas's eldest sister Marianne. He gladly took a seat across the table from Adam's sober, intelligent company.

"God, Phin, how the hell do you do it? I couldn't put up

with these fools for five minutes," Adam muttered, casting a sour look at the club's denizens.

Phineas signaled the waiter and grinned at Adam, still in character for the sake of anyone watching. He was a rogue and a rake, never serious, always seen with a drink in one hand, another man's wife in the other. Or so he made it seem. Adam was one of the very few who knew differently.

"I have made every man here think I am even more reprehensible than he is. They believe I am singularly focused on the pursuit of pleasure and that I care nothing for anything—or anyone—else. A gentleman in his cups will willingly babble his closest secrets if he thinks the man he's talking to is a bigger fool than himself. I make them believe they're talking to the greatest idiot in Christendom, and the information I want comes tumbling out."

The waiter proffered his whisky on a silver tray, and Phineas raised it to Adam before sipping. "The job is not without its pleasures, I assure you. Ladies adore rakes."

"Nor is the job without its torments, I imagine," Adam said. "I have no doubt a lot of useless drivel comes streaming out along with those brilliant gems of information you collect." He raised his glass in turn. "I applaud your gift for knowing the difference."

Phineas let his eyes roam the room, resting his gaze briefly on various faces as he spoke. "I know which gentleman is sleeping with his brother's wife. I know who has been forced to sign away his family estates to pay his gambling debts. I know who is hiding a fortune in smuggled brandy under his great house by the sea. I know which lord wears a corset to hide his belly, pads his stockings and wears high heels to impress a mistress years too young for him."

He met Adam's eyes. "And those are just the little secrets. I also know truly nasty things. I am the keeper of dozens of dangerous secrets that could ruin marriages, topple the government, or send seemingly upstanding lords into lifelong exile. I keep them all to myself, in case England ever has need of them." He rubbed a hand across his brow, trying to smooth away the frown as he looked frankly at his brother-in-law.

"Adam, I think it's time I got out of this line of work, before I become what they all believe I am."

Adam raised his eyebrows. "You? You're the most honorable dishonorable rogue I've ever met. The only one in fact." He grinned, but Phineas didn't return his smile. "Edmond wasn't wrong about you, Phineas. My brother knew how clever you were when he recruited you for this work."

"He picked me up out of the gutter after I told Carrington to go to hell and came to London to kill myself with drink and whores. I damned near succeeded," Phineas said bitterly.

Adam folded his arms and leaned back with a smile. "You managed to make your own way in this unholy city for three years after Carrington cut off your allowance, solely by gaming and watching what other men did. Edmond saw it had become a very useful skill, and simply helped you make use of it for more noble purposes. You could have stopped once you came into your inheritance at twenty-five."

Phineas scowled at him. "We both know why I didn't, Adam. If Edmond hadn't been killed—"

Adam held up his hand. "If Edmond had not been killed, then *he* would have married Marianne, *I* would have joined the navy, and we would not be having this conversation."

Phineas wished it was as easy for him to be glib about the lonely years he'd spent in the service of the crown. His work had been dangerous at times. For their own safety, he'd severed his ties to everyone he cared about, and he did not dare forge new ones. He glared at his brother-in-law and wondered yet again if serving his country in lonely secrecy was worth the cost.

"My grandfather is in Town, but I suppose you know that.

He's brought Miranda for her debut Season. I haven't seen Miranda in more than five years. Carrington believes everything he hears about me. Except for you, I am a stranger to my family. They don't know this . . . life of mine is for show, for England. No one does. Even Marianne despairs of me, and we were once close friends as well as brother and sister."

"She still loves you," Adam said. "My wife is unfailingly loyal. She will stand by you no matter how great the scandal."

Phineas tightened his hand around his glass, letting the cut crystal points bite into his palm. "Did you know she sends me letters, admonishing me for my behavior? They come with clippings from the scandal sheets, or segments from letters she's received from friends here in Town that mention me. Never in a good way. She believes I am utterly without honor or control."

Adam's expression hardened. "This isn't the time, Blackwood."

Phineas frowned, knowing by Adam's expression there was another mission afoot. He felt trapped, and he leaned forward, meeting his brother-in-law's flat gaze, feeling desperation swell in his throat. "My grandfather is staying at Blackwood House, keeping an eye on me."

Adam nodded. "Yes, I know. Marianne and I are staying with your great-aunt Augusta until the renovations to our town house are completed. Jamie's with us, and His Grace couldn't countenance a small boy underfoot. Too noisy. Look, it may make things more challenging, but—"

"Damned right it will," Phineas interrupted. "Carrington is going to be watching everything I do. He's already lecturing me like a child of five. He's insisted I be on my best behavior while Miranda's in Town, and that's to be some months, I understand. My family's presence is a perfect chance to affect my reform. No one would question it." He shrugged. "I might even marry, retire to the country like you and Marianne." He fleetingly thought of the eyes behind the mask in Evelyn Renshaw's ballroom, gazing at him with such admiration. If only it had been real. Longing made his throat ache.

"You can't," Adam sighed. "Your grandfather's presence may make your job more difficult, but you'll have to find a way around it." He paused, glanced around the room, then back at Phineas. "Did Evelyn tell you anything last night?"

Phineas's gut tightened. "Evelyn Renshaw is the most upstanding lady in London. She isn't going to let me seduce her, and she isn't going to betray her husband after a few cupfuls of strong punch."

Adam leaned in, his voice low. "We're not asking her to betray him. We just want to know where he is. We can find out what he's up to ourselves. We know he's not at his estate in Wiltshire, or at her manor in Dorset, but he must be somewhere."

"What does it matter?" Phineas asked bitterly. "What's one more smuggler? There's not a lord in England who doesn't drink contraband French brandy, or a lady lacking a gown of French silk and lace. Every footman, coach driver, and whore in London sips gin smuggled from France. There's no way to stop it." To prove his point he beckoned the waiter. "French brandy, please." The man nodded without a word and went to fetch it.

Adam ignored the demonstration. "Philip Renshaw is involved in something much more dangerous, much more important, than smuggling a few casks of spirits. Did you find anything when you searched his study?"

Phineas sipped the brandy when it arrived, swirling the acrid liquid in his mouth before swallowing it, feeling it burn his throat and warm his belly. He'd take mediocre whisky over the finest brandy any day. He fixed Adam with a cold stare. "Unfortunately not. There was a party going on, if you'll recall, and there was a woman standing right in front of the door that led to his office."

Adam's eyes sharpened. "What woman?"

Phineas looked into the dregs of his brandy, seeing her masked face, her painted mouth. "Damnedest thing. I have no idea who she was."

Adam laughed out loud, causing several heads to turn. Phineas grinned at them out of habit, but Adam ignored them and folded his arms over his chest. "A woman in London you don't know, Phin? I didn't think it was possible."

Phineas let the sultry memory of the mysterious woman nudge the corners of his lips back into a grin. "I got to know her better before the evening was out."

"What was her name?"

Yasmina. A sound like a sigh, as sweet as the exotic drift of her perfume. Except it wasn't her real name. He shifted in his seat.

"We didn't get to that."

"What was she doing there?" Adam asked, his voice betraying his anxiety, his brows drawing together. It made Phineas nervous. Prickles of warning crept up his back.

What *was* she doing there?

"Relax, Adam. It was a party. She was a guest like anyone else."

"Except you didn't know her," Adam snapped, as if that had been the worst sin Phineas had committed in the dark.

"Not by name. It was a masked ball, after all, but I'd know that mouth if I saw her again." He grinned, but Adam ignored the joke.

"The biblical sense notwithstanding, we still have need of information. Now more than ever."

"Why? It didn't seem all that important last time we spoke."

"Things have changed." The room was quieter now. Several tables had cleared out, their occupants off to an afternoon at the track or for luncheon at yet another fashionable club. Private conversations were easier to overhear.

"Look, we can't discuss this here," Adam muttered. "I'm late to meet Marianne and Jamie at Hyde Park. Ride with me." He made it an order, not an invitation, and didn't speak again until the Westlake rig swung out into the chaos of London's midday traffic.

"How was your voyage?" Phineas asked. Adam owned a fleet of merchant ships, an unusual thing for an earl, but his brother-in-law was not a typical peer. Several of his ships were used to gather information about Napoleon for the English crown.

"I saw Thomas Moore at Smuggler's City." That instantly bought Phineas's full attention. Napoleon had set up a safe and welcoming haven for English smugglers at Gravelines. In exchange for gold, English fishermen and sailors could buy all the contraband they could carry. Napoleon used the gold to pay his vast armies, and the smugglers provided the enemy with a great deal of useful information while drunk on cheap French wine.

"Moore, at Gravelines?" Phineas asked. "I thought he was running a booming business smuggling French prisoners of war out of England."

"Yes, he's making a fortune 'rescuing' officers who give their parole and promise to remain in England for the duration of the war. Probably even has a French priest to absolve them of their vow on the trip across the Channel. We have reports that most of the former prisoners run straight to Napoleon the moment their boots touch French soil, to report on what they've seen. It could do a lot of damage. All thanks to Moore."

"Is that what's so important?" Phineas asked. "Some

French officer with a tale to tell? What's Philip Renshaw got to do with that?"

"It's much bigger than that. Moore was only too happy to sell the information to me. He'd sell his own mother for a shiny ha'penny. Do you remember when King Louis of France arrived here, looking for asylum until Napoleon could be defeated?"

Phineas nodded.

"When he landed, two English lords offered His Highness their hospitality until the government decided what to do with him. One was the Marquess of Buckingham, and the other was Lord Philip Renshaw. Philip went to great expense to lure the king to his home. His mother was a French noblewoman, a cousin of the royal family, and he expected Louis to honor the connection. He did not. Instead, Louis walked right past Philip's magnificent coach and got into Buckingham's plainer one and went to his estates at Stowe. Philip hasn't forgiven the slight, and according to Moore, he's made a deal with Napoleon. He has promised to deliver King Louis to him, Phin."

Phineas's brows rose. "If Renshaw plans to kidnap him, surely a few additional guards could handle the threat.

Adam shook his head. "It's not just Renshaw. He could never manage this alone. Tom Moore says there's other English lords involved, some of England's most important men."

"Have we got names?" Phineas asked.

"Moore didn't say who they were. I don't think he knows. This goes higher than he can reach. He's worried, though. Such a plot would give the authorities a greater reason to clamp down on smuggling. Moore's afraid his business may suffer because of this." Adam smiled grimly. "That, and he says he's a patriot."

"If Louis were captured, paraded through the streets of

Paris to the guillotine, it would put England in a deadly position," Phineas predicted. "We'd look like fools. The French royalists and our allies would lose faith in us, some might decide to join Napoleon against us. England could lose the war, end up as part of Bonaparte's empire. Even if Moore isn't willing to become a French citizen, it appears Philip Renshaw might be."

"You see why we need you to play the rogue awhile longer. Are you sure there's no chance of charming Evelyn into revealing her husband's whereabouts? It would be the fastest, easiest way to—"

"Evelyn Renshaw is a model of virtue."

Adam grinned. "Come now, I have complete faith in your abilities. You've never failed before."

"Evelyn Renshaw has no interest in forbidden trysts. Not even the faintest whiff of impropriety touches her. When asked directly, she simply says Philip is away, and changes the topic of conversation. She is clever, and no amount of hinting or trickery can get anything out of her. She is immune to my charms, Adam."

"And the other lady? The one who stopped you from searching the study?"

"She didn't stop me exactly. She was simply standing in my way." Phineas couldn't resist a grin. "She wanted to play, so we played. And as they say, all work and no—"

"A dangerous game, wouldn't you say?"

"There was nothing sinister about her," Phineas said, but uncertainty blew a cold breath down the back of his neck. Why *had* she been standing in front of that door, staring at him? "Probably just bored with her husband, wanting a little adventure," he muttered.

"Need I remind you there's nothing sinister about you either, to most people? You appear to be a pleasant, harmless chap. But you are most definitely sinister, aren't you?"

The coach pulled to a stop in the green confines of Hyde Park, and Adam opened the door. "Marianne and Jamie will likely be at the pond," he said, climbing down.

Phineas followed him across the grass.

Sinister, was she?

He scanned the park, looking at every lady in sight, dismissing each one. None of them were Yasmina. He'd know that mouth, those eyes, anywhere.

Phineas prided himself on knowing people, especially women. He knew what pleased them. He imagined Yasmina's head thrown back in the dark, the glint of starlight catching the white column of her throat as he pleasured her. His mouth watered, remembering the taste of her skin.

He also knew how to lie to a woman's face when he had to, but in bed, when he made love to them, his bedmates got the real Phineas Archer. It was the only time he was truly honest, truly himself. He had given Yasmina his best.

His gut tightened. Had it all been a deception on her part? If so, she was very skilled at the game. His game.

He scanned a carriage filled with ladies as it passed, and quickly looked away. She wasn't among them. Not that it mattered. She couldn't hide for long. It would take him mere hours, a few days at most, to find her.

And when he did, he was going to make love to her with the lights on.

Chapter 6

"**M**ay I suggest something in pink today, perhaps with a lovely bit of décolletage?" the modiste asked, but as usual the young widow shook her head.

"No, make the gowns in pale gray or dark blue, please, with a modest cut," she ordered firmly.

The modiste's smile faded. In her opinion, the young Countess of Ashdown was too pretty to spend the rest of her life dressed in half-mourning. Behind her widow's weeds and a hideously unbecoming coiffure, she had a lovely figure and a natural grace. Her pale skin, her auburn hair, those large, luminous eyes—they were all glorious, and such features deserved to be shown off. In Madame's opinion, her client needed pretty clothes to attract a new husband, or at least a lover, someone rich enough to dress a mistress in the latest, most expensive styles.

Madame was not purely mercenary. She was also a Frenchwoman, with a romantic French soul. The widow had a delightful secret that Madame treasured. While the countess might insist upon wearing the most grim and unflattering gowns on top, she wore delightfully shocking undergarments beneath. The lady liked silk, lace, and pretty satin ribbons next to her skin where no one could see.

The modiste regarded the gray serge her client was rubbing between her fingers and pursed her lips, knowing a dreadful mistake when she saw one.

"Consider this blue moiré silk instead, Countess. It will turn the color of your hair to flame, and enhance your eyes." She draped a rustling length of iridescent fabric over the lady's shoulder. *"Voilà! C'est magnifique!"*

She stepped back to wait as the countess stroked the fabric wistfully, feminine longing clear in her eyes.

"It is still blue, as you requested, but a very subtle shade," the modiste coaxed. "In low light, it will look quite sober, but with a touch of elegance, and it will shimmer oh so gently."

Madame watched as the spark of delight in her client's eyes turned to regret. Without hesitation, she took the lady by the shoulders and led her to the mirror to see the transformation for herself. The spark returned, along with a becoming blush.

"We could trim the gown with violet ribbon instead of purple or black or gray. It would be subtle, elegant, and . . . how do you say it? Just the slightest bit *enticing*." Madame purred the last word, making it as sibilant and sensuous as the slippery fabric. Pride swelled in her ample bosom when the countess smiled at her reflection and her lashes swept down to hide the glint in her eye. Madame chuckled, knowing she'd not only made her point, but a sale.

Isobel's stomach filled with butterflies at the sheer daring of such a decision. What had gotten into her of late? First Blackwood, and now silk? The cloth was soft against her skin, and it had warmed like a lover the instant she touched it. Whatever would Honoria say? She glanced around her.

Lady Caroline Graves, a young matron close to her own age, was being fitted for a sprigged muslin walking dress with a pretty leaf-green jacket to match. As one assistant pinned and tucked, another was showing her silks and satins in a dozen brilliant and daring colors, not one of which was pastel. Isobel watched as they rolled out a luscious violet silk and Lady Caroline ordered it made up with a pink satin underskirt.

No one noticed Isobel amid the bolts of black and gray fabric, or knew that last night she had stepped out of the shadows and discovered how wonderful it was to feel pretty. She looked again at the moiré silk over her shoulder. True, it was flat blue when one looked at it, but if she moved, breathed, there was a shimmer that made her mouth water.

"Yes, I'll take a gown in the moiré silk," she heard herself say to the modiste. "With blue trim instead of violet, though," she added, forcing herself to be somewhat sensible. She raised her chin and met the modiste's eyes. "I need some nightgowns as well."

"Something lacy as usual?" The modiste brought forward a bolt of pink silk, so sheer it was a mere rumor.

Isobel cast a sidelong look at the vivacious Lady Caroline and imagined her in bed, attired in the same silk, as her lord husband came striding toward her, more purposeful and virile than Robert had ever been.

But in her imagination the face in the candlelight was Blackwood's.

"Yes," she breathed, dragging her thoughts away from Blackwood and bed. "You will list it on the bill as heavy flannel?"

The modiste gave Isobel a conspirator's grin. "As usual, my lady."

Charles and Honoria had no idea of her little secret, the one pleasure she indulged in, Isobel thought as she walked across Hyde Park to meet her son.

She was entitled to one secret, wasn't she?

What harm could it do, wearing silk undergarments instead of linen or wool? She found herself tempted to hum. She looked around, checking to see if Honoria or Charles or

Jane Kirk might be watching her, but no one was looking. No one ever looked at plain Isobel Maitland. Still, she hid her smile under her prim bonnet. What on earth had gotten into her? But she knew the answer to that.

Blackwood.

Her other secret.

At the pond, she found Robin playing with a toy sailboat with another boy about his age that she didn't know. His dark head was bent next to Robin's russet curls as they pushed the boat out onto the water with twigs. Nurse looked on from a shady bench with a placid smile as Isobel approached. The sack of bread crumbs sat untouched beside her.

Instead of crowding the bank as they usually did, the ducks hovered warily off shore, unsure of whether the ship in their midst was friend or foe. It carried no colors to advise them, and they regarded it as if half expecting the vessel to suddenly run up the Jolly Roger and begin firing.

"Hello, Robbie," Isobel said, crouching next to her son and his friend.

"Mama, this is James," he said happily, and the other boy regarded her with solemn gray eyes.

"How d'you do, ma'am?" He rose and bowed to Isobel, and Robin grinned and mimicked his friend.

"I see you remember how to greet a lady, Jamie. I'm proud of you," said a pleasant voice, and Isobel turned to see a well-dressed woman smiling at her. "His grandfather taught him how to make a polite bow, even if his jacket is torn and his knees are muddy."

Isobel looked at the lad again. He was indeed muddy, but no worse than Robin. A moment's panic swelled in her chest. What would Honoria say? She'd have to take him in the back door, sneak him upstairs, and give him a bath straight away. She reached out a hand to take Robin's, only to find her fingers clasped in a polite handshake.

"I'm Marianne De Courcey, Countess Westlake, and that muddy scamp is my son James, Viscount Halliwell."

"Isobel Maitland, Countess Ashdown, and this is Robin, Earl of Ashdown, and first lieutenant of the duck pond fleet, by the look of things."

Marianne Westlake laughed. "I am delighted that we happened upon Robin today. Jamie's father promised to join us, but it appears he's been delayed. Robin has been a most enjoyable companion."

"Robin doesn't often get to visit with other boys his own age," Isobel said.

Robin tugged her sleeve. "Mama, may we have the bread? We're going to pretend the ducks are Napoleon's fleet and James's ship is Admiral Nelson's flagship."

Isobel could not say no. "Only for a few minutes. We have to go soon. Do be careful near the water."

"James has playmates at home on our estate, but none here in London," Marianne said. "After the first day in Town he was bored. I brought him out today because my great-aunt threatened to lock herself in her dressing room to escape the noise. She isn't used to small boys, but you must find it the same with Robin."

Isobel stared at her. If Robin had made any noise at all, Honoria would have ordered a stern paddling, followed by a long lecture on deportment from Charles and hours of extra lessons. She watched now as James cheered the brave little ship's progress through the enemy duck flotilla, yelling at the top of his lungs. Robin watched silently. Isobel's heart broke all over again for her little boy. She did her best to make his childhood happy in little ways, but Robert had tied her hands. Honoria's word was law where Robin was concerned.

"Not exactly," she said.

"Well, they seem content now. Why don't we let their nurses watch them, and stroll along the bank?" Marianne suggested. "It's such a glorious day, and I'm glad to be out. My sister is in Town to make her debut, and I have spent every minute of every day for three months helping to plan it. My grandfather insisted that every detail be accounted for, right down to the last candlestick. After he got through with organizing Miranda's come-out ball, my great-aunt began planning her wardrobe. I almost wish I'd stayed in the country."

"Miranda? Good heavens, do you mean Lady Miranda Archer?" Isobel blurted out, and felt her face heat at her rudeness.

Marianne didn't seem to notice. "Yes! Do you know her? You couldn't possibly. This is her first trip to town since— well, in many years. She was only James's age when she was last here, and that was because she begged my great-aunt to bring her to see the menagerie at the Tower."

Isobel's stomach climbed up to lodge behind her collar button as she recognized the family resemblance between Marianne and Blackwood. James too looked like his uncle. Those solemn eyes, that dark hair.

"Good heavens, Countess, you do look pale all of a sudden!" Marianne said. "Come, let us sit in the shade for a few minutes."

Charm seemed to run in the Archer family. Marianne's smile held only concern as she led her to a bench. "I'm sorry," Isobel managed. "It just seems such a coincidence to meet you today. Only this morning my mother-in-law received an invitation to Lady Miranda's debut ball."

Marianne smiled dazzlingly. "Oh, then you'll be there. How wonderful! I shall have someone to gossip with!"

Isobel tried to imagine standing in a corner giggling with a friend over the ridiculous behavior of the *ton* as they danced past with their beaks in the air. She'd often seen other ladies gossiping with friends but never had such companions. Honoria did not approve of her dancing. She wondered how her mother-in-law would feel about giggling and gossiping.

"I think I will be unable—" Isobel began.

"Marianne, I'm late. My apologies, my dear," a male voice interrupted. "But look who I've brought with me."

Isobel looked up and gasped in horror. Beside the gentleman, Blackwood stood smiling down at her. Well, not at *her*. At Marianne. His attention fixed on her quickly enough at the strangled sound of surprise.

"We appear to have startled you, my lady. We mean no harm, I assure you," Blackwood said stiffly. She stared at him like a ninny, her tongue knotted around her tonsils. Blackwood frowned and slid a questioning glance to Marianne, and Isobel felt mortification slither over her frozen limbs.

Marianne threw herself into Blackwood's arms. "Phin! Oh, Phin, what a wonderful surprise. I'm so glad to see you. Let me look at you!" She drew back and stared up into his face. Blackwood's gloved hands were tight on his sister's sleeves, his eyes filled with warmth and love. Isobel's envious heart flipped.

"Forgive me, Isobel. It's been many months since I've seen my brother," Marianne said. "And you look dreadful, by the way, Phineas."

"Introduce us, if you please, Marianne," the other gentleman reminded her.

"Yes, of course. Where are my manners? Isobel Maitland, Countess of Ashdown, may I present my brother, Lord Phineas Archer, Marquess of Blackwood, and my husband, Lord Adam De Courcey, Earl of Westlake?"

He took her hand briefly, and Isobel felt fire streak up her arm to heat her whole body. "Enchanted," he murmured, but there was not the slightest hint of enchantment in his eyes. The same eyes that had been so warm and playful last night were a cold, fathomless gray. In a single frosty glance he assessed her, dismissed her, and looked away.

Barely aware of Westlake's greeting, Isobel pressed her hand against her skirt to still the tingle he'd left upon it, and felt bitter disappointment close her throat. Blackwood didn't recognize her.

"How is Jamie's ship doing?" Westlake asked, looking back toward the two boys.

"Adam designs ships as a hobby. Jamie is trying out his latest model today," Marianne explained to Isobel.

"It's hardly a hobby, Marianne. My ships are the finest and fastest merchant vessels afloat." Adam De Courcey looked more closely at Isobel, his dark eyes cool. "Maitland," he said thoughtfully. "As in Lord Charles Maitland?"

"He's my brother-in-law." Isobel tried to keep the apology out of her tone. The earl's eyes slid over her in cool appraisal before he looked back at his wife.

"Shall we be getting back to the boys?" he asked.

Marianne took her husband's arm, which left Isobel standing awkwardly next to Blackwood. She tried to move past him, but he bowed and offered her his arm.

"Allow me to escort you back to the pond, Countess," he said, his tone horribly polite. She laid her hand on his sleeve, instantly dizzy at the physical contact. She felt the play of his muscles under her hand, breathed in the scent of his soap. She glanced sideways at the line of his jaw and noted several tiny red marks at the edge of his cravat. Had she bitten him, scratched him? The little injury spoke of passion, reminded her of the taste of his skin, the feeling of his body moving within hers, as rhythmic a thing as walking.

She stumbled.

He righted her without the slightest change of expression, a firm and impersonal hand cupping her elbow momentarily.

Her heart pounded and she concentrated on each step, on

keeping her hand flat on his sleeve and resisting the urge to
curl her fingers around his arm and shake him until he looked
at her, *really looked at her*. She shot another quick glance at
his profile. Damn him, he was completely and utterly unaffected, while she was nearly panting with desire.

A frisson of annoyance shot through her. The daft man
had no idea he'd made love to her only hours ago. Of course, a
rogue like Blackwood was probably so used to such encounters that he forgot his lovers the moment they left his bed, or
in this case, his borrowed bench.

She swallowed a hysterical giggle. It was a very good
thing he did not recognize her. "Silly," she murmured under
her breath.

"Your pardon?" he asked, his eyes on her at last.

She felt her face heat. "Oh, it's nothing, Lord Blackwood."
She looked straight ahead, hiding under the brim of her
bonnet. "Nothing at all."

"You were Robert Maitland's wife?"

"Yes," she replied simply, focusing on the movement of
his polished black boots next to her gray skirts as they took
each step. "He's dead," she said, unsure of what else to add,
feeling the butterflies beginning to circle her stomach again
at the very idea of making polite conversation with Blackwood about her husband, of all topics.

He didn't offer condolences. In fact, he barely seemed
to have heard. She fumed silently. Really, the man hardly
deserved his reputation as a charming rogue. In the light of
day he was a complete boor. His gaze roved over every other
woman in the park.

Blackwood made it clear he found her dull in the extreme,
and she was, she supposed, compared to the fashionably
dressed ladies in his sights. Pride poked at her, goading her
to anger. He did not even find her worth the effort of polite
conversation.

She withdrew her gloved hand from his sleeve as if it burned and made a fist so tight the fine kid leather squeaked a protest. He paused to look at her, his expression patiently polite, the way one might look at an elderly and annoying dowager.

"Look, there are the boys." She hurried toward Robin, desperate to get away from him so she could gather her wits enough to bid Marianne a proper good-bye.

Her mind worked to come up with a suitable excuse not to attend Miranda Archer's debut ball, but her brain was filled with only one thing.

Blackwood.

She could not spend another evening in his disturbing company. He would not notice her, but she would be aware of every step he took, every society beauty he danced with.

She did not want to stand in the shadows and watch him spirit his next conquest away to the privacy of another dark garden. She shuddered, more with desire than disgust, even now. No, it was obvious her nerves could not handle the strain.

She would go home and compose a note refusing the invitation to the ball.

"Oh, Robin, you're very wet!" She bent to brush at the worst of the mud on his linen breeches. He grinned at her, flushed and happy.

"James has other ships at home. He said he'd bring them tomorrow. We're going to launch a whole fleet!"

"But Robin, we can't—"

"Oh, do say yes, Isobel!" Marianne caught her hand. "James would not have offered to share his precious ships if he didn't like Robin exceedingly well. Think of my poor great-aunt. She would be most grateful for an hour or two of silence, much as she adores Jamie."

Isobel looked down at James De Courcey's earnest face.

He regarded her with his uncle's intense gray eyes. She read the plea there that was absent from Blackwood's flat gaze.

"Yes, all right." She bit her lip, trying to think of a way to get her son out of his Latin lesson for the second afternoon in a row. Perhaps if Mr. Cullen accompanied them to the park and taught Robin the names of trees and flowers in Latin, it would suffice.

"Excellent! And you must come to tea sometime very soon, Isobel. Or I should call on you at Maitland House? Which would be better?" Marianne prattled on as if they'd known each other for years.

"We have appointments to keep, my dear," Lord Westlake said, taking his wife's elbow. "You can send a note."

"Just one?" Blackwood asked, smiling indulgently at his sister. "It usually takes Marianne at least six notes to arrange even the simplest tea."

Isobel smiled. She couldn't help herself. Blackwood was so handsome, so charming as he teased his sister. He caught her expression from the corner of his eye and turned fully to look at her. Isobel bit her lip, felt herself grow hot under his stare.

"Have we met before, Countess?" he asked softly. "You seem . . ." His brow furrowed for a moment as his eyes moved over her again. "No, I am mistaken," he said as his gaze reached the hem of her gray gown.

Pride commandeered Isobel's tongue and what was left of her wits. "No, my lord. I am most certain we have not. We hardly travel in the same circles." She could have bitten her tongue in half. She sounded as prim as Evelyn Renshaw, as rude as Honoria.

She watched his eyes narrow at the set-down, and she turned away in horror to rub at the mud on Robbie's coat. She felt the cold dampness soak through her glove to her skin, and stared at her palm. The glove was ruined. She shut her eyes and her hand, and waited for serenity to return.

It hadn't really been an insult. Not with his reputation. Nor was it truly a lie when she said they had not met. He had spent an enchanted evening with an exotic lady called Yasmina. He had most definitely not met dull, dowdy, and dutiful Isobel, and he'd just proven that he would never even *glance* at her, never mind— Well, never mind indeed.

She clutched her son's small hand like a lifeline to sanity. "We must be going." The words came out husky, breathless. She fixed her smile on Marianne, avoiding Blackwood's eyes. She could not look at him. Not now. Probably not ever again.

She managed a brief curtsy, turned away and let Robbie tug her toward Nurse, and safer ground. She dared to glance over her shoulder only once, but Blackwood's eyes were on a gaggle of chirpy females tripping along the path by the pond. She swallowed a bitter sigh.

She had been dismissed and forgotten.

Chapter 7

"Well, I liked her exceedingly," Marianne said as they drove away from the park. Jamie was asleep on his mother's knee, the precious model ship clutched under his arm.

"You can say that only because you never met Robert Maitland," Adam said with disdain. "Am I right, Phin?"

Phineas was only half listening. He assessed and dismissed another group of ladies—not one of them was tall enough or graceful enough to be Yasmina—and looked at Adam blankly. Marianne laughed and swatted his knee.

"Pay attention, Phineas! We were talking about Isobel Maitland. I liked her, but Adam did not. What did you think?"

Adam interrupted before Phineas could reply. "I did not say I didn't like *her*. I said I did not care for her husband, or her brother-in-law, for that matter. You are most unfair, sweetheart. I hardly know the lady well enough after five minutes in her company to form an opinion." He grinned at Phineas. "She set you on your ear, though. It was very smoothly done, was it not?"

An insult was an insult, and all the worse coming from a dull creature like Isobel Maitland. Phineas opened his mouth to say so, but Marianne cut in.

"Never mind, Phin. You'll have ample opportunity to

change Isobel's mind. She's coming to Miranda's debut. You can dance with her, escort her in to supper and charm her into thinking well of you."

Phineas suppressed a shudder. Dance with her? Escort her? Why should he?

"Are you certain she plans to attend?" Adam asked. "If that horribly dull gown she was wearing was any indication, it looks as if she's still in mourning, and won't be doing any dancing. Either that or she's about to take holy vows and become a nun, eh, Phin?"

Phineas didn't bother trying to answer. He'd almost forgotten how impossible it was to get a word in when Adam and Marianne were arguing, or *discussing,* a situation they felt passionately about. He had absolutely no intention of dancing with the insulting frump. He'd save his charity dances for deserving ladies like Great-Aunt Augusta and Evelyn Renshaw.

"Since when did you start noticing ladies' fashions, Adam?" Marianne sniffed. "And such a critic too! Of course Isobel's coming. She said she'd received an invitation."

Phineas glanced at her as she paused for breath, a rare occurrence with Marianne.

"Actually, I think I shall send a personal invitation to Isobel the moment we get home. Her son is a perfect playmate for Jamie."

"Ah, so that's it," Adam crowed. "Next you'll be declaring Phineas the perfect escort for the boy's mother too, and demanding that he come to tea with her, and squire her to the opera, and the theatre, and—"

Phineas stared at his brother-in-law in horror. Even in jest, making such a suggestion to Marianne was like waving a red flag before a bull. She'd charge it without a second thought as to how it would affect *him.*

"Adam, don't even—" Phineas began, but Marianne rounded on her husband, the fire in her eyes consuming every ounce of Adam's attention. Phineas ran a finger under his cravat. It was getting warm in the confined space of the coach.

"I don't see why he should not do so. She is a lovely person!"

"She's dull," Adam said.

"The cut and quality of her garments were of the best."

"She's prim."

"She has excellent manners! If you'd bothered to look, you would have noticed that her eyes were pretty, and she is a lady to her fingertips!"

"Despite her mud-stained gloves, I suppose," Adam muttered. "And you know very well that you'd have my hide for stockings if I dared to notice another woman's pretty eyes. And what about the set-down she handed Phin without so much as a blush? Phineas hardly deserves to be saddled with her. Did he do you some dreadful childhood wrong, that he owes you such a debt?"

"Really, Adam, it isn't going to—" Phineas started again, but Marianne was glaring at her husband, and Adam was glaring back. His sister never looked away first, and Adam was just as stubborn. Phineas sighed and gave serious consideration to throwing himself out of the moving coach.

When the vehicle pulled up at Augusta Porter-Penwarren's vast mansion, Marianne let the footman take her sleeping son, and stalked up the steps into the house in high dudgeon. Adam looked after her hungrily, and Phineas rolled his eyes. Fighting always ended this way for the Westlakes. No one would see either of them for the rest of the afternoon.

Adam waited until his wife entered the house and the door closed behind her before turning to look at Phineas. "There. That's settled. You understand what you have to do?"

Phineas raised his eyebrows. "Not in the least."

"Did you know Lady Isobel's husband was shot and killed

during a smuggling raid? Since her brother-in-law might like-wise be up to something he shouldn't be, I'd say Marianne's budding friendship with the widow makes a perfect opportunity to find out more. Use your seductive touch," Adam ordered. "Consider it duty, old man. It will also make Marianne happy, and it will keep you out of trouble while your grandfather is in Town." He glanced at the front door. "Look, I dare not let Marianne's anger simmer too long. I won't bother to ask you in. With Miranda's ball tomorrow night, it's sure to be hell's playground inside. My coach will take you wherever you wish to go."

Phineas watched him climb the steps two at a time, hot on his wife's trail, and ordered the coachman back to White's. In a single day his life had become even more of a complicated tangle of intrigue and mayhem than it usually was.

He stared at the model ship that had slipped from Jamie's hands in his sleep and now lay forgotten on the floor of the coach. He was tempted to redirect the coachman to the docks and get on the first outbound ship he came to. He shut his eyes and rubbed the idea away with thumb and forefinger. He could not, of course. He had work to do, and his sister was making her debut and had asked for his company.

Most of all, he wasn't going anywhere until he found Yasmina.

Chapter 8

Isobel slipped through the front door and headed for the stairs. She stifled a cry of surprise as Jane Kirk threw open the doors of the salon and pinned her to the wall with a look of triumph. She was caught. She peered over Jane's shoulder to see Honoria lounging on the settee, glaring at her.

"You are late again, Isobel. I hope there's a good explanation."

Isobel untied the ribbons of her bonnet, using the few seconds it took to compose herself before answering. She silently cursed Blackwood. He'd rattled her senses and she could barely think. Fortunately, Nurse had taken Robin through the kitchen and up the back stairs so Honoria wouldn't see him.

"Mud!" Jane Kirk said in horror, and Isobel looked up, expecting to find her son dripping pond water on the hall floor, but her mother-in-law's companion was staring at Isobel's soiled gloves as if dirt might be contagious. Instinctively, Isobel clasped her hands behind her back, but the footman was waiting. Slipping the gloves off, she handed them to him, and sent Jane a single sweeping glare before lowering her eyes demurely. Then she followed the blue and white striped carpet to her usual seat in the salon, a straight-backed chair across from Honoria.

"What have you been doing all afternoon?" Honoria demanded. With the point of a fat finger she indicated that Jane should refill her teacup.

"I had an appointment with my modiste," Isobel said. "I believe I mentioned it at luncheon."

Honoria sniffed. "It took rather a long time for a simple fitting. If the woman is so slow, we'd be better to switch your patronage to my modiste. She is more expensive, of course, but we could cut your allowance in another area—"

"No!" Isobel blurted. Honoria and Jane stared at her in open-mouthed surprise, resembling fresh-caught gudgeon in a fish market. She swallowed the lump in her throat and tried again. "No, thank you, Honoria. The shop was just busy today, with the start of the Season upon us."

"But you are a countess and you should receive the service due to your title."

Isobel raised her chin. No one ignored her title more thoroughly than Honoria herself, but there was no point in reminding her mother-in-law that she outranked her socially. "Of course, and Madame is always very prompt, but afterward I went for a stroll with Robin and his nurse in the park." She tossed out the small admission like bait to a hungry dog.

"Was the earl in the mud?" Jane asked, casting a look at Honoria that spoke of disobedience and dishonor.

"Of course not!" Isobel said quickly, praying that they did not send for Robin to check.

"Then where did the mud on your gloves come from, Countess?" Jane Kirk asked, her tone dripping with deference, and at odds with the glitter of suspicion in her eyes.

"A careless coachman, I'm afraid. I was splashed as he passed—slightly—when I left the modiste's," Isobel lied, her tongue thick and slow on the words. She managed a tepid smile as Jane handed her a cup of tea.

The clock ticked as Honoria assessed her in silence, chomping on a biscuit. It had been a horrible day. First, her indiscretion with Blackwood had plagued her. She still felt a wicked tingle at the memory. Then, the stupid man had not even recognized her. How could he be so dense? Her hands shook and she set her teacup down so the rattle of the china wouldn't give away her turbulent emotions.

Once Honoria released her, she would have to go upstairs and write a note to Marianne, making her excuses for not attending the ball. A headache perhaps, or a case of plague.

The door opened and Isobel jumped. The butler entered with a silver tray. "A letter has arrived for you, Countess."

"A letter?" Honoria screeched. "Who on earth is it from? Bring it to me at once, Finch."

The butler knew better than to argue. He crossed the room and held the tray before Honoria.

Isobel's throat tightened. What if it was from Blackwood? What if he'd recognized her after all? What would such a letter say? The wicked things he'd murmured in her ear flew through her mind. She pressed a hand to her hot cheek.

Honoria glared at the initials that indented the red sealing wax. "I don't recognize this seal," she said suspiciously as she unfolded the letter and read it.

Isobel waited, her heart climbing into her throat, her brain working frantically to think of a way to deny she had ever even seen Evelyn's garden, let alone—

Jane Kirk, who was reading over her mistress's shoulder, gasped. Honoria gave an odd squawk, and Isobel half rose from her seat, her heart thundering. She should have known he would not be discreet. She had flouted the terms of Robert's will, and now she would be banished, driven out, and would never see Robin again.

"I can explain," she pleaded, her head buzzing as if it were filled with bees.

"Countess Westlake!" Honoria cried. Isobel watched in

bafflement as a grin oozed over every jowly inch of Honoria's countenance. "Countess Westlake, granddaughter of the Duke of Carrington, sister to Lady Miranda Archer!" she said, as if she were announcing Marianne's arrival. "How on earth did *you* form such a connection?" she demanded.

Isobel's breath stuck in her throat. Honoria didn't look angry. She didn't look suspicious or vengeful. She looked utterly delighted.

The sight struck terror into Isobel's heart.

"I—" she began, and stopped, wondering if she dared admit the truth. "I—I met her just this afternoon."

Honoria clasped the letter to her bosom, her face wreathed in a ghastly yellow-toothed grin. "Her grandfather is a duke, her husband one of England's wealthiest earls! How fortuitous!" Even Jane Kirk was regarding Honoria with concern now.

"Do you know her?" Isobel asked, her voice a thread of sound.

"Know her? No, of course *I* don't know her!" Honoria turned to Jane. "Don't stand there gaping. Fetch Charles at once. He's in his study, I believe."

"Actually, my lady, he's in the billiards room," Jane murmured tartly.

Honoria wasn't listening. Her eyes were fixed on Isobel, glowing, as if lit by some unholy fire inside. Isobel schooled her features into the perfect dullness that had become second nature. She might appear as blank as a wall, but her cheeks burned as if she was too close to the fire, and her forbidden silk undergarment was clinging to her sweaty skin.

"What is it, Mother?" Charles asked impatiently, returning with Jane. He ignored Isobel entirely.

"Charles, you'll never guess who Isobel has become acquainted with!"

"The Prince Regent? King George himself?" Charles said without interest, taking a fresh-baked ginger biscuit from the tea tray and flopping into a wing chair.

"Countess Westlake!" Honoria crowed.

"So?" Charles asked, blowing biscuit crumbs over his waistcoat.

"I assume Isobel met her at the modiste's," Honoria said. She fixed Isobel with a sharp stare. "What did she purchase? What color was it, what fabric?"

Isobel couldn't recall a thing about what Marianne had been wearing, but she could have described every crease in Blackwood's cravat. "Actually, I met her by chance in the park. She was there with her son, Viscount Halliwell. He's the same age as Robin, you see, and they—"

"You allowed Robin to play in the park?" Jane Kirk began, but Honoria waved her to silence.

"And now she has sent you a personal invitation to her sister's debut ball!"

"She has?" Isobel croaked. If the vague spark of interest in Charles's eyes and Honoria's grin were anything to go by, she'd never be able to bow out of attending now.

"Yes!" Honoria handed the letter to her at last. "You should have told her we had received an invitation, of course, and mentioned Charles's name, and mine." Isobel tried to focus on the elegant script, but she recalled Westlake's flat expression when she had confirmed that Charles Maitland was her brother-in-law. Still, she saw an opportunity for Robin, and leapt at it.

"Robin gets on well with her son James," she said, raising her eyes to meet Honoria's. "In fact, Countess Westlake has invited us to tea so the boys can—"

"To tea!" The hectic fuchsia shade of Honoria's face was quite alarming. "Jane, go and fetch paper and ink. She must accept at once. It is a most marvelous connection! I will accompany you, of course," she said. Even Jane Kirk looked impressed now, though she tried to hide it.

Isobel clenched her hands in her lap, heard the paper crumple in protest and smoothed the letter against her knee.

"It will be some days before we can think of calling, Honoria. They are quite busy with arrangements for Lady Miranda's debut, and Robin has his lessons." She almost bit her tongue, saying such a thing.

Honoria ignored the objection. "Charles! Do you understand what this means? Isobel can arrange your introduction to Lady Miranda!"

Charles looked at Isobel as if seeing her for the first time. "Well, well. How fortuitous indeed."

"You shall court her, Charles, and Isobel will be there to speak well of you, to encourage the young lady to look fondly on you. Why, by the end of the Season you could find yourself betrothed to the granddaughter of the Duke of Carrington. How famous!" Honoria was giggling with pleasure now, her whole body vibrating with delight at her scheme.

The tea gathered itself into a tidal wave in Isobel's stomach. She wished she'd never met Marianne Westlake, even if it meant a friend for Robin. Just a slip of the tongue and Blackwood's name might come up. She leapt to her feet, and three pairs of sharp eyes fixed on her like rapiers, ready to kill the slightest objection to their plans. She fixed her gaze on the floor, sure her sins were written in her eyes.

"Would you excuse me? I have a slight headache."

For once she didn't wait to be dismissed.

Chapter 9

I f the sharp smell of fresh paint and the new draperies in this small salon were anything to go by, then Phineas was willing to bet that his great-aunt had had every inch of her elegant town house done over for Miranda's debut.

He had arrived early for two reasons. He wanted to see his sister before she set sail on the turbulent seas of the marriage mart. And, his great-aunt did not want him to be seen arriving at her front door with "polite" society.

He eyed the whisky decanter across the room and considered having a drink. It was going to be a long evening, and a trying one. Being in the bosom of his family was like sitting naked in a nest of vipers. He was sure to be bitten before the night was over, and perhaps before it even began, if his grandfather teamed up with Augusta.

He turned as the door opened, but didn't recognize the slender blond beauty until she hitched up her shimmering skirts and came at him running. He opened his arms and caught her.

"Phin!" Miranda hugged him, and his heart constricted. She was all grown up. She was wearing perfume, and silk, and a fortune in jewels. He laid his chin against her artfully styled curls, crowned with the glittering Carrington tiara, and wondered what had happened to the soft yellow braids he used to tug.

He breathed her in. Rosewater, like his mother used to wear.

It wasn't until she stepped back and smiled at him, her blue eyes lit with joy, that he recognized his little sister in the woman before him.

Phineas held her at arm's length and looked at her. She simpered and batted her eyelashes, already a practiced debutante. He kept the smile on his face so he wouldn't disappoint her. She'd obviously been well coached in how to attract a husband. Everything from her gown to her gestures was perfect.

In an hour or so gentlemen would be looking at Miranda as a potential bride, and she would be flirting with countless suitors. She was beautiful enough to attract entirely the wrong kind of attention. He felt his smile slip, and forced it back into place.

"Well?" she asked. "How do I look?" She was practicing her fledgling wiles on him, he realized, and he didn't like it in the least. She shouldn't flirt with rakes like him.

He was tempted to say she looked far too grown up, and remind her that the last time he'd seen her, she was rolling in the orchard with a litter of puppies, her knees skinned, her freckled face sun-kissed and filthy. "You look beautiful," he managed.

She smiled sweetly and smoothed a gloved hand over her white satin skirt. "Good. I have saved the second dance for you, right after Grandfather. I wanted it to be a waltz, but I have not yet been approved to waltz."

The idea of Miranda waltzing made Phineas uncomfortable in the extreme. He pictured a man's hand on her waist, his eyes fixed on her fashionably exposed bosom as they swept around the dance floor. His hands curled, resisting the urge to snatch the handkerchief from his pocket and tie it around her neck like a bib.

"Really?" He wondered if she would be foolish enough in her innocence to consent to a walk in the garden, should someone ask.

He stepped closer to her, but she didn't notice the protective gesture. She drew off one elbow length glove and turned to fuss with her curls in the looking glass. She pinched her cheeks and bit her lips to redden them, then raised sultry eyes to smile coquettishly at her brother's reflection.

"Yes, really. The patronesses of Almack's must give each debutante permission to waltz. I know you are not allowed access to Almack's, of course, because of your reputation, but Great-Aunt Augusta says there are rules that must be followed. I've spent the last year learning them, and I still don't think I know them all."

"Do you still like puppies?" Phineas asked.

"Puppies?" She accented the word with studied, elegant disbelief. She tossed her head, her eyes sparkling to rival the tiara. "I'm too old for puppies, Phin."

"No one should be too old for puppies." He wasn't going to let her out of his sight tonight. Any gentleman who came near her would have to go through him first. These men weren't puppies. They were full grown dogs.

She pulled on her glove with ladylike grace, smoothing the satin in place from wrist to elbow. "Do you know Richard Muir? Or Andrew Compton?"

He did. Their names on his sister's lips made him frown. "Why do you ask?"

"Because they are two of the most eligible gentlemen this Season."

Phineas frowned. Richard Muir was too old for Miranda and too fond of bedding other men's wives. Andrew Compton gambled more than he could afford to lose and had vowels all over town. Phineas held one of them himself, for an eye-popping amount.

Miranda rattled off the names of other wealthy, titled, single men. "You've made a list?" he asked in surprise.

"Of course. It wouldn't do to waste my time on someone who isn't suitable."

He scanned her face, read the seriousness there. She had all the tender sentiments of a banker recalling a loan. "How can you expect to fall in love with a name?"

"Love? How silly you are, Phin. What does that have to do with anything? I won't marry a title lower than earl, and he must have at least sixty thousand a year."

The shrewdness in her blue eyes gave Phineas chills. "You don't marry a title, Miranda. You marry a man. What if you fall in love with a mere second son? Or a vicar?"

She tilted her head like a seasoned flirt. "Don't be ridiculous! Grandfather would reject his suit, of course. As would I."

Before he could argue, his great-aunt swept into the room, resplendent in emerald silk and diamonds. Even at sixty, Lady Augusta Porter-Penwarren was a handsome woman. "Miranda, your guests will be arriving soon. It's time to go downstairs and prepare to greet them."

She looked down her aristocratic nose at her great-nephew. "I see you've arrived, Blackwood. I trust you'll remember who and where you are and behave yourself tonight. This is not a brothel."

He hadn't seen Augusta in more than three years, but the coldness in her eyes hadn't changed, nor had the unmistakable expression of distaste that a rake like him should be tied to her by blood. He bowed, resisting the temptation to horrify her by kissing her cheek.

"I promise I will not seduce a single debutante," he said with the roguish grin he used to charm older ladies and make them feel like girls again. It had no discernable effect on Augusta.

"You are the worst sort of rake, Blackwood. Unrepentant."

"Thank you, Great-Aunt." He stepped forward to offer his arm. "May I escort you downstairs?"

Augusta drew back as if the fine black wool of his sleeve was poisoned. "Certainly not! I expect you to slip in quietly once everyone else has arrived, and not disrupt the evening!"

She turned her back on him as Carrington entered the room, leaving Phineas standing with his arm extended. He lowered it and clasped his hands behind his back, taking care not to let his irritation show.

His grandfather's face lit with pleasure at the sight of Miranda. Phineas's jaw tightened. He had never seen even a vague shadow of the approval that now shone in Carrington's eyes. He reminded himself it was merely a hazard of his profession, of the illusion he had created. He stood apart from his family, like an unwelcome ghost in perfectly tailored evening clothes.

Miranda kissed Carrington's wrinkled cheek, completely unafraid of the old curmudgeon. "Grandfather, you look so handsome tonight. I shall feel like a princess on your arm."

Carrington smiled down at her, and Augusta adjusted the pleats at the back of Miranda's gown, making a loving family circle that Phineas was not part of. He cleared his throat and watched Carrington's joyful expression harden into the familiar harsh lines as he turned to regard his heir.

"I suppose I should be pleased you're on time, Blackwood."

"Actually, I'm early."

"I've warned him to stay out of sight until there's a proper crowd," Augusta said. "Perhaps no one will notice him."

Carrington looked surprised. "What? No, I think he should be downstairs. There are several eligible young ladies coming tonight. Do you recall what I told you, Blackwood?"

He didn't bother to reply, and Miranda looked up at her brother. "He thinks it's time you married, Phineas," she prompted. "Imagine it. We could have a double wedding."

Phineas looked at her fresh, virginal face and suppressed a shudder. They expected him to choose a girl like his little sister, a chit right out of the schoolroom with no experience of the world at all. That kind of wife held no appeal. He tried to recall the women he'd known in the past, the many bedmates and mistresses, searching his memory for someone whose conversation he had enjoyed as much as the pleasures of her body. Only one came to mind. A passionate lady in a dark garden.

"I haven't made my list, I'm afraid," he said, grinning at Miranda, who laughed aloud.

"Miranda!" Lady Augusta admonished. "Ladies do not laugh like horses."

Miranda clapped a satin-gloved hand over her mouth. "I'm sorry, Great-Aunt. I'll help you make a list of potential brides, Phineas," she said more demurely.

"A list? There's no need of a list," Carrington said. "The Duke of Welford's girl is making her come-out this Season. She would be suitable. Good lineage, and a very generous dowry. She has thirty thousand a year, as well. She'd make a fine marchioness, and an excellent duchess."

Augusta snorted in disbelief. So much for ladies not sounding like horses, Phineas thought. "Welford isn't going to countenance a scapegrace like Blackwood as his son-in-law! If he's to have a chance at the girl at all, he'll have to learn to behave." She sized him up with a soul-searing glare, as if she doubted such a transformation were possible.

Phineas couldn't resist the challenge. He held her gaze, slowly raising one eyebrow as he let a slow smile spread over his face. A practiced rake was irresistible to *any* lady when he set his mind on seduction, and he played his role well.

He watched two crimson spots rise like twin suns in Augusta's cheeks. She snapped open her fan and flapped it before her flushed face.

"I shall arrange an introduction to Welford's girl this very evening," she said to cover her confusion. "God help her, though. Come, it's past time we were downstairs."

Phineas followed his family down the polished oak staircase, two paces behind.

"Blackwood, you will stand at the end of the receiving line, next to Westlake," Augusta instructed. "I want you as far away from Miranda as possible."

Phineas ignored the insult, took his place at the entrance to the still-empty ballroom and glanced at his sister. He watched her adjust her posture, thrusting her bosom forward to best advantage, pouting moistened lips, and he cringed. They had turned a happy, loving child into the perfect debutante, ready to become the perfect society wife.

He knew the consequences of marrying for position instead of passion. Such matches were as cold as the cash boxes they were founded on. Bored husbands quickly turned to other women once an heir was born. Lonely, unhappy wives turned to men like him, settling for meaningless affairs in place of love. Surely if she knew, Miranda would want more than wealth to comfort her at night.

The guests began to pour down the marble staircase into Lady Augusta's elegant ballroom. The sibilant swish of silk and the trip of dancing shoes almost drowned out the sound of each exalted name as the butler announced the arrivals.

Phineas scanned the faces of the ladies waiting to enter. Yasmina had not yet arrived, but if she set one delectable toe into the room, he'd know. He bowed over the hand of a disapproving dowager who snatched her fingers away and hoisted her nose in the air as she sailed away on the tide of good society. He looked back at the crowd milling in the doorway.

Yasmina would be here. Every person of consequence in London was here.

All he had to do was wait.

Chapter 10

"**H**as your mysterious lady made her appearance yet?" Adam asked, taking two glasses of champagne from a passing footman and handing one to Phineas as they stood in the receiving line, waiting for the last guests to arrive. "I suppose she hasn't," he concluded when his brother-in-law didn't answer. "You're still staring at the door and watching every woman who enters like a hungry dog scenting meat. That's when you're not glaring at any man who dares to look at Miranda, of course. Quite out of character, Phin."

Phineas didn't appreciate the reminder that he was still expected to play the charming idiot and spend the evening collecting information and secrets, regardless of his family's presence.

"No, Adam, I haven't seen her yet," he snapped.

"Odd that the only place you've ever seen her is Renshaw House, and now she's the one woman in London you can't find. If she's connected with Renshaw's plans to kidnap the French king, we need to know."

Phineas watched Sir Harold MacKenzie bow over Miranda's hand, assessing both her bosom and the value of her jewels in a shrewd glance. The man was nearly as old as Carrington, and not nearly as well preserved. From her place next to Miranda, his great-aunt raised her lorgnette and glared at Phineas suspiciously. He forced himself to smile.

"Are you certain she wasn't foreign? French, perhaps?" Adam suggested in a low voice, dragging his attention back. "Perhaps she's left the city. Or the country."

Phineas shook his head. "No, she is as English as I am."

"Why, because she didn't scream *'mon Dieu'* in the moment of passion?" Adam asked sarcastically.

Phineas gave his brother-in-law a roguish grin. "They all scream *'mon Dieu,'* Adam. The English ones loudest of all."

Adam sipped his champagne. "The lady your grandfather is speaking with doesn't look familiar," he offered.

"That's Lady Morton. Too old, and much too short," Phineas said.

"And the lady in the yellow gown, there, with the Duchess of Welford?"

Phineas frowned. "That's her daughter, Lady Amelia. We just met her, if you'll recall." And he had discarded her as a potential bride in the same moment. The simpering, spoiled, horsey type of woman did not even appeal to him as a dinner companion, let alone a wife.

"And next to her?" Adam persisted.

"Miss Anna Charles. Too thin."

"The one with the lacquered fan in the corner?"

"Not her," Phineas said firmly. "Stop trying to be helpful."

"Are you sure you only saw her in the dark?"

Phineas sent him a look of irritation. "I'll know her when I see her."

"I must remind you of the urgency of doing so, Blackwood. You have a job to do, and—"

Marianne reached around her husband and poked Phineas. "Look, Phin, Isobel Maitland has arrived. And you said she wouldn't come!"

He hadn't said any such thing, Adam had. Phineas watched the widow coming down the stairs. She wore a gown of brownish-red bombazine that rustled like dry leaves in a graveyard. Her hair was pulled tightly back from her pale face in a severe style twenty years too old for her, and her huge hazel eyes flicked around the room like a pair of nervous hummingbirds before coming to rest on him. He watched her lips part as her face flushed almost as purple as her hideous outfit. She stumbled on the last step, and he reached out to catch her, gripping her elbows to steady her. The soft skin of her upper arm was warm, and he felt the flutter of her breath on his cheek for an instant.

She stared up into his eyes for a frozen moment before she pulled free, looking positively horrified as she stepped back out of reach.

So the widow thought a rake's touch would dishonor her, soil the memory of her dead husband, did she? What did she expect, that he had intended to ravish her on the spot? He'd have to be extremely hard up for that. He felt her newest insult keenly.

He let his disdain show in his eyes, but she didn't look at him again. The toes of her shoes seemed to be fascinating in the extreme. He pasted a carefully bored look on his face as Marianne leapt forward to fawn over the miserable woman.

There was worse to come. Hard on the countess's flat, sensible heels, a portly matron in a ruffled lavender gown descended upon him. He made himself smile charmingly and reach for her hand as she approached, but she pulled back with a gargantuan gasp. Her jaw dropped into a vast set of rippling chins that went all the way down to the overstuffed confines of the low neckline of her gown. She stared at him in horror, effectively blocking the staircase for everyone else.

"Charles, it's *him*!" she cried, her voice surprisingly high-pitched for such a large woman. Phineas had expected a tone like a low note on a pipe organ. She had the frame for it.

"Good evening, Blackwood," Charles Maitland said

sourly from behind the lavender behemoth, not bothering with any kind of smile at all. "Didn't think *you'd* be here tonight. This is my mother, Lady Honoria, the Dowager Countess of Ashdown." He joined Phineas in regarding the frozen woman, standing with her hands clutched against her bosom as if Phineas were a rat in her pantry instead of a marquess in a ballroom. "Make your curtsy, for pity's sake, Mother. It won't do to be rude to him."

Honoria Maitland dipped, and let her eyes wander over him again. Every one of the lady's chins flushed pink. "My my," she murmured. Charles frowned, and led her on to greet Carrington.

Phineas noted that Charles didn't bother to introduce his sister-in-law. The countess outranked her relations and should have been introduced first, but she trailed behind them like a shadow.

"I see Charles Maitland is here," Adam said with sarcastic brightness.

"Unfortunately," Phineas replied. Maitland would no doubt be in the card room for most of the evening. Once Charles had a few glasses of champagne and several tots of brandy, he would ask the man a few subtle questions about Robert Maitland's untimely death. Phineas glanced at the widow, wondering what it would take to loosen *her* tongue.

She moved to make her curtsy to Carrington, only to be knocked aside by Lady Honoria.

"Good evening, Your Grace!" Honoria shrieked at Carrington, dipping so low that Charles had to haul her back up.

Lady Isobel took a step backward and stood apart from her family, her eyes on her mother-in-law's broad backside. Her hands were clasped demurely, her arms white against the darkness of her dress. She looked delicate and dignified, unlike the other Maitlands.

"I suppose Lady Honoria thinks a man of Carrington's

years must be quite deaf," Adam whispered. "Won't be hard to overhear *that* conversation."

"Good evening, madam," the duke said, with the politely blank expression he reserved for people he considered social inferiors. Phineas knew that look well. He watched his grandfather's features harden to full ducal haughtiness as the vast lavender figure before him grinned like a pirate.

"Grandfather, this is Isobel, Countess Ashdown," Marianne said, but had to catch Carrington's arm and lean around Honoria to point out the slender widow. "Her son is a great friend of Jamie's." Phineas hid a smile as the old duke reddened at the impropriety of the awkward introduction.

Lady Isobel was jostled by people moving past her, as if she were invisible. But of course she was, Phineas thought. She was hardly the kind of woman to command attention in a crowd, or engender any emotion other than pity. She curtsied again to Carrington as her mother-in-law continued to stand like a wall between herself and the duke.

"Countess Ashdown," his grandfather murmured, his eyes roaming over her dowdy gown. "And where is the Earl of Ashdown this evening?"

"At home in bed, of course, Your Grace," Honoria put in before Isobel could speak.

Phineas watched Isobel blush. She didn't move a single submissive line of her body, but he didn't miss the flare of heat in her eyes before she lowered them. Her pulse hammered against the white skin of her throat in agitation, or fury, or embarrassment. Her hands were clasped so tightly her black satin gloves were wrinkled.

"Is he ill?" Carrington asked, looking from Honoria to Charles to Isobel, his brow furrowing in concern.

"Who?" Honoria asked, distracted. Her narrow little eyes had found Miranda. Phineas bristled. She looked like she was considering dining on his sister.

"The Earl of Ashdown, of course," Carrington said, looking at Isobel. "Your husband, madam?"

"He's dead," Charles said flatly, also staring at Miranda, who flushed uncertainly as Charles leaned toward her, all but drooling on her, his expression openly lecherous. Phineas started forward, but Adam grabbed his sleeve.

"Careful, Phin," he murmured. "What would Carrington say if you started a punch-up at your sister's come-out ball before she'd even had her first dance?"

Carrington was regarding Isobel in horrified surprise. She smiled, and it transformed her features. Slightly.

"My *son* is the current Earl of Ashdown, Your Grace. As he is only five, he is indeed at home in bed," she explained succinctly. Phineas didn't miss the furtive look of exasperation she sent Honoria and Charles, but they did, since it was gone almost as quickly as it appeared.

It was obvious the lady did not like her relatives by marriage. There was anger in the tilt of the countess's head, in the tight muscles in her jaw and slender neck, yet her face remained free of any emotion at all. Now that made her interesting, in his opinion.

If Isobel Maitland had a secret, he'd know it before the night was through.

Phineas glanced at his grandfather, still beset by Charles and Honoria. There was a dangerous tic starting under Carrington's right eye.

"Thank you for coming," the duke said pointedly, but the Maitlands would not be dismissed.

"How soon will you be taking offers for Lady Miranda's hand?" Honoria asked, and Phineas felt every nerve in his body heat. He finished the champagne in a gulp and set the glass down with exaggerated care.

"Steady, old man," Adam warned again. Phineas put his fist behind his back and watched Charles smirk at Miranda.

She swallowed nervously, the pearls around her neck bobbing.

Carrington's complexion reddened at the question, and Augusta snapped her fan open with a crack like a pistol shot.

"I will not be entertaining serious offers for some weeks yet," Carrington replied, his tone brittle. Phineas felt a warm flush of family pride. It was nice to see that there was someone Carrington disliked as much as his own heir. He felt a smirk tug at his lips, and looked up to find Isobel watching him. She looked away at once, fading backward into the crowd like a ghost, instantly subsumed into the crush of living bodies.

"Perhaps we should invite Charles to dinner, and pick his brain for secrets. He seems quite taken with Miranda," Adam mused, and Phineas shot him a hot glare.

"There are ways to get information that don't require torture," Phineas said.

"Good lord, Phin, I wasn't suggesting torture!"

"What else would you call dinner with a boor like Maitland?"

At the top of the stairs, the footmen closed the doors to the ballroom with a decisive thud, signaling that all the invited guests had arrived.

Phineas felt his stomach sink. *She* hadn't arrived. Either that or he'd been so distracted by the damned Maitlands that he hadn't noticed her.

As the orchestra struck up the first notes, and his grandfather took Miranda's hand and swept her onto the dance floor, Phineas scanned the crowd. It had been days since Evelyn's ball, yet he remembered how Yasmina smelled, how she tasted, how she felt in his arms.

He just had no idea what she *looked* like. He racked his brain, trying to put scanty clues together and assemble a woman.

She was tall, since the top of the little cap she'd worn had reached his ear. Several women present fit that description, but he knew all of them.

Yasmina had full, delicious breasts. They'd been hidden from view under her costume, of course, but he held them in his hands in the dark, heard her sigh, felt her nipples harden at his touch.

His hands curled against his sides as he stared at the ample and well-displayed breasts that filled his great-aunt's ballroom, trying to picture them naked, measuring them in handfuls.

He remembered her perfume, something exotic and unforgettable, but he could hardly prowl the ballroom sniffing ladies' necks. That kind of behavior would ensure he'd have more duels arranged for dawn than he could fight in a month, and he made it a rule never to be seen out of bed before noon. Rising early after a debauched night in the lowest gaming hells and gentlemen's clubs in London would hardly fit with the image of a carefree rake he'd so carefully cultivated. Nor would it do to be seen dueling for something as trifling to a rogue as a lady's honor.

He had no idea what color her hair might be, but he remembered her mouth. Her lips were full, and she'd tasted of champagne when he kissed her. There wasn't a single woman in view with a mouth full enough, or red enough, or mobile enough to be hers.

Phineas shut his eyes. He was standing in his aunt's ballroom, at his sister's debut ball, staring at the female guests with a very inconvenient erection.

Damn Yasmina!

He backed toward the nearest pillar, wondering if he could slip out of the room without anyone noticing. He needed some air. He needed—

"Eek!"

He stepped on something soft and turned. Isobel Maitland

stood in the shadows behind him, clutching the toe of her slippered foot awkwardly, her face furrowed in pain.

He instinctively stepped forward to shield her from the curious eyes around them as she recovered. It hardly seemed necessary. Her dull gown almost matched the heavy shadows that filled the corner she'd chosen. Her pale face floated in the gloom.

"Your pardon, Countess Ashdown. I didn't see you there," he said sarcastically, irritated that it should be *her* of all people. "I don't know how I could have failed to notice you in the dark."

She righted herself, leaning on the pillar, her bare, ungloved hand as white as the marble. "It's quite all right. I didn't expect you to back up, or I would have gotten out of your way, my lord," she said in the same frosty tone he'd used.

Despite her polite words, her eyes glittered in silent reproof and her lips were pursed in disapproval. It annoyed him that this dowdy creature should find him repulsive. Women of her sort usually found his attentions flattering.

"Are you enjoying the party?" he asked, knowing she was not—could not—from the dark corner she'd chosen to hide in. She blushed, the added color a distinct improvement to her looks. Her long lashes swept downward over high, elegant cheekbones. He had a sudden urge to snatch the pins out of her matronly coiffure, to loosen both her auburn hair and the lady herself and see what Isobel Maitland *really* looked like. "Perhaps you'd like some champagne?"

Her mouth rippled in response, but she folded her lips between her teeth, pressing the color out of them. "No thank you," she said primly.

He stood beside her awkwardly. It would be rude to walk away and leave her alone. He took the opportunity to study her as she stared at the tiled floor. Under purely masculine appraisal, without any bias for her shrewish personality, the severe hairstyle and lack of jewels, the feminine body under the ghastly dress was surprisingly good.

"Marianne is pleased that you came tonight," he said less harshly, but the comment merely earned him a sharp look of suspicion. "I am trying to make polite conversation, my lady. It would be helpful if you participated. You might say something about how many people my great-aunt has managed to cram into this overly warm room tonight, or mention the pleasantness of the weather. It needn't be witty, if that's a strain for you."

He hadn't imagined she'd understand the biting comment, but her eyes shot to meet his, a fire kindling in their golden depths.

"It has been a cold, wet spring, save for yesterday," she said, "and I understand that the number of people here tonight is due to the fact that there is a debut ball taking place. I would be surprised if there was an unmarried gentleman to be found anywhere else in London, given Lady Miranda's fortune and beauty. Marianne tells me that you are likewise seeking a wife, my lord, which possibly accounts for the vast numbers of ladies, wouldn't you say?"

He blinked at her, read the keen wit in her eyes. Marianne was right. She did have pretty eyes, he admitted grudgingly, molten pools of copper and gold, as if an alchemist had taken the lumpen lead of her appearance and transformed it into something precious. It annoyed him that this dull, difficult widow should have redeeming features.

"And you, Countess?" he asked coldly. "If I recollect, your husband died several years ago. Is it not time to come out of mourning and find another?"

The color in her face fled and she glanced around nervously. She met his eyes, her expression expectant for a brief instant, before she lowered her gaze to stare at his waistcoat.

Phineas felt a sharp jab of horror. Good God, surely she didn't think he meant it as an offer? Even if he did, it would have been a compliment to her, a marquess proposing to a peahen. It would hardly warrant the look of embarrassment on her face.

Perhaps she had loved Robert Maitland, and he had been boorish enough to remind her of her loss. He watched her sag under the cruel blow of his thoughtless comment. This was the moment to ask her a few questions about Robert, but he could not bring himself to flirt with *her,* of all women, to charm the information out of her.

"I did not mean to suggest—" he began, ready to console her, but she recovered instantly. Straightening her spine, she rose upward like a flower on a stem too fragile for the blossom. Her vulnerability fled and she regarded him with ferocity in her luminous eyes, pride clear in every elegant line of her body. Her breasts heaved under the hissing fabric of her dress as she glared at him.

"I believe the first dance has ended, my lord, and Lady Miranda is looking for you." She turned her head away to look out over the crowd, her long neck a white column of indignation.

Phineas realized he'd been dismissed. He didn't like it. Not from her. She should be grateful he'd taken the time to exchange a few words with her at all. It would surely prove the highlight of her evening, since no one else was likely to come near her. He bowed stiffly and walked away, not bothering to bid her good evening.

Isobel dropped her gaze to the black and white marble floor so she would not see him walk away from her, but her eyes were inexorably drawn to him, like a moth to a flame. He was a very stupid man, possibly the greatest fool she had ever met, and that included Charles and Robert and her father

too. She also tarred him with the sins of arrogance and rudeness. He had no idea who she was, who she had been to him.

She watched as he bowed gallantly to his sister and led
her onto the dance floor. He smiled lovingly at Miranda as
they danced. Isobel's toes curled and her breath caught in her
throat. She remembered the warmth in his eyes at Evelyn's
ball, eyes that never left hers, as if she were the most fascinating woman on earth. She felt her heart skip a beat, curl
into a tight, hard knot inside her empty chest. It had meant
nothing. The man was a heartless rake, an inveterate flirt and
not worth another thought.

But she bit the inside of her cheek as he executed the
dance's intricate steps perfectly, his athletic body moving
easily in time with the music, all masculine pride and
perfection.

Isobel licked her lips, suddenly dry, and longed for that
glass of champagne, but knew she dare not indulge while
Honoria was close by. She was forbidden to drink spirits at
social functions, in case she became intoxicated and found
herself contemplating an affair with an Italian musician, as
her mother had. She glanced at the orchestra. Not one of them
looked even remotely Italian. Nor was there a man among
them she would consider giving up everything for.

Not one of them was Blackwood.

The dance ended and Blackwood handed his sister to her
next partner and retreated to lean against a pillar near her own,
his eyes on the crowd. He did not even glance in her direction,
though she was not a dozen feet away. He took a glass of champagne from the tray of a passing footman, and she watched his
throat work as he swallowed. Her mouth watered, tasting the
wine vicariously.

His eyes were on Miranda, engaged in the next dance,
her smile bright and sweet and teasing. Blackwood's mouth
by contrast was twisted, and his eyes were hot enough to

burn holes in the fine black wool coats of the gentlemen who danced attendance on his sister.

He was protective, she thought, feeling a frisson of unbidden jealousy skitter across her nerves. What a hypocrite he was. He preyed on women, seduced them, then discarded them. He'd likely forgotten his encounter with Yasmina altogether. He'd probably seduced ten women since that night, though it was only six days ago. Not that she was counting. The memory of his body on hers made her gasp, shiver, and she forced herself to stay placid and unconcerned, though her heart threatened to burst from her chest and fall at his feet.

She watched in dismay as a giggling lady in the most fashionable shade of pink taffeta beckoned him to dance, and he went, smiling that rogue's smile of his. Every fiber of Isobel's being yearned to be held in his arms, flying around the dance floor. He swept by her corner a dozen times and never even looked her way, and she held her breath as he whispered something in the lady's ear that made her blush as pink as her gown.

Isobel did not dare to breathe, in case it came back out as a scream. She stood very still and waited for him to lead his pretty partner through the open French doors, but he did not. He bowed and chose another lady to dance with. Only dance. The heavy weight of bitter relief nearly dragged her to her knees.

She raised a shaking hand to her mouth to hide the twist of her lips, and resisted the urge to sob. It hardly mattered. No one was looking at her. Not even Honoria. She didn't just blend into the shadows. She was becoming one of them.

Chapter 11

"**G**ood morning, Blackwood. Isn't it rather early in the day for you to be up? I can't recall the last time I saw you in full daylight."

Phineas rolled his eyes at the jest and ignored the speaker, whoever he was. He was right, though. It was barely ten o'clock, and he'd been up for hours, but only because he hadn't been able to sleep. Yasmina still plagued his mind, and his body.

"I didn't get the chance to say hello to you at the ball last night. Your sister looked lovely, of course. Very lovely."

That got Phineas's attention. He stopped what he was doing, which was running his hand over the silken fetlock of a particularly pretty mare, and glanced up at Gilbert Fielding, an old friend he hardly saw anymore. Gilbert was impeccably respectable, and rarely descended to the kind of low places he himself frequented. He scanned the man's pleasant face, pleased to see it free of any lewd innuendo with regard to Miranda. He relaxed a little, letting the grim edges of his scowl soften.

"Fielding," he said by way of greeting, and stroked the mare's nose. She whickered her appreciation and buried her face in his greatcoat, searching for treats. Typical female.

"Looking for a horse?" Gilbert asked, and Phineas raised an eyebrow.

"Why else would a man get up at this ungodly hour and come to Tattersall's?" he asked. "I'm looking for a suitable riding horse for my sister. The nags in my great-aunt's stable are a trifle staid for Miranda." She'd mentioned it at supper last night while flirting with some *ton* fop. *He'd* send flowers this morning, but Phineas intended to make a grander gesture. He couldn't recall the last gift he'd given her. That had been one of the problems that kept him awake, trying to imagine how he might protect Miranda from predatory suitors, or at least distract her. He decided to buy her a horse.

The other problem was that Yasmina had not come to the ball. He was beginning to think he'd imagined her after all. A bitter mix of frustrated lust and disappointment brought the scowl back again.

"May I say that this lovely lass would be a perfect match for such a beauty as Lady Miranda?" Gilbert said as he ran a gentle hand along the horse's side, looking at her with clear admiration. Phineas wondered if he was thinking of the horse or the lady.

Phineas nodded to the trainer, and the lad moved off at a run to show the potential buyer the mare's paces.

"So what brings you here, Gil?" Phineas asked, strolling over to lean on the fence, his eyes on the mare.

"I've come to find a horse suitable for an army captain," Gilbert said morosely.

Phineas took note of the grim set of Gilbert's mouth. "Your father will have his way after all?"

Gilbert sighed. "So it seems. He insists I buy a commission in the army. He won't have his second-born son living a useless life. He has, bless his heart, given me reprieve until the end of the Season to find a rich wife if I can." He looked at the sky, which was threatening an icy spring downpour at any moment. "At least Spain is warm, I hear."

"Have you any prospects?" Phineas asked.

Gilbert pointed. "That gray stallion appeals to me. I like the wary look in his eyes, as if he's sensible enough to run the minute danger threatens, and take me out of harm's way along with him."

"I meant prospective brides, actually," Phineas said.

Gilbert's smile slipped. "No, not yet. The Season is young, however. Unfortunately, I am even more selective of potential brides than I am of horseflesh."

"Good teeth, strong legs, twenty thousand a year?" Phineas supplied.

"Twenty thousand? I'd settle for three, as long as we had some regard for each other. I want a *wife*, not just an income. Of course, a very wealthy wife could be just as easy to love if she were the right woman, don't you think? Take Lady Miranda, for example." He shot Phineas a glance, half hopeful, half teasing.

Phineas felt his lips twist bitterly. "Forget it, Fielding. Carrington expects her to marry a title, and you haven't got one."

Gilbert looked away, following the mare's progress from walk to trot. She was parading prettily, like a debutante making her way down Bond Street before an admiring crowd of gentlemen. "Poor devil, whoever her husband turns out to be. Anyone married to Miranda would also find himself related to you."

He said it lightly, without malice or insult, a jest to ease the awkwardness, and Phineas took it as such.

Gilbert gestured at the far paddock. "I think I'll go over and have a look at that stallion. I like him. His coloring will look well with a scarlet captain's tunic, don't you think? There's no use waiting until the last minute to choose a good cavalry horse."

Phineas watched him stride away with his head high. There was pride in every step he took over the muddy ground.

Gilbert was well aware of his lowly status as a second son and unlikely marriage prospect for any lass with a fortune, and he had callously reminded him of it.

He hadn't meant to offend Fielding. He was a decent fellow, Phineas thought, and in truth he liked him. Gilbert gambled, but never to excess. He drank, but was never unruly or mean when in his cups. He treated every woman—even whores and servant girls—with courtesy. He was a thoroughly likable chap, despite being born out of the money.

Phineas squinted at him. He supposed Fielding was good looking, though only a woman would be able to judge for certain. He'd make a respectable woman a decent husband, but he would make a dreadful army officer, in his opinion. Gilbert was too quiet and too polite.

Of course, he could put the matter in Marianne's capable hands. She'd find Gilbert a suitable lady, or die in the attempt. He racked his brain to think of a woman with money who just happened to need a husband.

Isobel Maitland sprang to mind. She was wealthy, and still young, and she was— He frowned.

Was what? Pretty?

He pushed the image of her fine eyes and sharp tongue out of his mind and pulled the collar of his greatcoat higher. She wasn't right for Gilbert.

It was starting to drizzle. He had hoped to take the mare to Miranda this morning, ask her to go riding with him in Hyde Park. The old Miranda would've gone no matter what the weather, just to try the horse. This Miranda would probably be afraid of getting her new handmade riding boots wet.

If only he could find a man like Gilbert Fielding for Miranda. It really was a pity he didn't have even a minor title, or a manor house, or even so much as a small dower farm of his own.

Phineas nodded to the winded groom as he ran up with the mare. The animal's fine dark eyes twinkled at him coquettishly, and she tossed her golden mane for him, arching her strong, supple neck to best advantage. She was a born flirt, and perfect for Miranda.

"I'll take her," he said.

Chapter 12

"**W**hat a pity Lady Miranda is out this afternoon," Honoria said for the third time, as she squinted at the painting above the mantel in Lady Augusta's drawing room, assessing its value. Isobel gritted her teeth at the naked greed in her mother-in-law's eyes. Honoria had already appraised the china cups by holding the delicate porcelain up to the light and looking at the maker's mark on the bottom.

"It's a Gainsborough," Lady Augusta said sharply, her eyes following Honoria like a Bow Street Runner as her guest snooped around the treasure-filled room. "He was a friend of my late husband's, and the scene was painted at my estate in Norfolk."

Isobel felt her own face heat at the pointed rebuke, since her mother-in-law hadn't the grace to look embarrassed.

"Indeed? Will Lady Miranda inherit the place from you?" Honoria asked, and Marianne choked on her tea in surprise. She looked at Isobel with mirth dancing in her eyes, but Isobel didn't see any humor in her mother-in-law's bluntness, and she didn't dare return Marianne's look in Honoria's company. With no one to share her amusement, Marianne instantly sobered. Augusta glared down her nose at the impertinent visitor without answering the question.

The clock on the mantel ticked, the only sound in the tense, uncomfortable silence. Isobel took a sip of tea, the small noise like thunder in the stillness. Her teacup rattled like a cymbal when she placed it gently back on the saucer. She jumped when Honoria spoke again, her voice shrill in the quiet room.

"Lord Charles was hoping to come with us this afternoon, but found himself otherwise engaged."

Lady Augusta looked bored. Marianne looked like she wanted to laugh, and Honoria blinked at both of them with so much inflated consequence that Isobel waited for her to burst.

In truth, Charles hadn't shown any interest at all in coming to tea. He'd been out at his club all night and arrived home after dawn. Once in bed, he refused to get up again to accompany them, no matter how many notes his mother had Jane Kirk deliver to his room. It had been nearly five when Honoria finally ordered the coach to go without him.

Honoria had not actually been included in the invitation, and Isobel wanted to fall on her knees and beg their pardon for inflicting her mother-in-law and Charles upon them. Charles might not have been present in the flesh, but Honoria filled the room with him, monopolizing the conversation with stories about him that only she would find interesting.

"Charles is with his man of affairs, going over the accounts from his properties at Waterfield Abbey, Ashdown, and Craighurst," Honoria lied. "He has made so very many improvements to the estates, you see." She leaned forward and whispered at Augusta. "He has realized huge profits in the past year. How I wish he had been my firstborn. My eldest, Robert, was never robust, and his disappointments in life—" She swung her great cow eyes toward Isobel, then back to Augusta. "—are what did him in at such a young age."

"Indeed?" Augusta murmured, her expression haughty. Isobel ignored the familiar insult. Honoria had said something far more remarkable, in her opinion. Waterfield Abbey and Craighurst were two of her estates, inherited from an uncle. They would someday belong to Robin, but Robert's will had given Charles the management of them. Just a week past, he had informed her that all her properties had *lost* money, and he intended to cut her quarterly allowance accordingly. Yet Honoria was bragging about the huge profits from those same lands. There was no question, of course, of her being allowed to see the accounts for herself. Isobel felt her spine stiffen with resentment and frustration she didn't dare show.

"Yes, indeed," Honoria continued, helping herself to another cream-filled cake from the silver tray on the table. "Charles will make a brilliant marriage, and the lucky girl will be most fortunate. There's not another man in England like him." That was certainly true, Isobel thought as she stared at the fanciful birds woven into the Oriental carpet.

"I've heard my husband say exactly that about Lord Charles, Lady Honoria," Marianne said tartly, but when Isobel shot her a quick look, her eyes were wide and innocent. "That he is unique in so many ways, I mean." Only Isobel heard the slight rebuke in her tone. Uniquely dull. Uniquely stupid. Uniquely greedy. She silently listed what she *knew* Marianne must be thinking.

"I believe we've stayed our fifteen minutes, Honoria," Isobel murmured. "We really should be going."

"Nonsense!" Honoria spluttered. "We are invited guests, Isobel, not ordinary callers. We can stay some while yet, I think. I have so much more to tell them about Charles."

Isobel bit her lip to keep from screaming out loud.

"Yes, do stay a little longer, Isobel," Marianne said. "Perhaps we could take a turn in the garden together. Would you mind, Great-Aunt?" she asked.

"I suppose since it is my house, I am expected to play hostess to your guest," Augusta said flatly. "I'd better send for another pot of tea, and more cakes. I daresay it will be highly beneficial to my health once De Courcey House is ready for you next week, and you may entertain your friends there. I shall have some rest at last."

Marianne smiled apologetically and patted her great-aunt's hand.

"De Courcey House?" Honoria asked avidly, her wide eyes swiveling from Augusta to Marianne.

"Yes, Lady Honoria," Marianne said. "It is my husband's London residence. It has been under renovations, and we had not imagined it would be ready so soon, but in a week we shall be able to move ourselves in, and give my great-aunt her peace again."

"I see," Honoria said. Isobel could almost hear the unoiled machinery of her mind struggling to turn. "Will Lady Miranda continue on here, or come to you?"

"She will stay here, as is proper," Augusta said sharply, glaring at the woman. "Any questions of courtship or offers of marriage will, of course, be directed to my brother at Blackwood House."

"Blackwood?" Honoria's smile faded and her voice quavered, as if he were a specter lurking behind her.

Actually, he was, having just come in with Lord Westlake.

"Good afternoon," he said dryly, and Honoria jumped with a warble of surprise and turned to stare at him with one plump hand splayed across her bosom where her heart would be, if she had one.

Isobel watched him return Honoria's look of horror with nothing more than a slight narrowing of his eyes. He bowed, and then he looked at *her*. The bored and painfully polite expression on his handsome face suggested she was the last person he had expected, or wished to see, in his great-aunt's drawing room. The flutter in her chest fell dead in the pit of her stomach.

Marianne rose to kiss her husband, despite the fact they had company. "Adam! You're back early. How wonderful."

Blackwood crossed to lean against the mantel, apart from the group.

Or perhaps he chose the spot to show himself off to best advantage.

Isobel tried to concentrate on staring at her fingertips, which were trembling slightly, but she could not resist peering at him through her lashes. His boots were speckled with dried mud, as if he'd been riding. They clung to his calves as though they were just a little bit in love with him too. His breeches were tan, smooth fitting, and went on forever. He wore a dark blue coat, a cream striped waistcoat, and a white cravat, the perfect picture of masculine elegance.

By the time she got to his face, which was flushed from the brisk spring air, she realized he was watching her ogle every inch of his body like a strumpet. She felt a blush start at her own toes and race to her hairline. His lips quirked enigmatically, neither a smile nor a grimace, and his eyes were unreadable. Suddenly there wasn't enough air to breathe in the vast salon.

"You remember Isobel, of course, Phineas," Marianne was saying.

"Of course. Good afternoon, Countess." He spoke without expression, but his eyes never left hers.

She felt Honoria looking at her with squint-eyed speculation, and the heat in Isobel's body was replaced by icy dread. She would be expected to account for knowing Blackwood later. The interrogation was bound to be long and grueling, the lecture afterward interminable.

She straightened her spine and stared into the amber depths of her tea as a trickle of cold sweat slipped between her breasts like an accusing finger. Beneath the plain wool of her gown, under the silken caress of her undergarments, her skin was alive with awareness of him. She gulped her tea, and burned her tongue. It didn't matter. It gave her something else to think of, or it would have if she *could* have thought of anything else. She prayed for him to take his leave, let the ladies enjoy their tea in peace.

"Do join us for tea," Augusta said, and Isobel's heart dropped to the carpet. "Marianne was about to take a turn outdoors with the countess, and you two can help me entertain Lady Honoria."

"Do you realize it's raining, Marianne?" Adam De Courcey said as he took a chair next to his wife.

Marianne sent her husband a dazzling smile that filled their corner of the room with love. Isobel drowned a sigh of longing with more tea, and burned her tongue again. She set the cup down before she did herself any further harm.

"Well then, we'll stay in, since you've arrived. I was just telling Isobel that De Courcey House is almost completed. Adam, I want to have a party when we are settled. We can send the invitations now, perhaps, and open the place next week with a grand event." She looked away from her husband's sudden frown and fixed glowing eyes on Isobel. "Will you help me plan it, Isobel?"

"We move in next week, Marianne," Westlake said. "The paint will hardly be dry. What kind of party do you have in mind? A small, intimate dinner, I hope."

"Not at all. A grand party, or—"

"A masquerade ball," Blackwood said.

Honoria's gasp of horror drowned out Isobel's own. She stared at him, but Blackwood's gray eyes were fixed on Westlake, who looked back at him with surprise.

"A masquerade?" Augusta said, scowling at each gentleman in turn. "Wretched things. You never know who you are speaking to."

"My feelings exactly," Honoria said. She'd had another cake, and there was a dab of cream on her topmost chin. "I can't abide masked balls." She gave a dramatic shudder that shook the settee, and sent the gob of cream into her cleavage.

"It would be challenging, if not impossible," Adam said. "Since the ballroom is still draped in sheets."

Marianne kissed him soundly on the cheek. "Then it will be a double unmasking! How brilliant you are, my dear!" Isobel sent a sideways look at Honoria, who wasn't at all shocked at the indiscreet display of affection. She was ogling a pair of silver candlesticks.

"What do you think, Isobel?" Marianne asked, and all eyes swung around to pin her to the settee.

"Me?" She racked her brain for a safe answer. "Why, I have heard that the Prince Regent himself likes masquerade balls," she managed. Honoria could hardly find fault with something she knew herself to be true.

"Then you'll come?" Marianne asked.

"I—" The frog in her throat, the knot in her stomach, the fact that Blackwood was staring at her, made it impossible to speak.

"Of course you shall attend." Honoria poked her in the ribs so hard Isobel nearly fell off the settee. "You went to Evelyn Renshaw's masquerade, and no harm came to you."

Isobel felt her body turn to water, icy fear melting into a puddle of horror.

"You were at Lady Evelyn's masked ball?" Blackwood asked. Her jaw locked. Her tongue glued itself to her teeth. She couldn't answer. She could only stare at him. Fortunately she was saved by Honoria, who turned the conversation back to her own concern, which was, of course, Charles.

"Will Lady Miranda be at your masquerade, Countess? I'm sure Charles would be happy to escort Isobel that evening. He loves masquerade parties almost as much as I do," she babbled, unaware that she had contradicted herself. Isobel slid her eyes to the floor.

She didn't hear Marianne's reply. She was aware of nothing and no one else but Blackwood. She knew without looking that his gaze was still fixed on her. She could feel it like a touch, moving over her hot cheeks. Dear God, what if he'd guessed at last, now, here in his great-aunt's drawing room?

With Honoria present.

She forced herself to look up, pretending to glance at the clock behind him, and silently willed him not to say anything, but there was no realization in his eyes. He was regarding her with flat speculation, like a curiosity in a museum.

Isobel's terror withered to a hard crumb of annoyance. She didn't know whether to groan at the man's utter stupidity or to laugh out loud.

"When is the ball to be?" Honoria asked.

Marianne considered. "I think a week from Thursday. Great-Aunt, may I borrow some of your staff?"

Augusta sighed. "I suppose you must. It seems an ill-conceived idea to me, and I for one will not be in attendance. I am certain I am already engaged on that evening."

Marianne smiled fondly, ignoring the protest. "Miranda will need a chaperone. Will you be coming as Minerva as usual?" she asked.

Augusta set her teacup down with a thump that rattled the delicate china. "Of course. Why waste a perfectly good costume?"

Isobel stared at the toes of Blackwood's boots, every nerve in her body on fire.

He'd suggested a masquerade.

He, who had hardly bothered with a costume at Evelyn's affair, since he'd only been there for one reason. She'd fulfilled his desire of the moment quite nicely.

Fire heated her skin and she swallowed a panicked breath, wishing she could run from the room. Honoria would insist that she attend Marianne's ball so Charles could woo Miranda. She would spend the evening in the corner, Isobel thought, watching Blackwood charm another conquest.

Her body stirred at the memory of his touch, ingrained forever on her skin. She shivered, and decided at that instant she hated him.

Chapter 13

"Charles Maitland has come into money," Phineas told Adam in the privacy of the study. Marianne's guests had gone up to the nursery to collect the young Earl of Ashdown, and Augusta had excused the gentlemen as no longer necessary.

Phineas quelled his annoyance. He'd come to give Adam some information, not to take tea with Charles Maitland's dreadful female relatives. Isobel Maitland had a way of setting his teeth on edge just by being in the same room.

Her gown had been particularly awful today, a dark blue atrocity trimmed with black ribbon and buttoned tight enough to choke her. She'd looked like a crow, perched on Augusta's jaunty cherry and green striped settee.

Until she blushed. The soft flood of color improved her. Slightly. He had quickly noted that he made her nervous, and he took malicious pleasure in that. She probably thought she was too good to be in the same room with a rake like him. It irritated him that he found her so distracting when he was in her company, when she obviously held him in such low regard.

"Has he?" Adam murmured, only half listening. He was looking over a letter Phineas had brought him, written by Lord Philip Renshaw to his wife, and stolen by Phineas before the lady ever received it. When Adam was finished, he would take it back to her, and use both the information and the lady's reaction to her husband's message to further their search for him.

As always, Adam studied every word of the brief note with painstaking care. Restless, Phineas crossed to the window and stared out through the rain-washed glass. Out of habit, he scanned the sidewalk and park square in front of the house for anything suspicious. There was nothing, of course, since it was pouring rain, and this was Mayfair, not the London docks, and respectable people remained indoors in such weather.

He turned back to Adam. "Maitland paid several large gambling vowels last night," he reported, trying to hurry him along.

"Perhaps he won at the tables, then. A lucky throw of the dice. It's bound to happen once in a while to even the unluckiest gambler."

"Yes, but he usually pays only his smallest debts when he wins, and only because no one would game with him again if he didn't. He does it with bad grace. Or he did, until last night. I don't think I've ever seen Maitland smile before. It's an unpleasant sight."

"Really?" Adam picked up the letter yet again. "Odd, Philip's letter is two weeks old. If I read his code aright, he's telling Evelyn she'll receive money too, just like Charles. I assume that's what 'await a visit from my man of affairs with a draft' means."

"I don't think it's a code, Adam. If it says await money, that's what it means. Philip is not a subtle man. The only question is what, or who, the source of these windfalls might be. Philip has more debts than Charles."

Adam frowned. "Charles is likely only a smuggler. A man that dull could hardly be connected with Renshaw's plans. We can ignore him for the moment. We need to find Renshaw as quickly as possible, before the plot to kidnap the French king becomes a monumental disaster. I have men watching the ports, but there's been no sign of trouble, or Philip, for that matter, other than this letter. We're also keeping a close eye on King Louis, just in case. Any theories as to where Philip might be?"

"Philip is somewhere near the sea, probably on this side of the Channel," Phineas replied. "The messenger I took this letter from still had sand on his boots, and he smelled of fish. The man swears he doesn't know anything, and was simply given a handful of coins to come to London with a letter to deliver to London along with his catch."

Adam sniffed the letter, which of course smelled of nothing more than parchment and perfumed ink. "No one else was able to figure out how Philip was sending messages to his wife. The post is watched, and so is everyone who comes in or goes out of that house. How did you get hold of this?"

"One of Evelyn's maids is from Hythe. The girl receives regular visits from her brother, with packets of fish and gifts from her mother."

"Yes, our man reported that some time ago," Adam said.

"Did he notice that the maid's brother is a different man every time?"

Adam grinned. "You're brilliant, my friend."

"So is Philip Renshaw, Adam, or at least he's more clever than we thought. We still don't know who he's working with. He's a step ahead of us, and that's dangerous."

"He can't hide forever. I have confidence you'll find him, even if no one else can. What about the masked woman? Do you know if she's connected to Renshaw yet?"

Phineas sighed, and paced back to the window, wondering again if the mysterious Yasmina played a part in this. He still hadn't found her, and there wasn't any place in London he hadn't looked.

Below the window, the Maitland ladies were getting into their coach at last. He watched Isobel climb in after her mother-in-law. The wind lifted the dark hem of her skirt to show a flash of trim white ankles.

"Is that a new coach?" Adam asked from beside him, oblivious to Isobel's charms.

Phineas frowned, realizing he'd been distracted by the countess yet again, and turned his attention to the vehicle. "No, the coach isn't new, but that matched pair of chestnuts pulling it was up for sale at Tattersall's the other day. They're expensive cattle."

"So Charles *has* come into some money, and not from the tables," Adam mused. They watched as the coach moved off down the street in the rain.

"Lady Honoria told us at tea that he's been turning a fine profit on his estates," Marianne said from behind them, and Adam jumped.

"My dear, I didn't hear you come in." As her husband kissed her forehead in greeting, Phineas crossed to the desk and pocketed Renshaw's letter before his sister saw it.

"Did you enjoy tea with Lady Isobel?" Adam asked.

Marianne sighed. "Yes, I suppose so. It would have been more enjoyable without Honoria Maitland eating all the cakes and monopolizing the conversation. I am convinced Charles Maitland is the dullest man on earth."

She looked up at her husband with a worried expression. "Adam, I think he wants to marry Miranda. We must take steps to see that doesn't happen. I like Isobel, but I could not abide being tied to Honoria by marriage."

"What *did* Honoria say about Charles?" Phineas asked, digging for information. His grandfather would never agree to a match between Miranda and Charles Maitland, but watching the man's attempt to charm his sister would be unpleasant enough. If he could prove Charles was guilty of smuggling, it would make it impossible for him to woo Miranda at all.

Marianne made a face and sat in the wing chair next to the desk. "Oh, she told us how clever he was, and how handsome. He just purchased a curricle, and had it painted bright blue to match 'a certain young lady's eyes.' Ugh!" She gave a shudder of revulsion.

"A new curricle?" Adam asked, casting a sideways glance at Phineas, who watched dangerous sparks flare in his sister's eyes as she noted the look.

"What is it?" she said crisply. "Do you envy Charles his new toy? I thought your ships and your collections kept you happy enough." She rounded on her brother. "And you, Phineas. How dare you come to tea looking like you were up all night?"

He raised one eyebrow and gave her his most rakish grin. "I was, dear sister." He'd been to three parties, hoping to find Yasmina. Then he spent several hours following Charles Maitland through the worst gaming hells in the city. The man had the stamina of a cockroach. Phineas had greeted the dawn outside Evelyn Renshaw's mansion, lurking in a cold and dirty morning fog, waiting for the messenger.

Marianne's eyes took on a rapier sharp gleam. "That means you are either taking Grandfather's edict seriously and looking for a bride at all the premier parties, or you're up to no good. Don't think I didn't see you staring at the ladies' bosoms at Miranda's debut."

She tapped a manicured fingernail against her chin and narrowed her eyes in a way that instantly had Phineas on his guard. "My guess is that you are between mistresses, Phin. You look tired and drawn and—unsatisfied."

"Marianne!" Adam said in a horrified voice. Phineas stood still, bemused by his sister's speculations. Was his sister trying to get him laid? Which of them was the rogue now?

"Well, he does. Look at him, Adam. Something is preying on his mind, and whatever else preys on a rake?"

Adam bristled, looking as prim as the widow Maitland. "Phineas's social life is not a suitable topic of discussion. His choice of—" Adam's mouth worked as he searched for a polite description.

"Women? Bedmates? Whores?" Marianne inserted saucily.

Adam glared at her. He was a gentleman to the very toes of his impeccable boots, and expected his wife to be a lady in all things, despite her spirited nature. "I do not wish to continue this unseemly line of conversation. Change the subject at once, Marianne, if you please."

Marianne sent Phineas a look that suggested the conversation was not at an end, and he could expect to be badgered about his personal life later. Adam should use her to spy for him, Phineas thought. She'd be a master at it, especially interrogation. There was no hiding a secret from her.

"What do you wish to discuss instead?" Marianne asked sweetly, clasping her hands in her lap, sitting in the big wing chair like an angelic child.

"Begin with why you decided to announce a masked ball at De Courcey House *next week*."

"Brilliant, wasn't it?" Marianne crossed to the decanter of whisky on the side table and poured a small amount into a tumbler. Phineas expected her to offer it to her ruffled husband, but she sipped it herself.

"A masquerade ball will be a tremendous amount of work. Have you thought of that?" Adam asked.

"Well, the masked part was Phineas's idea," Marianne said, finishing her whisky and grinning at her brother.

Adam looked at him sharply. "Yes, it was, wasn't it?"

Phineas kept his expression bland and studied a small watercolor painting of Augusta's late husband that hung on the wall behind the desk. His sorrowful countenance was a poignant reminder that marriage killed a man early.

"We'll have to find you a suitable costume," Marianne mused, circling her husband, examining him like a modiste with a challenging client. "A pirate perhaps, or Sir Francis Drake. Something suitably nautical."

"Even if Phin doesn't, I hate costume balls," Adam said, his eyes still boring into Phineas.

"Unless they serve a purpose?" Phineas suggested.

The light in Adam's eyes kindled, then flared to full comprehension.

It was a fool's bet that Yasmina would attend Marianne's ball, of course. He knew that. But if there was one chance in a thousand that she'd appear again in the delectable harem costume, with the pink half mask over her teasing eyes, he'd gladly take those odds. He was looking forward to facing the challenge of all those tiny pearl buttons once more. He hadn't had a woman since he met her at Evelyn's. No other woman held the appeal she did. His sister wasn't entirely wrong about the reason for his haggard appearance.

"A purpose?" Marianne jumped on the comment. "What purpose could a masquerade serve?"

"To open our town home in grand style," Adam said, kissing her. "Have you made a guest list?"

"Do be sure to ask Evelyn Renshaw for her list of invitees," Phineas murmured.

Marianne was neatly distracted, like a hunting dog thrown a scrap of meat. "Of course. I hear the Renshaw ball was a triumph."

"Who would have imagined Lady Isobel was there?" Adam marveled. "Did you happen to see her, Phin?"

Phineas felt his lips twist at the mention of her name. He'd been busy that evening with far more delightful company, and he left early, with his buttons in his pocket.

"I must have been in another part of the room. I never bother with the wallflowers and shepherdesses."

Marianne glared at him. "Well then, you must tell me who to invite to please you, Phineas. Remember that Miranda will be present, and likely dressed as a shepherdess. It is one of the few costumes considered appropriate for young ladies, widows, and sensible matrons."

"Then we can expect you to come dressed as a shepherdess?" Phineas teased, and Marianne rolled her eyes.

"Certainly not! I plan to be the belle of the ball. In fact, I think the whole affair will be delightful, don't you, Phineas? Do try to convince Adam that this will be fun."

Adam groaned in dread, his eyes pleading with him. Phineas hoped that in return for his suffering, Yasmina would be there.

This time he'd know everything about her before the evening was over.

Chapter 14

Isobel looked at the two costumes Sarah had set out side by side. Honoria had chosen the first one, and even Sarah was scowling at the black nun's habit. It was made of rough and shapeless linen, poorly dyed to an unidentifiable color somewhere between green and black. The heavy wimple resembled an angry bat, poised to attack unfortunate sinners.

"You're certain Lady Honoria has left for the evening?" Isobel asked, grimacing at the horrid costume. "And Miss Kirk went with her?"

"Yes. They went to a card party at Lady Conrad's," Sarah replied. "She's a second cousin of Miss Kirk's uncle, or some such connection. Miss Kirk said that Lady Conrad is expecting the Prince Regent to attend, and there are two dukes and a royal mistress on the guest list. Lady Honoria wasn't about to pass up an opportunity like that for the costume ball of a mere earl. She insisted that Lord Charles attend Lady Westlake's ball, though. Will he notice if you switch costumes?"

"He only just arrived back in Town this afternoon. Honoria won't have had time to discuss my masquerade disguise with him," Isobel said. She looked longingly at the other costume and reached out a hand to touch it. The shimmering pink satin warmed under her fingertips like living flesh.

The gown had been her mother's, a confection of lace and

satin in the latest style of two decades past. Lady Charlotte Fraser had been as famous for her sense of fashion as she was infamous for her scandalous love affair.

Sarah picked up the fan beside the gown and opened it, blushing at the painting of a scantily clad lady sailing through a rose garden on a swing that unfurled. She turned her attention to the powdered wig, covered with dainty silk rosebuds, and the embroidered dancing slippers. A pair of lace gloves so delicate that a spider might have spun the threads for them completed the ensemble.

Isobel imagined her mother wearing this gown, flirting shamelessly with a man who looked just like—

Blackwood.

She snatched her hand away from the satin as if it burned and twined her fingers together in a tight knot of resolve. She would not—could not—think of him tonight. Nor would she think of her mother, for whom pleasure had been more important than her only child.

"Where did he go?" Sarah asked.

"What?" Isobel struggled to focus on the maid's plain and honest face without seeing the delectable marquess.

"Lord Charles—he was gone for nearly a week."

"He went down to Waterfield, I believe," Isobel murmured. Not that anyone told her where Charles had disappeared to for six days. She had seen the yellow sand on his boots as his valet carried them past the door of her room earlier, on his way to polish them. Waterfield Park was the only Maitland holding by the sea.

Actually, it was *her* holding, inherited from her uncle. She had spent her summers there as a child, playing happily on that same golden sand. Visits to Waterfield had stopped when her mother left. For months afterward she had had nightmares of walking along that yellow beach, searching for Charlotte. She swallowed the bitter taste of her mother's betrayal and looked away from the satin gown, to consider the nun's costume.

How ironic that Honoria chose it, since Waterfield had once been a medieval abbey. In Isobel's opinion, the satin would make a far better disguise than the habit, given that her usual wardrobe resembled the drab garment so closely.

If she wore the lovely gown, and Honoria caught her, there'd be more penance to pay than any nun ever endured. But Honoria was out for the evening.

She took a deep breath. "I'll wear the pink satin," she said, and Sarah grinned like a conspirator as she bundled the horrid habit into the bottom of the wardrobe.

Isobel stood before the mirror and raised her arms as the maid slipped the petticoats over her head. Waves of taffeta and lace washed over her with a sibilant swish, cascading to her ankles. A second layer flowed over the first, then Sarah held the satin gown high and Isobel ducked under it.

It skimmed down over the curves of her body from breast to hip like a second skin, settling itself gracefully over the petticoats. Dried rose petals and sprigs of lavender fell from the folds of the gown, and the ghost of their scent circled the room and hovered.

Isobel gaped at herself in the mirror. She was the image of her mother. The russet hair was the same, and so were the hazel eyes, except she remembered that her mother's eyes perpetually glowed with mischief and merriment, unlike her own sober gaze. The familiar longing for her mother sprang unbidden, tightening Isobel's throat. She recalled the sick sensation of disbelief she felt when her mother had left.

Harlot! The image in the glass flinched as she heard her father's harsh voice caw the word in her mind. The day his wife fled, he had made his daughter kneel in front of her mother's portrait and listen to a lecture on the wicked nature of women, and the particularly lewd character of Lady Charlotte. She hadn't wanted to believe any of it. Her beautiful, laughing mother couldn't be *bad*. And she couldn't be gone. But she was.

Charlotte the Harlot, the servants had taken to calling her. The ugly whisper filled the empty house, split it wide open, becoming a mighty wind that filled the whole world with her mother's shame. The more people sniggered at the scandal, the more her father despised Charlotte's daughter.

Charlotte the Harlot's motherless child learned to become Isobel the Invisible. Only Lord Denby, her mother's brother, had tried to comfort her. He brought her gifts and curiosities from his travels abroad, but never what she really wanted, which was news of her mother. Isobel knew he visited his disgraced sister in Italy, but Lord Fraser had forbidden anyone to speak of his wife, and Denby's visits with Isobel were carefully supervised. If Charlotte ever wrote to explain, or thought about her abandoned child at all, Isobel never knew of it.

After her uncle's death, Robert had decided that his principal home at Craighurst was to be rented out, and her uncle's personal items, which included several trunks filled with her mother's belongings, were packed up and shipped to Maitland House, where they were stashed carelessly in the attic, of no interest to anyone but Isobel. She prowled the attics on rainy days, searching for some clue to her mother's flight, but found nothing except memories in the perfumed gowns and garments of the finest silk and satin. If Honoria had known that Charlotte Fraser's belongings resided above her head, she would have ordered them burned.

Isobel watched in the mirror as Sarah laced the back of the gown and drew the ribbons tight. The snug, low-cut bodice thrust her breasts upward, turning them into two luscious peaches in a frothy bed of lace that barely concealed them. The more Sarah tugged, the higher her breasts rose, and Isobel stared at the plump mounds in amazement. It was an excellent disguise. Even if she didn't wear a mask, no one would recognize her, since she doubted anyone would be able to raise their eyes above the lush display of pulchritude under her chin.

"You'll want to cover those up," Sarah said, and tied a lace fichu over Isobel's décolletage. She stood back and looked at her mistress critically. "You still look too pretty by half, my lady. Pink becomes you well."

Then she removed the wig from the box and made a face. "Mind you, this horror will fix that quick enough."

Isobel touched one of the pretty silk rosebuds that adorned the hairpiece. "It just needs a little dusting, perhaps." She blew on it, and a cloud of white powder flew about the room. Sarah coughed and waved her hand, holding the wig at arm's length.

"Are you certain, my lady? This old thing is probably filled with rats' nests, or hordes of biting fleas."

"Nonsense," Isobel said, sweeping her skirts aside so she could sit at the dressing table. "It's been carefully stored. With that on my head, I'll be completely disguised. Not even Lady Honoria would know it was me." But it wasn't Honoria she was worried about.

Blackwood.

She kept her spine straight and stared fiercely into the reflection of her own eyes in the mirror as Sarah set the wig in place.

I will stay away from Blackwood tonight, she pledged. Far away.

Surely that wouldn't be difficult, she reasoned, now that she knew how arrogant he was, how superior. He was a cad, a womanizer, a rake, and—

And it was no use. Listing his faults made no difference. Just the thought of his slow, lusty grin made her heart flip. What would she do if he smiled at her that way tonight?

The wig transformed her. The hair swept back from her forehead in thick waves, swirling into a cloud of curls so delicately blond they were almost white, before it rose high at the back of her head in an artful twist of ribbons and roses to reveal the naked length of her neck. Isobel smiled.

No one else was going to say it, so she silently complimented herself. She looked beautiful. Just like Charlotte. She opened the patch box and applied a tiny black half-moon to her cheek. Charlotte stared back at her from the mirror, elegant, seductive, and flirtatious. Everything Isobel knew she was not.

Sarah set to work pinning the wig firmly into Isobel's hair so it wouldn't come loose. "You'd better stand very still tonight," she warned her mistress. "If this wig doesn't fall off, then that low bodice is sure to fail you."

"I will be very careful indeed," Isobel promised. Extremely careful. She would not allow herself to be tempted.

She would not dance.

She would not flirt.

She would not so much as glance in Blackwood's direction.

Still, her mouth watered, remembering every caress they'd shared at the last masquerade ball. In the mirror, she watched the blush rise from her bodice to her hairline to belie her good intentions. She shifted restlessly, every inch of her skin alive, all too aware of what Blackwood was capable of doing to her composure.

"Almost done," Sarah said, mistaking the cause of her agitation.

Isobel pulled the lace fichu more tightly over her breasts and fidgeted with the knot that secured her modesty. Even if she did find herself forced to speak with him tonight, for politeness' sake, she would do no more than that.

She would not allow herself to be tempted, she promised, glaring a stern warning at Charlotte's image in the mirror. She would not abandon *her* child for a moment of pleasure in a man's arms.

She would not walk with him or let him kiss her.

Not that he'd be tempted if he discovered it was plain Isobel under the eye-popping costume. If all else failed, she could remove her mask and reveal herself. That should drive him off in a fit of lust-shriveling horror. She felt a little of that shrivel herself just imagining being forced to such an extremely humiliating measure, but there was Robin to think of.

Isobel opened her jewelry box. It contained few pieces of any value. Her father had not allowed her to keep any of her mother's magnificent jewels. There was a string of pearls that were her grandmother's, a small garnet brooch her uncle had given her for her sixteenth birthday, her wedding band, and a miniature portrait of Robin. She'd painted it herself, several years ago, when he was barely two and his face was still round as a ball and baby-sweet.

She kissed the little painted cheek and handed the necklace to Sarah, who fastened the delicate gold chain around Isobel's neck. She tucked the portrait into her bodice, near her heart. It would remind her what was most important in her life.

Sarah wrapped a long dark cloak over Isobel's shoulders and helped her tie the satin mask, securing the ribbons behind her head. She handed Isobel the lace gloves and the fan that completed the disguise.

Isobel opened the fan and held it before her chin. "How do I look?" she asked her maid.

Sarah grinned. "Like no one I know."

Charles was waiting downstairs in the salon, a tumbler of brandy in his hand. He wore a plain black domino over evening clothes. A black half mask lay on the table next to the half-empty decanter. He tossed back the rest of his drink and turned to glower at her as she entered in a rustle of petticoats, her costume hidden under the black cloak.

"It's about time you made your appearance," he muttered,

hardly looking at her. "I've been waiting for nearly an hour. At this rate we'll be the last to arrive."

He stomped out of the house without bothering to offer his arm. He didn't assist her into the coach either. The footman took her hand while Isobel struggled with the unfamiliar bulk of her old-fashioned skirts. She settled across from Charles as the coach jerked forward.

"Well disguised, aren't you?" he said, peering at her in the dim glow of the streetlamps. "I wouldn't recognize you if I didn't know you." He took a flask out of his pocket and drank deeply. Lamplight flashed on silver, and the acrid smell of brandy filled the coach. Charles was surely drunk, or well on his way to being so.

"Isn't that the point?" she dared to ask, her lip curling in disgust as he took another swallow of brandy. "To be well disguised?" He hadn't even bothered to put on his mask.

"Mother left word that I'm supposed to watch you tonight, but I have better things to do than nursemaid you, so just stay out of my way and behave yourself, d'you understand?"

"Of course," Isobel glared daggers at him from the dual protection of her mask and the darkness.

"Did Lady Marianne tell you what Miranda will be wearing?"

She had indeed. Miranda would be dressed as a medieval princess, forsaking the shepherdess costume for something more unique. "She'll be dressed as a Greek goddess," she told Charles. "I assume I can find you in the card room as usual if I do need you?"

"Did I not just tell you to stay away? Are you simpleminded?" Charles demanded, his breath a dragon's plume of brandy fumes. She turned her head away and didn't bother to reply. She knew which of them was simpleminded, and it most certainly wasn't her. Anger and disgust made her bold.

"How was Waterfield?" she asked.

"Waterfield? Who told you I was there?" he demanded, his tone low and suspicious. "It was that damned Jane Kirk, wasn't it?"

"No, Honoria mentioned it at luncheon," she lied. "I haven't been there in years. Is the estate earning well?"

"What?" he demanded, sounding confused.

"It is *my* estate. I haven't seen a statement of accounts since before Robert died. He used to show me the quarterly reports from all my properties," she bluffed, daring to ask since Charles was drunk and likely wouldn't remember the conversation in the morning.

He moved fast, like a snake striking unexpectedly. He grabbed her knee and squeezed, his grip merciless. Red-hot needles of pain shot up her leg and she gasped, but the pressure and the agony only increased. He was enjoying hurting her.

"Please—" she began, but he let go suddenly as the coach turned a corner and knocked him off balance. She clutched her stinging limb in horrified surprise as he struggled to right himself.

"Damn you, hold your tongue!" he said, his words slurred and sloppy. "It's none of your affair what happens at Waterfield, do you understand? I'll tell Mother if you interfere, and then you'll see what impertinent questions earn you. You're nothing but a burden on this family, my dead brother's useless widow. You aren't even worth the air you breathe."

Her heart rose in her throat, making a reply impossible. His eyes glittered dangerously in the low light, and Isobel shrank back against the squabs, letting the shadows swallow her.

Putting a hand under her cloak, she touched the little portrait of her son, letting the throbbing pain in her leg fuel her resolve.

For Robbie, she could bear anything. They could take everything else from her, so long as they left her her son.

Chapter 15

Highwaymen and pirates stormed St. George's Square, eager to see the Earl of Westlake's newly renovated London home. They paused on the threshold just long enough to present their invitations to the liveried footmen.

Charles pinched Isobel's arm as they entered the marble foyer, squeezing until it hurt. "Remember, I don't want to be bothered by you tonight," he growled in her ear. Then he was gone, leaving the bruise as a reminder of her duty.

She watched him shoulder through the throngs, heading for a lady dressed as a Grecian goddess. She scanned the room for Miranda and saw a costumed princess in the opposite corner from where Charles was going. Isobel flicked her fan open to hide a malicious little smile. Miranda was safe.

The ballroom basked in the gleam of a thousand candles set in high crystal chandeliers and gilded wall sconces. From the ceiling, painted cherubs grinned down at the guests. The sharp odor of new paint competed with the sweet fragrance of the flowers that adorned every corner. Goddesses, kings, and shepherdesses trod a gleaming floor inlaid with mahogany and ebony to form a huge compass rose that reached all four corners of the room, a tribute to the earl's ships.

Due north, Marianne and Adam held court, costumed but unmasked, and surrounded by their guests. Isobel hesitated, unwilling to push through the crush of bodies to reach her friend. Out of habit, she looked around the room for a quiet corner to make her own for the evening, out of the way of both harm and temptation.

Then she saw him.

Tonight he was Sir Walter Raleigh, in a short brocade doublet, trunk hose, and long leather boots that climbed his thighs. The familiar jeweled sword was once again draped around his lean hips. He looked handsome, virile, and dangerous.

He was leaning against a marble pillar near the door, his bored posture at odds with the anxious set of his mouth as he scanned the room.

Anger hit her like a flash of lightning. Looking for another conquest, was he? She glared at him, knowing the scathing look was lost under her mask.

She took a step forward, planning to sweep right past him without so much as a glance as she crossed the room to the secluded spot she'd chosen, but he shifted, just the slightest movement, his long legs changing stance, one hand coming to rest on the hilt of his sword. Sharp desire pierced her to the quick, and she drew a breath as his head turned, froze where she was and waited for his eyes to touch her, bracing for it.

His bored gaze flicked over her and away, and she let out the breath she'd been holding. There. It was done. He had not recognized her, and she did not interest him tonight. A deluge of disappointment drowned fury, resolve, and lust all at once.

But his eyes swiveled back, stopped on her and locked. She saw the change in him, felt it. His body tensed and his jaw dropped as he looked her over from head to toe. He hadn't moved, but if he had slid a hand over her skin it could not have been more electrifying.

Run, her mind said. *Run, before it is too late to stop this.*

But it already was.

The room was too hot, and he was the source of the fire.

With trembling fingers she untied the knot at her breast and whisked away the fichu, needing to breathe. Candlelight and sultry air fell on her breasts, but she felt no cooler for it.

His eyes flowed over her again and stopped at her breasts. She saw his chest heave as he drew a deep breath. She almost swooned, a mixture of desire and doubt making her heart hammer, her knees too weak to hold her upright, but the crowd did not allow the space to fall. They closed in around her, pushing past like a torrent, cutting off her view of him, and she struggled to stand against them, to regain good sense and turn away, but she was rooted to the spot.

She shut her eyes and sent up a plea to the Fates to take the matter into their capable hands and decide what would happen next.

She felt his hand close on her arm and almost sobbed with relief. She breathed him in, the now familiar scent of his soap, his skin, his desire.

"Yasmina?" the word was a guttural hiss.

That was all it took. In a single instant she was Yasmina again, not plain Isobel. Yasmina was playful and daring. She took what she wanted, made this man drool with lust. She was everything Isobel Maitland was not but wanted to be. And plain Isobel wanted it very much at this moment.

She felt Yasmina smile, wide and slow. "I thought I recognized your sword."

His palms slid down the tight satin of her sleeves to the bare flesh of her forearms, warming every inch. He clasped her hands as if he were afraid she might flee and stood staring down at her through the slits in his mask, his eyes a knowing glitter that made her nipples swell like rosebuds, her mouth water, her breath catch in her throat.

He took a step closer, shielding her from the crowds as they pushed past. She could feel the heat of his male body, the strength and power of him.

He put an arm around her waist and bore her toward the wall and a little respite from the crush. She leaned against the polished paneling and looked up at him, and he put a hand on the wall behind her, making an intimate space for two in the midst of the crowd. He didn't say a word, just stood with his eyes on hers.

"You're staring, my lord," she managed, suddenly afraid he'd recognized her. She couldn't bear it if he laughed now, or was angry that the exotic Yasmina turned out to be only dull, frumpy Isobel. She realized she was trembling, waiting for his answer.

"Yasmina," he muttered again, a hint of very flattering awe evident in his voice. He leaned close enough to breathe her in, and she instinctively arched toward him and placed a hand on his chest. She could feel the throb of his heart under her palm, and her fingers curled against the damask of his tunic.

"Not tonight. Tonight I am Charlotte." The name tripped off her tongue unbidden. Why hadn't she said Marie Antoinette or Lady Anne or any other name but *Charlotte*?

He grinned at her, his rogue's grin, the one that made a woman's heart flip and her toes curl. A woman might do anything under a smile like that, even forget her own name and all good sense. Isobel shut her eyes and took her hands off his chest, clenching them at her sides, knowing if she touched him again, she would be lost.

"You look delicious, Lady Charlotte—or is it Queen Charlotte?" he asked, playing the game she'd foolishly started. She smiled as the compliment thrummed through her veins like liquid fire. His eyes dropped to her breasts, and the intensity of his gaze made her feel naked. She ran a fingertip over the velvet ribbon that edged the low bodice, checking that nothing had escaped and now lay exposed.

"That's a very fetching gown, Your Majesty," he drawled,

following her finger with his own. She clasped his hand before she melted under the tickling caress and set it safely on her waist instead. She did not wish to give up his hands on her entirely.

"This? This is a very old gown, my lord," she said truthfully. She let her eyes roam over his costume again, daring to flirt, needing to look anywhere but into his eyes. "May I say I am pleased to see that you have put more effort into your own costume tonight? You quite do your sword justice now."

He chuckled. "My sister chose my disguise. Mari—"

"Are you Sir Walter Raleigh or Sir Francis Drake?" she interrupted, not wanting the real world to intrude, not now. She reached out and touched the hilt of the sword, running a fingertip over the large ruby. The jewel's cold smoothness contrasted with the heat and softness of her satin bodice, a sensual, dangerous comparison.

She watched his throat bob as he swallowed hard, but he didn't answer.

"Cat got your tongue, my lord? You're staring again."

"I am trying," he said slowly, as if speaking was a new and difficult skill. "I am trying to resist the desire to pop your breasts out of that gown right here in the middle of my sister's ballroom."

Her eyes drifted shut and a small gasp of pure desire escaped unbidden from her parted lips, and she knew she would do anything, follow him anywhere. She cursed her weakness even as she leaned into him, surrendering her strength to his. He would push back the coldness of her real life, the fear, and replace it with pure, scintillating pleasure.

Phineas breathed her in. After weeks of searching every ballroom, salon, and brothel in London, he'd found her.
Yasmina.
He should tear her mask off, demand to know who she

was. Charlotte, was it? The Queen of England was named
Charlotte, so were a thousand other noble ladies. He stared
down at her. Under her mask, her eyes were closed, her
cheeks flushed, her luscious lips slightly parted and begging
for a kiss. His own mouth watered. He *needed* information
from her, but he *wanted* something else entirely.

He was standing in Marianne's elegant ballroom with an
erection that could knock holes in the freshly plastered walls.
She ran her tongue nervously over her lower lip, moistening
it, the soft flesh gleaming in the candlelight.

"Hell," he muttered, and grabbed her hand, dragging her
through the crowds as fast as he could clear a path.

"Phin!" The sound of his name made him wince. He felt
Yasmina try to pull out of his grip as Marianne called to him,
but he held her tight and glared at his sister without stopping.

"Not now, Marianne."

Undeterred, she plucked at his sleeve. "But there's someone I want you to meet!"

He watched his sister's bright eyes flick over his companion briefly, before her eyes came to rest on the lady's pert
breasts. Her jaw hit the starched Elizabethan ruff she wore.

He stepped around his frozen sister, and she disappeared
behind them, swallowed by the crowds. He'd explain tomorrow, when his brain was functioning again and he could think
of something other than the pressing need to make love to
this woman.

Yasmina?

Charlotte?

He pushed through the crowds, ignoring anyone who tried
to stop them, desperate to find a place to be alone with her,
needing to touch her, to kiss every satin-clad inch of her,
whoever she was. They'd get to that afterward, he promised
himself.

He opened the first closed door he came to and pulled her

inside. The honorable scent of leather and old paper assailed him. Westlake's library. It would do as well as any other room, he thought. A soft carpet, a deep settee, the top of Adam's wide mahogany desk—

A loud gasp stopped him before he'd gone three paces, letting him know that the room was already busy. He stopped so fast that Yasmina crashed into his back. Six *ton* matrons, shepherdesses all, stared at him.

"Damn," Phineas muttered under his breath as they recognized him. Their eyes bulged with indignation. Six fans snapped open and fluttered, and a twitter began behind them.

Adam, dressed as Henry VIII, came toward him, his eyes on the woman behind Phineas, his expression bland. Phineas instinctively stepped in front of her, shielding her.

"Ah, Blackwood, I was just showing Lady Moresby and Lady Kelton some family portraits." He sounded so calm that Phineas had the sudden desire to hit him. "Do join us." Phineas glanced up at the magnificent oil portrait of Carrington glaring down at him in dour disapproval, and backed out of the room without a word. He was leaving Westlake in the awkward position of having to explain his ungainly intrusion. The old hens were probably clucking already, squawking over his lack of manners and speculating as to who his companion might be. Adam surely was.

Phineas winced. He still didn't know the answer to that himself.

Even if he'd wanted to, he could not have introduced her. He could tell them how she tasted when he kissed her, how her breasts felt in his hands, or describe the soft sounds she made when he slid slowly into her body, but he couldn't tell them her name.

Damn them all. Right now he had a very urgent need for privacy. Once he'd loved her, and satisfied them both, he'd find out who she was and make a hundred introductions.

He needed a place where they wouldn't be interrupted. He could hardly take her upstairs with Jamie asleep in the nursery. Marianne would call him out, shoot him dead and mount his head in her new sitting room.

He looked down the length of the hall, trying to remember where the passage led and which rooms might be unlocked and unoccupied. Hell, he'd take a curtained alcove behind a potted palm in the ballroom right now. He forced his lust-fogged brain to work. To the right there was the morning room, the dining room, and the stairs to the kitchens. Beyond that was the door that led into the garden and Adam's pride and joy, the conservatory.

"We should go back to the ballroom, my lord," she said at his elbow.

"The conservatory," he muttered.

"What? No, I think—"

She looked so delicious that he dared to swoop in for a kiss, if only to stop her objections. Her lips clung and her body cleaved to his. She wanted him as much as he wanted her, but not *here*. Anyone could walk by. He stared down at her luscious mouth.

"Do you like cherries?" he asked, running a thumb over the ruby flesh of her lower lip.

"Yes," she said on a sigh. "That is, I want—" She flicked her tongue out over her lips, and he was instantly as hard as a post.

"I know," he growled. "Come on."

He pulled her into the conservatory. It housed dozens of exotic plants, collected by Adam's ships from around the world. Adam also grew strawberries, cherries, and oranges year-round to please Marianne. The room was hot and dark, the heavy fragrance of flowers and fruit a powerful aphrodisiac. Not that he needed one.

He pushed through the foliage. The setting was perfect

for a casual seduction, but a trifle awkward for what he had in mind. They'd made do with a bench before, but he'd spent weeks imagining this woman in a proper bed, for a night, a week, or a month. In the same way Adam carefully catalogued his collection of plants, Phineas had listed the things he wanted to do to Yasmina once he found her.

It was almost pitch-dark in the glass house, and as dense as a jungle. The faint lights of the city beyond the high garden walls lessened the blackness only enough to see the dark lace of leaves and branches against the glass ceiling.

Phineas pushed past pots and clinging vines with clumsy desperation, not daring to let go of her hand. He reached the trunk of the cherry tree, ran into it, actually, and turned, tugging her into his arms.

She pressed her body to his with a needful cry, her mouth crashing hard into his in the dark. He molded the length of her luscious body to his, devouring her, thrusting his tongue into her mouth, reveling in the taste of her. She was everything he remembered her to be.

More.

"Yasmina," he muttered. "Charlotte." Whoever she was, she was a marvel of feminine perfection.

He spread his legs, drew her between them, and she pressed her hips against his, rubbing, soft little gasps of desire escaping from her lips, the satin of her gown whispering sensuously as she moved. The sword was in the way again, but this time he pressed the ruby clasp and let it fall to the ground with a careless clatter. There was no need to tell her what he wanted. She already knew. He marveled at that, and the fact that their hands unerringly found what they sought in the darkness.

Her perfume washed over him like a tidal wave, and he groaned and slid his fingers down the plump warm slopes of her breasts to scoop them out of her scanty bodice like ripe fruit. Her nipples peaked instantly under his thumbs and she gasped and threw her head back, thrusting herself into his hands, his mouth. She fumbled with the laces on his doublet as he struggled to free more of her body from the tight bodice. He wanted to touch every inch of her incredible skin, softer than the satin of her gown.

"Laces," she sighed, guiding his hand to the ribbons that tied the back of her gown, and he expertly unstrung her. He gasped as her hands slid inside his open tunic at the same moment, her touch electrifying. She pinched his flat nipple, and the sensation shot straight to his groin.

"Yasmina," he growled, using the name he knew best, the one that had resounded in his mind for weeks. He slid down the smooth tree trunk, pulling her on top of him. She straddled him, leaned forward to kiss him, her naked breasts brushing his chest. He was enveloped in a fragrant cloud of lace and satin, and he struggled to find a way through the tangle of petticoats and frills, seeking paradise. He wished he still had the sword handy. Or a machete. He could smell the sweet musky scent of her desire under her skirts, and it drove him wild.

At last he felt warm, soft, bare flesh. She moaned as he touched her, and he slid his hand upward along the inside of her quivering thighs, over the silk of her skin until he brushed the curls at her center. He inserted a finger into her, felt her tremble and sigh. She was wet, ready for him, and he stroked the soft petals of her flesh. He caught her cry, kissing her hard, using his tongue in her mouth as he used his finger below, driving her release higher.

As she collapsed against him, he could feel her heart pounding against his in the darkness, and he couldn't resist a private grin of pure masculine pride at his accomplishments as a lover. He wanted to be good, especially, earthshatteringly good, for her.

She was murmuring as she slid a hand down to find the ties of his Elizabethan breeches to free his erection. Her hand closing around him was almost too much. He'd waited weeks for this moment.

"Now," he commanded, grasping her hips, lifting her and positioning her. She plunged down onto him and shivered in renewed climax almost at once. It undid him, and he thrust into her, hard and fast, holding her buttocks in his palms, feeling the silken skin, the warm, feminine flesh, the flex of her muscles as she moved on his body, strove for pleasure in time with him. In the faint glimmer of light he could see her white breasts above him, the nipples dark and round, the long pale column of her neck.

"Take off your mask," he said, holding his release until he could look into her eyes, even in the dark. It was like trying to control a team of runaway horses. He was on the edge, buried deep in the hot, tight paradise of her body.

She made a soft sound of denial and moved her hips against him, swiveling in a provocative, needy little circle that made him forget everything, even his own name, let alone hers. He thrust into her, unable to do anything else.

As she cried out, he clasped his hands around her hips, pressing into her as far as he could go. The molten waves of his release rolled on endlessly.

He clasped her against his chest, still inside her, caressing the smooth planes of her back, the jut of her shoulder blades, the softness of her neck. Once he could breathe again, he'd question her. He'd know if she lied, and he opened his mouth to tell her so, but she kissed his throat, licked at the corner of his mouth provocatively, convincing him questions could wait for a few moments. He turned his face to kiss her properly.

"How did people manage to make love with all these petticoats and laces?" he asked.

She laughed, the sound vibrating through him. "I assume they took them off," she said.

"And used real beds," he suggested. She didn't reply.

He touched her face, running his finger under the edge of her mask, over her high cheekbones, along the seam of her mouth. She caught his fingers in her teeth and shifted her hips, indicating without words she wanted more.

He stroked the warm skin of her thighs and buttocks, dipped between, teasing her, and laughed against her mouth as she sighed. "You'll have to wait for a few minutes, greedy wench," he said. "I assure you it won't be long." He already felt the desire to take her again, his mind ready for her, even if his body required a brief respite. There was time for love play and a few pointed questions between kisses. He ran his lips over the fragile curve of her jaw, the corner of her mouth, the tip of her nose. "Take off your mask," he breathed into her ear. It was a command, not a plea.

Instead of responding, she stiffened and moved off him. Cold air rushed to claim the heated flesh where her body had rested on his. Could there have been a more pointed refusal? He felt the loss of her acutely.

"Come back," he said without moving, not daring to, in case she fled. He heard the soft rustle of her clothing in the darkness, saw the faint shimmer of satin as she righted her garments.

"I should go back to the ballroom before I am missed," she said softly. "Oh, no. I need you to lace me up again." She said the last shyly.

He could hear her agitated breathing in the dark. She hadn't gone far.

"Leaving so soon? But I promised you cherries," he drawled.

She laughed. "There really is a cherry tree in here? I will forgive you if there is not, you know."

He got to his feet and reached up. The cherries hung in clumps above him, and he grabbed a handful of the cool, smooth fruit and pulled. One burst and he felt the juice running over his hand. He held them out to the shadowy form he hoped was Yasmina. He could very well be offering Adam's prized cherries to a potted plant. "See?" he asked.

"It's too dark to see anything," she replied, her voice a little to the left of where his hand was extended.

"Where's your mouth? Let me feed you." He shut his eyes as he felt her hand on his, the touch tentative as she guided his fingers to her lips, sucking the juice from them with a sigh of amazement.

"Blackwood! There really are cherries!" she said, as if she'd still expected to discover he'd been lying to her. He frowned at the sound of his name on her lips and wondered what else this woman knew about him. Prickles of warning shot up his spine.

He put a cherry against her lips. She bit down, and the squirt of juice hit his fingers, the sensation erotic. He leaned forward, finding her mouth, sucking the sweet taste from her lips and tongue. He was hard again, ready for her in a rush of urgency.

"God," he gasped, dropping the cherries in his hand and reaching for her. "Tell me your name," he begged, his voice ragged.

"Call me Yasmina," she sighed, nuzzling his neck, her breath warm against his skin. "Or Charlotte. What difference does it make?" She kissed him, her lips clinging to his to silence him when he tried to speak again. He pulled away, heard her grunt with frustration.

"Tell me your name," he said again, his hands on her shoulders, holding her away from him, tormenting them both in the name of duty. "I need to know how to find you. If this is going to keep happening—and I sincerely hope it will—I want to know what to call you, where to send flowers, or a basket of Westlake's cherries."

She rubbed against him like a cat, and he reached under her skirts again. She pressed against his hand and fumbled for his erection, drawing him toward her. He went, unable to resist, kissing the long column of her neck.

"This cannot keep happening, Blackwood. It should not have happened at all," she murmured.

"Which time?" he asked, nuzzling her ear, nipping the lobe until she relaxed in his arms, let him bear her backward beneath the cherry tree, their fall cushioned by her petticoats.

"Both times. Neither time. Never, ever again," she said on a wistful sigh, parting her legs, drawing him to where she wanted him. He resisted the urge to thrust, teasing her, needing information before he gave in to desire.

He caressed her breast, rubbed his thumb over her needy nipple and felt it swell.

"Are you married?" he asked her. "I can be discreet—"

She stiffened. "No, of course not!" she said, trying to pull away, but he wouldn't allow it. "Please—"

He cupped a hand behind her head, drew her mouth back to his, gentling her with a drugging kiss. He ran his hand over her throat, traced the delicate lines of her jaw as he slid his hand behind her head, under the curls of her wig. She had a tiny mole on the back of her neck, and he ran his finger around it.

"Please," she whispered again. She was writhing beneath him.

He hovered, making foreplay out of the interrogation. He'd make her give up a secret for every caress she craved. He was already sweating. The game would require the utmost willpower. Not that he couldn't—

Light streaked across the floor as the door creaked open.

"Blackwood?"

Phineas was on his feet in an instant, squinting at the silhouetted form in the doorway. He would have reached for his sword but it was lost in the dark. His lover scrambled into the shadows with a horrified gasp and a hiss of satin, but Phineas kept his eyes on the intruder.

"Adam," he growled, recognizing Westlake's voice. Damn him, he probably wanted to give the old cats a tour of his conservatory too, now that they were finished in the library.

Phineas hurriedly straightened his clothing before his brother-in-law marched into the glass house with half the *ton* in his wake and created a scandal London would be talking about for the next decade. He strode to the door, intent on keeping everyone out, glaring at Adam like an angry bear.

Adam's eyes searched the dark foliage, and Phineas's fist curled, ready to punch the curiosity off his face. He stepped into the hallway to face down any society matron who dared look at him with outrage and shock, but Westlake was alone. Phineas turned to his brother-in-law. If this was about his damned sense of propriety, then—

"Duty calls, Blackwood. We've got to go." Adam's voice didn't carry even a hint of apology for the interruption.

Phineas squinted at his brother-in-law's face, read the urgency there. His anger sharpened to keen alertness.

"What's wrong?"

"Not here," Adam muttered through gritted teeth, and looked pointedly into the darkness behind Phineas.

He followed Adam's gaze. "I need a minute."

"No more than that," Adam replied. "This can't wait."

Phineas went back into the conservatory.

"Yasmina?" he called softly. She didn't answer. There wasn't even a telltale rustle of clothing to betray her hiding place. She must be horribly embarrassed. Or she was a master of subterfuge. An uneasy feeling prickled along his spine, but he pushed it aside and concentrated on lacing his doublet. There was nothing he could do about it now.

"Yasmina, I have to leave," he said to the shadows of the leaves and branches. "I'll be back before the ball is over. Wait for me." He dared not say more. She didn't reply, and Adam was waiting. He returned to the hallway.

Adam's expression was cool and unreadable. He expected a lecture for using Adam's sacred conservatory to stage a seduction, but that sin was obviously less important than the matter at hand.

Phineas followed him out through the kitchen and into the mews behind the house, where a carriage was already waiting.

"What's so bloody important?" he demanded, and settled back against the squabs as the carriage pulled away at a gallop.

Isobel huddled behind a row of huge clay pots and waited until everything was quiet. Fear and the coldness of the flagstones crept into her bones and made her teeth chatter. The room smelled of cherries, rich soil, and sex.

With shaking hands she straightened her clothing as best she could, awkwardly tying her laces over her shoulder, cramming her wayward breasts into the bodice as far as they'd go. She wiped away tears of regret and stood for a long moment near the door Blackwood had shut so firmly behind him, gathering the courage to leave the dark sanctuary, knowing she must be gone before he returned. She would go home at once, of course, and send the coach back for Charles.

She ran a hand over her clothing and mask to ensure all was in place. Opening the door, she squinted at the light for a moment. Blessedly, there wasn't a soul in the hallway. Biting her lip, she picked up her skirts and hurried back through the throngs of people in the ballroom. She didn't stop until she reached the safety of the Maitland coach.

She watched the lights of Mayfair waver through a haze of tears.

It took just a single glance from him to melt her determination. Even now, despite the fact that she'd very nearly been caught in Blackwood's arms, her body craved his. Disaster had loomed over her and still she wanted more. Charlotte indeed.

She was just like her mother.

She shut her eyes. She regretted everything now—her costume, her weak will, even the decision to attend both this ball and Evelyn's.

But most of all, she regretted that he'd left her so soon.

Chapter 16

"They brought in a man we need to talk to," Adam explained. "He came across the Channel with documents that suggest they plan to move against King Louis sooner than we thought. Sorry I had to interrupt you. We can't wait to question him." He spoke with quiet formality, and didn't sound sorry in the least.

"You do understand why I had to interrupt you, don't you?" he asked then, a tinge of irritation in his voice. "Beside the fact that my wife was giving a ball not twenty yards away and my son was asleep upstairs."

"You sound like my grandfather," Phineas said.

"Was it her? Your mysterious masked lady?"

Phineas's mouth tingled from kissing her, and his body ached for more. He didn't want to share her with anyone, especially Adam, but he knew Adam would keep asking. "Yes. It was her."

Adam sighed. "Good. At least you know who she is now."

Phineas didn't dare answer that. He knew she wasn't married. He knew she had a tiny mole on the back of her neck. He knew she liked cherries, and him. But *her name* remained a mystery. One he would have solved by now if not for Westlake's bloody interruption.

"Well? Who is she?"

"You saw her. Did you recognize her?" Phineas countered.

"I saw her for all of fifteen seconds before you whisked her away. She was wearing a mask and a wig. Apart from that, the only thing I noticed was—" He stopped, and Phineas bristled.

"What?" he demanded, knowing the answer but determined to make Adam say it anyway. He pulled his hand into a fist in readiness, wanting a reason to fight, any reason.

"Her costume was rather low-cut."

Phineas was about to launch himself at his brother-in-law when Adam began to laugh. "What the hell is so funny?"

"You. I've never seen you twitterpated over a woman. It's fascinating."

"Oh, is it? I suppose it's never happened to you, you stiff, unfeeling—"

"Of course it has," Adam said blandly, ignoring Phineas's anger, "The moment I set eyes on your sister."

Phineas fell back against the squabs, the wind knocked out of him. Adam *loved* Marianne. But he wasn't in love. He wasn't the kind of man who fell in love, and despite his grandfather's edict, he wasn't the marrying kind either. He would probably wake up tomorrow morning and realize he'd had his fill of the mysterious Yasmina, and her charms had paled in his imagination.

Except he knew by the stubborn jut of his erection that wasn't going to happen.

They arrived at Horse Guards and the coach came to a halt. He didn't wait for the footman to open the door.

"Phineas?" Adam caught his sleeve.

He turned so sharply he nearly knocked Adam flat. "What?"

"Just remember you don't know who she is. She might be a spy, or a courtesan, or someone completely inappropriate to be a marchioness. Don't lose your heart to her. Or your nerve. Not now."

He met Adam's eyes with a hard glare intended to tell the

nosy bastard it was none of his business. He was in complete control, as always. When he got back to the conservatory he'd see to it that she answered every question. He turned to climb the steps.

"Come on. Let's get this over with."

Illuminated by only a single candle and the scant light from a brazier, a man sat tied to a wooden chair in a basement cell. The contents of a battered leather satchel, including opened letters, a knife, a pistol, and a few personal items, lay on a table.

"Is this some kind of joke?" the man demanded in English, eyeing the costumes Phineas and Adam wore. Phineas ignored the question and looked at him carefully. He was dressed like an ordinary English fisherman, right down to his heavy, salt-caked boots. He held Phineas's eyes boldly, as if daring him to find anything wrong with his disguise.

"You're French," Phineas said quietly.

He flicked insolent eyes over his captors. "I can't tell what you two dandies are. I've never seen clothes like yours before. Why am I being kept here?"

"He's Henry VIII and I'm Sir Walter Raleigh. You can't get more English than that," Phineas said. "We need to know why you're in England. Who sent you, and who were you waiting for?"

The man's grin slipped a little, but he didn't reply. He slid his eyes away from Phineas's stare and looked at the embroidered bear's paw shoes Adam wore. "I like your slippers, sweeting," he quipped. "Like I told the bastards who jumped me, I was in that tavern looking for a whore. Perhaps you'll do. I just got paid for a fine catch o'herring."

Adam didn't even twitch at the taunt. He sat down and crossed his legs as if the ridiculous shoes were a pair of his fine Hessians.

Phineas went through the items on the table. The letters were in some kind of code, folded but without seals. The pistol was still loaded, and the knife was spotless. There was a small pouch of coins on the table as well. He picked up the handkerchief that lay incongruously amid the other items like a duchess among rogues. It was a fine square of linen, edged with lace. The monogram in the corner was a single curling letter M, pierced through with an embroidered rosebud.

"Where did you get this?" he asked.

"It's a gift for my wife."

"She'll be a widow, then," Phineas said in French, and watched the man's eyes flicker. "Unless we find out what you know."

"I don't know anything," the prisoner said, his English accent losing the sound of the sea, becoming careful in his agitation.

Phineas picked up a letter and scanned it, pretending to understand the coded contents. "Look, Westlake. This could get him hanged for treason." He handed the page to Adam.

Adam glanced at it. "Or as a French spy."

"I'm not!" The man objected. "I'm not a spy!"

"Then explain this," Phineas said, holding a second letter in front of the man's face. His complexion turned as pale as milk in the candlelight. Phineas picked up the pistol and cocked it.

"It's not mine," the man tried. "I found the satchel on the beach."

Phineas grinned at Adam. "I love when they lie." He laid the pistol across his wrist and pointed the barrel at the man's long Gallic nose.

"Is that blood on your shirt?" the prisoner asked, his voice an octave higher. Phineas glanced at the cherry juice staining his ruffled linen cuff, and forced himself to concentrate, not to think of her lips wrapping around the sweet fruit and his fingertips, or the delicate scrape of her teeth and the spurt of juice as she bit down.

"Yes," he replied. "Your partner refused to tell me what I wished to know, and it got messy." He spoke lightly, as if they were discussing the weather. The man shifted, and the ropes that bound him to the chair creaked, but held fast.

"Is he dead?" Adam asked Phineas, playing the game.

Phineas merely smiled, letting his teeth flash while his eyes remained cold, dead pools of shadow. He hadn't moved the pistol.

"Look, I'm only a fisherman," the prisoner tried again, but the careful English accent failed him entirely now.

"'E say ee's a feeshermon," Phineas mocked.

"I'd say he's a friend of Lord Philip Renshaw," Adam said.

"Who?" The man looked genuinely confused.

"Or Robert Maitland, perhaps, the late Earl of Ashdown? Or his brother Charles?"

The man shut his eyes, gathering his wits. "Look, there's a dozen estates, and a hundred lords of La-di-dah near Hythe. I don't know any of them."

"This could take all night," Adam sighed.

"Not at all," Phineas said smoothly. He aimed the pistol and fired. The prisoner screamed and the chair toppled backward. Crimson drops of blood splashed the stone wall, gleaming in the candlelight, and trickled toward the floor like cherry juice.

Adam leapt to his feet. "What the hell have you done, Blackwood?"

"I haven't got time for this," Phineas muttered. He grabbed a pitcher of water and dashed it over the prisoner's blood-spattered face. He came to with a splutter, and Phineas righted the chair with the prisoner still tied to it. The man's left ear-lobe was gone, his rough shirt stained with blood.

"You shot me!" the man blubbered.

"Looks like I missed, actually. Blame it on the drink," Phineas said, and passed the pistol to Adam. "Do me a favor and reload, will you, old man?"

"*T'es fou!* You are mad!" the man cried, his eyes darting from Phineas to Adam.

When Phineas took it, he felt Adam's hand clutch it tight for a moment, a subtle warning. He met his brother-in-law's eyes. "I have no intention of staying here all night. If he knows nothing, then why keep asking him?" He lowered the pistol to rest against the man's temple. The prisoner whimpered as the cold metal touched his sweaty skin. Phineas cocked the pistol slowly, the click of the mechanism satisfying, deadly.

"Do you have any last words you'd like us to give to Lord Philip, or Napoleon, or whomever is in charge of this fool's errand you know nothing about?"

The man blubbered. The acrid smell of urine filled the room as he wet himself in terror. "It's not Lord Philip!" he screamed.

"Then who's in charge?" Phineas insisted, grinding the muzzle into the man's cheek. "I want his name!"

"It's not a man!" the prisoner screamed in French. "It's a woman, for God's sake. An *English* woman."

"Who is she?" Adam demanded, grabbing the man's rough collar. "What's her name?"

"I don't know, I swear it," the man sobbed. He swung his eyes toward the table, not daring to move his head against the pistol. "The handkerchief is a token. I was to give that to the man in the tavern, and he would pay me for the letters. That's all I know, I swear. I am a carpenter from Normandy, I live in Gravelines. Someone asked me if I wanted to make some money. My wife is with child and I—"

A cold slick feeling of dread crept down Phineas's spine. He felt Adam's eyes on him.

"Phin," Adam said. "Is it her, your masked woman? Who the hell is she?"

But Phineas's eyes were on the prisoner. "Yasmina." He growled the name. "Does that mean anything to you?" he demanded.

The Frenchman miserably shook his head.

Twenty minutes later they were back at De Courcey House. Many of the guests had gone, and Phineas and Adam hurried toward the conservatory. Four footmen accompanied them, armed with pistols and lanterns.

The soft light of dawn crept through the glass ceiling. Phineas searched the shadowy folds of the plants and found nothing. He looked at Adam, who stood waiting grimly as each footman shook his head.

Phineas dug his fingers into the bark of the cherry tree and looked at the discarded fruit on the ground. He bent to pick up a small silk rosebud, lost from the wig she'd been wearing. A rose like the one stitched on the handkerchief.

"My lord?" A footman dropped something in Adam's palm. He examined it and then held it up to Phineas. A small portrait dangled at the end of a broken chain.

Phineas held it up to the light. "It's a child. Is it Jamie?"

"No. This doesn't belong to Marianne," Adam said. "Jamie's hair is fair. This child has brown hair, or perhaps it's red. Hard to tell even if it's a boy or a girl."

Phineas clutched the little portrait in his palm. "She said she wasn't married."

"Phineas, we have to find her," Adam said soberly.

"I know," he replied.

This time it was more than a personal quest for an intriguing lover. If she was a spy, then she was damned good at it. She'd tricked him, fooled him twice and slipped away. Now, for the honor of England and his own sanity, he had to find the delectable Yasmina, and outwit her.

Chapter 17

"**O**ur first ball at De Courcey House was a marvelous success, I must say," Marianne gloated as she and Isobel strolled through the park the next afternoon. "I believe it was one of the premier events of this Season. I shall have to convince Adam to make it an annual event. I shouldn't admit it, but there were so many guests I didn't have the opportunity to greet everyone. That would be quite unforgivable if it hadn't been a masquerade. You were there, weren't you?"

Despite the warmth of the spring sun on her face, Isobel felt cold.

Marianne hadn't recognized her?

She forced a smile. "Of course I was there. Your town house is lovely." Especially the conservatory.

Marianne put her arm through Isobel's. "Good, then we can gossip. What was your costume?"

It hardly seemed possible. Marianne had *seen* her. So had Lord Westlake and a library full of sharp-eyed *ton* matrons. Afterward she hadn't slept a wink, certain gossip and scandal would follow her out of the conservatory like the ills of Pandora's box.

"I was Char—er, a shepherdess," Isobel choked out the lie. "Blue muslin, with a yellow ribbon on my hat." She pulled her black woolen shawl more tightly around her shoulders as Marianne frowned, trying to recall the costume.

Isobel watched her son playing happily by the pond with Jamie and felt shame. Was there a person in this world she loved as much as she loved Robin? Oh, what she'd risked for a few moments of selfish pleasure!

Desire for her lover stirred.

She had to admit that Blackwood was her lover now. He made her feel alive and happy, and if she had the chance to make love to him again, she knew she would be powerless to resist the temptation. Even now her body ached for him, ignoring common sense. The only solution was to stay as far away from him as possible.

She smoothed her fingertips over her cheek where the skin was still tender from his kisses, and resisted the urge to sigh.

Marianne shook her head at last. "No, I'm certain I didn't see you, but the crush was dreadful." She leaned in to whisper, "I think there might even have been a few people present who were not invited guests."

Isobel's eyes widened. "Really? How do you know?"

"Well, for one, there was a most extraordinary lady with my brother, dressed in pink. I most certainly didn't know *her*."

"Oh?" The light spring air suddenly grew thick, difficult to draw into her lungs.

Marianne pursed her lips. "I can only assume she's Phin's latest amour." Her expression turned avid, hopeful. "Did you see her? She had a beautiful costume, all pink satin, lace and ribbons."

"Er, no," Isobel croaked. "Did you see her face?"

"Well, I might have, but her costume—well, I mean, it was very . . ." Marianne held her gloved hands in front of her chest. Quite a way in front of her chest. Isobel felt her face heat. "It was very—*distracting*. Fortunately she disappeared almost as quickly as she appeared, which was for the best. A single hop in one of the country dances and she'd have been Blackwood's newest scandal, and Adam can't abide a scene."

Isobel stumbled. Scandal. Ruin. Disgrace.

"Oh, good heavens, I've shocked you," Marianne said.

Isobel's icy fingers crept up to her collar, wrapping her shawl around her neck so tightly she nearly choked. She made herself let go.

Blackwood's newest scandal.

Honoria was sure to hear about the lady in pink *somewhere*. She loved gossip. Her mother-in-law would ask her if she'd seen the woman. What if Charles remembered her costume?

"Let's sit down, shall we?" Isobel said, and sank down on a nearby bench without waiting for Marianne to agree. Under her dowdy gray gown her heart pounded.

The ducks immediately congregated at their feet, paddling in place, eavesdropping. They'd quickly learned to avoid the corner of the pond where Jamie and Robin were playing.

"Actually, I'm quite worried about my brother," Marianne said, sitting beside her.

"Really?" Isobel asked, curiosity mixing with icy dread.

"My grandfather wants him to marry this year. He's thirty-two, you see, and I heartily agree it's time, but Grandfather has chosen the Duke of Welford's daughter, Lady Amelia, for him."

Jealousy ignited in Isobel's chest. She didn't even know Lady Amelia, but hated the duke's daughter Blackwood would share his life with. She studied her gloved hands and tried to still the black emotions churning in her belly.

It was ridiculous. She couldn't marry him, and she couldn't keep letting him make love to her in dark corners at masquerade balls. She resolved to refuse any future invitations to masked events, and to strictly avoid even speaking to Blackwood.

Especially at his wedding.

"Mind you, I want him to find a bride," Marianne said,

"but I do hope it won't be Lady Amelia. She isn't the right sort of girl to make him a good wife."

Isobel forced her hands to unclench from the painfully tight fists they'd formed. "Why isn't Welford's daughter right for him?"

Marianne snorted. "He'd be bored in a week with a milk-and-water child like Amelia! He would look for amusement elsewhere, with someone like the lady in pink, and he'd be just as miserable as he is now. He needs a woman of spirit to bring him to heel and keep him there."

"And who might that be?" Isobel asked, stiffening her spine, steeling herself to hear the name without reacting, but Marianne surprised her, turning her spine back to jelly in an instant.

"That's where I need your help. Do you know anyone who might be suitable? You watch carefully, observe people at every event. You must know a lady who might be—"

Isobel leapt to her feet in astonishment. "Oh, Marianne, don't ask me that!" she cried, her frayed nerves snapping under the strain. Careful and observant, was she? What would Marianne say if she knew the truth? She could no more help her friend choose a wife for Phineas than she could fly. Oh, how she wished at this moment that she could! Unfortunately, she was rooted to the earth, with Marianne's curious gaze fixed on her.

"Why, Isobel, whatever is wrong?" Marianne asked, as stunned as Isobel by the outburst. Isobel watched in horror as her friend's eyes widened with sudden understanding and her hand flew to her mouth "Oh! Oh, of course, now I see."

Isobel's stomach rolled. "You do?" She waited for Marianne to recall that the lady in pink looked very much like her. Sitting down again, she tried to think of an excuse, a reason for her behavior, a convincing lie. She felt as if she'd spent weeks doing nothing but making up lies.

But Marianne patted her hand. "Of course I understand. You were very much in love with your husband, weren't you? I mean, you must have been, to mourn him for so long after—"

The shocking supposition had Isobel back on her feet in a second. "No!" she said, the word torn from her. "No, Marianne, you are quite wrong. I didn't love Robert Maitland. Nor did he love me!" She couldn't bear to have her friend think that she had loved a man as dull and hateful as Robert.

"You didn't love him?" Pity warred with shock in Marianne's eyes.

Isobel knew she had said too much. She bit her tongue until she tasted the iron bitterness of blood, and stared at the ducks, still listening with pebble-eyed fascination.

"Please don't ask me to suggest someone for Blackwood. I cannot." Her heart clenched in agony as she retreated behind a mask of bland placidity, trying to calm her emotions.

"Well of course not! I can only imagine you have a very poor opinion of marriage, if your own was so unhappy," Marianne said. She rose to her feet and laid her hand on Isobel's arm. The soothing touch, and the pity that came with it, were most unwelcome.

"Have you considered marrying again?" Marianne asked. "For love this time?"

Isobel swallowed the bitter lump that rose in her throat. "I can never marry again."

"Why not?" Marianne asked. "Many widows take a second husband. Not all men are bad. Westlake is a wonderful husband. You're young, and you're pretty. I'm sure if you came out of mourning, you'd have more offers than you could count."

Isobel clenched her jaw on the despair that hovered just below the surface of her skin. Her legs were trembling with the effort of staying calm. A bead of sweat rolled between her breasts, as intimate as Blackwood's caresses.

Marianne leaned closer. "Have you considered taking a lover?"

Isobel's jaw dropped, and Marianne giggled. "It's not so shocking as that, Isobel! Many ladies do, you know. Someone discreet."

Marianne's expression sharpened and she tapped a gloved finger against her chin as she scanned the selection of gentlemen in the park. Isobel couldn't force an objection past the leaden lump clogging her throat. She didn't want another lover. She wanted—

"Blackwood!" Marianne's eyes lit up as she turned to Isobel with a wide grin.

Isobel shut her mouth with an astonished snap. Marianne laughed.

"Oh, Isobel, I've shocked you yet again. I didn't mean taking *him* as your lover, though gossip says he's very accomplished in bed. I meant that he is sure to *know* someone. Phineas spends enough time lurking in the shadows of the demimonde, and Adam says that he knows everyone in London."

Isobel put a hand to her temple, where a headache was starting to throb. "Marianne, if Honoria knew I was even having such a conversation, you can't imagine what she would do, what she *could* do!" she pleaded. She cast a desperate look at Robin, soaked and happy.

She doubted very much Blackwood would be at all discreet once he stopped laughing at his sister's request. Everyone in London would laugh.

Everyone except Honoria.

"I have to go," Isobel said, and picked up her skirts, moving quickly toward Robin.

"Isobel, wait," Marianne called, hurrying after her. "Surely you want to be happy."

Tears threatened now, but Isobel refused to let them fall.

Oh, yes, she wanted to be happy, but she would never consider trading Robin's happiness for her own. She was not Charlotte, not now in the crisp light of day after a night of indescribable passion, *not ever.*

She fixed a placid smile on her face, hiding behind Isobel the Invisible's imperturbable mask once again. "I like my life the way it is, Marianne. I have Robbie to raise, you see, and that's quite enough."

Marianne sighed. "But if that's true, why are you crying?"

Isobel touched her hand to her cheek. It came away wet. She had not shed a single tear since her mother left. Not when her cold marriage was arranged, not when Robert died, nor even when his will was read. Her heart skipped a beat. She knew who her tears were for.

Blackwood.

Chapter 18

"**W**hat a glorious morning!"

Phineas glanced dubiously at Miranda as she rode beside him on the pretty little mare. Above them, dark clouds threatened rain before the morning was out, and a brusque wind swatted irritably at the feather in her fashionable hat. She seemed scarcely aware of the horse under her, though his gift delighted her when he presented it, and for a few moments she'd been the girl he remembered.

Today the polished debutante was back, and she was preening and posing for the other riders they passed. She flirted shamelessly with the gentlemen of means and good *ton*, and looked down her pert nose at everyone else.

"Have you named her yet?" he asked, gesturing to the mare.

Her gaze turned coy. "I think I may have to call her Kelton."

"Kelton?" Phineas frowned. "Whatever for?"

She giggled, and the insipid sound grated across his nerves. "Oh, Phineas! After Viscount Kelton, of course. I think he's the one I will marry."

"Kelton?" Phineas demanded again, more sharply this time. "The man is an idiot."

"He's heir to an earldom, and he has eighty thousand a year."

"He has a ridiculous lisp that makes it impossible to have a conversation with him without getting wet, and he's about as bright as a burnt-out candle."

"I think he's charming, and his estate in Hampshire is said to be one of the most beautiful homes in England. I am looking forward to redecorating it."

"If it's so beautiful, why redecorate?" Phineas asked.

"Oh, Phin, you are silly. It's what new brides do. I will put my stamp on his heart *and* his home."

"It will be difficult to put a stamp on Kelton's heart. I doubt he has one. I saw him kick a puppy once," Phineas muttered.

She sent him a look that said he was trying her patience, and straightened herself in the saddle as another gentleman rode down the track toward them.

Phineas was relieved to see it was Gilbert Fielding, someone sensible to talk to. "Gil!" he called, beckoning to him. Gilbert came, but his eyes were on Miranda. "You bought that stallion, I see."

"And you bought the mare," Gilbert replied, tipping his hat to Miranda, who blushed under Gil's scrutiny. "She suits you well, Lady Miranda. She is almost as lovely as her rider."

"Thank you, Mr. Fielding," Miranda said, and batted her lashes as she stroked the horse's neck.

"Isn't it a fine morning?" Gilbert asked her, and Phineas cast another glance at the glowering sky, then looked at Miranda.

She smiled. A real smile, not a simper, the kind with teeth and warmth. Phineas frowned. That kind of smile used to be reserved only for him.

"Yes, it is a lovely morning. I was just telling Phineas it was, but he disagreed with me."

"Phineas, how unchivalrous you are," Gilbert joked, his smile as bright as Miranda's. "I daresay wherever Lady Mi-

randa goes, it's a lovely day, no matter what the weather."
Phineas stared at Gilbert. Odd. He'd never sounded like an
idiot before.

Miranda blushed and made a show of patting the mare
again, and the silly conversation turned to banalities about
parties and horses. Phineas stared down the track, waiting.
He had things to do, mysteries to solve, a lady to find.

He'd spent the wee hours of the morning sitting in his
study with the few scant clues to Yasmina's identity lined up
on the desk before him.

The jeweled slipper would be more at home in a harem
than in dirty London.

The portrait miniature was a fond and indistinct watercolor of a baby, but there was no name or date to give him a
clue. The child gazed out at him with bronze curls, solemn
eyes, and a rosebud mouth that might have belonged to any
infant in England.

The last two items disturbed him most. The monogrammed handkerchief was made of the finest Irish linen and
the most delicate French lace. It was a smuggler's token, a
symbol of betrayal and treason. The embroidered rose looked
much like the tiny silk flower Yasmina had left behind in the
conservatory. Too much. He still had the uneasy feeling in
his gut that usually meant trouble. It haunted him, like the
soft sweetness of her perfume, her damned drugging kisses,
her luscious body. He shifted in the saddle, silently cursing
a very inconvenient erection.

"Phin, do pay attention. I've asked you twice if you're
ready to ride on!" Miranda said, and he turned to her. She
tossed her head, making the feather in her saucy hat bounce
for Gilbert's sake, looking at him out of the corners of her
eyes with a mischievous half smile. She kicked the mare into
a trot. Phineas nodded to Gilbert and followed his sister, fully
aware that Fielding stood by the track and watched them go.

"Planning on naming the mare Fielding instead?" he asked.

Miranda sighed. "Possibly. What is Lord Fielding's title?"

Phineas grinned. "Lord Fielding is his father's title. Gilbert hasn't got one. He's a second son. His father is an earl, though."

"Does he have a fortune?" she asked.

"Not a farthing."

Annoyance kindled in her blue eyes. "Does he have anything to recommend him other than a handsome face, a fine horse, and a charming manner?"

"Well, he's a decent shot, an honorable fellow, and pleasant company. Isn't that enough?" Phineas said. "And those were his own teeth he was grinning at you with, I believe."

"Teeth!" Miranda muttered. The debutante was back, raising her chin in disdain. "Too bad. I shall have to marry Kelton after all."

Phineas noted that she completely forgot to flirt with the next gentleman they passed, much to the man's dismay. She glanced over her shoulder instead, to where penniless, titleless Gilbert Fielding was riding away, sitting tall in his saddle.

Phineas wondered if Gil would christen his stallion Miranda.

Chapter 19

"There's a gentleman from Waterfield Abbey to see Lord Charles, my lady," Finch said, hovering in the doorway of the library where Isobel was pretending to read. Blackwood's face filled every page. She put the book down.

"I see. Does Lord Charles wish to use this room?"

"Er, no, my lady. His lordship is out, and so is Lady Honoria. The gentleman has asked to speak with you," he said, his tone apologetic. "He's come a long way, and it seems urgent, if I may be so bold. I told him I would see if you are at home."

Isobel hesitated. She should ask Finch to tell the man to come back when Charles was available, but Waterfield Abbey *was* hers. If there was urgent news, didn't she have the right to hear it?

"Please show him in, Finch." She got to her feet and clasped her hands, waiting. The man entered the library and stopped near the door. He bowed, his expression grim, as if unsure of his welcome.

"Good day, my lady. I'm Jonathan Hart. I'm the steward at Waterfield Abbey."

Isobel smiled. "Of course. I remember you from my time at Waterfield as a child, Mr. Hart. Do sit down."

He took several more steps into the room but remained on his feet, holding his hat before him like a shield. "I'd prefer to stand," he said grimly.

His expression was respectful but hardly friendly as he met her eyes briefly before lowering his gaze to the carpet. Confused, Isobel sat down in the chair nearest him. Her bold confidence in her ability to handle the matter on her own quailed.

"Finch mentioned there is an urgent matter you wish to discuss. I'm afraid Lord Charles isn't here—"

"Actually, I was hoping to see *you*, my lady."

"Me?" Isobel asked, surprised.

"It's about conditions at Waterfield. The servants haven't been paid, and Lord Charles has dismissed many of them from their posts. There's also a number of repairs that can't wait." His eyes kindled with frustration. "I've sent a number of requests to Lord Charles for money to buy livestock and seed and the supplies I need to keep the place in good repair, but I have not received anything from him. When he's there, he ignores me. I can't run the place on nothing."

Isobel stared at him. Honoria had boasted to Marianne that Waterfield was making a good profit under Charles's brilliant management. Charles had recently bought new horses and an expensive curricle.

"I hadn't heard. Is there some mistake, perhaps?"

Mr. Hart thrust a sheet of figures at her. "I have the expenses listed, my lady. I know you likely hate the old place now, in light of what happened there, but it's prime land, and the people are good-hearted, hardworking souls. It's a shame to see it fall to ruin under the circumstances—"

"In light of what happened there?" Isobel repeated, confused.

"Yes, my lady. We were all very sorry, of course. Our condolences were sincere, I assure you, but—"

"To what are you referring, Mr. Hart?"

"Why, to Lord Robert's death, my lady." The man looked as confused as Isobel. He cast a quick look at the door, as if he wanted to summon help, or flee.

"But what has my husband's death to do with Waterfield? He died at Ashdown Park." She wondered if the man was befuddled. He'd been steward of Waterfield for nearly thirty years. Was age making him forgetful?

He shook his head, and she noted his eyes were sharp and clear, his expression sure. "The Earl of Ashdown, Lord Robert, your husband, died at Waterfield. I was there when they brought his body up from the beach. I helped bury him in the churchyard, in accordance with Lord Charles's orders."

Isobel's stomach knotted itself. Honoria had told her Robert died of a fever in his bed at Ashdown Park. She clasped her hands to keep them from shaking. Honoria had not even allowed her to attend the funeral. He'd been interred quickly, she said, for fear his illness might be catching.

"How did he die?" she asked quietly.

The man shifted his feet, looking at her as if he feared she might be daft. She held his gaze steadily. "Why, he was shot of course, Countess."

Heat rose under her collar and she clutched the list of expenses in her lap, barely aware of the crackle of the paper in her hand.

"Shall I call someone for you, get you a glass of water, perhaps?" he asked, his brow wrinkling in concern.

"Under what circumstances was he shot?" she asked.

Hart looked sympathetic. "Smugglers, my lady," he said in a half whisper. "They told me it was a highwayman, but there are no highwaymen on the beach at night. They'd be on the roads, wouldn't they?"

"I see." Isobel rose to her feet and crossed to the window, staring out at the street without seeing it.

They'd lied to her about her husband's death.

Robert had been shot by smugglers. Surely that wasn't possible. There was some mistake. But in her gut she knew Hart's account was true. He had no reason to lie.

"Begging your pardon, my lady, but about the list, and money?" Mr. Hart asked after a few moments, his tone desperate.

She shut her eyes, realizing that she was powerless to help him. She had no access to her own funds. She turned to look at him. "I have your list, but I must speak to Lord Charles." His face fell, and she held out a hand. "Truly, I'll do what I can, Mr. Hart."

"I see." Hart sighed, his shoulders drooping. "Then I shall do my best to speak to his lordship when he's next at Waterfield." He made a stiff, awkward bow. "Good day to you, Countess. I'm sorry to have troubled you." He turned toward the door.

"Mr. Hart?" Isobel called after him.

"Yes, my lady?" he said, and his eyebrows rose hopefully.

"How often is my brother-in-law at Waterfield?"

"Why, very often, my lady. Once a month or more."

"I see. Will you wait?" She hurried past him and went up the stairs, furious. They had lied to her about her husband's death. She opened the door to her room and crossed to her jewelry box. She took out her hated wedding band, and the emerald betrothal ring too. If Mr. Hart sold them, they might fetch enough to pay a few months' wages. Her hand hovered over her grandmother's pearls for a moment before she scooped them up. She turned to go back downstairs.

She made it as far as the doorway, then turned and stared back at the jewelry box.

Dread closed her throat.

Her fingers crept up to her neck, but there was no chain there. She moved toward the dressing table and reached out with numb fingers to touch the edge of the lid. She whispered a prayer as she opened the box again.

The blood drained from her limbs, and she sat down heavily on the little chair before the mirror. The portrait of Robin was missing. She hadn't noticed until now.

She knew exactly where it was.

Chapter 20

The ladies of Maitland House gasped as Phineas arrived for tea, uninvited and unwelcome.

He stood beside his sisters and Adam and smiled charmingly at the three females gaping at him.

Honoria's pale blue eyes nearly bulged out of her head.

The second woman stared at him like he was a cream cake and she was starving. Her eyes roamed over him, and she gave a shivering little gasp and laid a hand to her cheek. No one bothered to introduce her.

Isobel blinked at him in pinch-lipped shock as if a cat had dragged him in bloody and left him on the rug at her feet. "Lord Blackwood," she murmured through clenched teeth, as though his name was a second corpse. "We didn't expect you." She dipped a stiff curtsy and turned away, her cheeks scarlet.

"Jane, more teacups will be needed," Honoria said as she dragged her eyes off Phineas and looked at the bemused woman beside her. But she didn't move. She was still gazing at him, her eyes wide, her lower lip caught in her teeth, so he smiled at her again, and watched hot color flood her sallow face, knowing besotted females were often the most useful.

"Jane Kirk!" Honoria said more loudly, elbowing the woman so hard she nearly fell over. "Go and fetch the tea, I say!"

Miranda sidled closer to Phineas under Charles's stare, which even made Phineas queasy. He squeezed his sister's hand and crossed the room to take the seat Honoria indicated, a chair well away from her own.

The salon's decor reminded Phineas of an expensive brothel, where the art, the lavish fabric, even the vases and knickknacks, were chosen for their extravagant cost, rather than any real sense of taste. The effect of such things in a countess's sitting room was garish. Given Isobel's long mourning, he had expected the house to be a shrine to Robert Maitland, but there wasn't a single portrait or memento to be seen.

He decided that the room must owe its extraordinary decorations to Honoria and Charles rather than Isobel. Honoria held court in an expensive ruffled fuchsia gown, cut in a style meant for a debutante, not a plump matron of sixty. Charles looked like an overfed pasha, in a green silk waistcoat and sporting a large ruby in his cravat.

Isobel was a respite for the eyes. Her dove gray gown was soothing amid the clutter, like shade on a hot day. Her vibrant hair was a bonfire against the ashen dress. He had to admit she looked elegant and rather pretty, even with her back and neck stiff with indignation at his presence.

She took a seat across from his, and left the responsibility of serving tea to her mother-in-law and Jane. He watched her, refusing to believe such a dull woman could be in charge of a ring of smugglers. She was probably afraid of the dark, and he'd wager she never touched strong spirits. She obviously had no passion for silk or French lace.

She caught him staring, and her eyes widened as she met his speculative gaze. Hot color rose in her cheeks and she looked away, pursing her lips. He damned her for being so outraged that he had dared to enter her home. He stretched out his legs, made himself comfortable. She pretended to concentrate on her tea.

Her hands on the china cup were long-fingered and delicate. She cast another bird-quick glance at him, her eyes bobbing over him in hasty appraisal, from the knot in his cravat to the toes of his boots, before darting away again. Her becoming blush deepened, and he noted the throb of her pulse above her prim collar.

Phineas was well aware of the effect he had on women. He shocked them, like Honoria, or bemused them, like Jane Kirk, but Isobel's reaction baffled him. She acted as if he'd caught her naked. It was a most intriguing reaction from the dull widow.

He made her nervous just by sitting across a room from her. She kept a pale imitation of a polite smile on her face, but a perpetual blush belied her agitation. From time to time she sent him sideways looks from under her lashes, and he found himself waiting for those glances, counting them.

He wondered how she would react if he touched her hot cheek, pulled her into his arms and kissed her. Arousal stirred unexpectedly and he shifted in his seat.

The devil! He was *not* attracted to a frumpy little snipe like Isobel Maitland. He would, of course, do his duty if he had to, but bedding her for information about Charles would hardly be a pleasure. Well, perhaps for her.

He forced himself to look away, to concentrate on the conversation.

"I understand you hold a property down the coast from my own, Countess. A place called Waterfield Abbey?" Adam said, subtly steering the discussion.

"It was one of my uncle's estates, my lord. I have not been there since I was a chi—"

"Did you know Charles controls *seven* estates?" Honoria interrupted, directing the question to Miranda, who blushed, unsure how to reply.

"How many of them are by the sea?" Adam asked.

"Oh, Adam!" Marianne rolled her eyes. "Do forgive my husband, Lady Honoria. He grew up by the sea, and is obsessed with ships and tides and the stars."

"I see," Honoria said, as if such an occupation was highly improper for an earl. Her predatory smile returned as she looked back at Miranda. "Are you enjoying your Season in London, my dear? I hear your name everywhere. You are quite the most successful debutante this year. Charles is considered one of the most eligible gentlemen, you know."

"Thank you, my lady," Miranda said, her tone wooden. "I am enjoying the parties very much, and I like to ride in the park when the weather is fine."

"Do you?" Honoria cried. "Charles! You must take Lady Miranda riding! Actually, he has a brand new curricle you might enjoy taking a turn in. The chestnuts he bought to pull it are perfectly matched, almost twins."

"Thank you," Miranda replied, "but I'm sure I have appointments arranged for some time to come, my lady."

"Perfect!" Honoria crowed, undeterred. "We have a week or two yet until the finest weather is upon us. By then, no doubt, you will have plenty of time. I shall write to your great-aunt so she may put it on your calendar."

Miranda looked ill.

"It has been a very mild spring, hasn't it?" Adam tried again. "The flowers are a welcome sight, but I am looking forward to seeing my roses bloom. Do you like roses, Countess?"

"I prefer violets, my lord," Isobel said quietly.

"You must come and see Adam's conservatory, Isobel," Marianne said. "He collects exotic plants, including violets . . ."

Phineas watched Isobel blush again, and slide an anxious glance at her mother-in-law, who was still grinning at Miranda like a tiger with prey in sight. Isobel did not look at *him*, though her eyes went everywhere else as Marianne prattled on.

It didn't matter. He was remembering the conservatory in the dark, with far more luscious company. He and Yasmina had probably crushed quite a number of Adam's exotic plants in their haste to renew their acquaintance, violets included.

He shifted in his chair and looked around the room again, making note of the cabinets and drawers. Later, when he returned at night, he would know where to search.

"Perhaps it's time we took our leave, my dear," Adam said to his wife, interrupting Honoria before she could launch into more gushing praise of Charles. "We wouldn't want to overstay our welcome."

"Of course. I'll go up to the nursery and fetch Jamie. Isobel, will you show me where it is?"

Phineas got to his feet. "I'll accompany you as well, if I may. I haven't met Jamie's new friend." He met the look of horror on Isobel Maitland's face with a firm and steady gaze. She quickly looked away, and he had an unexpected urge to put a hand under her chin, to raise her face and read what was hidden in her eyes.

"Charles and I will happily keep Lady Miranda and Lord Westlake company until you return," Honoria said. "Jane, accompany Isobel upstairs, in case Lady Marianne needs anything."

Phineas watched Isobel's lips tighten as she led the way out of the room. Marianne linked arms with her friend as they climbed the stairs, and chattered in her ear.

Phineas glanced at the doors leading off the hall. One stood ajar, and he paused, feigning interest in a painting, peering through the open door. A large desk squatted in the center of an unremarkable room. "I see Lord Charles keeps a library," he said to Jane Kirk conversationally.

"He uses it as his study," she simpered. "There *is* a collection of old books, which I believe belonged to the countess's father, but *she* is the only one who reads them," Jane added, looking daggers at Isobel's back as the two countesses climbed the stairs.

"Are there any family portraits?" Phineas asked. Jane's thin brows slammed together in bafflement. "I have an interest in portraits," he lied, giving Jane an encouraging smile. A widow as devoted as Isobel probably kept a life-sized picture of her dead husband hanging over her cold, lonely bed, if only to hide a safe full of yellowing love letters. He very much wanted to see her room.

"Portraits," Jane parroted. "Well, there are three paintings of Lady Honoria in the house, one of Lord Charles, and one of the late earl, Lord Robert."

"Would it be possible to see them?" Phineas asked. "I knew Lord Robert. I would be most interested to see if the artist did him justice."

Jane looked as if she might melt if he smiled at her again, so he did. "Ohhh." She raised a trembling hand to her flushed cheek and led him upstairs.

By the time they reached the second floor, Isobel and Marianne had already disappeared up the stairs to the third. He waited as Jane opened a set of oak doors just wide enough to slip into the room.

The countess's suite was decorated much like the salon downstairs. Insipid shades of lavender and purple assaulted the senses. The cloying scent of perfume hung heavy in the air. Unfortunately, the door to her bedchamber was closed.

"There it is," Jane said, pointing to a portrait of Robert Maitland that hung in the place of honor over the fireplace. Robert looked back at Phineas, a thinner, fair-haired version of Charles. His pale blue eyes were Honoria's, as was the thin, selfish mouth.

"He was a handsome man," Jane sighed. "This painting doesn't do him justice."

Phineas turned, and found a picture of Lady Honoria gazing down at him from the opposite wall. Now why would Isobel keep a portrait of a woman she disliked in her rooms?

"How extraordinary. I would have thought such an impressive portrait of Lady Honoria would have pride of place downstairs. Of perhaps in her own rooms," he said.

"Oh, but this *is* Lady Honoria's room. She took over the countess's suites when Lord Robert died. Lady Isobel has a smaller room down the hall. Lord Charles occupies the earl's apartments, of course. And there *is* a portrait of Lady Honoria in the library, and another in the dining room, but this one is her favorite."

"Does Lady Isobel keep a portrait of Lord Robert in her suite?" he asked, hoping it would be that simple.

Jane sniffed. "No. She has a small watercolor of the sixth earl, Master Robin, that she painted herself. She also has a miniature of her own mother, but she keeps it hidden, and thinks no one knows." Her eyes turned shrewish. "If Lady Honoria knew Charlotte the Harlot's portrait was in this house, she'd be very displeased. I could tell her if I wanted to, of course."

Lady Charlotte Fraser was Isobel's mother?

He remembered the bawdy songs and salacious tales of Charlotte the Harlot. The scandal was still fresh when he arrived in London. He'd been eighteen at the time. Isobel must have been a child.

"We should find the countess, I believe," he said, but Jane took a bold step toward him, her thin lips puckered for a kiss. He hesitated. A kiss would ensure her silence, possibly win him more help later if he needed it, but he could not bring himself to lower his mouth to meet the servant's shriveled lips, not while Yasmina's lush mouth filled his mind.

"We should rejoin Lady Isobel, Miss Kirk. I do not wish you to get into any trouble for merely showing me a portrait."

Her jaw dropped and she stared at him. Her ugly purple blush perfectly matched the room's decor. He kept his expression cool until she lowered her eyes.

"This way, then, *my lord*. Up the stairs and to the right," she said tartly.

He followed her down the hall. "*That* is Isobel's room," Jane said as they passed a narrow door at the end of the hallway. By Phineas's estimation, it was right above the library, facing the street. He wished he had the opportunity to slip inside now, to satisfy his curiosity, but Jane was already halfway up the stairs, her expression closed and unhelpful. He'd probably have to ravish her on the spot to get any more information. It would be easier—and more pleasant—to come back later and find what he needed on his own.

Laughter bounced through the open door of the nursery, and he paused on the threshold. Jamie and the young Earl of Ashdown were sprawled on the floor playing a game of cards. Marianne sat beside them, carefully guarding her hand against Jamie's attempts to cheat.

To his surprise, the happy peals of laughter were coming from Isobel as she took a trick from Marianne. She was lying on her stomach, her knees bent, trim legs folded upward and crossed at the ankles.

Phineas stopped where he was. Isobel Maitland was not just pretty. She was beautiful. He'd never seen her smile, but she was grinning at her son with so much adoration in her eyes that his breath caught in his throat and a pit of longing opened in his stomach. Something elusive flitted through his brain as he watched her.

"Countess!" Jane Kirk interrupted the fun, a pruny look of disapproval on her face as she glared at Isobel. "The marquess has come to fetch his sister and Lord James."

The smiles on all four faces instantly faded. He felt like a storm cloud over a picnic. Isobel righted herself in a lithe, graceful motion, covering her shapely legs and ankles, taking Robin's hand to stand silently before him, her face scarlet. Through tight lips she introduced Phineas to her son, both of them regarding him with solemn hazel eyes, as if he, and not Jane Kirk, had spoiled the game.

It was a look he was used to. He'd seen it often enough in the eyes of his family, and anyone else who imagined they were better, smarter, more respectable than he was. He felt his mouth twist bitterly.

"It's time to go, Marianne," he said, still looking at Isobel. She was flushed from playing, and a few fragile curls had crept free of the tight hairpins to frame rosy cheeks. He couldn't seem to look away from her. Didn't want to. Her eyes held his, her thoughts unreadable in the luminous depths.

Then Jamie launched himself onto Phineas's leg, where he clung like a fox terrier, demanding attention. Phineas grinned and ruffled his nephew's dark hair.

"Phin, the Maitlands are also attending the theatre tonight," Marianne said. "I thought Isobel might sit with us, but she won't agree. Use your famous charm to convince her."

"I'm sure Lady Honoria would not approve," Jane Kirk said, and everyone looked at the servant.

"Why ever not?" Marianne asked, eyeing the bold servant coldly. Jane had the good sense not to answer.

"It's a kind offer, Marianne, truly," Isobel said, "but I really must keep Honoria company."

"I'm sure Lord Charles would be pleased to sit with you, Countess Westlake, especially if Lady Miranda is attending the play," Jane Kirk suggested pertly.

Marianne glared at her. "Hold your tongue! You have forgotten your place, Miss Kirk. I am speaking to the countess, and you are interrupting."

Phineas hid a smile. Marianne sounded like Great-Aunt Augusta, but it needed to be said, and it appeared that Isobel was too busy staring at the floor to rebuke Jane.

There was more here than just an impertinent servant. Jane Kirk was glaring at Isobel from the corner of her eye. She'd even moved to stand between the two countesses. Perhaps Jane was a poor relative and had more standing in the family than he thought. Under her withering glare, Isobel's expression was fixed once more into placid nothingness. All traces of the radiant beauty had flown.

"Come, Marianne, Adam is waiting," Phineas murmured.

Isobel came out of her trance and bent to kiss her son on the top of his head. "I'll see you later, Robbie," she whispered.

"He has lessons this afternoon, Countess," Jane reminded her, and again Phineas waited for Isobel to correct the impudent servant, but she did not.

He moved aside to allow Marianne, Jamie, and Isobel to precede him out the door. He pointedly stepped in front of Jane Kirk.

Isobel's back was stiff as she descended the stairs ahead of him, her shoulders tight. She had pride, and it had obviously been wounded. Whatever she was in this odd household, it appeared that Jane Kirk had some power over Lady Isobel. Another secret, perhaps?

His senses tingled. Now that he knew the layout of the place, he would come back tonight. This odd visit had tripled the number of questions he wanted answers to.

Chapter 21

Isobel couldn't believe it. Blackwood had been in her salon.

Well, not *her* salon, Honoria's, which was worse. Honoria had raged over the infamous rake's audacity all afternoon, saying he quite ruined the mood of the day, though Isobel could not see how, since he'd said almost nothing.

He just sat staring at her.

He made her feel as if she were a curiosity in the Tower Menagerie, or a clockwork toy that might be amusing if only it were wound. She was wound, all right, so tightly she thought she'd break in half with the tension.

She'd almost run out of the room in sheer relief when Marianne suggested they go upstairs to the nursery, but he asked to come along. He disappeared with Jane, and she'd hoped he had decided to wait downstairs after all.

She'd been giddy once the terrible strain of his presence was lifted, and perhaps she did get a little carried away while playing in the nursery, but she hardly expected him to appear in the doorway and catch her sprawled on the floor.

He'd just stood there, staring at her, his expression unreadable, until she thought her heart would pound its way out of her chest and land at his feet.

Even now, hours later, as she drove to the theatre with Honoria and Charles, he wouldn't leave her be. She stared out at the passing city, knowing he would be at the theatre. Her body prickled with nerves, and she pressed a hand to the throbbing pulse at her throat.

"Charles, you'll have an opportunity to pay your respects to Miranda tonight," Honoria said to him. "Take Isobel with you to the Westlake box. She'll keep Marianne busy so you may speak with Miranda more intimately."

"What do you want me to do, Mother, propose, or have my way with her while Isobel distracts her family?" Charles barked a laugh at his own jest.

"Really, Charles, there's no cause for that kind of talk," Honoria said. "Are you drunk?"

"I wish," he grumbled. "Look, the chit doesn't like me. I'd marry her fast enough, if only for her fortune, but she hasn't shown the slightest bit of regard for me."

Honoria shifted in her seat. "Isobel, I can only lay this at your door. Have you been using your influence with Marianne?"

Isobel's stomach churned. At least in the dark she didn't have to smile. "Of course," she lied. "But Marianne says that His Grace expects Miranda to not only marry money, but a title."

"A title, eh?" Charles growled. "I'd have one if not for—"

"Charles!" Honoria stopped him, but Isobel felt the hairs on the back of her neck rise.

If not for Robin.

If her son didn't exist, Charles would be Earl of Ashdown, and fit to marry a duke's granddaughter. She glanced at her mother-in-law's shadowed profile, waiting for Honoria to defend Robin, but she said nothing, and fear jabbed at Isobel. A connection to a duke would benefit Honoria as well.

Panic shook Isobel to action. "Did Mr. Hart meet with you yesterday?" she asked in a rush. "He came to see me while you were out, and he says there are repairs that need—"

Charles buried his fists in the collar of her cloak, jerking her forward. Isobel struggled to pull away but he held her fast.

"You spoke to Hart?" he snarled. "You dare to interfere with things that don't concern you?"

Isobel struggled against his grip.

"You met with Jonathan Hart?" Honoria demanded. "Alone? Charles, let her go. She can't tell us anything if you're choking her."

Charles released her, and Isobel fell backward against the seat, gasping. "Since Robert saw fit to leave everything in my capable hands, he must have believed you did not have the sense to manage important estates. He wanted you to concentrate on raising Robin."

But she didn't raise Robin, Isobel wanted to scream. She had no say at all in how her son was brought up. She felt ice cold sweat prickle between her breasts. She swallowed, but the knot of fear remained. "No one was home. He insisted on seeing someone, and Finch thought—"

"Do not lay this at Finch's doorstep!" Honoria said shrilly. "It's the kind of thing your mother would have done, sneaking around behind our backs. You owe us everything, Isobel, including the roof over your head. I hope you haven't forgotten that. We shelter you, clothe you, and ask only obedience in return. If you weren't the mother of Robert's heir, you could do as you like, go where you wish, but Robin must be brought up without the taint of scandal attached to his name."

"Yes, Honoria," Isobel said through clenched teeth. Anger and fear warred in her breast as the familiar threat rose up like the grim reaper. They could take Robin from her, and she would be powerless to stop them. She clenched her fists. She would never, ever let that happen. She straightened her spine.

"Mother, I think the time has come to do something more final," Charles began, but Honoria waved her hand, a shadowy, frightening thing in the semidarkness of the coach, which silenced him at once.

"We will discuss it later, Charles. *In private*." She turned to Isobel again. "What did Mr. Hart say to you about Waterfield, Isobel?"

That Robert had died there, shot by smugglers. Isobel wondered what other falsehoods lay buried with Robert. Anger rose, but fear advised her to tread cautiously.

"H-He said nothing of importance, really. He merely said that seed was needed for the spring planting, and several cottages had been damaged by winter storms and wanted repair." The lie marched off her tongue neatly enough, but it sounded false, and she braced for a blow or a pinch from Charles. It didn't come. Isobel wondered if they could hear her heart pounding.

"Is that all?" Honoria said.

"Yes," Isobel managed.

Honoria let out a heavy sigh. "How impatient of the man! Charles has been busy touring the other Maitland holdings. If Hart was a better steward, then he would have managed these things himself. He should be dismissed, Charles. There are plenty of competent men—"

"No!" Isobel cried.

"It is not your business," Charles grated.

"But Mr. Hart worked for my uncle. He was at Waterfield when I was a child. It would be wrong to turn him away after so many years of good work."

"You see, there's the proof that Robert was right," Honoria said. "You are too stupid, too sentimental, to manage important estates."

Isobel's indignation made her unwary. "But I haven't been to Waterfield since I was a child. If I went there, saw what was needed, perhaps I *could* help. I could take Robin there for a few weeks. There's a beach, and he might—"

"Damn you, Isobel!" Charles snarled.

"No." Honoria's tone was ice. "The boy would fall behind in his lessons. It's best he stays in Town. He needs constant discipline." Bitterness filled Isobel's mouth. Silence fell over them like lead.

"Actually, now that I think about it, I might allow you to take Robin for a holiday in the country after all," Honoria said a few minutes later.

"Mother! Not to Waterfield, surely!" Charles hissed.

"I was thinking she might go to Ashdown Park, or to a more secluded manor, perhaps, with Jane."

"His tutors could travel with us," Isobel said, snatching at the possibility, but again Honoria waved her hand for silence.

"*If* I decide to allow it, you must do something for me in return, Isobel."

"What?" she asked, bracing for whatever dark favor Honoria might ask of her.

"At the interval of the play tonight you will accompany Charles to the Westlake box. You will advise Lady Miranda what a wonderful husband Charles would make her, and you will be convincing. I want to see her smile at him, to accept his invitation to go driving in the park."

Isobel shut her eyes. They wanted her to lie. She would rather tell Miranda that the lowest footman in her grandfather's service would make a better husband than Charles Maitland.

The dilemma gnawed on her resolve with small sharp teeth. Could she ruin an innocent girl's life to get Robin away from Charles and Honoria?

"Isobel? Do you understand?" Honoria prompted. "There will be no visit to Ashdown if Charles does not wed. In fact, if he does not marry Miranda, I cannot see that there is any point in continuing your friendship with Marianne Westlake at all. Perhaps that connection should be severed for good."

A wave of despair left Isobel trembling. They would take everything. Her son's happiness, her only friend, even the job of a loyal steward she cared about. How she hated them! Her mind worked frantically to find a way around helping Honoria and Charles to ruin another woman's life the way they'd destroyed hers.

"Do you understand what I expect you to do?" Honoria demanded again.

Isobel's jaw tightened. She needed time to come up with a way out, a way to protect her son. For now, there was only one thing she could do.

"I understand perfectly," she said succinctly.

Chapter 22

Miranda clutched Phineas's sleeve as the curtain fell for the interval of the play. "Oh, good heavens, Charles is coming over here!" He felt his sister shudder as Honoria waggled her fingers at Miranda across the theatre.

Marianne waved back, and Miranda grabbed her sister's hand. "For pity's sake, Marianne, waving will only encourage them!"

Marianne tugged her hand away and raised her opera glasses to follow Charles's progress. "At least he's bringing Isobel with him!"

Phineas's gut tightened. He was supposed to be on his way to Maitland House, but if he left now it would look like a snub to Charles and Isobel. Not that he cared what they thought of his manners, but Charles might be suspicious, and his job was easier when no one suspected a thing. The arrest of the French agent was sure to have made someone nervous.

The Duchess of Welford rose. "We really must be getting back to Welford. He slept through the whole of the first act. If I don't go and wake him, he'll sleep through the second act as well. Come, Amelia, bid Blackwood good-night."

Marianne lowered her opera glasses and turned to her sister. "Quick, Miranda, go with Her Grace and Amelia to the Welford box. If Charles follows you there, then go on to Colonel Lord Hollister's box, with Her Grace's permission, of course."

"Oh, Mother won't object," Amelia said eagerly. "Anthony is here with his mother. Lady Hollister is my godmother."

"Isn't it undignified to be racing about the theatre to avoid someone?" Adam asked. "Miranda could simply remain here, preserve her dignity and say hello if he comes over. There is no guarantee he's even heading this way."

"He most certainly is, Adam. I know it in my bones," Marianne argued. "Off you go, Miranda, or it will be too late."

With a giggle, Miranda and Amelia fled.

Marianne fixed her husband with a scathing glare. "One would almost think you wished to see her married to that toad!"

Adam rolled his eyes. "I think I'll go and order some champagne. I'll leave you to your wicked schemes, my dear. Coming, Phin?"

Phineas rose to go, but Marianne caught his arm. "You can't leave me alone to greet Charles Maitland! Whatever will I say to him? We need to give Miranda time to make her escape. You don't mind, do you, Phin? Wouldn't you like to say hello to Isobel?"

He most definitely did not wish to say hello or anything else to Isobel. He wished to go and search her brother-in-law's desk, and rifle through Isobel's drawers, but a lady's entreaty, even when that lady was your sister, left a gentleman no choice but to bow and acquiesce to her wishes.

Phineas pasted a smile over gritted teeth and sat down, hoping there'd still be time to slip away once Marianne began to chatter to her friend. He tapped his fingers on his knee as he waited impatiently.

He leapt to his feet when Isobel Maitland entered with Charles.

"Isobel! What a lovely gown," Marianne gushed. "How pretty you look tonight."

Phineas glanced at her dress. The subtle blue-green shimmer of the silk enhanced the copper of her hair, brought out the golden lights in her eyes and made the soft flush of her cheeks, well, charming. The delicate embroidery around the neckline of the gown drew his eyes to her bodice and the feminine curves beneath. He felt his chest tighten, and told himself it was merely curiosity, not interest in what lay beneath her clothing.

Still, as she passed him to reach Marianne, her gown brushed over the fine wool of his breeches, a caress as sensual as skin on skin, and he felt a jolt of awareness of Isobel Maitland as a woman.

"Where is Lady Miranda? Charles asked, not bothering with greetings.

"Off to pay her respects to the Duke and Duchess of Welford," Marianne replied. "Isobel, do sit down. Adam went to get some champagne. Would you like a glass?"

"I shouldn't," Isobel murmured.

"Oh, go ahead. It might loosen your tongue," Charles said cryptically, and Phineas watched Isobel blush.

"Stay here with Countess Westlake," Charles said. "I think I'll go pay my own visit to the Welfords." Then he left as he'd come, with no regard to anyone.

Even Marianne was momentarily stunned into silence by his rudeness. Isobel stared at the floor, her face as red as her hair, as Marianne recovered enough to organize everyone.

"Take Miranda's seat, Isobel. She won't be back until the play ends. The duchess will keep a close eye on her. What do you think of the play?"

Isobel gracefully took the seat in front of Phineas, and sitting behind her, he only half listened to the conversation. Etiquette demanded he remain until Adam returned, and he stared at the back of Isobel's head, cursing the delay. As usual, her hair was twisted in a matronly bun, drawn upward with skin-pulling tension, every strand as stiff as a bowstring.

She ignored him completely, so he moved his feet to remind her of his presence, and she jumped and shot him a wary glance.

So she was aware of him. The tightness in her shoulders said so as she turned away again. She was nervous, but whether that was due to him or another cause, he couldn't tell. She sent sidelong glances at the Maitland box from time to time, where Honoria sat like a great pink silk spider in the dark, the glittering orbs of her opera glasses alternately trained on Charles, still racing about the galleries behind the boxes, and Isobel.

Poor Charles arrived at the Welford box just as the lights dimmed for the second act, only to find Miranda and Amelia had gone on to the Hollister box, and all he could do was pay brief respects to Welford before taking his leave, since the duke did not invite him to sit.

"I should go. The second half is beginning," Isobel said, rising. Phineas got to his feet as well, and they came nose-to-nose for an instant. She stepped back quickly, almost falling, and he caught her elbow to steady her. The skin above her glove was unexpectedly cool and soft. She made an odd little sound of distress under her breath and pulled away as if his touch burned.

Something about that sound, soft and needy, prickled in the back of his brain, but Marianne grabbed Isobel's other arm.

"Do stay here with us, Isobel—you'll miss the start of the second act if you walk back now, and I cannot send you away unescorted. Phineas is so engrossed in the story, you see, and I know he'd hate to miss a minute. Adam should be back any moment with the champagne."

She fixed her brother with a conspirator's squint, but he

looked at Isobel, ready to escort her back if she wished, regardless of Marianne's insistence that she stay. But her eyes were soft and wide, so clear he felt he could drown in them. He drew a breath of surprise as another jolt of sexual awareness shot through him.

Marianne shook Isobel's arm, breaking the spell. "Look, Charles is safely back with Honoria, and Amelia and Miranda are sitting with the Hollisters. Since everyone is comfortable, the matter is settled. Do sit down, Isobel."

Adam returned with a waiter bearing champagne, and Phineas watched Isobel's eyes slide shut as she sipped the effervescent golden liquid, saw her lick a drop of wine from her lip in the semidarkness, leaving a gleam of wetness on her mouth. He frowned.

Where had he seen that before?

The curtain rose, and Isobel turned to face the stage. Contrary to what Marianne had told her, Phineas wasn't engrossed in the play at all. He knew he should be on his way to Maitland House, but would now have to wait until there was a sword fight or a love scene on stage to keep the audience's interest. The *ton* attended the theatre more to look at each other than to watch the entertainment they had paid to see. The slightest movement toward the exit now was sure to cause a hundred pairs of opera glasses to turn in his direction.

Marianne was whispering to Isobel, a sibilant twitter that nearly drowned out the players. Phineas rolled his eyes. Did Marianne ever stop talking? Half the audience was glaring at her. At this rate it would take a fire in the pit for him to get away unseen.

He glanced at Adam for help, but his brother-in-law was watching the play as if it were the most fascinating thing on earth. Impatience fizzed in Phineas's gut. He'd have to wait. Charles, he knew, would go on to his club afterward, but Isobel, dull widow that she was, would likely go straight home to bed. Even if she and Honoria had another party or ball to attend after the theatre, he couldn't be certain when they would arrive home, or how much time he'd have. At this rate he'd end up lurking in the shadows outside Maitland House in the cold rain, waiting for the last light to go out. While not impossible, it would be riskier to search the place if they were at home.

Waiting for another night was out of the question. They needed information now, and there were other leads, other suspects to tumble, if the Maitlands didn't provide anything useful.

Marianne was still whispering without a pause. She would chatter through the whole rest of the play, now that she had someone to talk to.

Phineas stared at the little frill of untamed curls at the nape of Isobel's white neck. Those wayward tendrils were the only soft thing about her. In the dark, her pale neck and shoulders looked like they'd been carved out of marble. It was easy to imagine her as a statue of a Grecian goddess in a forgotten corner of a dusty museum. The only flaw on her perfect skin was a tiny mole on the back of her neck, nearly hidden by her hair.

Odd. Yasmina—or Charlotte—had a mole in the same place. He remembered caressing it, drawing circles around it with his fingers as he kissed her.

Phineas's heart skipped a beat. Then it stopped entirely as he stared at the spot. He forced himself to breathe. He blinked at it in the low light, hoping it was a speck of lint, a bit of dirt, a blemish that could be explained away or flicked off with a fingernail.

It was indeed a mole. Horror gripped his belly, pushing the champagne back up his throat. Adam leaned in as well, putting his head next to Phineas's, squinting along with him at the mark.

"Spider?" he asked quietly.

Phineas didn't answer, Couldn't. He stared, willed the spot to disappear. It didn't move.

It couldn't be.

She couldn't be.

His mind raced. He silently took Isobel Maitland's measurements in the dark, sitting, and from behind, which told him nothing. He shook his head, trying to find some difference between Yasmina and . . .

Isobel Maitland?

Disbelief chased horror in dizzying circles around his stomach, rising to crowd his throat, and he coughed. She turned and met his eyes. Shadows fell like a mask across the upper half of her face, leaving only her mouth illuminated in a band of light, her lips softly open. His stomach plummeted to his shoes. He'd know that mouth anywhere.

Isobel Maitland was Yasmina, and Charlotte, and—

She was Isobel Maitland.

He sat in stunned silence, no longer seeing anything but her slender neck and that damned mole. He wanted to grab her, turn her to face him, stare into her eyes and read that it wasn't true.

Instead he ran a finger under his cravat and thought of the way she'd made love to him with utter abandon. She was the most passionate woman he'd ever known.

He alternated between fury, disbelief, and horror for the rest of the play.

And now that he knew the identity of his mystery woman? Would he make love to her again?

His erection was sudden and powerful, providing a definitive answer to that question.

He was Isobel Maitland's lover.

He tried to think of reasons it could not possibly be true. Instead, his mind stacked up evidence against him, one heavy volume after another until he felt crushed by the weight of the proof.

Isobel had been at Evelyn's, according to Lady Honoria, though he hadn't seen her.

Oh yes, he had. How could he have forgotten those eyes, that mouth?

She'd torn the buttons off his breeches! He squirmed in his seat.

Marianne had invited Isobel to her masquerade as well, though he would have sworn he hadn't seen her there either. In his defense, it had been extremely dark when he made passionate love to her and fed her on Westlake's prize cherries.

The truth was unavoidable.

He pinned the mole with a hard glare. *She* had known exactly who *he* was all along. She must think him a complete idiot. It was lowering in the extreme. He was a spy, for God's sake, a man who took pride in being able to do his job better than any other spy alive. He saw the unseen, unearthed the most closely guarded secrets, exposed the most heinous lies. How the hell had she managed to fool him for so long?

Weeks.

He didn't like it. Not in the least. He was the one who made fools of others, men who deserved it. He shifted again, uneasy. Had he deserved it? A bitter taste filled his mouth.

Phineas was scarcely aware of the play ending. The curtain dropped, the crowd applauded, and he sat lost in thought, trying to imagine confronting her, demanding answers. What would she say? Hell, what would he say? For weeks he'd imagined nothing more complicated than all the ways he was going to make love to her when he found her, but they were in a crowded theatre, and he could hardly demand an explanation now. He could only let her walk away, thinking her secret was still safe.

That was probably for the best. He needed to think, to

decide what he would do, what he would say when he got her alone.

How the hell was he going to explain this to Adam?

"Phineas, you go and collect Miranda from the Hollisters," Marianne instructed as the house lights were lit. "Adam, you escort Isobel back to the Maitlands. Honoria always seems a trifle shocked when Phin shows up, and we've done quite enough to rile Charles tonight. I don't think we should upset his mother as well. Imagine the miserable ride home if Isobel had to sit and listen to them complain about our manners."

Isobel offered Phineas the briefest of curtsies, and he bowed. Neither of them said a word. He watched Adam take Isobel's arm. He could see Yasmina in her now. How had he missed it? It was clear in the graceful sway of her hips, in the slender delicacy of her figure. He recognized every curve. The shimmer of the dress emphasized her long legs.

Legs that had been wrapped around his body as he made love to her.

Now he knew where he'd heard that soft, desperate little sound.

As if she could feel his eyes on her, she looked over her shoulder at him and bit her lip, blushing. He was instantly hard.

Even now—especially now—he wanted her body every bit as much as he wanted an explanation.

Chapter 23

"**H**ave you found your mystery woman yet?" Adam asked, and Phineas looked up at him in surprise, wondering if Adam—and everyone else—had known all along, and this was some colossal joke at his expense. But his brother-in-law's expression was businesslike and cool, without a trace of mockery.

"I have some leads," Phineas said.

"Need I remind you that time is of the essence? Even if she is a delightful playmate, if she's guilty, you must give her up."

Anger rose. "If your wife hadn't kept us playing elaborate games of blindman's buff with Charles Maitland, then I might have some leads for you now. I intended to search Maitland House tonight while they were all conveniently at the theatre, but I couldn't get away, not with Isobel Maitland camped in our box!" Her name stuck to his tongue like thick honey.

"You might have said something," Adam said calmly.

"Like what?" Phineas demanded, pacing the floor. "Excuse me, Countess Ashdown, but I have to go and find proof that you and your bloody brother-in-law are guilty of smuggling and possibly even plotting a royal kidnapping?"

"I meant you might have said something to me, not to Isobel. I could have helped you get out of attending the theatre tonight. I know you only went because Marianne and Miranda insisted. We could have put them off with an excuse." He regarded Phineas with a frown. "Do you know something I don't? I personally can't see how Charles Maitland is clever enough to be doing anything more heinous than *buying* a few casks of smuggled brandy. And what could Isobel possibly have to do with anything Charles is involved in? That woman is afraid of her own shadow."

Phineas fixed him with a hard stare. He'd thought the same thing a few hours ago. "What if she isn't, Adam? What if she's part of the game, and her clothes, her hair, her whole life is an elaborate disguise?"

"Isobel Maitland?" Adam could scarcely say her name for laughing. "Perhaps you *have* been in this line of work too long, my friend. *You're* the one with the secret life, remember? She's a dull, timid widow, and I doubt there's much mystery—or anything else remotely intriguing—under those dowdy frocks of hers."

If Adam only knew. Phineas cast another glance at Carrington's smug, painted face and turned toward the door.

"Where are you going?" Adam asked, rising from his chair.

"To get some answers," Phineas growled.

Chapter 24

J ane Kirk had said that Isobel used the library to read, but there wasn't a trace of her in the room. It smelled only of Charles's tobacco and brandy.

He tried to picture her here, both as dowdy Isobel and as Yasmina. His eyes fell on a thick, soft rug by the dark fireplace, and the image of her body spread out beneath his sprang into his mind. He looked away, shaking off the distraction, but he was all too aware that she was right above him, in bed. He lit a candle and forced himself to concentrate on the job at hand.

He knew the places lords and ladies hid their secrets. Everyone used the same places, and every servant—and men like him—knew exactly where their masters kept the evidence of their misdeeds.

Phineas checked the bookshelves first, running his hand over the embossed spines. Poetry, novels, plays, exactly the kind of thing one would expect a proper widow to read.

But Isobel Maitland was anything but proper.

He checked the shelves for hidden panels or false books that might hold something more sinister than bad verse, but aside from uncovering the maid's secret—she only bothered to dust the lower shelves—he found nothing.

With every sense on alert for even the quietest movement

outside the door, he picked the locks on the desk drawers
with quick efficiency.

He found the usual bills, lists, and letters, which were
often the most incriminating records of all. He scanned each
one quickly.

There was a receipt for a room at the inn near Hythe,
but not the same one where they had caught the French spy.
There were several bills from prominent London modistes,
and he scanned the long list of items purchased under Honoria's name, but there was nothing more sinister there than six
yards of imported lace, probably French.

There were also accountings from an exclusive Bond
Street haberdasher, and a boot maker that catered to the
wealthiest male members of the *ton*. It appeared that the
Maitlands had been spending a great deal of money. At least
Charles and Honoria had. The only receipt in Isobel's name
was for several unglamorous items listed as "personal garments constructed from heavy flannel."

Of course, Charles was a wealthy man and could afford a
lavish lifestyle. How else could he withstand losing so regularly at the tables?

Phineas found a crumpled letter from a man named Hart,
requesting money for urgent repairs at Waterfield Abbey.
The list of necessary funds was meticulously itemized. He
frowned. They were the most basic of costs, the kind no steward should have to beg for, and no responsible landowner
would allow to go unpaid unless he was penniless.

Phineas opened another drawer and found the account
books. The Maitland estates had all seen poor harvests and a
drop in income since Robert's death, suggesting that Charles
was a poor manager. At this rate the rich earldom of Ashdown would be ruined by the time young Robin came of age.

He turned the pages, checking the figures for each estate.
Every one was failing.

Except Waterfield Abbey.

What he read made him gape, hold the candle closer and look again. Unlike the other properties, the Waterfield accounts showed a huge income, scribbled in under crop yields and wool sales. A mistake perhaps, or an outright lie, if the steward's request was genuine.

Phineas frowned and looked at the letter again. It was addressed to Charles, not Isobel. Other than the flannel garments, there were no receipts, bills, or letters in her name. He wondered if she knew Charles was running her properties into the ground, or if she even cared.

It wasn't unheard of for absentee landowners to bleed their country estates dry for the money to support an extravagant life in London, but it would be almost impossible to enjoy the kind of lifestyle Charles did on the income from just one property, especially if those profits belonged to Isobel, or were supposed to be in trust for her son.

No wonder Charles wished to marry Miranda. It wasn't his sister he wanted, but her fortune. Phineas's mouth twisted.

Of course, something illegal and dangerous would pay well enough to provide the kind of money Maitland was spending.

It warranted more investigation, and a closer watch on Charles, and Waterfield.

Phineas put the ledger back and closed the drawer. He knew Charles's sins might add up to more than the petty smuggling of brandy and gin for himself and a few wealthy friends, but if they did, he wouldn't find the evidence here. That was the kind of secret a man buried deep.

He blew out the candle and stood in the dark, letting his eyes adjust, finished with Charles's secrets for the moment.

Now it was time to find out what game Isobel was playing.

Chapter 25

There was no light under her door, but he pressed his ear to the panels for a moment to make certain everything inside was silent before he lifted the latch.

The soft drift of her perfume hit him like a blow to the gut as he entered her room. He closed the door and leaned on it, heart pounding.

Light from the street crept through a crack in the drapes, and he could see Isobel's red hair spread across the pillow, glowing like sin.

He'd been wrong. Her room was typical and feminine. Her bed was not a hard wooden cot, but a four-poster. A dressing table, wardrobe, and chest of drawers made up the rest of the furnishings. Soft rugs covered the floor.

He crossed to stand beside her bed.

Even in the shadows he recognized the line of her jaw, the shape of her ears, the curve of her luscious mouth. How could he not have noticed?

Desire rose, heavy and immediate, a bone deep need for her. It made him angry. She'd played him for a fool and still he wanted her more than he had ever wanted any woman. Perhaps he *was* a fool. Or she was a master at whatever wicked game she was playing.

In a quick move he had hold of her, one hand clamped across her mouth, his arm pressed across the fullness of her breasts, pinning her to the bed. She woke instantly, stiffened in his grip, and he felt her draw breath to cry out. Her fingernails scrabbled at his hand. Her muffled scream vibrated through him.

"I advise you to be very quiet, *Yasmina*," he growled. She stilled at that, and he felt her shock in the quick indrawn breath, cool against his palm. He stared into the glitter of her eyes, watched them widen with surprise and fear. He let her read the anger on his face.

She moaned, and that was a sound he recognized. It shot straight to his groin. He was half lying across her body, using his weight to pin her down, all too aware of her soft curves as he pressed her into the mattress.

He lifted himself off her before he forgot why he'd come. He held her with one hand on her mouth, the other on her shoulder, and even that slight contact made him ache for her.

"I want to hear your explanation, Countess, but if you scream when I take my hand off your mouth, I will take you somewhere where it won't matter how much noise you make. Do you understand?"

She nodded, a jerky, frightened motion that was barely possible under the tight grip he had on her jaw. She reached up to touch his hand, a careful, pleading pat, or a tentative caress. He didn't release her.

"I am going to light the candle. I want to see you without masks or disguises. I want to look into your eyes when you tell me exactly why you've been lying to me for weeks."

She squirmed, tried to shake her head, daring to deny it even now as he held her captive. "Do you understand?" he demanded.

She nodded again, grunting something into his hand. He released her, heard her gasp for breath as he lit the taper beside her bed. She sat up then and stared at him, her eyes huge in her white face.

She ran her fingertips over the red marks his fingers had left on her skin. Her hair was an untidy jumble over her shoulders, a cloud of red silk.

His eyes widened as the coverlet fell to her waist. Above the pool of linen, she looked like Venus rising from the waves, wearing nothing but a froth of sea foam. The scrap of lace that clung to her breasts was more enticing than if she'd worn nothing at all.

He wondered what had become of the heavy flannel she'd bought and paid for. He clenched his fists and fought the urge to run his fingers down the slopes of her breasts, press his lips to the hollow between them, tear the damned lace off with his teeth. His eyes locked onto the tempting shadow of her nipples, peeking through the delicate fabric, and he turned away to wipe the sweat from his brow and gather his wits.

Grabbing the chair from her dressing table, he set it close enough to the bed so he could see her face, read her eyes, but couldn't touch her.

She still hadn't said a word. She merely watched him like a terrified vixen caught in a trap, unsure if he would caress her or kill her. He let her wonder.

He sat down and crossed his legs, hiding his erection, aware that he was on dangerous ground. His composure was legendary, except with her. The intimate sight of her in bed, in a whisper of lace that was more sin than clothing, was making it hard to think about anything else. He wasn't sure if he was the biggest dupe in London or the luckiest bastard alive.

He let his eyes travel over her again, trying for an impression of disinterested insolence, but enjoying the view.

She gasped and snatched the blankets up to her chin.

"Don't bother. I know every inch of your body, Isobel. By feel, if not by sight."

If he expected her to whimper, or cry, or scream, he was

disappointed. She freed one arm and pointed to the dressing gown at the end of the bed.

"Hand me my robe," she ordered, her tone regal.

Phineas was tempted to toss it out the window for effect, but the sight of her naked shoulders, the knowledge that there was almost nothing covering her charms under the blanket, was a dangerous distraction.

He gave her the robe, a gray flannel monstrosity, and watched as she shrugged into it awkwardly, allowing her no privacy. She wrapped it tight and tied the sash around her waist with shaking fingers. Decently covered, but still sitting in her bed, she folded her arms over her breasts like a queen holding court and glared at him.

"What do you want?" she demanded in a low voice, and glanced at the door as if expecting someone to burst into the room.

"You aren't going to deny it, then. Thank you for that small courtesy at least. You *are* Yasmina. And Charlotte."

Hot color flooded her face, and her eyes closed in a sweep of copper lashes.

"Who would you have been when next we met, I wonder?"

"How did you find out it was me?" she asked in a tight whisper. "I didn't think you knew." He watched her knuckles whiten as she gripped the collar of the robe tight against her throat.

He reached into his pocket and brought out the harem slipper. He tossed it onto the counterpane between her feet. The little bell jangled.

"Oh," she murmured.

Next he dangled the miniature portrait in front of her eyes. She snatched at it, pulling it out of his hand, and stared down at the little painted face, her expression bleak.

"Young Robin, I assume?"

She nodded, and closed her hand over the little picture

protectively. She looked up at him, her expression fierce. "Now that you know, what do you intend to—" she began, but Phineas held up his hand to stay her. He wasn't finished.

He got to his feet as he took out the silk rose and the handkerchief. He held them in the candlelight, watching her, scorching her with the unspoken accusation before he let them drop.

Her reaction wasn't what he expected. She tossed her head with an angry snort and glared at him, her lip curling. She pulled her feet away, as if the items had burned her right through the bedclothes. He felt a surge of triumph in his breast, the thrill of retribution, and braced himself for tears, pleas for mercy, and—

"How dare you?" she demanded, keeping her voice low, casting another quick look at the door.

He folded his arms over his chest. "You aren't going to deny that these belong to you, are you, Isobel?"

She pushed back the covers and reached for the little silk rose, rising to her knees on the bed as she shook it at him.

"*This* is mine. It fell out of my wig when we—" She stopped, a blush spreading over her pale cheeks. He raised a lazy eyebrow and slid another sultry gaze over her body, showing her he remembered every touch, every kiss.

With a soft cry of fury, she threw the rosebud at him, and it hit his cheek, so light it was more a caress than the slap she intended it to be, but he flinched, surprised.

She pointed at the handkerchief still lying on her bed, and her eyes bored into his, filled with indignation.

"That little souvenir, my lord, is not mine. It obviously belongs to one of your other *conquests*." She filled the word with venom and spat it at him.

He didn't believe her. He leaned toward her. Kneeling on the bed, she was the same height as he, and he came so close their noses almost touched. She didn't flinch or look away.

In her rage, she forgot to hold onto the neck of her robe. The candlelight caressed the delicate bones of her throat, and deepened the tempting shadows between her breasts. He grabbed the handkerchief, brought it between them, held it before her eyes.

"You haven't even looked at it, Isobel. How can you be so certain it isn't yours?" He unfurled it like a battle flag, so she could see the initial and the embroidered rose.

"It is not mine," she insisted. As quickly and as gracefully as a cat, she slipped off the bed and stalked past him.

"The rosebud, Isobel. The M for Maitland. *Look* at it," he demanded, following her.

With her nose in the air, she crossed to her dresser, opened the drawer, drew out a plain linen square and thrust it into his hand.

"*This* is mine," she said.

It bore her initials and the Ashdown crest. There was no lace, and no rose.

"There's a dozen more in the drawer, all alike, if you wish to look on your way out, Lord Blackwood."

She stood in the middle of her room and glared at him. Her prim flannel robe was at odds with the lace that trailed below the hem, and her bare feet were white and vulnerable against the darkness of the carpet. Her hair swept around her like a cloak, loose, glorious, and simmering angrily in the low light. His breath caught in his throat.

The intimacy of the situation was overwhelming. He stood and stared at her, crushing the damned handkerchief in his fist.

"Why, Isobel? Why me?"

A little of the fury went out of her eyes, and she looked away for an instant. "Is that why you came? To fish for compliments? Do you expect me to tell you what a magnificent lover you are?"

"It would be a place to start. Why didn't you tell me your name when I asked?" He dared to take a step closer. "I know you enjoyed it. Both times." Her head shot up and she drew the breath to deny it, but he held up a hand. 'Magnificent lover' was your description, Isobel."

"I believe you enjoyed yourself as well, my lord," she said boldly.

He took another step toward her. The hushed fall of his boots on the carpet was the only sound. He didn't stop until he reached her and they stood toe-to-toe, and she had to tip her head back to meet his eyes. "Now who's fishing for compliments?" he asked, and pulled her into his arms, swooping down to capture her mouth with his.

Isobel was powerless to resist. Fury melted under the heat of his touch. He'd broken into her bedroom like a thief and tossed another woman's handkerchief at her, but pride was no match for her desire for this man. She sank into the kiss, reveled in it, marveled that her need for him only grew stronger the more she tried to sate it. She was drugged by the sensation of his body against hers, by the scent of his skin, by his lust for her.

She reached up a hand to his chest and felt the tiny portrait in her fist.

Robin.

With a surge of dread, she pushed him away. This was not anonymous anymore. This was a dangerous, high stakes game she could not win. She would lose everything if—when—Honoria found out. She stared at the door, her heart pounding, but the house was quiet. She wrapped her arms over her robe, hugging it to her, holding the portrait so tight in her hand that the filigreed edges cut into her palm.

He was staring at her, and she shut her eyes. He'd come for an explanation, but she didn't have one, couldn't tell him the truth.

"Are you mad, Blackwood? I cannot do this!" she said, taking refuge in anger.

He put his hands on his hips and frowned, breathing hard, but made no attempt to touch her again. "Why not? It's not as if it hasn't happened before, and this time the luxury of a bed would surely enhance the pleasure."

She let her eyes roam over him, tempted still, despite the risk. He wore black, which should have made him sinister, dangerous, but he looked magnificent. *Magnificent*. There was that word again. It should be *his* word.

"No!" she said, trying to mean it. Weak, that would be her word, and he would be the cause of it. "Honoria's room is right down the hall! Robbie—*my son*—is upstairs." She held out the portrait, and it dangled between them like a talisman against calamity. "I am not one of your conquests. I have a reputation to protect, Blackwood."

He stepped right over her good intentions and cupped her cheek, running his thumb over her hot skin. "I think we know each other well enough that you may use my Christian name, Isobel. It's Phineas. Say it."

His voice was low, dark and seductive, and she rubbed her face against his palm like a cat in heat. "There is nothing Christian about you," she whimpered. He laughed, and she shut her eyes, the sound vibrating over every nerve. "Please, Blackwood," she begged.

"Close enough," he muttered, and with very little effort and no warning at all scooped an arm under her knees and lifted her as if she weighed nothing. He carried her back to the bed and dropped her on the rumpled sheets.

She scrambled backward and clambered off the other side, putting the dangerous, seductive surface between them. She could see his erection through the dark wool of his breeches, and she shut her eyes against the flood of desire.

"Look, Isobel, I'm willing to play your game," he said.

"No one need know. We can keep our affair discreet. You can even continue to snub me by day, if it salves your conscience. I've grown used to it."

She stared at him, saw he meant his offer in all serious- ness. Her heart was hammering against the fragile cage of her ribs. Her knees barely held her upright. She clung to the bedpost, wishing she were as hard and unfeeling as the carved oak. She wanted nothing more than to fall onto this bed with him, but he was a craving she could never satisfy. She wanted more, everything, when she could not afford to have any.

"This is not an affair," she said.

He gave her a slow, wicked grin that frayed the raveling edges of her willpower. "Then what is it?" he asked.

What indeed? "It's a mistake. It was never supposed to happen," she murmured, wondering which of them she was trying to convince.

He didn't look like he believed her. She didn't believe a word of it herself. He was the best thing—and the worst— that had ever happened to her. "I didn't know—that is, I didn't think it would—" She stopped before she said too much, spoke a truth that would not let her go back to a world without him.

"You like what I do to you, Isobel. You like how I make you feel."

She moaned her denial, adding the lie to her sins, sure she would burst into flames in punishment at any moment, or worse, that Honoria would open the door and find her here, with him.

"Please, Blackwood, you've got to go." She closed her eyes so she wouldn't see him leave. Instead, he came around the bed, and she sighed when he pushed his hands through her hair.

"You have beautiful hair. I had no idea it was red. All

those weeks, trying to imagine what you looked like without a mask, a hat, a wig. I didn't guess you were a redhead."

She couldn't pull away from the simple, sensual caress. "I suppose you thought I was blond. Most of your amours seem to be blond."

She felt her face heat and wondered if she'd given away the sad fact that she'd watched him from the shadows for months before Evelyn's masquerade.

He merely lowered his mouth to hers. "Not anymore," he whispered against her lips. She opened her mouth as if it was a natural thing between the two of them, let his tongue find hers, held onto his broad shoulders and stood on her toes, pressing the length of her body against his.

A muffled thump in the hallway made her jump. Terrified, she pushed him into the dark corner behind her and stood in front of him, staring at the door.

She braced for the door to come crashing in.

"Hide!" she hissed, and did her best to press him into the shadows.

Chapter 26

Isobel had no idea what the ungodly noise in the hall might be, but surely it meant discovery and disaster.

Blackwood was in her bedroom, and there was no way to explain him away.

She waited for the door to crash open, for Honoria's screams of outrage. Charles would come running, and probably Jane too, and her shame would be complete. She flinched as another thump echoed through the house.

She felt Blackwood's hands on her shoulders, moving her aside. "Thank you for your kind offer of protection, sweetheart, but I'm quite capable of defending myself." He stepped in front of her, pulled a pistol from the small of his back and cocked it.

"What are you going to do with that?" she demanded in a shrill whisper. "Please, it's only Honoria, arriving home from a party. Perhaps she's downstairs looking for something to eat to help her sleep." Another crash shook the room. She stared at the door, but it remained closed.

"Something to eat?" he muttered. "Sounds more like she's hunting big game in the hallway."

"It doesn't matter! You've got to leave! Go down the back stairs, out through the kitchen," she instructed as she hurried toward the door, but he caught her arm.

"Isobel, wait—"

She shook him off. "If you aren't leaving, at least hide!"

She looked around, searching the intimate space of her bedroom for somewhere big enough to conceal a man his size.

He stepped past her and locked the door. Now why hadn't she thought of that?

He crossed to the window and pulled back the drapes a fraction, and she followed. A coach stood in front of the house, with a familiar portly silhouette on the curb next to it.

"It's Charles!" She drew back, afraid he would look up, see her in the window, or worse, see Blackwood there. She blew out the candle, leaving them in darkness.

Blackwood opened the curtains fully and stood watching whatever it was that Charles was doing. What *was* he doing?

Isobel held her breath as two men came down the front steps with a crate and carried it to the coach.

"Is Charles going out of town?" Blackwood asked. He sounded calm, barely even curious, but his avid gaze never left the coach.

Charles was directing the loading of the vehicle. The men weren't Maitland servants. They had rough, lean faces. "I don't know. He sometimes goes to Waterfield Abbey."

"Does he usually depart in the middle of the night?"

She shrugged, uneasy. "It's in Kent, a long journey." It was the only explanation she could think of, but it sounded false even to her. She saw the glint of coins in the lamplight as Charles paid the men. They melted into the dark.

Blackwood turned to her as Charles climbed into the coach. "I have to leave, Isobel, but this discussion isn't over. If it's too distracting in your bedchamber, then I'll call on you tomorrow. We can have this conversation in your drawing room."

"That's impossible! You can't call on me here!" He raised an eyebrow and waited. "Honoria wouldn't like it."

"This isn't about Honoria, Isobel. It's about what you and I want, and I for one still want an explanation."

She retreated into the shadows and pulled the flannel robe around her body. "There isn't one, don't you see? It was just a moment's pleasure. There isn't anything else to say, Blackwood. Forget it ever happened. It cannot happen again."

"And what am I supposed to do when I meet you in my sister's salon?"

She felt the sting of tears but forced herself to meet his eyes. "You must show as much disdain for me as you did before you knew."

His mouth tightened, and she sensed he was not satisfied with that. Still, he turned away at the sound of the coachman's order.

He opened the window wide and stuck a leg over the sill.

"What are you doing?" she hissed.

He cupped her chin and kissed her quickly. Her lips instinctively curved to his, a perfect fit. He pulled away too soon. "I still say this isn't over, Isobel. I need—" He stopped and shook his head. "But this isn't the time." He climbed out her window and disappeared silently into the dark.

Isobel watched Charles's coach pull away from the curb, clumsy under the heavy load. Blackwood emerged from the shadows, on horseback, and followed. At the corner of the street, he turned to look at her, his expression unreadable. Then the darkness swallowed him and he was gone.

Chapter 27

Charles joined Isobel at the breakfast table without so much as a grunt of good morning. He was still wearing his evening clothes, and he ordered Finch to bring a decanter of brandy. He filled his teacup to the rim, twice, and left his food untouched.

Isobel's own breakfast tasted like ashes in his silent, moody company.

Wherever Charles had gone last night, with Blackwood in hot pursuit, she had not expected to see her brother-in-law this morning. She'd hoped to have a quiet breakfast and time to compose herself, but Charles's presence made the tension almost unbearable. Her heart skipped a beat.

Blackwood knew.

Those words had echoed in her mind since he appeared in her bedroom, then disappeared again almost as mysteriously. *He knew.*

He left by climbing out the window, and she'd been too distracted by his presence to find that immediately surprising. It wasn't until she was getting dressed this morning, after a sleepless night, her fingers shaking as she buttoned her prim gown, that she wondered exactly how the Marquess of Blackwood had gotten into the house, and her bedroom, at all.

He'd climbed down the side of the house like a squirrel and followed Charles as he went about his unsavory business.

By the time she finished dressing her hair—the hair he'd said was beautiful—she was beginning to suspect that the Marquess of Blackwood was something other than a gentleman. Or a rake.

Isobel's stomach lurched as the door to the breakfast room opened and Honoria entered. Jane Kirk was with her. She carried the morning post along with a notepad and pencil, ready to write her mistress's instructions for the day.

"Charles, look what's arrived!" Honoria trilled, waving an invitation in Charles's face. He silently refilled his teacup and sent his mother a look of irritation. Isobel glanced at Jane, who was looking over her dress to ensure it met Honoria's strict standards of dullness. Isobel was certain it did, but underneath, her heart pounded a rapid tattoo.

There was a man in my room last night, she was tempted to crow to the gimlet-eyed companion, *and not just any man—*
The Marquess of Blackwood.

She lifted her toast to her lips but set it down again, untasted. He would not be there again, and she felt the loss keenly.

"Charles!" Honoria chided her son. "This is an invitation to Lady Augusta Porter-Penwarren's musicale evening! I knew Lady Miranda favored you. Obviously, she simply wishes to be pursued more forcefully."

Charles snatched the engraved card out of Honoria's hand and squinted at the elegant script. He tossed it back on the table with a sneer. "This invitation is addressed to Isobel, Mother. It does not mention me at all, or Miranda Archer's longing to have me pursue her forcefully or any other way." He glared at Isobel. "In fact, I would think that since it mentions *only* Isobel, it is a clear and pointed indication of the lady's desire that I cease my attentions to her."

Isobel sipped her tea, striving to be invisible. It was uncharacteristically astute of Charles to notice such a subtle snub. Honoria would now blame her for Miranda's lack of interest.

She hoped Honoria would refuse the invitation. Blackwood was certain to be there, and she could not bear to be in the same room with him now that he knew the truth. Every glance, every gesture, would be sweet, dangerous torment.

"What did you say to Lady Marianne last night?" Honoria demanded, fixing suspicious eyes on her.

Isobel swallowed. "Why, I told her that Charles was handsome, clever, and rich, just as you told me to," she lied.

"And what did she say to that?"

She had sent her sister racing around the theatre to avoid him, exactly as Charles suspected. He was watching her now, his bleary gaze daring her to lie again.

"She said that Miranda had a number of suitors, Charles among them of course, but she had not decided on any of them as yet," Isobel said carefully.

"And the Duke of Welford's girl? Did you discuss her?"

"There's a rumor that she's to marry the Marquess of Blackwood," Jane Kirk murmured, and Isobel's heart lurched painfully. Even Jane Kirk had heard the news, then. Had Blackwood already proposed? Isobel felt a fizzle of indignation that he should come to her in the night, with his promise to another woman still warm on his lips. Honoria gasped in horror at Jane's tidbit of gossip, obviously as shocked as Isobel.

Jane waved to the footman to pour out a cup of tea for her stricken mistress, but Honoria pointed to the brandy decanter at Charles's elbow. The footman poured a small glassful, and Honoria gulped it.

"Blackwood is going to marry a duke's daughter?" Honoria cried. "He seems to have the devil's own luck, that man."

"He *is* the devil," Jane interjected, and Isobel shot a quick glance at her. Jane's mouth was set in hard lines of scorn.

"Charles, now you *must* convince Lady Miranda to marry you!" Honoria insisted. She picked up the invitation from the table and waved it again. "We will both accompany Isobel. Lady Augusta can hardly object. Isobel is in deepest mourning, after all."

Isobel's heart sank. Not only would she have to face Blackwood, but she would have to do it under Honoria's watchful gaze.

"I'm not going," Charles said peevishly. "I don't want to."

"But Charles!" The warble of dismay in Honoria's voice quickly hardened to iron. "I must insist. You must marry and set up your nursery as quickly as possible. If anything were to happen to the boy, you would be earl, and an earl needs an heir. You must safeguard the Ashdown title."

The teacup slipped from Isobel's nerveless fingers, but she ignored the clatter. She looked at Honoria's ruthless face as she talked about the death of her only grandson.

"What could happen to Robin?" she croaked as terror squeezed her breakfast back up her throat.

Jane, Charles, and Honoria turned to look at her, their eyes cold, as if they were discussing a stranger instead of *her son*. She clenched her fists, forcing herself to sit still, not to scream and race for the nursery.

"What could happen to Robin?" she asked again, unable to think or say anything else.

"Children die all the time, Countess," Jane said. "Most wives breed more than one son." She smirked at Isobel, as if pointing out her failure to do so.

Honoria folded her arms over her vast bosom, her eyes returning to her own son. "Charles, you will attend—"

But Charles shot to his feet, tipping over his teacup as he rose. The brandy flowed across the white linen like blood.

"I said no, Mother. It seems plain enough that I'd need the title *first* in order to marry bloody Miranda Archer. Go to the damned musical evening yourself, if you think it will do any good. I see no point in making a fool of myself any further." He glared at Isobel, as though it were her fault, and she braced herself to bear the brunt of his rage, but he turned on his heel and left the room.

Honoria watched the door for a moment, as if she expected him to come back. Even Jane looked surprised.

Honoria sniffed at last. "Jane, write a note of acceptance to Lady Porter-Penwarren at once. Tell her I will accompany Isobel."

Jane scratched the reminder on her list. "Anything else, your ladyship?"

But Honoria had already turned to her. "Isobel, I am disappointed in your efforts on Charles's behalf. When do you expect to have an opportunity to speak to Lady Miranda or her sister again?"

Isobel clenched her hands in her lap, trying to still the trembling, her heart still caught in her throat for her son's sake.

"I have no outing scheduled with Countess Westlake today," she managed. Honoria narrowed her eyes, and her lip curled dangerously.

The unspoken threat was clear in her mother-in-law's eyes. There was only one way for Charles to be earl. This time, Isobel knew, she would not lose something so trifling as an outing in the country with her son. This time they meant to take Robin from her forever.

She wondered if Charles was capable of killing his own nephew to get what he wanted. Panic rose, and she forced it down.

"What do you suggest we do about this?" Honoria demanded.

Isobel's brain raced. "Perhaps you might consider sending Lady Miranda a bouquet of flowers from Charles," she suggested, surprised at how calm she sounded. The posies would end up on a dung heap, but Honoria need not know that. The gesture would buy her precious time.

"An excellent idea. Jane, see to it," Honoria said.

Isobel listened to the scratch of the pencil on the paper, panic rising, threatening to drown her.

She needed help, and she knew who she had to ask.

Chapter 28

Marianne and Miranda arrived at Blackwood House just in time to catch Phineas coming home as the sun rose. He'd obviously been out all night, since he was unshaven and still in evening dress.

Marianne didn't miss the fleeting look of irritation on his face as she sailed across the entry hall toward him like an attacking frigate, but she'd caught him, and there was no way he could instruct Crane to say he was not at home. He glanced at the clock, then back at her in surprise. She was well aware it wasn't a suitable hour for paying calls, but this couldn't wait.

"You look dreadful, Phineas," she scolded, instead of saying good morning.

"You, on the other hand, look lovely," he said sarcastically, eyeing her fashionable bonnet as if it were the silliest thing he'd ever seen. "Coffee, please, Crane," he ordered. "I'll escort the ladies to the salon."

Miranda slumped onto the nearest settee. She looked as tired as Phineas, worn-out by the endless social whirl, the late nights, and countless parties a debutante had to endure.

"Are you on your way in or out?" Marianne asked her brother indelicately, though she knew the answer. "No wonder you sleep until afternoon. I assume you are regularly out all night doing unsavory things like seducing widows and teaching orphans to cheat at cards."

"Seducing widows?" He looked at her sharply. "It's a little early for you as well, isn't it, Marianne? I believe the fashionable hour for morning calls starts at three. You're seven hours early. Did you come specifically in the hope of catching me misbehaving?"

"Adam is routinely up by six," she countered. "I breakfast with him every morning. I came early because I wished to see you before Carrington gets up. He, I believe, rises by nine."

"That's because he's in bed by ten o'clock every evening," Phineas muttered. "What did you want to see me about?"

She pulled off her gloves and gave him her sweetest, most beguiling smile. "I have a favor to ask you, dear brother."

His eyes narrowed suspiciously. "And what might that be?"

Crane entered with the coffee tray before she could reply. "I'll pour, Crane," she said impatiently, and waited for the door to shut behind him.

"I wish to speak to you about Isobel Maitland."

Was it her imagination or did he suddenly turn a dreadful shade of green? She poured a cup of coffee and passed it to him. He ignored it, his gaze fixed on her with disturbing intensity.

"What about her?" he asked in a dark voice she supposed was meant to be a warning that he would rather discuss anything but dull Isobel.

She raised her chin stubbornly. "I know you'll think I'm interfering in things that don't concern me. Adam certainly does, but I can't help it. Isobel is a wonderful woman, and she deserves to be happy."

"And she isn't? Perhaps that's because she's a widow, still in mourning. One can hardly expect her to be jolly," he said blandly. Too blandly. She grinned, and he quickly picked up his coffee cup and hid behind it, but it was too late. She'd seen the spark of curiosity in his eyes.

"It's been two years since Robert Maitland died. It's time Isobel went on with her life, found another man."

He put the coffee cup down with a clatter. "She wishes to remarry?"

He looked horrified by the very idea. Marianne bristled. How unjust of him to find Isobel unworthy of love because of her appearance! "No, but that doesn't mean she couldn't take a lover."

"Marianne!" Miranda gasped.

"A lover?" Phineas repeated stupidly. He looked as shocked as Miranda.

"Yes, a lover," Marianne said. "Perhaps with the right man, she'll consider marrying again, once she sees—remembers— how pleasant it can be to have a man in your bed."

"Great-Aunt Augusta would be scandalized to hear you talking like this, Marianne!" Miranda said breathlessly, but her eyes kindled with delight. "Do you have someone in mind? He'd have to be a very boring gentleman, used to the company of very dull ladies."

Phineas rose to splash whisky in a glass and swallowed it in a single gulp. Warning bells went off in Marianne's mind. Was he thinking she'd come to ask *him* to fill the position, so to speak? She pressed her hand to her lips to suppress a giggle.

"Not you, Phineas," she said bluntly. "You'd be all wrong for Isobel. I was thinking your friend Gilbert Fielding might do nicely."

"Gilbert Fielding!" The shriek came from Miranda as she leapt to her feet to glare at Marianne. Her rabbit fur muff tumbled to the floor and sought sanctuary under the settee.

"Fielding?" Phineas asked calmly, but his eyes were cold and hard, his jaw tight.

She forged ahead. "Yes, why not? He's handsome, personable, discreet—"

Phineas's "He's leaving for the army in a few weeks" and Miranda's "He's looking for a wealthy wife" came out almost at the same moment.

Marianne smiled. "Then that makes him doubly perfect! After a brief affair, he will be conveniently gone, unable to spread gossip if he's so inclined. On the other hand, Isobel inherited several properties from her uncle, I believe. If Gilbert marries her—"

"He can't!" Miranda squeaked.

"Why ever not?" Marianne demanded, peeved at the objection. She had expected Miranda to be her ally. Archer women were champions of love, especially when it involved secrets and matchmaking. They lived for such opportunities.

Miranda had gone red and was blinking back a shimmer of tears. "Perhaps there's another lady Mr. Fielding prefers. Perhaps another lady cares for *him*."

Phineas ignored Miranda's tears. "Have you spoken to Gilbert about this, Marianne?"

Marianne laid a hand over her chest dramatically. "I? I'm a lady, Phin! I can hardly go around making indecent proposals to gentlemen, now can I?"

"Adam would lock you up."

"Of course he would! That's why I came to you. You are experienced in delicate matters like these. You could ask Mr. Fielding without the slightest embarrassment. For all I know, you do this all the time for friends in need. I only need you to ask him. After that, I could make all the arrangements for Isobel to—"

"No." He threw the word at her like a dagger.

"No!" Miranda cried.

"No?" Marianne blinked at them both. "How can you say

no? I thought you were a champion of illicit romantic encounters, Phineas!"

He looked more angry than hurt by her cutting assessment of his character. "I am not a procurer, Marianne. Gilbert Fielding's love life is his own concern."

Marianne's smile slipped. The idea that Phineas might refuse to cooperate had not occurred to her. "A simple introduction, perhaps—" she tried.

"No," he said again, even more sharply, and held up a hand as she opened her mouth to object. "This discussion is over, Marianne." He sounded almost as prim as Adam.

"Then perhaps you know another gentleman who might do? Someone equally handsome and discreet?"

His eyes burned like coals, searing her. "Does Isobel know you're doing this? Did she ask for your help?"

"Good heavens, of course she doesn't know! I am doing this out of the goodness of my heart. I can't bear to see anyone unhappy, including you, Phineas. Have you found a bride yet? I could help you next."

He didn't answer. He merely crossed the room and opened the door of the salon and stood beside it. "No," he growled again, this time through gritted teeth.

"No to what?" Marianne persisted. "Helping Isobel or finding you a bride?"

"No to continuing this conversation. I need a bath and sleep, if you don't mind. You can stay and wait for Carrington if you wish, but I'm going upstairs."

Marianne rose to her feet and glared at her brother. "Come, Miranda, it appears we're being dismissed," she said, stung. She paused to placate Phineas with a kiss on the cheek. "If you're meeting Adam today, I trust you won't repeat any of this to him?"

"Wild horses could not torture it out of me," he muttered coldly.

"Will you at least think about Isobel's plight?"

He didn't answer her, but there was an odd look in his eye before he flicked his gaze away, a hunger, or maybe she was mistaken and he just wanted breakfast and sleep.

Miranda advanced on her brother. "Don't you dare say a word to Mr. Fielding either, Phineas!" she commanded, her chin in the air.

He gave Miranda a gentle smile and touched her cheek, wiping away a tear. Marianne frowned. Obviously, her sister was also exhausted and overwrought. A nap was in order there too.

She sailed toward the front door. How foolish her siblings were being! Anyone who didn't know them better might think they were jealous.

And of what exactly? They could always count on her help too, later, once she'd assisted her friend.

Marianne pulled on her gloves and stepped out into the soft morning sun, her mind already turning to other ways to help Isobel find a lover.

Chapter 29

"**A**h, Blackwood. You are perusing the selection of young ladies, I see," Carrington said.

Phineas was standing in Augusta's salon, waiting for the evening of aural torment to begin.

"Lady Amelia and her parents will be here tonight," his grandfather continued, scanning the room, nodding to the ladies already gathered. They gazed back hopefully, but their eyes were on him, not the duke. Phineas felt a prickle of warning shimmer up his spine.

It looked like every earl's daughter, every peer's unwed sister, was here tonight. His grandfather's grin confirmed it.

"Amelia sings rather well, I'm told. Nice to have a wife with talent," Carrington hinted. "She will be performing tonight, along with Augusta's famous soprano, and that violinist she admires. In fact, there are a number of talented and eligible young ladies who intend to sing or play the pianoforte."

"I've heard Lady Amelia is being courted by Colonel Lord Hollister, and Lord Henry Morton, and the Earl of Silcox," Phineas said. Carrington's smug expression slipped a little.

"Yes, but I daresay Welford would accept your suit above theirs. Amelia's an obedient girl, biddable. That's a sterling characteristic in a wife. She'll marry where she's told to, and you need only say the word."

The word was no. Phineas had no interest in marrying Lady Amelia or any of the other debutantes that Carrington had invited for his benefit. In fact, he had decided not to marry at all.

After Marianne's unsettling visit, he had spent the rest of the morning wanting to kill Gilbert Fielding or any other man who might take his place as Isobel's lover.

By midday the realization that he couldn't manage to turn his thoughts to anything besides Isobel had put him in a bad mood, made him irritable and restless. He couldn't afford to be so constantly and completely distracted by a woman.

He'd taken out his annoyance on everyone around him. Burridge bore the brunt of it as Phineas dressed for Augusta's musicale. Phineas had rejected the first four cravats his valet offered, though there was nothing wrong with any of them.

As Burridge tied an artful knot in the fifth cravat, Phineas came up with a solution. He would ask Isobel Maitland to become his mistress.

The arrangement would be formal, and exclusive.

He immediately felt better, but still went through three waistcoats before he chose one. As Burridge presented each garment with exaggerated patience, Phineas realized he was nervous, anxious to have her answer.

Once she'd agreed, he would find a private place and let her rip the damned waistcoat to shreds.

In the morning he'd rent a discreet house for their trysts.

As his valet helped him into his black evening coat, he realized there was a chance she'd refuse him. Only at first, of course, and it would be only a token resistance to soothe her sense of propriety. He could be very persuasive. A kiss, a lick, a caress in the right place, and he'd have her. Still, he decided, it was better to be safe. Once he had arranged for the house, he'd visit the best jeweler in Mayfair and buy her something shiny as an enticement.

He watched as Burridge brought out his evening shoes and gave them a final polish. Phineas had never seen Isobel wearing jewels. He had no idea what she might like.

Pearls were right for a widow, but too staid for a woman as passionate as Isobel.

Diamonds would make him appear too eager.

Emeralds were too showy, the kind of stones a mistress flaunted in public, with her lover as a mere secondary accessory.

No gem shone with as many colors and facets as Isobel's eyes. He'd seen them glazed with passion, glittering with fury, and glowing with love when she smiled at her son.

Burridge cleared his throat and held out the shoes, waiting. Phineas put them on, and picked up his cloak, gloves, and hat. After seeing about the house and the jewels, he'd visit the modiste who made naughty little nothings of lace and silk for London's most alluring courtesans. He'd order a dozen. No, two dozen. Such delicate fripperies were likely to tear easily in the heat of passion. He nodded to Burridge as he placed his hat on his head and checked his appearance in the mirror. He made a mental note to order extra buttons for all his breeches from now on.

As he settled himself in his coach, Phineas frowned. His investigation of Charles Maitland could be a problem. Isobel might not like it if and when they had to arrest Charles for treason. By then, of course, their interest in each other might have cooled.

But what if Isobel was involved in Charles's illicit activities? Then he himself could be compromised, possibly even implicated in any treasonous schemes the Maitlands were involved in. Hell, he might be already, if Isobel had taken note of him following Charles the other night. If she'd warned her brother-in-law, then the game would be lost, and he would be to blame.

He sat back against the squabs. There wasn't a damned thing he could do about it now. He could only wait, and hope that Isobel Maitland was not a mistake that would cost him everything.

"Look, there's the Earl of Clifton's daughter," Carrington said, forcing him back to the present. "She's not as wealthy as Lady Amelia, but she would make an excellent marchioness. And Lady Wheaton is here with her niece. Fine lines to her. Good breeding stock."

Phineas wondered if each lady had been tested for soundness of wind and limb before Carrington allowed her inclusion on the guest list.

"Well? Where will you sit, Blackwood? There's a space open next to the very wealthy Miss Caroline Petry."

Phineas suppressed a smile as Lord Henry Morton took the spot and Caroline turned her horse-toothed grin on the man, dazzling him before his bottom had even hit the seat.

Then Isobel entered the room, and he wasn't aware of anything or anyone else. She stood out like a black rose in a posy of wildflowers. He waited for her to look at him, but Marianne accosted her and steered her toward Gilbert Fielding.

Jealousy swept over Phineas as Marianne made the introduction herself and Gilbert smiled at Isobel, his eyes roaming over her with polite interest.

He vowed that if Fielding so much as touched Isobel's hand, he would call him out and shoot him. He realized he already had his glove off in readiness, and put it back on and smoothed his expression into a bland smirk.

Carrington chuffed as eligible young ladies took their places next to eligible young men. "You've waited too long yet again, Blackwood. Amelia is already seated next to Lord Collingwood," he growled.

"Shall we tell him to move?" Phineas asked, and Carrington reddened.

"You'll have another opportunity to speak to Amelia at supper. I expect you to present yourself to her and the other young ladies I've mentioned. *Pick one.* I will see you at breakfast tomorrow morning, at nine o'clock sharp, and I want the name of your chosen bride by then, is that clear?"

"Perfectly, Your Grace," Phineas replied, his gaze drifting back to Isobel as Gilbert bent close to listen to some remark she was making. He imagined the satisfying crunch Gilbert's jaw would make under his fist.

No one was going to make love to Isobel tonight but him. He would be the one surrounded by her hair, her perfume, her body, the one who heard those soft little noises of pleasure she made in the heat of passion.

As if she'd read his mind, Isobel turned to look at him. She blushed from the modest neckline of her drab gown to the roots of her hair as he raised one eyebrow and smiled, making it clear what he was thinking. Her lips parted slightly, and he read suppressed desire in the stiff lines of her body.

Then he heard the snap all the way across the room.

Chapter 30

Isobel felt Blackwood's stare like a caress, a touch on her skin that she could feel everywhere at once. She felt the distance between them and the intimacy of their connection.

He smiled. How could she make polite conversation when there was no mistaking what he was thinking? She could not give in to temptation tonight. She had to speak with him, find a few moments of privacy to— The fragile ivory fan she was holding snapped in her fist, as overwhelmed by the tension as she was.

"Isobel!" Marianne cried, and Mr. Fielding reached for her hand.

"Are you injured, Countess?" he asked. He took the broken fan and held her hand gently in his. "Perhaps if you remove your glove—"

But Isobel felt Blackwood's eyes on her more strongly than she felt Fielding's tentative, careful touch. Her skin heated anew and she snatched her hand away. "I'm quite fine."

"How kind of you, Mr. Fielding," Marianne said. "Are you certain there is no injury?" she asked Isobel.

"It's plain to me that she's perfectly well," said Miranda, glaring into Isobel's eyes instead of looking at her hand.

Isobel was aware of Blackwood watching, but he did not

come forward to see if she was hurt. It was better he stayed away, she thought. She would surely melt if he touched even just her hand. The idea made her quiver.

"Places, if you please, ladies and gentlemen!" Augusta's butler called.

"Mr. Fielding, if you would escort Isobel—" Marianne began, but Miranda put her hand on his arm, interrupting.

"Look, there are still two seats in the front, Mr. Fielding. Shall we take them?" she asked, sweeping him away without a word of farewell.

"Miranda!" Marianne called after her, but her sister was gazing at her escort, and he had obviously forgotten Isobel. "Well of all the cheek!" Marianne began, but Isobel caught her sleeve.

"Lord Westlake is trying to get your attention," she said, and Marianne hesitated. "Go ahead. I'll find a seat on my own."

Isobel walked toward the back of the room, and Blackwood watched her move in his direction. She clasped her hands together, drawing her wits around her like a cloak. "I need to speak with you, my lord," she whispered in a rush as she passed him. "Is there somewhere to talk?"

She answered the teasing question in his eyes with a flat stare, and he bowed, sobering. "Meet me in the corridor after the violinist finishes his first piece."

She forced herself to nod, to step away from him and take her usual seat among the dowagers and wallflowers.

Phineas gritted his teeth as the violinist raised his weapon to his chin and brandished the bow like a cudgel. He left the room at the instrument's first scream and paced the corridor. He needed a private place to ask Isobel to be his mistress before he seduced her, but every room of Augusta's magnificent mansion was open to guests during her parties, so that they might see and envy her magnificent collections of art and silver.

There was a small sitting room on the second floor, currently being used by an artist Carrington had hired to paint Miranda's portrait. The masterpiece was to remain unseen until it was unveiled at Miranda's betrothal ball. It was the one room that would be closed to guests tonight, making it perfect for private discussion.

The wail of the violin ended with a squeal, like an animal in pain given a merciful death. Phineas stood in the shadows and waited until Isobel stepped out of the salon. He felt a jolt as her eyes met his, and she put a hand to her throat. The evidence of her desire did nothing to soothe his own. He curled his fingers against the fine wool of his coat, resisting the urge to touch her.

"Upstairs, third door on the left," he murmured. "I'll follow in a few minutes."

In the salon, the trill of a feminine voice rose, filled the room and spilled out into the corridor in search of more distant victims. Phineas fled, taking the stairs two at a time, following the faint echo of Isobel's perfume.

Beyond the half-open door the room was dark. He could smell the earthen odor of paint and the tang of turpentine. He grabbed a candle off a side table and carried it inside.

"Isobel?"

"Here."

He heard the rustle of her gown in the dark. Her face was white in the gloom, her eyes bright. He kicked the door shut and set the candle down on the table.

She was looking at the portrait of Miranda, and he crossed to stand beside her. A pair of familiar laughing eyes gazed at them from the canvas.

"She looks like you," Isobel said. "Only blond."

"She looks like my mother," Phineas corrected. He

glanced at Isobel. She was stiff and uncertain, not daring to look at him. Not the bold Yasmina who had torn open his breeches to get what she wanted.

"I take after my father," he said, looking back at the painting, feeling a trifle uncertain himself, now that he'd come to the moment of asking her to be his mistress. "The Archers are dark haired and tall with plain gray eyes."

She looked at him. "Gray eyes remind me of the sea. Robert's eyes were brown."

His gut twisted at the mention of Robert Maitland's name. Had she loved him?

"You wished to speak to me, Countess?" he said a trifle sharply.

She drew off her gloves, twisting the black satin in white hands. "Yes," she breathed, "I—I did. I do."

She hesitated, blushing.

"I think I know what you want, Isobel," he said, and stepped forward to caress her hot cheek. She let her eyes drift shut, reveling in the simple touch, making it erotic. He brought his other hand up, held her face, brushed his mouth over hers, a mere prelude to the kiss he hungered for, but she pulled away.

"Don't!" she said, her voice husky. She held up a hand to ward him off, took a step backward. "I won't be able to say this if you touch me. We'll just end up on the floor, or on that settee."

Phineas read desire in her eyes and her fierce struggle to control it. It took all his strength to stay where he was. His senses were on alert, his nerves on edge, and he was hard as a rock. Her eyes flicked over him and paused, aware of his condition.

She moaned, a small, breathless sound that made him harder still.

Then she drew herself up, lifted her chin, and her eyes hardened.

"Lord Blackwood, I am in need of your services."

He blinked. It was hardly the passionate, husky cry of desire he'd hoped for, but it would do for a start. He grinned.

"Then perhaps the settee won't be so bad after all?"

She glanced at the room's sole piece of comfortable furniture and pursed her lips. He stepped forward, put his hands under her elbows and pulled her close. She slid her hands into his coat, pressed her palms against the fine linen of his shirt, and he began lowering his lips to hers with an agonizing slowness meant to tease. His mouth watered in anticipation, his need for much more than a kiss rampant. She sighed, clasped her hands around his neck and raised herself on tiptoe. She moaned with relief as his mouth touched hers at last. She tasted sweet, and he deepened the kiss, pulling her closer, caressing the supple curves of her back, her hips, and her buttocks through the dark silk of her gown. She rubbed herself against his erection.

"God, Isobel, why is it always like this with you?" He looked down into eyes glazed with passion, and tugged her toward the settee, holding her with one hand, loosening his cravat with the fumbling fingers of the other.

She jerked out of his grip and shot across the room, as far away from him as she could get. She pressed the back of her hand to her mouth and shut her eyes.

"Isobel?" he demanded, setting his hands on his hips, staring at her in frustration. "What the hell are you playing at? Do you want this or not?"

She did. Even from across the room he could read the answer in her eyes. "I need to talk to you, and if you're touching me, I can't even think, never mind speak. Stay there, if you please, until I'm through." The last was a tart little command.

"And then?" he asked, unable to resist.

She blushed again, and it was all the answer he needed.

"Say what you will, then." He leaned against a table, folded his arms over his chest, and gave her his full attention.

"I may be wrong about you, Blackwood, but I don't think I am. You came to my room, got into the house somehow," she said. "And then you climbed out the window as if it's something you do all the time."

Alarm prodded his spine like the cold barrel of a loaded pistol. She was searching his face. He set his features into unreadable lines.

"You're not the only lady in London with a window," he suggested, but she tossed her head.

"You saw Charles come out of the house with those men. That's why you left. They aren't Maitland servants, by the way. I've never seen any of them before."

"It was dark," he suggested. "You may not have seen what you thought you did."

"Then I did not see you ride after him?" she demanded.

A pair of sharp daggers joined the pistol. He narrowed his eyes and met her question with a guarded scowl.

She looked away first and began to pace, making short, nervous circuits of the rug. "Look, I know Charles is involved in things that can only be done in the dead of night. I am not as stupid as they imagine. Perhaps Honoria has no idea, but I know there's something wrong, something sinister, going on."

"Every gentleman in London goes out at night, Isobel, and most don't tell ladies what they're up to. It may seem sinister, but it's probably just—"

"How many gentlemen load their coaches with heavy crates to visit clubs and brothels?" she demanded.

None that he knew of. He waited, keeping his face blank.

She sent him a look of entreaty. "If you are what I think you are, then I am hoping you'll help me."

"And what do you think I am, Isobel?"

"A Bow Street Runner, perhaps. Someone who investigates people engaged in suspicious activities." She cast a glance over him, took in his elegant evening clothes, from his fine linen cravat to his patent leather shoes, and he saw uncertainty bloom in her eyes. She snapped her gaze back to his face. "If that's what you are, Blackwood, then I need to hire you," she finished.

He stood very still. She was extremely perceptive. In all the years he'd been doing this, no one else had ever suspected he was anything more than a bold rake. He groped for the right words, some platitude to dismiss her suspicions, allay her fears, shut her mouth, but he was curious.

"You wish to hire me? To do what, Isobel?"

She bit her lip, and he read fear in her eyes. "Charles has, um—suggested that if Robin were dead, then he would be Earl of Ashdown. He believes he could marry Mir—well, marry anyone he wished, if he had a title." He saw the glitter of tears in her eyes, but she blinked them away and looked at him fiercely.

"I don't want you to harm Charles. I just want you to find out what he's doing, so I can have something—some knowledge, a threat of my own—to keep my son safe."

He scanned her face and saw that she believed what she was saying, that she could save her child by confronting Maitland with her knowledge of his sins.

She had no idea that a man ruthless enough to harm a child would have no scruples about killing the boy's mother as well if she got in his way. A pit opened in his chest and filled with revulsion for Charles Maitland.

"Why don't you simply take Robin and leave Maitland House? Wouldn't that be easier?" he asked.

"Robin is Charles's ward. I cannot take him anywhere." Her tone was a hard pebble of frustration.

"But you're his mother. When Sir Alan Denby died, he left

you his fortune and several estates, did he not?" She looked up at him, eyes wide, as if surprised he knew that, but it was common enough knowledge.

Especially if one happened to be a spy, or a Bow Street Runner.

"Why not just take Robin and go to one of your own estates? Surely the Maitlands could be bribed."

Dignity warred with humiliation in her eyes. "I have no money."

His brows shot up. Isobel should be one of the richest women in England. Unless Charles had lost her fortune as well as his own at the tables.

"Then how did you propose to hire me?" he asked softly.

She bit her lip for a moment and blushed. "I will become your mistress for a time," she said.

He almost fell off the edge of the table. It was that easy? No house, no jewels? He reminded himself to keep his wits sharp, especially now. "For how long?" he asked.

A flicker of irritation passed over her features. "I suppose we'll need to come to an agreement, but will you help me?"

He crossed the room slowly, half expecting her to flee, but she stood her ground. He read a kaleidoscope of emotions in her eyes as he approached, hope and fear and courage and embarrassment and desire. She had bared her soul to him, and it lay in his hands. He kept those hands at his sides, knowing she was right. If he touched her now, they wouldn't get this conversation finished.

She began to babble, and the closer he got the faster the words tumbled out. "There's something happening at Waterfield Abbey, I think, in Kent. My steward—well, Charles's steward, since I don't manage the estate—needs money, and I don't understand why there isn't any. I have not been there for many years, not since my mother's . . ."

She paused as he reached her, standing so close she had

to tip her head back to look at him. She wasn't telling him anything he didn't already know, but he let her go on. "I think Robert died at—" The rattle of the door latch froze the words on her lips. She gasped as the door slowly swung open, a look of horror transforming her face.

They were seconds from being discovered.

Chapter 31

The rattle of the latch was as loud as a rifle shot in the quiet room. Isobel spun, too stunned to do anything but watch the polished handle lift. It glinted in the candlelight, and the door creaked open. Yellow light raced across the floor to touch her shoes and climb her skirts.

Caught.

With Blackwood, his newest scandal.

Except this time it would be her scandal, and it would cost her everything. Horror turned her limbs to stone.

She barely felt his hands on her shoulders as he tugged her into a curtained alcove she hadn't even noticed and pulled her tight against his chest in the scant space. She could feel the rapid beat of his heart under her own. She tried to push him away but he held her. The makeshift closet was narrow and dark, filled with the shadowy shapes of easels, paintbrushes, and canvas. There was no room to stand *but* in his arms. She gasped, and the sweet reek of linseed oil invaded her lungs.

Her ears pricked at the unmistakable rustle of taffeta as someone crept into the room.

She clenched her fists against the hard muscles of Blackwood's chest, pushing, but he wouldn't let her go. In a moment they'd find her in his arms and—

"Come on, Evelyn. I want to see this portrait I've heard so much about!"

Isobel felt her pupils expand as her knees turned to dust. *Honoria!*

Blackwood pressed her face into his shoulder, stifling her gasp of horror. She sucked in clean linen, sandalwood soap, and the familiar smell of his body.

He held her close, silently offering his protection, but it was a sanctuary with no security at all against what she feared most.

"I believe Augusta wishes to keep the portrait unseen until it's been completed," Evelyn Renshaw said in a nervous whisper.

Honoria snorted, not bothering to keep her voice low now that the door was shut behind her. "The door wasn't locked, and the girl *is* going to marry Charles. Since the portrait will no doubt come to hang in my salon at Maitland House, I don't see why I should not see it now."

Isobel cringed at the smugness in Honoria's tone. She felt Blackwood stiffen, and glanced up at him. He was watching the two women through a narrow gap in the curtain. In the dim light the muscles of his jaw stood out and his eyes burned like brands.

"Miranda Archer has agreed to marry Charles?" Evelyn asked, incredulous.

"As good as," Honoria murmured. "There are just the formalities to be dealt with." She made an ugly sound of distaste. "Well! If this is the portrait Lady Augusta has been talking up all over town, then I must say I'm disappointed. It's not really *like* the girl, is it?"

"I think it's lovely. It captures her vivid spirit," Evelyn said diplomatically.

"Well, that spirit will be curbed once she's married to Charles," Honoria said. "The Maitlands do not put up with impropriety, even when it masquerades as 'spirit.' One black sheep in the family is quite enough, and it has taken years to breed the Fraser whore's influence out of Isobel."

Mortification heated Isobel's skin from ankles to hairline, but Blackwood's hands tightened, caressing her, soothing her. She didn't want his pity. She glared up at him, arching away like an angry cat, but he held her easily. He captured her mouth and kissed her as if she were worth more to him than gold or rubies or any other woman on earth.

She clung to his lips, feeling the sting of tears as her heart opened like a rose in her breast. Honoria's voice became a distant, meaningless buzz under the moist heat of his mouth on hers, the sensation of his breath on her cheeks, her eyelids. He did not see the shame in her, she realized. He made her feel beautiful, almost loved.

"But I'm sure Charles knows where Philip is!" He broke the kiss at Evelyn's shrill cry, and his hands tensed on her shoulders as he peered out at the two women, his expression sharp.

"What makes you think Charles would know?" Isobel instinctively tensed at the dangerous edge in Honoria's voice.

"I received a letter from him, telling me Charles would visit me, bring me a message that Philip felt he could not write," Evelyn said, less dignified now.

Isobel heard the click of heels, the rustle of clothing, the creak of the polished floorboards as Honoria paced.

"And did Charles bring you this message?"

Honoria's voice was closer now. Isobel realized she must be right outside the thin curtain, close enough to hear the faintest breath. Her stomach shrank against her spine.

"No," Evelyn said, her voice breaking on the single word.

Honoria's sigh was like a hurricane. "Then it was probably just a passing comment. Perhaps Philip merely asked Charles to give you his regards, or to ask after your health. I'm not surprised he hasn't relayed such trifling mush. Charles is not the kind of man who would be comfortable delivering declarations of love and devotion."

"Where did he see my husband?" Evelyn demanded.

"How would I know that?" Honoria spluttered. Isobel frowned. Charles did not go anywhere without Honoria knowing.

"But you *do* know, don't you?" Evelyn cried out, then fell silent. Seconds ticked by. "You won't tell me, and I suppose there is no point in arguing, but please ask Charles to give Philip a message from me when he sees him next."

"If you wish to send your husband a *billet doux*, you should write it and post it yourself. Charles is not a courier," Honoria replied coldly.

"My message is simple enough. Even Charles will remember it, and delivering it should cause him very little discomfiture." Evelyn's tone was now calm, dignified. She would not beg for this favor. Isobel felt a surge of admiration.

"*If* he sees Philip—" Honoria began, but Evelyn interrupted.

"*When* Charles sees my husband, he can tell him that I am tired of waiting for him to come home." Isobel heard footsteps.

"Where are you going?" Honoria demanded.

"Back to the salon. We should not have come up here."

"No, perhaps not," Honoria agreed, her tone icy. "It is never advisable to pry into other people's business."

"Are we discussing my husband, or the portrait?" Evelyn asked.

"Take it as you will. Your marital woes are best kept private. If Philip has left you, it certainly isn't Charles's fault."

Evelyn's gasp at the cutting insult covered Isobel's own.

"I think we had better go downstairs before you become completely distraught, Evelyn."

"Yes, I suppose we must," Evelyn murmured, sounding defeated.

The two women left the room and the latch fell back into place, leaving Phineas and Isobel alone again.

Chapter 32

Blackwood opened the curtain. "They've gone."

Isobel leapt away from him, her eyes on the door as she sought the safety of the shadows. Honoria's malevolent presence hung in the air with her heavy perfume.

"Isobel?"

She was trembling and her lips were pinched in her white face, her eyes huge. She jerked her gaze toward him and he saw the glitter of tears in the candlelight.

"I'm sorry, Blackwood. I never should have involved you in this. If Honoria finds out what I've done . . ." Her mouth twisted and she paused, unable, or unwilling, to tell him what she feared, but he understood well enough. His anger rose.

"Letting the most disreputable rake in London bed you?" he asked bluntly.

"There are consequences for one's choices. Dire ones. I know that, and still I let myself *feel* something, *want* it. I know better. There are things, precious things, *people*, who must be considered, protected, ahead of our own desires," she stammered.

"What the hell are you talking about?"

"I should not have come up here. I should not have t-told you about Charles, or asked you to f-follow him. It's too dangerous." She raised her chin, her face carefully blank. "Please forget I said anything."

"Too dangerous?" he demanded. "For me or for you, Isobel?" He strode toward her. "What about your other offer to become my mistress?"

Her eyes flashed, a small explosion of anger. "That would be the most dangerous thing of all." She picked up her skirts and moved toward the door.

He caught her arm as she passed him, refusing to let her leave. Her hand curled over his sleeve in a desperate caress.

"Please let me go, Blackwood. I should be downstairs, tucked away in the corner of the salon where I belong, alone, or at home with my son. I should be anywhere but here with you. The price is too high."

"Is your precious reputation really worth that much to you?"

She flinched, surprise clear in her eyes, and he knew he was mistaken. There was something else, then, a secret she wasn't willing to share. His skin prickled.

"It would be better if we did not see each other again," she said, trying for hauteur as she looked pointedly at his hand on her arm, but her voice wobbled.

He tightened his grip. "I can see the desire in your eyes, Isobel. I can feel it when I touch you, even now." She pulled away from his hold on her as if that would stem the need.

"I cannot explain, Blackwood."

She ran a nervous hand over her dress, patted her hair, her eyes on the door, making herself ready to leave the room, and him.

"Look, they've gone. I doubt anyone else will have the audacity to come up here. Stay with me, Isobel. I'll lock the door." He wanted to see her face as he made love to her without masks or darkness to hide behind. He wanted to prove to her that she could not live without him.

"I—I can't," she said, her eyes drinking him in as if she truly intended this to be the last time she saw him. She took a step toward the door, but he caught her wrist again, his fingers on the hectic pulse point. She looked up at him. "Every time I touch you, it becomes more difficult to stop. If I do not leave now, this very minute, then I will lose—"

"You said your son was in danger. Do you now believe you imagined it?"

She shut her eyes. "No." The single word was small and desolate. "I think I believe it even more, since Evelyn and Honoria—" He felt a shudder run through her. She looked up at him. "Whatever Charles is involved in, it's dangerous, isn't it?"

Risking much, he nodded. "Does Charles know Philip well?"

Isobel frowned. "I suppose he must, though I've never heard Charles speak of him."

"Does he receive letters from Philip?"

"I don't know. Honoria is the first one to see the post when it arrives."

"Even Charles's?" he asked.

"Everyone's," Isobel said bitterly. "She reads my letters before I do, decides which invitations I am allowed to accept."

Phineas frowned. Isobel Maitland might well have been the richest woman in England, but she had no money. She was a young, beautiful woman, free to remarry or take a lover, yet she hid herself away in widow's weeds and shadows. She had no privacy, yet she had secrets. Secrets like him. And she was afraid. He swallowed, unwilling to let her walk away into whatever danger faced her.

"Isobel?" He loosened his grip on her wrist just enough to slide his hand up the length of her arm, drawing her closer. He lowered his head, and she let her eyes drift shut.

"Yes?" she breathed, caught in the same dizzy whirlpool of longing he was.

"I accept your offer," he whispered in her ear, and ran his lips down the silken length of her neck.

"What offer?" she murmured, tilting her head to give him better access.

He gave her his most devastating grin. "Your offer to become my mistress."

She stiffened. "But I can't—"

The door opened again, and this time there was no time to hide.

Chapter 33

"**O**h!" The startled gasp came from Marianne. "I was expecting the room to be empty. What on earth are you two doing in here?" Her eyes roamed over them, and Isobel felt her skin heat, aware of the shocking intimacy of the situation, though they now stood a dozen feet apart.

"I was showing the countess Miranda's portrait," Blackwood said, his voice cool, as if he had not just been kissing her, about to make love to her. Her body still tingled, but he looked perfectly calm. "And what brings you up here, Marianne?"

"Same thing, actually." She moved in front of the canvas. "I know Augusta put this room off limits, but Miranda asked me to come and have a look at her portrait. She's afraid Senor Condotti hasn't got her smile quite right and he's made her look like a child. What is your opinion, Isobel?"

Isobel swallowed the lump in her throat. "It's lovely. It captures her vivid spirit perfectly," she managed, and winced, realizing she was parroting Evelyn's polite description.

Marianne turned her attention to her brother. "And what do you think, Phin? Your opinion will mean more to Miranda than anyone else's." She made a face and crossed to straighten his cravat. "You're dreadfully rumpled, aren't you?" Isobel turned away so Marianne wouldn't see the blush scorching her cheeks.

"The portrait isn't finished." Blackwood pulled away and smoothed his cravat himself.

"No, but I can also see what Miranda means. He's given her a sweet girl's smile instead of the knowing look of a grown woman," Marianne pointed out.

"She *is* a girl," Blackwood insisted. "She looks like a young lady of quality, just as she should. She's not a hardened courtesan."

Marianne frowned. "Well of course she's a lady! I didn't mean to suggest otherwise. If you truly knew anything about women, Phineas, you'd know that every lady Miranda's age wishes to look older and more worldly, and every matron of an age with Isobel and myself wishes to look younger. Isn't that so, Isobel?" Marianne turned to enlist her help in the argument.

"I—" Isobel began.

"Isobel is hardly in her dotage!"

"I did not mean to suggest she was!" Marianne replied. "I only meant that ladies are more sensitive to their appearance than men." She touched a hand to her expertly styled curls, and the diamonds interwoven in the dark brown locks glittered. "Isobel is a beautiful woman."

Blackwood sent her a look that confirmed his sister's appraisal, but it was interrupted as the door opened yet again. He turned with a frown. "I thought access to this room was forbidden. By the end of the evening, everyone in London will have seen this portrait. If Augusta had thought to sell tickets, she could have made a second fortune."

"Phineas!" Miranda's face peered around the half-open door, blue eyes wide. "I had no idea you'd be up here. Oh, and Marianne, and Lady Isobel." She scanned the dark corners of the room. "Charles isn't here, is he?"

"No, of course not," Marianne said. "This room is closed to guests this evening. Who's that with you?"

Isobel watched Miranda blush. "I brought Mr. Fielding to see my portrait."

"Good evening," Gilbert Fielding said sheepishly, stepping into the room.

Marianne drew herself up to indignant attention. "You brought Mr. Fielding *upstairs*? *Alone*?"

Miranda raised her chin. "We aren't alone. You're here, and Phineas, and Lady Isobel."

"This argument could go on for the rest of the evening without any point at all being made, Fielding," Blackwood said. "Since Miranda wants your opinion, let's have it, and we can all return to the salon."

Gilbert considered the painted face and compared it to the real one. "It hardly does her justice at all. It would be like trying to paint the scent of a rose, or the feeling of the wind on your skin. Even the most skilled artist could not capture such beauty."

The sweet smile Miranda bestowed on Gilbert matched the one on the canvas very well, in Isobel's opinion.

"Have you considered a career in politics or the Church instead of the army?" Blackwood asked. "You appear to have a talent for poetic speeches."

Marianne sniffed. "It's time we all went back downstairs."

Gilbert offered his arm to Miranda as Phineas moved toward Isobel.

"Oh, no," Marianne said. "Phineas, you escort Miranda. Mr. Fielding, would you be so kind as to take Isobel downstairs?"

Isobel felt Blackwood's eyes on her, saw the muscles in his jaw tighten as she laid her hand on the fine, cool wool of Gilbert Fielding's sleeve. Miranda shot her a look of pure ire, and Marianne marched them all down the stairs like matched horses set in tandem.

Chapter 34

"**H**ave you considered seducing Isobel Maitland?" Adam asked.

Phineas stared at his brother-in-law across the width of the oak desk.

"For information, I mean, about Charles's activities, and his connection to Philip Renshaw," he added, smugly cheerful about the idea. "I understand the idea has no personal appeal, but it's for England, and the sake of this mission.

"Surely you've had to charm unattractive women before," Adam continued, mistaking his hesitation.

Phineas wanted to punch the superior smirk off his face, but it was true enough. He steered the conversation in a safer direction. "Has anything turned up about Maitland's midnight activities at the Bosun's Belle Inn?"

Adam sat back in his chair. "No, not yet, but one of my sailors is working for the landlord. He'll report to me directly if there's anything important. It might take time, though, and there are faster ways to learn what we need to know."

Phineas ignored the hint. "Does your man know Charles by sight, or Philip Renshaw?"

"No, but Gibbs knows a gentleman when he sees one, especially if he's as out of place as a mermaid in a net full of herring."

Phineas didn't laugh at the joke, and Adam frowned, obviously disappointed, and shifted in his seat. "You're on edge, Phin," he said. "That makes me nervous. Isobel might know something that could speed our investigations considerably."

"Isobel Maitland is Marianne's friend, Adam. What's your wife likely to say about this?"

"Do you think Isobel would tell her?" he asked. "Surely ladies don't discuss their conquests. Women are discreet creatures when it comes to intimate matters."

"You're discreet, Adam. Marianne is like a ferret on a mission to sniff out every secret in London, and if ladies didn't talk about their conquests, my job would be impossible."

"Marianne doesn't gossip. She's merely observant. If I were to put it delicately, I'd say it ran in the Archer blood."

Adam held Phineas's mocking stare for a moment before getting to his feet and crossing to look out the window. "Ah, well, never mind Isobel, then. I suppose every man has limits to what he's willing to do for his country. I don't blame you."

He turned, an unpleasant gleam in his eyes that set Phineas's teeth on edge. "There is another way. We could use Miranda. Charles Maitland is interested in marrying her. We could use her as bait, lure him in and—"

"No," Phineas said, loathing for Charles and dislike for Adam warring in his gut.

"No?" Adam asked softly, waiting for Phineas to agree to use Isobel instead. He didn't.

"Charles is a dangerous man, Adam. I've spent years apart from my family to keep them safe. Using Miranda is out of the question."

"I see. Then it looks like tumbling the widow is the only way, wouldn't you say?"

"Do you ever think of anything other than who you can use for your own ends?" Phineas demanded.

"Not my ends, old man. For England."

There was a knock at the door. "Come," Adam said.

The butler entered and bowed. "Her ladyship requests your company for tea, my lord. Her guests have arrived."

"Thank you, Northcott. We'll be right down. Come and join us, Phin."

"Who's here?" Phineas asked, straightening his coat.

Adam grinned at him. "Isobel Maitland."

"I hope you don't mind that we're in the morning room for tea," Marianne said as she welcomed Isobel into the sunny yellow room. "It's such a pleasant room, and I don't feel I have to stand on ceremony with you." The furniture was more comfortable than fashionable, and the windows were thrown wide to take advantage of the warm day and the lovely view of the garden.

"Good afternoon, Lady Isobel," Gilbert Fielding said, rising to greet her.

"You remember Mr. Fielding, don't you, Isobel?" Marianne chirped.

"Yes, of course. How nice to see you again so soon, Mr. Fielding."

"Isn't it?" Marianne gushed. "Now you sit here, Isobel, and Mr. Fielding can take the chair beside you. There. Isn't that cozy?"

Isobel took her seat, noting that Gilbert Fielding looked uncomfortable in the intimate surroundings. "Should we save a place for Lady Miranda?" he asked.

"Oh, Miranda won't be joining us today," Marianne said. "But Adam will be here shortly, and we'll be as happily paired as turtle doves."

Turtle doves? Isobel felt her face heat, and Gilbert Fielding cleared his throat, his cheeks as red as her own. Marianne smiled sweetly at them both, as if she had a dove trapped behind her teeth.

Adam arrived at last. "There you are, my dear. I expected

to find you in the salon. Isn't that why we had it redecorated, so you could show it off to guests?" He kissed his wife's cheek.

Behind him, Blackwood stood in the doorway.

Isobel felt her heart tie itself into an intricate knot.

He merely brushed her with an impersonal glance before he fixed Fielding with a hard glare. Isobel's heart unraveled again. Without his eyes on her, she was able to fold her hands in her lap and paste a calm smile on her face.

He took the seat opposite to hers, a few feet across the room. He was at once too close and too far away. She was aware of every small movement he made, every breath he took. He hardly seemed similarly affected. He crossed his legs with casual ease and frowned at Gilbert Fielding. He appeared to be measuring the distance between her chair and Gilbert's with a cold eye. She noted the tic in the taut muscles of his jaw.

Perhaps he was angry that Fielding had tried to steal a kiss from Miranda. Whatever it was, with the lion's share of his attention on Gilbert today, she felt shut out of the sun.

"I didn't expect to see *you* this afternoon, Phineas," Marianne said. "Did you come by for a reason, or are you just here to see if Adam can come out to play?"

"Do I need a reason to visit?"

"Of course not, but I would certainly have planned to take tea in a larger room if I knew we'd have so many guests," Marianne replied. "I was only expecting Isobel and Mr. Fielding. I asked Northcott to fetch Adam to keep the numbers even, male to female."

Turtle doves, Isobel recalled. And now there was a hawk in their midst.

Blackwood raised his eyebrows. "Then I suppose I am the gooseberry. Was there to be dancing later? We could ask Northcott to send a carriage for Miranda to make six."

Gilbert Fielding brightened at once. Marianne glared at

her brother. "Don't be silly, Phin. There's hardly room for dancing."

"Perhaps if we moved the chairs back a little," Adam offered. "Mr. Fielding seems quite crowded. Phineas could move over there, next to Isobel."

"Don't be ridiculous, Adam. Mr. Fielding isn't crowded at all. In fact, I think if we asked him, he'd declare himself to be very comfortable indeed next to Isobel. Isn't that so, Mr. Fielding?" Marianne asked.

"Any closer and the lady's reputation would be in tatters," Phineas muttered. Isobel met the ice in his eyes with a quelling glare of her own. Whatever was the matter with him?

"I am indeed comfortable, Countess," Gilbert said, looking anything but, in Isobel's opinion. She blamed Blackwood.

"You would have a wonderful view of the garden, Gil, if you were to lean to the left and look out the window," Phineas suggested. And it would move him away from her, Isobel realized with a frisson of annoyance.

"And you have a charming view of Isobel, Phineas," Adam said brightly. "May I say that's a lovely, um, bonnet, Countess?" he said awkwardly, after searching her person to find something admirable. Her hat was a poor choice. It was plain black straw, with no adornment at all. Isobel blinked at the earl, and was surprised to see him blush.

Phineas was glowering at her bonnet as if it were indeed the dullest piece of millinery in the world. She gave the black straw a defiant pat as an uncomfortable silence fell over the room.

"The weather is very fine today, don't you think?" Isobel asked Gilbert, trying to make conversation with the least threatening person in the room.

"Indeed, Countess," Gilbert replied, smiling politely. "It reminds me of the kind of spring days we get in Kent, don't you agree?"

"Kent?" Marianne brightened. "Yes, I understand you have a property by the sea, Isobel. Waterfield Abbey, isn't it? Adam counts a fascination with the histories of England's great houses among his interests." She elbowed her husband in the ribs.

"Waterfield was a convent until the Reformation," Adam recited. "Henry VIII dismantled it, and gave the lands to the Denby family."

"Don't you think that's fascinating, Mr. Fielding?" Marianne asked. "Does your father's manor lie very near Waterfield?"

"Yes, indeed. I grew up hearing the stories of those times," Gilbert said.

"Fine bedtime stories, I can imagine," Phineas drawled. "Nuns raped, chapels looted, crops burned."

Everyone looked at him in surprise.

"I can't imagine what's keeping the tea," Marianne murmured, for once having nothing to say. "Phineas, if we're keeping you from an appointment, don't feel you must stay."

Phineas's eyebrows rose at the thinly veiled dismissal. "I have no plans at all for this afternoon, Marianne, and I am most interested to hear Gil's stories."

"But surely you cannot be interested in what Isobel and Mr. Fielding have in common," Marianne said, her gaze so pointed it would have punctured and deflated a lesser man than Blackwood.

"You'd be surprised what interests me," Phineas said, glaring at his sister, who glared back. There seemed to be a whole unspoken conversation going on between them, one that made Isobel extremely uneasy.

At last the butler arrived with tea. "Thank God," Gilbert murmured under his breath. Isobel overheard, and they grinned at each other with complete understanding.

"What's the jest?" Marianne asked eagerly.

"Nothing at all, Countess. Just a thought about Kent," Mr. Fielding managed, and smiled at Isobel again, a warm conspirator's grin.

"I see," Marianne purred. She shot her brother a sharp look of triumph.

She poured the tea then, and Isobel handed out the cups. Phineas's fingers brushed hers under the saucer, and she met his eyes. His gaze was filled with a cool speculation she didn't understand. He took the cup, breaking the contact between them.

Marianne served the cake. "Mmm, Cook has sent us a bowl of cherries. Isobel, you would hardly believe it, but Adam grows cherries in the conservatory."

Isobel stared at the ruby fruit in the china bowl. She dared not look at Blackwood, but she felt his eyes on her. She flicked her tongue over her lip, almost tasting the juice.

"Try one," Marianne said, and held them out to her.

She didn't have to taste them. She already knew how intoxicating they were. She remembered the coolness of the fruit and the heat of his mouth, the taste of the sweet juice mixed with the salt of his skin.

She could not look at him now, didn't dare, knowing he was also remembering the intimate details of that night. A surge of longing swept over her like a tidal wave.

"Adam worries they're not as tasty as wild fruit. I find them very sweet," Marianne continued. "We would be glad to have your opinion."

"They are a cross between English varieties and a type from the South Seas," Adam explained, but Isobel barely heard. Whatever their origins, they were the most succulent, delicious, erotic cherries in the world.

She took one in her naked fingers. The flesh was cool and firm. It glowed like venal sin.

Her mouth watered as she brought the fruit to her lips,

caught it in her teeth, felt the shocking spurt of juice hit her tongue. She drew a breath and looked at Blackwood. He stared back, his eyes heavy lidded, a banked fire in their depths. She felt desire stir, tighten her nipples and swirl between her thighs. She stared at his mouth, remembered his kiss, flavored by the tang of the fruit. She swallowed the cherry, pit and all.

"Well?" Marianne asked.

"Delicious," Blackwood murmured.

Marianne swung to look at him. "You haven't even tried one!"

"No, but I've enjoyed them before."

"Ah, yes," Adam murmured. "You're no stranger to the temptations of my conservatory, are you, Phin?"

Did Westlake know? Isobel felt her skin heat, but Blackwood looked unaffected as he glared at his brother-in-law. She remembered Adam's voice in the dark doorway at the masquerade ball. She licked her lips but tasted the sweetness of the fruit again.

Obsession.

Sin.

She wanted more.

She read the heat in her lover's eyes, felt awareness and desire threaten to overwhelm her. She dragged her gaze away from his.

"I really should be going. Robin has a fencing lesson this afternoon." She could not remain in Blackwood's disturbing presence, not with cherry juice on her lips, and act as if nothing had ever occurred between them.

"One of my ships is in port," Adam said. "I am taking Jamie down to see it this afternoon. Perhaps Robin would like to accompany us," he suggested.

"I have no doubt he would love it, but his fencing master is waiting," Isobel hedged.

"Adam has men on board who would be glad to show the lads their skills with a blade," Marianne coaxed. "He could still have his lesson."

"But Honoria is expecting us."

"Send a note home with your coachman, and stay," Marianne pleaded. "I'm sure Mr. Fielding would be delighted to see you home later."

"Or perhaps you could do it, Blackwood," Adam suggested. Isobel's heart leapt in surprise.

"But Mr. Fielding would be *delighted* to take care of Isobel." Marianne glared at her husband.

Gilbert smiled apologetically at Isobel. "Alas, Countess, while it would be my pleasure to be of assistance, I have only my horse. I doubt you'd want to ride pillion down Bond Street."

The idea was so ridiculous that Isobel giggled. She cast a glance at Phineas and the happy sound died on her lips. He was regarding Gilbert with a steely frown.

"I would be happy to lend you my carriage, Mr. Fielding," Marianne suggested.

"But Phineas's coach is right outside, the horses already harnessed," Adam said. "It would be no trouble for him to see Isobel safely home."

"It would be my pleasure to take you wherever you wish to go," Phineas said. Isobel felt her knees weaken at the double meaning.

"I really can't—" she started, but Marianne leapt in.

"Really, Mr. Fielding. It is no problem at all to call out my carriage. You could tie your horse to the back."

"This is Mayfair, not a country village, Marianne," Adam said.

"Perhaps it would be best if I—" Isobel tried again.

"I daresay you're keeping Fielding from his usual afternoon pastime, Marianne," Phineas said. "The eligible young ladies ride in the park at this time of day, don't they, Fielding? Can you afford to miss the opportunity of a sunny afternoon to find a wealthy bride?"

"Phineas!" Marianne puffed up with indignation at the insult to her guest. "Aren't you in the market for a bride as well? I hear Lady Amelia rides every afternoon."

"And who would be left to take Isobel home?" Phineas drawled.

Isobel had had enough of Blackwood's incomprehensible behavior. If he was angry with her, then there was no need to take it out on Mr. Fielding. The poor man had gone quite red at his insult.

"I can see myself home, Lord Blackwood. I hope you will have a care in the park. Your reputation is likely to frighten away your potential bride, if your insulting manner does not," Isobel snapped.

She kept her eyes locked with his and dared him to look away first. He held her gaze.

After a long moment Gilbert cleared his throat and Marianne set her teacup down with a clatter.

Isobel dropped her eyes, mortified that she'd let him goad her. She concentrated on smoothing her expression—and her unruly passion—to placid nothingness, but her heart was pounding in her throat.

"I think Mr. Fielding should see to Isobel, since he was here first," Marianne said.

"Hardly," Phineas muttered, looking at Isobel. She knew exactly what he meant.

"It's a simple matter, gentlemen," Adam said. "It shouldn't have to come to a duel to decide it. Perhaps we should let Phineas take Isobel home, Mr. Fielding. I daresay it would improve his reputation, and hopefully his temper, to be seen with such a fine and moral widow."

Fielding gave Isobel a bemused look, as if he wondered

what all the fuss was about. She was wondering herself. She smiled at him, if only to irritate Blackwood.

"I am ready to leave whenever you are, Countess Ashdown," Blackwood said coldly, rising to his feet, sketching a mocking bow.

"Let her finish her tea at least, Phineas," Marianne snapped. "She'll also need to send a note to Lady Honoria. Perhaps you'd like to visit the conservatory as well, Isobel. I'll get a basket and you can pick some cherries for Robin's tea." She rang the bell to summon pen, ink, paper, and basket.

"Would you like to join us, Mr. Fielding?" she asked, pointedly turning her back on her brother.

"Er, no, thank you, my lady. I really must be going," he said politely, bowing over Isobel's hand. "I look forward to seeing you again, Countess, and discussing our mutual recollections of Kent."

"That will be a pleasure." Isobel curtsied as his lips brushed her knuckles impersonally.

Phineas plucked her hand out of Fielding's grip in a proprietary gesture.

"Your note, Countess?" Isobel felt her pulse increase at the simple touch that was too hot, too familiar, too disturbing in the crowded room. "Shall I dictate?" he offered. "If you hurry, we could follow Gilbert through the park. Perhaps you'd like to advise Honoria and Charles you'll be bringing him home to dine."

She blinked at him. Now what on earth did that mean?

Chapter 35

Phineas handed Isobel into his coach and settled himself across from her. She hadn't looked at him since they left the morning room, but the hot color in her cheeks had told him she was very aware of his presence.

Damn Marianne and her matchmaking, and while he was at it, damn Adam for his permission to seduce Isobel. And damn Gilbert Fielding, and damn Isobel for being charmed by the handsome, respectable, penniless fool.

And damn himself too. Isobel brought out emotions he prided himself on being incapable of feeling. He'd never been jealous before in his life, if that's what this was. Perhaps it was just lust. Watching her eat a cherry was the most erotic thing he'd ever seen. The last time they'd shared the fruit in the dark, both of them were half naked. At tea, in company, he'd been as hard as a bloody pole the moment she bit into the lush fruit. He'd barely restrained himself from dragging her across Marianne's morning room and taking her on the tea table.

His famous self-control was in tatters, and his mind was turning to mush.

"Isobel . . ." he began, and she turned to meet his eyes. The same desire shimmered there, and he groaned, catching her as she threw herself across the coach and into his arms with a cry.

He pulled her close as her mouth landed hard on his.

She still tasted of cherries, and he devoured her like a starving man, unable, unwilling, to resist. He felt her hands on his cravat, ripping at Burridge's carefully tied knot. After that all rational thought vanished.

Isobel was on fire. The moan she had been holding in all afternoon escaped as he cupped her breast through the dark muslin of her gown, a throaty, needy sound she barely recognized as coming from herself. She wished she were allowed to wear pretty, low-necked gowns, so she could feel his bare palms on the warm, naked weight of her breasts, but the dress wouldn't budge. Inventive man that he was, he suckled her nipples through the fabric of her ugly gown, driving her mad.

"Blackwood!" she gasped as he lifted her and set her astride his hips. She tugged her gown out of the way with shaking hands and pressed her naked flesh against his erection. He still wore his breeches, and the rough fabric and the jostling of the coach made it almost unbearable. She fumbled for the buttons, but he laid his hand on hers.

"Allow me, sweetheart. It's broad daylight." He opened them with one hand as she watched, freeing himself. With the other, he caressed the warm wet petals of her flesh with maddening slowness.

"Blackwood," she whimpered again, pleading this time, rubbing against his hand.

He didn't need a second invitation. He grasped her hips and impaled her, filling her with one hard thrust. She moaned and arched, settling him more deeply inside her, joined to him at last, filled.

He dragged her forward and kissed her, sucking her lips and her tongue, and she could taste cherries on their mingled breath. Then she was lost to the desperate friction.

"Isobel!" he groaned, coming deep within her body in a heated rush.

She clung to him, resting her forehead on his, kissing his sweat-soaked face, and felt his heart beating against her breast. Still embedded in her, he reached between their bodies and stroked her, and she gave herself up to the pleasure of what he was doing.

Phineas watched the muscles of her throat tense as her skin flushed. She cried out his name as her release claimed her. Unmasked, in daylight, she was more beautiful than he had ever imagined. He gathered her against his chest and held her, her breath warm on his neck. He stroked her hair, her back, the silk of her thighs, not wanting to let her go. Too soon, he felt the coach turn a corner and slow.

He knocked on the roof. "Drive through the park," he ordered the coachman. "Or we could find an inn," he murmured in her ear.

She sat up, still perched on his lap, her body still joined to his, and blushed as if she'd realized for the first time where they were.

Masculine pride swelled. In his arms, she'd forgotten everything, her pride, her stiff sense of propriety, and especially bloody Gilbert Fielding.

Isobel wriggled off his lap, her face flaming, and he let her go. She sat on the edge of the seat opposite and straightened her clothing. He had a tantalizing glimpse of white thighs before she tugged her dark skirts over them. Her bonnet was askew, and a pretty frill of displaced hair framed her flushed cheeks under the black straw. Her mouth was swollen from his kisses, her eyes still wide. She looked like a woman who'd been pleasured in the back of a coach, and he'd willingly bet it was the first time for that.

"I know an inn just outside the city," he said. "We could spend the rest of the afternoon there. I want you again, Isobel, every lovely inch of you, naked, and in a real bed."

She bit her lip, looked tempted for a moment, then shut her

eyes, as if she could dispel desire so easily. "I am expected at home," she said. "I didn't mean to—"

"I'm very glad you did," he drawled.

She blushed. "I meant I did not expect to see you today," she said, watching as he buttoned his breeches. His cravat was a hopeless mess, so he pulled it off and tucked it into his pocket. "That is, I didn't plan on *this* happening. I went out to take tea with Marianne and Mr. Fielding, not to—"

The sound of Fielding's name set Phineas's teeth on edge.

"And I did not expect to see you with Gilbert Fielding," he said, and cursed himself for sounding like a jealous fool. She looked at him with dull surprise, as if he hadn't the right. He recognized the simple truth that Gilbert was much more suitable for a respectable widow than a rake like him. Didn't she deserve to be happy?

Hell, didn't he?

"You seem to like Gilbert," he said, striving to keep his tone even as his anger grew. "Were the two of you acquainted as children?"

"No not at all, but he is a pleasant man, and it appears we have much in common."

Much in common? What in hell did that mean? He searched for some common ground *he* shared with Isobel. They shared passion and fire. She'd reduce a milksop like Fielding to ashes.

"Do you intend to take Gilbert Fielding as your next lover?" he asked bluntly, wanting her to feel a little of the pain, the frustration, that roiled in his breast. "Is that why seeing me —and this—was so unexpected?"

"What kind of woman do you think I am?" she gasped.

"I know exactly what kind of woman you are, Isobel." His eyes scorched her mouth, her breasts, to make his point.

"Well, I doubt Mr. Fielding is that type of man," she said

in a strangled voice, looking away. A flush of color bloomed over her throat and face.

He wanted her to look at him, to see him and not think of goddamned Gilbert bloody Fielding, but he had to know. "You mean he's the marrying kind, I suppose. You do know he wants to marry money?"

She looked confused. "Yes, I've been told that. Still, I think he will make a pleasant enough husband."

The hard knot of jealousy grew like a tumor. "Good God, Isobel. Do you have hopes he will offer for you? Make *you* a pleasant husband?" he demanded, the question tearing itself out of his throat.

"He has not made any such offer!" she protested.

"He will. He's desperate. He'll propose the instant he smells money."

Her jaw dropped at the insult. He had meant to direct it toward Gilbert, but it came out wrong.

"How dare you? What does it matter to you? You're going to marry Lady Amelia. I hear she has plenty of money—"

Rage burned through him. "We're talking about you, Isobel. Answer me. Do you intend to marry Fielding?" He waved a hand to indicate her dowdy, love-rumpled gown. Despite her dishevelment, she held herself with dignity. "I thought you were still grieving for Maitland. You must have loved him very much to mourn this long." He wanted to be loved like that.

Suddenly, it mattered more than anything else.

Her eyes kindled with anger. "That is not your affair, my lord."

"Ah, but it is, Isobel. Our lust is mutual, sweeting, every single time we meet. You offered to be my mistress, and if you intend to marry, have the courtesy to let me know. I am not above adultery, but—"

With a cry of fury she drew back her hand and struck him. It wasn't a ladylike slap. He felt his lip smash against his teeth and burst. The iron taste of blood filled his mouth.

She pressed a hand to her own lips, anger and wounded pride at war in her eyes. "Order the coachman to stop. I wish to get out."

"No. I won't let you run from me again. Damn it, Isobel, ever since I met you I've dreamed of nothing else but you, I haven't touched another woman. I haven't *wanted* any other woman. If you want to marry again, then marry me."

Her eyes widened in shock. "What?"

His heart thumped against his ribs. For an instant his tongue refused to move. He hadn't meant to propose, but he knew at once that it felt right. It was what he wanted.

"Marry me, Isobel. Be my wife."

She blinked at him, her throat working, her eyes filling with tears. He waited for them to overflow, for her to fall into his arms and say yes.

"No."

It came out in a whisper, and he thought he'd misheard her. His heart turned to lead.

Her eyes were wild and she fiercely dashed her tears away. "I cannot marry you! I should not even be in the same room with you, or the same coach. The price is too high."

"Isobel, I don't understand. I thought you knew that I'm not what I appear to be."

"*You* don't understand, Blackwood! It is *I* who am not what I seem!"

What the hell did that mean?

She scrabbled at the door handle, her tears flowing unchecked now, and he watched her, numb, bewildered. "Isobel, wait. Surely I deserve an explanation!" he said, trying to catch her hands, to stop her and make her look at him. She shook him off, and her attempts to open the door grew even more frenzied.

He didn't understand. He, the man who prided himself on reading people, knowing what they were thinking, feeling, what they wanted, had no idea why she'd rejected his proposal.

"Let me go, Blackwood, please," she begged as the door opened. He barely had time to knock on the ceiling to stop the coach before she half tumbled, half jumped from the vehicle and disappeared into the crowds. He pressed a knuckle to his split lip, but the pain of her parting souvenir hardly mattered.

Jane Kirk stepped out of the milliner's shop in time to hear a savage curse as a gentleman reined his horse to avoid a woman fool enough to jump from a carriage in the middle of the street. The woman didn't even notice, just ran on, sobbing. Jane almost dropped her parcels as she recognized Isobel. She glanced around, wondering where the countess had come from so suddenly and in such a state. Her eyes narrowed.

The Marquess of Blackwood sat in the open doorway of his coach staring after the widow. Jane smiled until her lips hurt.

She checked to see if Lord Philip's latest letter was still tucked securely in her bodice. It wouldn't do to lose that. Honoria was waiting for it. The paper crackled reassuringly under her fingers. She hurried on her way, looking forward to delivering the note, now that she had a most titillating tale to tell as well.

Isobel and the Marquess of Blackwood. My my.

This changed everything.

Chapter 36

*B*lackwood had proposed.

   The incredible, unbelievable words echoed in Isobel's head on the long walk home. It had been a horrible, wicked thing to do.

She loved him.

And she hated him.

For a moment she had felt the terrible temptation to accept, to let him take her away, to marry him and damn the consequences.

But that was what her mother had done. Had Charlotte been happy with her choice? Was she so much in love that she had not felt the pain of leaving her child? Even now the agony of Charlotte's abandonment, and the idea of leaving her own son, was a raw ache in Isobel's chest.

She could not abandon Robin, no matter how miserable Honoria made her life, or how much she loved—

Blackwood had proposed.

Damn him!

He had wanted an explanation, a reason why she refused him. Was it so obvious she loved him? She had tried to hide her feelings, but she'd been in love with him since the first moment she laid eyes on him.

How could she tell him her dead husband still ruled her life from the grave, that his will ensured she would never be free? She was beholden, enslaved, to Honoria, a bondage she endured willingly for Robin's sake. Phineas could not ask her to choose between her love for him and her son. It was impossible. The pain left her breathless. She could not do it, would not.

By the time she climbed the steps of Maitland House, she knew she had to find a way to leave London. If she stayed in Blackwood's mesmerizing, tantalizing sphere, she would be unable to resist. She would end up just like her mother. Isobel the Harlot. Robin would grow up hating her.

She would promise Honoria anything, plead on her knees if necessary, to go to Ashdown or Waterfield, or wherever they'd allow her to take Robin. Perhaps if Robin were out of sight and out of reach, Charles would forget he even existed. Away from London, she could keep her son safe.

And she could forget Blackwood.

Never, her heart whispered as Finch opened the front door for her and she handed him her bonnet and gloves.

She glanced in the mirror. Her face was tearstained, her eyes puffy. Her lips were swollen from his kisses. Her gown was rumpled from the wild lovemaking in Blackwood's coach.

Her body still tingled.

She needed to go upstairs and change her dress, compose herself, before seeing Honoria to make her plea.

The door of the library was slightly ajar as she passed, and she winced, knowing she'd need to slip by unnoticed, or be prepared to explain her disheveled appearance if she were caught. She was too tired to think of a believable excuse.

She paused outside the door and peered at Honoria's broad back through the crack. She wore a vivid shade of green today and was pulling on her gloves in preparation to go out.

"Is the new man in place at Waterfield?" Honoria asked Charles, who sat at the desk.

"Yes. One of Renshaw's men."

Isobel's skin prickled, and she froze outside the door to listen.

"And I assume everything else will be ready on time? We cannot afford any mistakes now, Charles."

Charles hesitated. "There are one or two minor details left to see to."

Honoria hissed her disapproval.

"Mother, be reasonable. How was I to know Hart would prove difficult, or the innkeeper would demand a larger payment?" Charles asked peevishly. "And Renshaw's demands have been endless."

"Just tell me you took care of the situation at Waterfield properly," Honoria snapped.

"I did exactly as you suggested," Charles replied. "All anyone knows is that Hart has left Waterfield and there's a new steward. I put about a few rumors of mismanagement so people will believe Hart was turned off for incompetence."

Isobel pressed a hand to her mouth to suppress a gasp. She had begged them not to fire Jonathan Hart. She shut her eyes. She should not have mentioned that Hart had come to see her. She wondered where he'd gone, if he had a family.

"Does anyone suspect that he's dead?" Honoria asked.

Isobel's eyes widened. "Dead?" she whispered. The word was flat and dark and ugly. Her heart began to hammer painfully against her ribs.

Charles laughed. "Only the fish that ate him, I suppose."

Horror squeezed Isobel's throat, cutting off her air. She couldn't have heard them correctly. Surely Honoria and Charles hadn't *killed* a man. Not for incompetence.

But they had.

She felt her stomach churn. Her panicked thoughts flew up the stairs to the third floor, to the nursery, where her son was.

Children die all the time.

She picked up her skirts and flew up the stairs, fear pounding in her throat, prodding her to run. She had to get to her son. She had to take her child away, far, far away where the monsters could never touch him, never hurt him.

Children die all the time.

So did grown men like Jonathan Hart.

Half an hour later she clutched Robin's hand as they descended the stairs. "We're going on an adventure, Robbie, but we must be very quiet, and very quick," she whispered.

"Will Jamie be there? Will we visit one of his papa's ships?" her son asked, running a hand along the polished oak railing.

"I don't know, darling." She wished he'd hurry, but she didn't want to frighten him.

"Lord Westlake tells me stories about the sea. Can we visit the sea?" he chirped.

"Isobel."

Charles's gruff voice slashed across her fragile nerves like a knife. He stood at the bottom of the stairs, waiting for her. Jane Kirk stood behind him, a cruel imitation of a smile on her hard face. Isobel's heart climbed her throat.

"Where do you think you're going?" Charles asked, his piggy eyes sharp on her.

Isobel squeezed Robin's hand to keep him still.

"I'm taking Robin to the park," she managed.

"It's nearly tea time," Charles said.

"Your gown is a mess, Countess," Jane noted. "Whatever have you been doing today?" she asked, smirking as if she knew. Charles too regarded her with odd speculation.

"Mother will want to see you when she gets home," he said. "Go back upstairs and wait."

Isobel's chest tightened, her head buzzed with terror. "Come Robin, let's go back upstairs," she said. She would find another way.

"No, I'd like to hear his Latin," Charles said. "Come here, boy."

Robin shrank into her.

"Now!" Charles roared.

But Robin didn't move, and Isobel clung to her son, unable to make her fingers let go. Charles jerked his head at Jane, and she ascended the steps, her footsteps echoing through the house like a death march. She took Robin's free hand and dragged him away from his mother. Isobel let go, because she had to, so he wouldn't be frightened or hurt. Jane turned the boy over to his uncle and sent Isobel a look of triumph that chilled her blood.

Children died all the time.

Chapter 37

"**L**ady Marianne is in your study, my lord," Burridge informed Phineas, waking him up.

"Probably here to see Carrington. Let him know she's arrived," Phineas muttered, and shut his eyes against the daggers of light trying to impale his aching eyeballs. He'd prowled the docks until dawn, looking for anyone who might know of an unusual shipment due at the Bosun's Belle in the next few days.

There was no better way to get information than by drinking with a sailor, and usually no better way to drown the memory of a woman, but his throbbing head was still filled with visions of Isobel perched on his lap, her head thrown back in the throes of passion.

He pulled the pillow over his face, but his valet nudged him again.

"Burridge, go 'way if you know what's good for you."

"Her ladyship asked me not to tell His Grace she was here. It's you she wants to see. She told me if I didn't wake you straight away, then she'd come up here and do it herself, and I believe she would, my lord. She's a formidable lady for a countess."

A less flattering description came to mind. He tossed the pillow aside and winced at the harsh morning light. "Then you'd better get me ready to hold court."

* * *

Three-quarters of an hour later he found Marianne pacing his study. Judging by the empty tumbler, she had eschewed Burridge's tea in favor of a tot of whisky.

She turned to face him, looking pointedly at the clock. "I've been waiting nearly an hour, Phineas. Ladies don't take that long to dress."

"Burridge insisted I look my best." He gave her a mocking bow that made his head hurt.

"You still look six shades of dreadful. You really must give up your life of dissipation."

He ignored the barb. "Fresh tea, some breakfast, perhaps?"

"Coffee," she said, and he ordered it, and slid into the nearest chair.

"What brings you out at dawn?" he croaked, though it was nearly ten.

"Gloves," she said triumphantly, dropping them on the table and looking at him like a governess admonishing a naughty child.

They were lady's gloves, black satin, elbow length, and very plain. He knew at once who they belonged to. If he picked one up and sniffed it, it would carry the faint trace of her perfume.

He did not want to have this conversation with Marianne. Not now. He forced his split lip into a roguish grin. "Do they have something to do with me? I never tell a lady's secrets, Marianne."

She raised her eyebrows. "They are Isobel's gloves, Phineas. Aunt Augusta found them in the portrait room and gave them to me, in case I knew to whom they belonged. I wondered why Isobel was in that room with you. She was gone from the salon for quite some time, and when I considered it, so were you, and you can be sure I considered it most carefully after I noted the way the pair of you were looking at each other at tea yesterday."

"Have you ever considered a career as a Bow Street Runner?" he asked.

She frowned. "I came to have a serious discussion, Phineas, and I'm not leaving until I get one. Now, about you and Isobel—"

"You are mistaken in your assumptions, Marianne," he said flatly.

"Am I? Her gloves were behind the curtain, Phineas. What on earth would Isobel have been doing there, if you please?"

Kissing him. Holding him. Hiding from fears he didn't fully understand.

"Perhaps she was looking for the necessary," he said baldly, hoping to shock Marianne and throw her off the scent, but the look in her eyes told him she was not going to let this rest with a flippant, easy answer. He let out a long breath.

"Have you spoken to Isobel about this?" he asked. He watched as his brazen sister lowered her eyes and actually blushed. His stomach rolled with dread. "Oh, Marianne, what have you done?" he asked.

The bold stare returned with a vengeance. "I? You are the one who let me make a fool of myself, asking you to arrange a tryst for Isobel with Gilbert Fielding. How mortifying! Of course I haven't spoken to her. I've embarrassed myself enough, thank you. That's why I'm speaking to you."

Fielding's name rang painfully in Phineas's head. "If it's any comfort, I think you were right about Gilbert, Marianne. He's a good man, probably perfect for her."

"Oh, Phineas, don't be a fool! Gilbert Fielding is in love with Miranda, unfortunately, and Isobel . . . well, I've seen the way she looks at you. It's how I looked at Adam when

I thought I couldn't have him, while I was still betrothed to Edmond."

He had thought he was being discreet. No doubt so did Isobel, but he remembered all too well how the secret passion that burned between Marianne and Adam had been obvious to everyone.

He shut his eyes. "Look, nothing will come of it, and it's best forgotten. Gilbert must marry money, and since Carrington will never let him marry Miranda, Isobel is his next best choice. He'll make her a pleasant husband."

Marianne snorted. "For the most famous lover in London, you know damned little about love! No woman wants to be any man's 'next best choice.' Nor does any woman worth the name want a 'pleasant' husband."

"Isobel is what he needs," he insisted stubbornly. "And he is probably what she needs."

"Fool. *You* are what she needs!"

"Not in her opinion, Marianne. Will you leave this alone?" he demanded. Isobel's heated refusal of his proposal still stung, even after several barrels worth of ale, or rum, or possibly both. He rubbed his aching temples, wishing Marianne gone with the rest of the heartless bow-legged women.

"In her opinion? What does that mean? Just how far has this gone,

He dared not answer that, but had to give her something, or she'd keep him here all day.

"I proposed to her, Marianne. She refused me." That admission was surely less damaging to Isobel's reputation than tales of stolen cherries and masks and anonymous trysts in dark corners.

Marianne leapt to her feet with a gasp. "Oh, Phineas, you didn't! What on earth would make you do something so foolish? You barely know Isobel! Is this a joke of some kind? You obviously have no regard for her. It was a cruel thing to do, and I'm not surprised she said no. She has *reasons* for not wanting to marry again!"

And they were as plain as the black dress on her back. "She loved Maitland," he muttered, still stunned by the idea that Robert Maitland could engender such passion. "My offer was genuine, by the way," he said, but Marianne ignored that.

"Loved Maitland? Good heavens, it was quite the opposite. It was a very unhappy match, and she's not eager to repeat the experience."

He frowned, puzzled now, and Marianne's expression softened with sympathy.

"You really meant to marry her? Poor Phin. You're hardly her type." She poured out a cup of coffee and sat down next to him. "Here, you look like you could do with this." His stomach curled in objection. "Now tell me why you proposed."

He set the coffee down untouched. "Carrington wants me to marry. Isobel would have done as well as anyone else," he said, hoping Marianne would think he merely wished to upset the duke by choosing the most unlikely wife possible, and drop the subject. But something Marianne had said tugged at him. "If Isobel didn't love Maitland, why does she still wear mourning for him?"

Marianne shook her head. "I don't know. Maybe to warn away suitors who only want to marry her for her fortune. Or perhaps she thinks Honoria and Charles expect it of her. If that's the reason, then her loyalty is misplaced. Neither of them is in mourning. Phineas, I don't think things are as they should be in that house."

Neither did he, but there was damned little he could tell Marianne about it.

"Poor Isobel is so unhappy, and now I understand. You're obviously the reason."

"Me?" Phineas asked. She did not seem unhappy in his arms. However, he recalled her fear for her son's life, and the tortured look on her face as she leapt from the carriage after his clumsy proposal. Fortunately, Marianne didn't wait for an explanation.

"Yes, you. Your offer was badly timed. She doesn't need a husband. Not yet anyway. What she needs is a lover." She held up a hand when he opened his mouth to protest. "I know I suggested Gilbert Fielding, but that was before I realized how you felt about Isobel. Perhaps *you* could seduce her."

Phineas wondered if Adam had put his wife up to this. "Marianne, have you considered that perhaps this is not your concern?"

"Of course it is! Isobel is my friend, and you are my brother. I assume you're quite proficient at seducing ladies, given your reputation. I doubt if all the stories are true, of course, but where there is smoke, there's fire." She looked at him with a gleam in her eye. "It *isn't* all true, is it?"

Was this what men felt like when he cornered them and badgered them until they could only tell him the truth? It was damned uncomfortable. He remained stubbornly silent.

"Well, it doesn't matter," she said at last. "The important thing is finding out just what Robert Maitland did to Isobel. They were only married for three years before he died of fever."

Phineas's head came up. "What?"

She rolled her eyes. "Do pay attention. I said they were only married a few years."

"And she—you—believe he died of a fever?"

She frowned at him. "Whatever is wrong with you? Isobel told me he did, so why shouldn't I believe it?"

Because it wasn't true. Robert Maitland had been shot to death on the beach at Waterfield, by smugglers. Which side he was on, smuggler or innocent fool, was cause for speculation. Was that Isobel's secret?

"It was sudden, and he was away from London at the

time. He's buried in the family crypt at Ashdown Park," Marianne said.

Robert Maitland lay under a plain stone in the churchyard at Waterfield. It was recorded in the thick dossier Adam held on the man.

"That aside, if we knew what Robert did to make Isobel so unhappy, you could fix it, couldn't you?" Marianne hinted again, leaning toward him like a conspirator.

Or perhaps the secret lay in what Isobel had done to Robert. He avoided Marianne's penetrating gaze. His skin was on fire and his head ached.

You don't understand! It is I who am not what I seem!

Suspicion rolled through his stomach and tried to claw its way up his throat.

In his cup-shot brain, Lady M laughed.

Chapter 38

"**H**onoria is ready to see you now," Jane Kirk said the next morning, unlocking the door to Isobel's room.

Isobel had been pacing the floor all night, dressed and ready, awaiting Honoria's summons like a condemned prisoner.

Her teeth clenched at the sight of Jane's oily smirk. She loved to see her in trouble, but this time she looked particularly smug.

"I see you changed your gown. Not that it will help you," Jane said coldly as they walked along the hall. She leaned close to Isobel. *"She knows."*

Isobel's heart skipped a beat, but she kept walking, giving the appearance of calm even if she didn't feel it. What did Honoria know? That she overheard her conversation with Charles, perhaps, or knew that she'd tried to take her son out of the house?

"I saw you with Blackwood. You were getting out of his coach on Bond Street yesterday. Your dress was rumpled and his lordship wasn't even wearing a cravat. I came to the only conclusion I could."

Isobel's feet stopped of their own accord.

"So I was right!" Jane crowed. "You're his whore. I told

Charles at once, of course, and Honoria as well, when she arrived home. They hardly believed it."

Isobel's knees turned to water, and she put a hand against the wall to steady herself. "You told Honoria?"

"Of course," Jane said sweetly. "It will be good to be rid of you at last, lady high and mighty!"

Isobel stared at Honoria's spy, read the malice in her eyes. "Why?" she asked, forcing out the single word.

Jane's lips twisted bitterly. "You really don't know?" She tossed her chin. "I suppose they never bothered to tell you. *I* was supposed to marry Robert Maitland. It was all arranged. The Maitlands were poor, and my father may have been a cit, but he had money, and I inherited every penny. I was going to be a countess until you showed up. Your father was willing to pay a devil's ransom to be rid of you, so Robert married you instead, and I was given a place in the household, companion instead of countess, because Charles still wanted my money." Jane leaned close to Isobel. "He wouldn't even marry me. Now it's your turn to be left with nothing!"

Isobel swallowed, but the lump in her throat would not move. Jane would never know how sincerely she wished things had been different, and Jane had been Robert's bride.

Now, thanks to Jane's hatred, her worst fears were about to come true. She had gambled everything precious for a few moments of pleasure in Blackwood's arms, and she'd lost.

Isobel the Harlot.

Isobel the Fool.

She was not invisible now, and there was no way to explain this away.

Jane grabbed her arm roughly, tugging her forward. "Come on, they're waiting, and I wouldn't miss this for anything."

Isobel pulled free. "Take your hands off me," she commanded, and met Jane's eyes, letting her read the disdain in her expression, the difference in their station that would never change. Jane slid her eyes to the floor.

"You'll only make it worse for yourself if you dawdle. Honoria hates to be kept waiting," Jane muttered.

Isobel walked down the stairs, concentrating on taking each step with dignity, though her heart pounded. She had to find a way to keep Robin safe.

Jane slithered past her and skittered along the corridor to knock on the door of the salon before opening it.

"She's here, Honoria," she gushed.

Isobel took a deep breath and smoothed her expression, determined not to let them read fear or guilt on her face. Her legs trembled but she held herself with grace.

Charles did not bother to rise. His eyes slid over her from hairline to toes, and he sniggered. Isobel felt her skin grow hot.

"Well well. Who could have imagined this?" he said. "Blackwood with *you*? I'll have to check the betting book at White's. Perhaps it was a wager, or a dare."

Behind Isobel, Jane giggled.

"You may go," Honoria said to her companion.

"But I thought we were—" Jane began. Isobel did not bother to look at her. Her eyes were on Honoria's cold countenance. At least she'd be spared the indignity of Jane's presence. She waited for the door to close.

No one invited her to sit, so she stood, her back straight, her eyes on the wall.

"Is what Jane told us true?" Honoria asked.

Isobel could tell them Jane was mistaken, that Blackwood had merely been seeing her home from tea at Marianne's.

"I—" she began, and closed her mouth. She was tired of lying, tired of subterfuge. Charles and Honoria had far greater sins on their souls than she did.

But there was Robin to consider, and surely accusations and admissions would only put him in greater peril. She lowered her eyes so they would not see the hatred burning there. She clenched her fists in the folds of her gown.

"I must assume the worst, since you won't answer me," Honoria said. "You are your mother's daughter after all."

Isobel's stomach curled in upon itself in mortification, but still her tongue remained glued to her teeth. *Speak up, deny him. Save yourself*, fear needled her.

But pride would not allow it. She did not regret Blackwood, even now. "I have done nothing wrong."

"Nothing wrong?" Honoria trilled. "Not by Charlotte Fraser's low standards, perhaps, but Robert's will was plain enough about what we expect of you. We can no longer have you living in this house, Isobel, or remaining in this city, bringing scandal and shame upon us."

Blood drummed in Isobel's ears. She had been found guilty, and all that was left was to wait for the sentence. Did they still put wanton women in convents? She stood very still, her limbs stiff, everything but her ears and eyes numb, useless.

"We've decided you will marry again," Honoria said.

"What?" Isobel croaked. Could Blackwood have spoken to Charles? A frisson of hope cascaded through her, but Honoria's cold expression dashed the possibility of any reprieve.

"We've had an unexpected offer from someone in the North."

"Far, far North." Charles chuckled.

Honoria quelled him with a glance. "You will leave tonight."

Just like that? She felt her limbs loosen, and reached out to grip the back of the nearest chair. "Who—Who is he?" she asked.

"It hardly matters," Honoria said. "You can't stay in

London, and we have to tell people something once you're gone."

Isobel shut her eyes. They had sentenced her to death. Just like Jonathan Hart.

There would be no wedding. She would simply disappear.

"What about Robin? What will happen to my son?" Her eyes flew from Honoria to Charles. There was no compassion, no regret, in either face.

"Obviously the boy cannot stay in London now," Honoria said. "None of us can. This scandal will ruin us all."

Charles smirked. "You wanted the boy to have a holiday by the sea, didn't you?"

Honoria's head whipped around. "Charles! Be silent!"

"What difference does it make now?" Charles asked, but he subsided into sulky silence.

"Waterfield?" Isobel gasped. Where Robert had died, and Jonathan Hart had been murdered. The ugly rush of color in Honoria's face confirmed it.

Fury replaced Isobel's fear. "No!" She could not, would not, let them murder Robin.

She fought for an idea, a way to save them both, but Charles was smirking at her, his eyes cold and dark and empty, and Honoria's mouth was a tight pucker of disdain. "No!" she said again, her fists clenched. "I will not let you harm him!"

Charles laughed as he crossed the room to grab her arm and twist it painfully behind her back. "You'll do as you're told for once."

She clenched her teeth against the pain, refusing to give him the satisfaction of making her cry out.

Charles pulled harder when she refused to move toward the door, but she stood her ground. "I want to see my son," she said to Honoria, fighting the pain. If she had Robin in her arms, could look into his eyes, she'd think of something.

Honoria turned away. "No. You are not fit company for an impressionable child. Don't make more of a fool of yourself than you already have," she said coldly. "You will go to your room and get ready to leave. I have already ordered your maid to pack a few things for you. If you make a fuss, I shall send Jane up with a sleeping draught. For the boy's sake, you will cooperate."

She dangled that last thread of hope for Isobel to cling to, a promise that Robin would be safe if she did as they wished. She knew it was a lie, and fought to free herself from Charles's grip, but he twisted viciously, until a moan broke from her throat. She sagged, the agony unbearable, made worse by imagining the pain and terror her helpless child would endure.

Honoria smirked, her eyes glittering. "So your pride is broken at last. You should have thought of the consequences before you became Blackwood's whore."

"Why don't you write the brat a letter while you're waiting?" Charles said mockingly as he dragged her up the stairs. "We might even let him read it."

A letter.

Charles shoved her into her bedroom, and Isobel crossed to her desk and began to write. She barely heard the key scrape in the lock.

The door opened again, and Isobel leapt to her feet. A bottle of perfume spilled, and she snatched up the letter she'd been writing before it was ruined. She hid it behind her back and faced the door, her heart hammering in her throat.

It was only Sarah.

The maid frowned. "What's going on around here today, my lady? Lord Charles had to unlock your door for me. There are four maids packing for Lady Honoria, and no one seems to know where she's going. Now they tell me I'm to pack a box for you. Jane Kirk is all smiles and secrets as well. It's a horrible sight."

"They're leaving?" Isobel asked. The letter slipped from her fingers, slithered to the floor. "Sarah, where's Robin?"

"Upstairs, of course, having his tea," Sarah said calmly. Her eyes widened. "My lady, you're as pale as death. Are you ill? Is something wrong?"

Isobel forced down the panic that rose in her chest. She needed a clear head. "Very wrong. I need your help, Sarah. Can you slip away, deliver a letter?" she asked.

"Of course."

Isobel was grateful that she didn't ask any questions, though she knew Sarah must be curious. She picked up the note and folded it with shaking hands.

"It's for the Marquess of Blackwood."

Sarah's brows shot up to her cap, but she tucked the letter into her apron pocket and turned to go without asking any questions.

"Sarah? Tell him to hurry. I need him."

Chapter 39

Marianne left her brother's house with a mission. Phineas deserved to be happy, and so did Isobel. Thanks to a pair of lost gloves and Phineas's misguided proposal, she could see now that Isobel and Phineas were perfect for each other. They just needed a well-meaning friend to help them see it. And since she was deliriously in love herself, who better than she? She smiled at Crane as she crossed the front hall, her boot heels clicking purposefully on the marble tiles.

Adam would forbid her from interfering if he knew, tell her again how planets and stars managed to orbit the sky without any help from her, but this was Phineas, her handsome, eligible, lonely brother, and Isobel, her dearest friend. Since the sparks were already there, it would hardly require interference on an astronomical scale to bring them together. Just a nudge, a push in the right direction, should do it. It could hardly even be called interference, now could it?

Crane opened the front door and preceded her down the front steps to instruct her footman to open the door of her coach. It wasn't necessary, but Crane was a butler who liked to put the stamp of protocol on every duty, no matter how trifling.

Marianne considered. If she was going to convince Isobel

and Phineas to become lovers, then she'd need to rent a house, set up a love nest, and—

A figure came hurtling along the sidewalk and crashed into Crane. He fell into the open door of the coach, his bottom in the air, his polished shoes kicking at the wind. The footman holding the door caught the young woman's arm before she toppled in on top of the poor man.

Marianne stopped on the steps and watched the melee. Crane scrambled to his feet as the woman straightened her plain bonnet and apologized. "I'm sorry, I'm sure. I was in a hurry and I didn't see you there."

"Aren't you Sarah, Isobel's maid?" Marianne asked, recognizing the girl.

"Yes, my lady." Sarah dipped a curtsy.

Crane glared at her as he straightened his coat and brushed at imaginary specks on the dark wool of his breeches. "Young woman, the servants' entrance is around back, but hooligans who go about plowing into their betters need not apply!" He turned on his heel and climbed the stairs to the front door.

Sarah blinked at the butler's retreating back. "I'm not here about a position! I have a letter for the marquess." She held it up to one of the footmen as Crane disappeared into the house. "See?" she asked tartly.

Marianne snatched it from the maid's hand before the footman could move. "Is it from Countess Isobel?" she asked, though she could see that it was. Isobel's feminine scrawl swirled across the fine vellum, and the note was drenched in her violet perfume. That could only mean one thing.

A love letter!

Delight raced through Marianne's body. She itched to break the seal and read the words of love Isobel had written to Phineas. Had she reconsidered his proposal?

If she knew what the letter said, she could better plan her matchmaking schemes to suit.

She was curious, as well. She had never received a love letter, at least not one on paper. Adam didn't write poems or notes. He sent bouquets of flowers to her room. Each flower had a meaning, and each meaning added to the message he wished to convey. It was never as simple as "I love you." It could take all morning to look up each flower and puzzle out her husband's thoughts, which were usually very romantic indeed. Still, there were times she wished he would just scrawl a note and leave it on her pillow.

She smiled at Sarah. "I'll deliver this for you. I'm just on my way in to see Blackwood," she fibbed.

Sarah dipped another curtsy. "Thank you kindly, my lady. I must get back."

Marianne watched her go. This was going to be fun— secret love letters, romantic trysts, even a wedding to plan, perhaps. She tingled with excitement.

A lady's laugh, all too familiar, rang out from the street.

"Miranda?" Marianne called, but her sister didn't hear her. She was riding with Gilbert Fielding, and they only had eyes for each other. Augusta's footman, obviously sent to chaperone, was lagging much too far behind his charge.

She watched in horror as Miranda leaned toward Gilbert, obviously about to make a cake of herself by falling into his arms in the middle of the street, right in front of the home of the notorious Marquess of Blackwood. Another Archer scandal was in the making, and this one would not be Phineas's fault.

She could not stand by and let her young and impressionable sister fall in love with Gilbert Fielding. Carrington would never allow her to marry him, and Miranda would end up with a broken heart.

Marianne knew from experience that a woman did not want to marry elsewhere when she imagined herself in love. She was spoiled for any other man by that first bloom of passion, and especially so if the match was doomed from the outset. Carrington and Great-Aunt Augusta would disown Miranda if she married against their wishes. Gilbert Fielding might be handsome, but he was penniless. How long would love endure with no money to sustain it? Without family connections or dowry, Gilbert would still need to join the army to earn his bread, and Miranda would face a miserable life of following the drum. It was unthinkable.

Marianne stuffed Isobel's letter into her reticule and crossed the street to stop disaster.

Chapter 40

I sobel lit the candles in her room with shaking fingers. The bright flame hurt her eyes for a moment, then pushed back the edges of the darkness. She stood in the circle of light and listened to the sounds of Maitland House moving around her.

Upstairs, Robin would be in bed by now, fast asleep, unaware of the danger he was in.

No one had come for her. Not Blackwood, not Charles or Honoria. Even Sarah had not returned. But soon, now that it was dark, they would drag her away, and she would disappear forever.

She wondered how they planned to do it. Would they take her to the sea and drown her like Jonathan Hart? Or perhaps they'd just shoot her, like Robert. She imagined Robert Maitland's fleshless hand reaching for her from the grave, and clenched her own fist.

She would not go without a fight.

She crossed to the window for the hundredth time and looked again, searching the street for a tall dark-haired knight on a white horse, galloping to the rescue, but the cobbles were empty.

Her breath caught in her throat as a coach turned the corner and stopped in front of the house.

The front door opened and yellow light lit the side of the

coach. The identifying crest was draped in black, making the coach sinister and anonymous.

She glanced at the door of her room, expecting them to burst in, making herself ready to fight for her life, but it remained closed, the hall outside silent.

She turned back to watch as a long shadow slid down the front steps.

Honoria.

Jewels glittered at her throat and wrists as she disappeared into the dark vehicle in a slither of blue satin, as if she were going to a party.

Charles followed his mother. He stood on the step of the coach, and the harsh shadows made his face ugly. His fingers were fat and white against the darkness as he reached for something.

Or someone.

Isobel felt the scream gather in her throat, tear loose and rip her heart out with it.

"Robbie!" She shrieked her son's name as Jane Kirk led him out. He tottered down the steps on sleepy feet, his hair mussed from bed.

Isobel twisted the latch on the window, but her fingers were clumsy and it wouldn't budge. She pounded on the glass in desperation, clawed at it, her eyes on her child. "Robbie! Come back!" she yelled, but he didn't look up, couldn't hear her. "Run!" she howled, but Charles lifted him into the coach.

She had only a glimpse of his white face before they shut the door.

Only Jane Kirk, left standing on the sidewalk, turned to look up at her, her smile malicious.

Isobel watched as the coach carrying her son, her very life, drove away.

Jane turned on her heel and climbed the front steps. The door closed, leaving only the darkness of the empty street.

* * *

"Really, Isobel, you'll only harm yourself," Jane said. "There's no one to help you."

Isobel's throat was raw, her hands bruised from pounding on the door, calling for Sarah, for Finch, for *anyone* to release her from her prison and help her save her son.

Only Jane came, and just to mock her through the keyhole.

"I'm in charge now, and I have some of Honoria's laudanum. If you don't stop yelling, I will drug you."

"They're going to kill Robin, Jane! Even you can't be so coldhearted that you'd let them harm an innocent child!" Isobel cried.

"Innocent?" Jane growled the word. "The brat bears the taint of Fraser blood, doesn't he? It's better if he dies."

Isobel fought the crushing weight of desperation and tugged at the lock again. "What are they giving you to stand by and let them do this? I will give you more!"

Jane laughed. "You can't give me what I want! I'm going to take it for myself. I'm going to marry Charles, and then I shall be Countess of Ashdown, and *my* son will be the next earl, just the way it was supposed to be."

Isobel shut her eyes, seeing a truth Jane did not. "Don't be a fool! Charles wants to marry a woman with a title, and money!"

"Money?" Jane scoffed. "In a few days the Maitlands will be back, the richest family in England. They will buy and sell titles. Unlike you, I know all the secrets in this house, and they'll do what I want from now on, or I'll tell."

"Jane, they'll kill you if you cross them. You'll die," Isobel whispered through the crack.

"What did you say?" Jane asked.

"Charles will kill you."

"Charles will do as I say if he doesn't want to hang for treason! By morning you'll be gone for good, and I'll be on my way to Waterfield." She heard Jane's footsteps retreat down the hall.

Waterfield! Panic rose in Isobel's throat. She had wanted Robin to have a holiday by the sea. Charles and Honoria intended to give him one.

She had to hurry or it would be too late. She needed to find a coach, or at least a horse, but first she had to get out of this room, and out of Maitland House.

The streetlamp stared in the window, a soulless eye in the darkness, an intrusive busybody, just as it had been the night Blackwood came to her room.

The night he'd climbed out her window.

She crossed to the window and pushed on the unyielding sash. Taking off her shoe, she smacked the stubborn latch until it gave in at last and opened with a squeal. She leaned out, taking a deep breath of damp night air. The ground was invisible in the darkness. She shook off a wave of dread. It was the only way.

Blackwood's way.

He'd made it look easy. Isobel swung her leg over the sill and hovered for a breathless moment between two worlds. Her fingers clung to the frame, but there was no time for hesitation.

She forced herself to let go, and lowered herself over the edge.

Marianne sighed as she reached the quiet sanctuary of her own salon at last. It was past ten when she left her great-aunt's house after a bitter struggle with Miranda. A long talk had yielded nothing but hysterical tears and threats to elope if she could not have permission to marry the man she loved.

Augusta had sent up tea laced with laudanum, and Marianne waited until her sister fell asleep. Hopefully, Miranda would see sense in the morning, but her heart ached for her.

Gilbert Fielding was charming, handsome, and exactly the kind of first love a woman never forgot.

Adam wasn't home, and Northcott could not say when he was expected. Marianne looked up at the portrait of her husband. Were all Archer women fated to fight for a happy ending with the man they loved? She dropped her reticule and gloves with a sigh.

The scent of violet perfume rose like a shade, and Marianne smiled. She'd entirely forgotten Isobel's love letter. Reading it now would soothe away the cares of the day, give back her faith in true love.

She unfolded it and scanned the scrawled note. Her smile melted in a gasp of horror.

It wasn't a love letter.

It was a plea for help.

She dropped the note and ran to the door. "Northcott! I need my coach at once!"

Chapter 41

"**T**his is bigger than we thought, Phineas," Adam said quietly. "According to Gibbs, Maitland's package isn't a package at all. It's a person."

Phineas's interest kindled. He looked at Adam over the width of his desk. "Does Gibbs know who?"

"Not yet. Someone important, though. The innkeeper has made over his best room. Not just clean sheets either. That would be a miracle in itself in a dockside inn. Apparently Charles has provided silk bed curtains, Turkey carpets, French wine, beeswax candles and silver candlesticks, among other luxuries."

Phineas's brows rose. "The French king?"

Adam looked away. "Louis XVIII is still safely tucked away at Aylesbury," he said, dismissing Phineas's question with odd abruptness. "Any other ideas? Your Lady M, perhaps?"

Phineas felt a chill run up his spine as he met the suspicion in Adam's eyes. "Hardly *my* Lady M, Westlake."

"For your sake, I sincerely hope not. She's proven remarkably elusive for you, hasn't she? Can I count on you to do your duty, no matter who appears at the inn tonight?" Adam asked.

Phineas felt his stomach rise. What if Isobel turned out to be Lady M? Could he shoot her, arrest her, watch her hang for treason? He looked up to find Adam watching him, his eyes wary.

" 'For England, Anything'? Isn't that the pledge, Westlake?" he asked smoothly. Adam's shoulders relaxed and he smiled.

"Let's have a drink, shall we?" he said, and took a heavy stone bottle from his latest cargo. He poured two glasses and raised a toast. "To unmasking Lady M."

The sweet liquor slid down Phineas's throat like acid.

An hour later, in the black and stinking alley behind the Bosun's Belle, Phineas felt the cold and unmistakable nudge of a pistol behind his left ear.

"Well? Are you going to rob me or rape me?" he asked, carefully reaching for his own weapon.

"Stand down, lad. Lord Blackwood is on our side." Phineas recognized Westlake's familiar voice and the pistol was withdrawn at once. "My men have orders to shoot anyone suspicious, Phin, and you most definitely fit the description."

"What's happening inside?" Phineas asked, shoving his pistol into his coat.

"According to Gibbs, the package is already tucked away upstairs. I have men in the alley and in the taproom, but no one has been able to get upstairs to have a look," Adam replied. "The innkeeper has an army of toughs on hand tonight, and their prime duty is keeping anyone from climbing those stairs."

"Any clues as to who's up there?"

"No," Adam sighed. "Gibbs didn't see her arrive—if it *is* a woman, of course."

Phineas peered cautiously over the fence at the lighted windows of the top floor of the inn.

"If you're considering climbing a wall or scaling the rooftop to see for yourself if it's her, my friend, then don't. I wasn't joking about the number of men waiting for trouble," Adam told him.

"Hardly necessary, old man." Phineas pointed through the jagged fence. "Look at all the torches in the yard. They must still be expecting someone. Or someone *else*, at least."

They drew back against the fence as the clop of wooden heels echoed up the street. Adam cocked his pistol and held his breath, but Phineas put a hand over the barrel as a dockside whore sauntered by without seeing them. She disappeared into the inn to look for custom or to spend her wages on gin.

A distant rumble made Phineas's ears prick, and he stared down the street, waiting as the sound grew louder and closer, moving toward the Bosun's Belle. The ring of iron-clad wheels on the cobbles told him it wasn't a local wagon or a simple handcart.

"Is this it?" Adam murmured, craning to see, his face yellow in the flickering torchlight that spilled from the inn. Phineas pulled him back into the shadows as men filed out of the inn to watch the coach arrive.

"Possibly," he muttered as the horses came into sight, a fine pair of matched grays. Charles Maitland owned a pair of grays.

You don't understand. It is I who am not what I seem!

Isobel's frantic words echoed in his mind again, and Phineas scowled at the oncoming vehicle, wondering if she was inside.

"Crests are covered," Adam muttered.

"It's Maitland's coach," Phineas replied. "I recognize the horses." The shades were drawn, sealing the coach's occupants away from prying eyes, making them anonymous. His stomach clenched. Isobel, his lover, the only woman he had ever proposed to, might be inside, and she could still turn out to be Lady M.

He would be just as guilty of treason as she, since he hadn't told Adam. The parson's noose was suddenly a macabre joke.

Phineas took a breath and pushed off the wall, crouching low in the coach's broad shadow, running alongside as it maneuvered through the narrow gateway. He heard Adam's indrawn breath, knew he hesitated only a second before following.

Once inside the yard, Phineas rolled away from the vehicle, landing in the doorway of the stable with Adam right behind him. Surprised horses stomped indignantly at the intrusion. Phineas slid into the shadows and waited for the shout that would come if they'd been seen, but every eye was on the coach as it came to a halt in the torchlit ring.

He stared at it, waiting for it to open, to reveal the man—or woman—inside, but for a long moment nothing moved.

Phineas stayed motionless in the moldy straw. The acrid smoke of burning pitch stung his eyes and dried the back of his throat. He blinked away sweat and watched the yard shimmer in a haze of dust and smoke. Leveling his pistol at the door of the coach, he steeled himself to shoot whoever got out first if he had to, even if it turned out to be the woman he loved.

Chapter 42

Isobel dangled from the side of Maitland House in the dark, trying to find a foothold.

Blackwood made this look like the easiest thing in the world, damn him, while she had almost fallen twice.

She had no idea how long she'd been out here, kicking her feet in the wind, so to speak, but her progress was dreadfully slow.

Her fingers ached, her arms were shaking with fatigue, and she clamped her teeth together to keep from shivering. She should have thought to bring a cloak, or a shawl. Or a ladder.

She almost lost her fragile hold on the wall as another coach turned the corner. The horses were moving fast, the clatter of hooves almost deafening in the quiet of the narrow street.

They'd come for her.

Her heart leapt in her chest, pounded against her ribs, strongly advising her to run, or fly, or climb, as fast as she could.

Turning her head, her cheek scraped the rough brick, and shock leapt through her whole body at the sting. She looked up at the window of her room, still only a few miserable feet above her. The curtains sailed outward on the night breeze, beckoning her back to safety like a lover's arms, but she could not go back. She would not.

Robin needed her.

She lowered one foot and prayed for a toehold. Below her the door of the coach swung open, and she heard the creak of the steps being lowered. She shut her eyes for a moment, wishing herself truly invisible, a shadow on the face of Maitland House. Fear lent her courage to find the next handhold. She had to get to the ground before they discovered her room was empty and came looking for her.

She heard the sound of running feet on the sidewalk, a light, urgent, feminine staccato. Without a bonnet or cloak, the figure was immediately recognizable.

"Marianne!" she called out, her voice a rusty croak. She wondered if Marianne had even heard her, but her friend whirled, scanning the street.

"Up here."

Marianne's face tipped upward in the glow of the streetlamp, and the shocked gape of her open mouth swallowed the whiteness of her face.

"Don't ring the bell," Isobel said softly, but Marianne was already pushing through the hedge, coming toward the base of the wall.

"Oh, Isobel, I stole your letter. I'm so sorry, I thought— well, never mind, Adam was right all along about not interfering, it seems, though I'll never tell him so. I came as soon as I could." She paused. "Are you going up or down?"

"Down," Isobel panted. "They've taken Robin. I need to—" Her foot slipped and she gave a whimper of fright. Her fingers constricted on the brick, and her body pressed hard against the pitiless wall and clung.

"Isobel! Wherever did you learn to do that?" Marianne asked.

Blackwood.

His name echoed in her brain. He had not received her note, that's why he hadn't come. Still, her heart nagged, she'd refused him, run away. She shut her eyes, forcing herself to concentrate on reaching the ground, getting Robin back safely. Her foot slipped and she swallowed a cry of frustration. Oh, how she wished Blackwood here!

But he wasn't. She forced herself to move again, and her satin slipper snagged on the rough brick. Blackwood had done this in boots and his feet were bigger. The wind tugged at her skirts. Breeches, she decided, must make all the difference.

Then Marianne touched her foot, and Isobel knew she was almost safe. She sagged in relief and her foot slipped. Her torn fingers refused to hold on any longer and she tumbled backward.

The kindly hedge—and Marianne's body—broke her fall. The two countesses lay panting in the shrubbery for a moment, tangled in their petticoats, trying to catch their breath.

Isobel dragged herself upright. "Marianne, I need to get to Waterfield Abbey." She looked at the Westlake coach, parked by the curb. "May I take your coach? They have Robin, you see, and I have to get to him before—" Tears cut off speech.

It didn't matter. Marianne grabbed her arm. "You can't go alone, and this is partly my fault. I'm going with you."

Isobel didn't argue. She plucked a twig out of her hair and climbed into the coach.

"Kent," Countess Westlake ordered the driver.

"Kent, my lady?" he asked in surprise. "The one next to Sussex?"

"Precisely. And hurry if you please," Marianne said, then bent to rummage under the seat. "Adam keeps pistols here somewhere," she told Isobel, and a moment later grinned and held one up. The dim light gleamed on the sinister metal of the barrel.

Isobel recoiled. This wasn't a game. Guns were sober, deadly things. She imagined the pistol in Charles's hand, aimed at her son.

She swallowed the bitter taste of anguish and replaced it with determination as Marianne passed the weapon to her.

"I'll teach you how to use it."

Chapter 43

Phineas wiped the sweat from his brow and stared at the dark windows of the coach. He imagined Isobel sitting demurely inside. Then he pictured her in *his* coach, perched astride him as he made quick love to her, her face flushed as he pleasured her, her ugly bonnet askew. His finger twitched on the trigger of the pistol.

The door of the inn crashed against the wall, and a burst of noisy song and the thick smell of sour ale followed the innkeeper out of the taproom. He stalked across the yard to the coach, his shoulders hunched belligerently.

The coach window slid open and Charles Maitland's face appeared, fat and sallow in the golden light.

"Ho, there, *my lord*! Your bloody 'package' is eating me out of house and home! Says he won't go until he's finished his meal," the innkeeper complained. "I agreed to do this for the gold, and I'm going to need more money. Fine French wine doesn't come cheap, and he's already had three bottles of the best."

Adam nudged Phineas. "Not Lady M, then. Any guesses as to who the gentleman might be?" he whispered.

"We'll know in a few minutes, I think," Phineas replied. "It appears the Maitlands have come to fetch him." He tried to see into the shadowed interior of the coach. Was the man another of Isobel's lovers? The idea knotted in his gut.

"You've been well paid, damn you," Charles snapped. "Enough of your insolence! Send the gentleman out at once." But Phineas noted that Charles's voice quavered and his tone lacked conviction. He mopped his face with a handkerchief.

The innkeeper folded his beefy arms over his chest, also aware that Charles was afraid, or nervous, or both.

"I said the payment wasn't enough."

Charles's mouth worked without sound. He wasn't quick enough to come up with the kind of reply that would put the greedy landlord in his place. Phineas raised an eyebrow and waited to see what Maitland would do.

"Bring the gentleman down at once, if you please, my good man, and I'll see that you get the reward you deserve."

Phineas's gut clenched at the sound of the familiar female voice coming from the coach.

"Honoria?" Adam croaked in surprise, a little too loudly. One of the henchmen turned and frowned suspiciously at the dark stable. Phineas set his finger back on the trigger of his gun, but the man turned away again.

"Charles, go inside, fetch him down," Honoria commanded.

"Wait a minute—" the innkeeper began, but Charles was already getting out, more afraid of Honoria than the bully, it seemed.

"I'll pay you when his lordship returns," Honoria promised, her tone so sweetly cajoling it made Phineas's teeth ache.

"Another hundred," the innkeeper demanded, peering into the coach. "Or some o' the jewels you're wearing will suffice, if they're real. Is that an emerald?"

Charles hesitated, half turned, his hand fisted on his walking stick.

"Go and get Lord Philip at once!" Honoria insisted, her shrill voice making a dog bark in another yard.

"Renshaw?" Adam hissed. "Blackwood—"

He didn't have to say more. Phineas felt the same chill race up his spine. Renshaw was here to exact his revenge on the French king, and the Maitlands were clearly part of the plot. The mission instantly went from dangerous to deadly. And it was personal too, if Isobel was involved.

"And you thought Maitland was just a petty smuggler," Adam muttered. "It appears treason is a family affair at Maitland House."

Phineas shut his eyes. Isobel had played him for a fool, taken his game and twisted it, using him. Anger tightened his jaw, and he stared at the dark window of the coach, waiting for a glimpse of russet hair.

"Would you care for a glass of ale while ye wait, my lady?" the innkeeper asked Honoria companionably, sure now of his payment. "The gent said you've got a long journey ahead of ye tonight."

"How indiscreet of him," Honoria said stiffly.

The man grinned. Phineas supposed he meant the smile to be charming, but he was missing three teeth, and his eyes were hard as stone, making him frightening in any light.

Phineas wished he could see Honoria's face, but a lady bold enough to come to a rendezvous in this part of London wasn't likely to be intimidated.

"If I can be of service again, my lady, you just come and see me. I like dealing with the person in charge," the man said. "Your son doesn't understand the business, if you ask me, doesn't know how to strike a bargain to everyone's advantage the way we do."

Honoria didn't answer. The innkeeper took it as encouragement and leaned closer to the window. "Now you and I, my lady, I think we could rub along together very well indeed. I have friends willing to expand the business, take in lace and fancy wine as well as brandy and gin. I know a few gentlemen o' the sea who also have goods to sell, if an investor such as yourself makes it worth their while. More money for all of us, to my way of thinking." He spoke smugly, addressing the pompous Dowager Countess Honoria Maitland with the familiarity of a fellow conspirator.

"Pirates too?" Adam hissed with a shipowner's dismay.

The door opened again, and Philip Renshaw appeared, pulling on his gloves. Charles followed him. "I barely had time to finish my meal, inedible as it was," Renshaw complained.

"My lord, time is of the essence," Honoria called from the coach, waving a handkerchief to get his attention. She leaned out, adorned with a fortune in jewels that would make any smuggler or pirate drool.

"I trust all is in readiness?" Philip said gruffly.

"Of course! Everything is just as you wished. Get in at once, if you please," Honoria said, opening the door herself and beckoning with a satin-clad hand. She turned to the innkeeper as Philip got in. "Open the gates at once. You have delayed us long enough."

Someone leapt to obey her imperious command, but the innkeeper grabbed Charles roughly by the collar before he could board the coach. "Not so fast, *my lord*. What about my money?"

The flash of the gunshot lit the inside of the coach, the roar deafening. The innkeeper spun, lifted into the air as his face dissolved in a red mist. Phineas swore and cocked his pistol, on his feet now, ready for trouble. Adam was on one knee, taking aim at the nearest man, yelling for his sailors to move in.

"Charles, get in," Honoria shrieked as the big man fell into the dust.

Leaderless, the innkeeper's men panicked. Torches crashed to the ground and died, leaving the inn yard nearly dark. Charles clambered onto the coach as the driver's whip snapped over the horses' heads. In the chaos, Honoria was screaming orders to hurry as the landlord's men began firing at the vehicle and anything else that moved.

As the coach passed the stable door, already picking up speed, Phineas leapt onto the side. He couldn't let them escape, and he had to know if Isobel was inside.

The pain in his shoulder was sudden and intense, tearing the strength out of his arm. As the coach took the corner hard and fast, he landed on the greasy cobbles, the breath driven out of his lungs. He could feel hot blood flowing over his shoulder, mixing with the icy mud that instantly soaked his clothes. He couldn't do anything but watch the Maitland coach disappear down the dark street at a full gallop. He shut his eyes in frustration.

Where the hell was Isobel?

Adam helped Phineas into the salon at De Courcey House, and he collapsed onto the settee. "Send for a doctor," he ordered Northcott. "And wake her ladyship. We'll need some bandages."

"I'm all right, Adam," Phineas grumbled. His arm was mostly numb, though his shirt was soaked and sticky with his own blood. Adam's men had splashed rum over the wound and forced a goodly measure down his throat as well. He smelled like a sailor on a payday binge.

He forced himself to sit up. As soon as she finished wailing over him, Marianne was likely to shoot him again for getting blood on her new settee. He held his head in his hands and waited. A glance at the makeshift bandage showed blood leaking through the linen. The wound needed stitching.

"Her ladyship is not at home, Lord Westlake," Northcott said calmly "She went out a little while ago. Perhaps I could be of assistance?"

"Went out?" Adam asked. "Where is she?"

"I don't know, my lord."

Phineas drew in a sharp breath, which was a mistake. His head spun and spots appeared before his eyes, threatening to pitch him into oblivion. He leaned forward.

There was a crumpled letter half hidden under the tea table. He reached for it with his uninjured arm.

The smell of Isobel's perfume hit him like another bullet.

Adam was grilling Northcott for clues as to where Marianne might be.

"Perhaps at Lady Porter-Penwarren's?" the butler suggested.

Phineas turned the letter over. Odd. It was addressed to him at Blackwood House. How the hell had it ended up here, on the floor of Adam's study? He knew, of course.

Marianne.

He read it, and read it again. The pain in his shoulder disappeared as every sense came to alert. A rush of dread ran over his battered body like a runaway horse.

"Adam, you'd better look at this," he said, and held out the letter.

Adam's face paled as he read the scrawled note.

"Why would Isobel Maitland write to you for help? She barely knows you."

Phineas didn't reply. "Northcott, did they bring my horse back?" he asked, forcing himself to stand.

Adam held up a hand. "You're in no condition to go anywhere, Blackwood. I'll send someone—"

"Marianne is with her, Adam. I found the note here, on the floor."

He watched the emotions cross his brother-in-law's face as Adam puzzled out just what that meant. It took only seconds. It was the first time Phineas had ever seen him sweat.

"Northcott, get my coach," Adam said brusquely, then turned to Phineas. "You can explain on the way to Maitland House."

* * *

"How the hell could you let this happen, Blackwood? *My wife* is in danger," Adam growled after Phineas told him everything. The thought of Marianne in peril had Adam crazed, his usual dignity forgotten. "You might have told me the truth before now. If someone hadn't saved me the bother, I'd shoot you myself."

Phineas gritted his teeth against the jolting of the coach and his own fears. "Marianne wouldn't be in danger if she hadn't stolen the letter. Neither would Isobel."

The bullet wound ached, and he clenched his fist against the pain. He stared out the window, gauging how much longer it would take to reach Maitland House.

"When this is over, I intend to marry Isobel," he said aloud.

Adam drew a sharp breath. "Marry her? Don't be a fool. The woman is a traitor."

Phineas frowned. "She's in danger, Adam, a victim."

"Is she? I seriously doubt it, but your gullibility has certainly put Marianne in jeopardy." He leaned forward. "Look at the evidence, Blackwood. That's supposed to be what you're good at, isn't it, when lust isn't clouding your judgment?"

Phineas felt his stomach twist as Adam counted Isobel's offenses off on his fingers. "She prevented you from searching Philip's office the first time you met. Does a respectable widow strike you as the kind of woman who goes around seducing strangers?"

The idea nipped at Phineas with sharp little teeth. "It wasn't like that," he muttered.

Or was it?

"And the night of Marianne's ball, she seduced you again. I had to drag you out of her embrace to question a suspect. A suspect with Isobel's handkerchief in his possession, if you'll remember."

"Coincidence," Phineas said. "There's no proof the hand-kerchief belongs to Isobel."

But the sick feeling grew. M was for Maitland.

Adam sat back. "If it's any comfort, you weren't the only one fooled. Her disguise is brilliant. She plays the role of a mousey widow to perfection. I was certainly gulled. Unfor-tunately, so was my wife."

Phineas didn't reply. Doubt rushed in, stabbing merci-lessly, and Adam twisted the knife. "There is also the addi-tional evidence that Isobel's husband and her brother-in-law have both been involved with smuggling. And Renshaw, of course. Isn't Evelyn a friend of Isobel's?"

"She's a friend of Marianne's as well," Phineas objected. "Isobel was a girl when she married Maitland!"

"And shortly after her marriage she inherited Waterfield Abbey. That's when Robert was killed, Phineas, while smug-gling, or worse. I think it's clear his widow has moved on to greater misdeeds." He had the gall to look pitying. "I'm sure you could think of other times when Isobel's behavior was suspicious. I doubt you've told me everything."

There was the scanty lace negligee she wore the night he'd confronted her in her bedchamber, a most unwidowly garment. And her desperate fury when she denied the hand-kerchief was hers.

Phineas shut his eyes. Adam was right. He must be. The evidence was clear enough. He'd been utterly fooled by a spy cleverer than himself, and Marianne had walked right into the ultimate trap Isobel set for him. If he'd received the letter, been lured into her web of deceit, he wouldn't have been at the Bosun's Belle tonight.

His skin prickled.

When they got to Maitland House, he didn't bother to knock.

Chapter 44

"What are *you* doing here?" Jane Kirk demanded rudely as Phineas strode down the hall. She stood in his path at the foot of the stairs, glaring at him. "It's too late to be paying calls, my lord. Far too late."

"Where's Countess Westlake?" Phineas asked the insolent servant.

"Don't you mean Isobel, your whore?"

Phineas ignored the taunt. "Answer me!" he bellowed.

Jane flinched. "Lady Marianne isn't here."

Phineas glanced up the stairs, but Jane quickly stepped in front of him. "Leave this house at once!" she ordered, but he saw the panic in her eyes.

"Why, Jane? Who *is* upstairs?"

Her eyes widened as he loomed over her. He caught sight of himself in the mirror behind her. His shirt was bloody, his coat torn, and his eyes were hellish hollows of fury. He looked more like a brigand than a marquess.

"You can't see Isobel!" Jane insisted shrilly. "They're sending her away. This is *my* house now. I'm going to marry the earl, and I'll be countess, and bloody Isobel will be nothing." She gripped the banisters with ugly claws, a mad gargoyle guarding a treasure.

"Isn't he a little young?" Phineas asked. Had Jane gone mad? It appeared to be a hazard of living in this house.

"Not the child," she smirked. "Children die all the time. *Charles* is Earl of Ashdown. Or will be very soon."

Phineas's blood ran cold.

Isobel's letter wasn't a ruse.

She wasn't part of the Maitlands' plots. She was a victim, and so was her son. Relief flooded through him, then dread, as he read the gleam of madness in Jane's eyes.

"Where is the boy, Jane. Is he upstairs?" he asked, advancing on her.

She laughed. "He's gone," she said merrily. "Gone with Honoria and Charles for a holiday."

His heart skipped a beat. It meant Robin had probably been in the coach at the Bosun's Belle. Phineas shoved past her to climb the stairs; he had to find Isobel. He prayed it wasn't too late. Jane came after him and grabbed hold with surprising strength, tugging on his wounded arm. "You can't go up there!"

With a grunt of pain, he pulled free. Jane shrieked as she lost her balance and tumbled down the stairs.

Phineas didn't turn to see what had happened to her. He climbed the stairs. Adam would be coming in through the back any minute, and he could see to the servant.

The door to Isobel's room was locked. He didn't have the time or the patience for niceties. He drew his pistol and kicked the door in.

A figure by the window thrashed, and Phineas spun, aimed, and found himself menacing a pair of curtains that billowed in the breeze coming through the open window. "Isobel?" he called.

He opened the wardrobe, checked behind the bed curtains, but the room was empty.

He crossed to the open window and looked down. Had she fallen, or jumped, or been pushed? The wild hatred in Jane Kirk's eyes sprang to mind, and his heart skipped a beat.

Then he remembered how Isobel had watched him climb out of her window.

"She wouldn't," he murmured. But someone had. The bushes below were crushed and broken.

Clever girl!

She'd waited in vain for him to come in answer to her letter. Her son was in danger and she'd had no other way. His breath caught in his throat as he imagined her trying to climb down the side of the house for what was undoubtedly the first time, afraid, alone and in the dark.

Stupid woman!

He looked again, expecting to see her lying beneath the window, neck broken, but the shadows were empty. He frowned, searching the street. If she'd survived the climb, then where the hell was she?

He looked around the room for a clue. The bed was rumpled, the wardrobe empty. The soft hint of Isobel's scent floated on the air, coming from the overturned bottle of perfume on the little desk. Out of habit, he crossed to open the drawer. Locked. He broke it open. Sheets of monogrammed stationery lay in an orderly stack next to quill pens, sealing wax, and a signet with her initials.

Everything was in perfect order. But perfect order always made him suspicious. Order hid the deepest secrets. He reached into the back of the drawer.

Phineas shut his eyes as a thin panel of wood shifted at his touch. Isobel had secrets after all. The kind of secrets she kept behind a false panel in a locked drawer.

Angry, he ripped it out, reached inside, and touched—

Silk?

He pulled it out and held it up. A silk chemise, pale pink, unfurled with a sigh and warmed in his grip.

Surprising, perhaps, and most definitely titillating, but

hardly criminal. Distracted, he crammed it into his pocket and reached for another hidden garment, a gossamer nightgown, sinfully cut, as fine as the one she'd been wearing the last time he was there. He swallowed hard, imagining—

"What's that?" Jane Kirk demanded. The garment was so sheer he could see her right through it. She was leaning against the open door, her eyes burning in her pallid face. She crossed the room and snatched the nightgown out of his hand, examining it with a gasp of shock. "This is silk, and expensive! She isn't allowed to wear such things!"

"Why can't Isobel wear silk?" Phineas asked.

"Because of the *will*," Jane hissed. "Because she might get ideas if she were allowed clothing such as this. Ideas like *you*." She dropped the garment as if it burned. "It hardly matters now."

Her cold smile chilled his blood.

"Where is she?" he demanded. He would have grabbed her shoulders, shaken the information out of her, but his arm was throbbing and fresh blood dripped from his sleeve.

Jane laughed and approached him. "You don't need her. If you want the Countess of Ashdown, my lord, then take me." She rubbed a hand over her breast and grinned. "This is my room now, my bed. I'll wear the silk, even put on her perfume, if you like."

Phineas felt revulsion coil through his gut, and fought to keep it from showing on his face. He reached into his pocket and pulled out the embroidered handkerchief, holding the rose and the letter M before Jane's eyes. "What about this? Will you hold it, caress me with it?" he asked.

Her smile faded. "Where did you get that?" she whispered, not touching it.

"Who is Lady M, Jane? Is it you?"

She squinted at him as if he were daft. "M? It isn't an M."

She moved back toward the door. "You want to know? I suppose there's no danger in showing you, since it all belongs to me now."

Phineas followed her down the hall to Honoria's suite, his pistol tucked in his belt where he could reach it. Where the hell was Adam? Perhaps he'd found Marianne. His heart clenched, fearing the worst, since nothing good had happened tonight.

Jane held the candle high and gazed around the room with a satisfied smirk. "When I marry Charles, I will make Honoria give up this room. It will be mine, and so will the jewels," she said. "They will all need to be reset, since they belonged to Isobel's harlot of a mother, but I don't suppose stones hold a taint. There's an emerald as big as my eye. Honoria doesn't think I know, but I see everything that goes on in this house, I know all their secrets."

Phineas's flesh crawled at the cold pride in her eyes. Every nerve was on alert as she pointed at Honoria's portrait.

"There." Jane's bony finger cast a black shadow across her mistress's painted visage. She scuttled forward to touch the wooden paneling under the portrait, her nails scrabbling on the wood. A hidden latch clicked, and she opened a small recess filled with documents and a stack of velvet jewelry cases. She pulled out a narrow box.

"See?" she said, pointing to the monogram on the box. "It's the same W, the same rose." She gave him a mocking smile. "It's not an M, it's a W, for Waterfield. That handkerchief belonged to Isobel's mother. There were more, but Lady Honoria sent them off with letters to a certain friend of hers."

"Philip Renshaw?" Phineas guessed.

Jane's eyes narrowed. "How did you know?" She opened the box and gasped. "No!" She threw the empty case to the floor and picked up another.

Phineas leaned against the wall and stared at the embroidered W.

It was the symbol for a place, and a plot, not a person.

"They're gone!" Jane howled. "All the jewels are gone! Honoria took them with her!"

Adam appeared in the doorway. He looked haggard, his pistol drawn. "Marianne isn't here. I found the servants locked in the cellar, but they swear they don't know anything." He frowned at the sight of Jane, still searching the empty cases, moaning. "What's happening in here?" he asked.

Phineas bent to pick up the handkerchief Jane had dropped and held it out. "You are wrong about Isobel. Her note said that she and Robin were in danger. It wasn't a trick. Charles and Honoria took the boy with them earlier. He was probably in the coach at the inn."

Adam's jaw tightened. "Miss Kirk, where is my wife?" he demanded, grabbing her arm.

Jane looked up, her brow furrowed. "How would I know?" she asked rudely.

"You seem to know more than any servant should," Adam replied. "Was my wife here this evening to see Lady Isobel?" He shoved his pistol against her temple. "Answer me!"

Jane jumped away from the gun with a cry, and bumped into the heavy gilt frame of Honoria's portrait.

For a moment the huge picture shuddered, as if the painted face was coming to life. Jane gasped, and stared up as it tipped forward. "Honoria!" she screamed, but it was too late. Her mistress was upon her, and the heavy frame thwacked her on the head with a dull crunch. She crumpled under the weight of the portrait and lay still.

Phineas sank into a chair, too small and delicate for a man's frame, and probably for Honoria's as well. Adam tucked his gun into his belt and turned away from the fallen servant. "You're bleeding again, Phin," he said coolly.

He crossed and pulled the bell, and a maid appeared, her eyes widening at the sight of the legs sticking out from beneath the portrait, and at Phineas's battered appearance.

"Hot water and bandages," Adam ordered. "Laudanum as well, if you've got it."

"Where's Lady Isobel?" the girl gasped, forgetting her manners. She pointed to the portrait. "She isn't—"

"It's Miss Kirk," Phineas said. "Lady Honoria knocked her senseless."

The girl's eyes glared at the parts of Jane that stuck out from under the canvas. "She locked us in the cellar, told Nurse that Lord Charles and Lady Honoria were taking Robin away, had the poor woman in a panic, and Isobel—" She paused, eyes frantic. "If you please, my lords, where is Lady Isobel?"

Phineas's vision wavered and he leaned forward, fighting to stay conscious. He stared at the scattered jewel boxes on the floor, and the W mocked him, whispered to him. He drew a sharp breath and looked at Adam.

"It's a W, Adam, not an M. It stands for Waterfield Abbey. Honoria has been using Charlotte Fraser's handkerchiefs to indicate a place, not a person. I think it's a safe bet she and Charles are on their way to Waterfield now, with Renshaw, and Isobel is following, to save her son. Marianne is probably with her."

He watched Adam's complexion fade to ash. "Waterfield? God, Phineas, no! They're walking into a trap!" He ran a hand through his hair.

"What the hell do you mean?" Phineas demanded.

Adam stared at him, his lips tight, his eyes flat and hard.

Phineas got to his feet slowly. There was something— everything—that Adam wasn't telling him. "What trap?" he demanded.

"The kidnappers came to Aylesbury for King Louis yesterday," Adam said finally. "We let them abduct an imposter so we could follow them to the real conspirators. If Renshaw is on his way to Waterfield—" He swallowed. "If Marianne gets in the way—"

Phineas felt his stomach drop into his boots. "You didn't think to tell me this?"

Adam raised his chin. "Sorry, old man. I thought you were losing your touch. All the talk of retiring and mysterious masked women. And you've been playing games with Maitland's sister-in-law. I wasn't sure I could trust you." He hesitated, his eyes hollow. "Can I?"

Phineas didn't bother to answer. Adam's mistrust was as bitter as the pain of the bullet wound. It was going to be a long night, and a hard ride to Kent, and the pain was only going to get worse. "Any whisky or brandy available?" he asked the maid.

But she was kicking away the empty jewel boxes, reaching into the safe for a vial of laudanum. "It looks like she's taken everything, as if she wasn't coming back!" she said, and dislodged a sheaf of papers from the safe. They landed on the floor at Phineas's feet, and he picked them up, felt his head spin. He stuffed them into his pocket, gritting his teeth against the pain. He'd read them later.

"Phineas?" It sounded like Adam was speaking to him through a tunnel. "Fetch some bandages," his brother-in-law barked at the maid, snatching the laudanum out of her hand. "I'm leaving you here, Blackwood," he said as the maid left the room. "I'll go to Waterfield myself."

Phineas pulled his battered body upright and knocked the vial out of Adam's grip. "There's no way in hell I'm staying behind. Isobel asked me for help, and I damn near let you convince me she was a traitor. I am going to find her and Robin, and once this mission is over, I'm resigning. I'm going to marry Isobel, and you can find someone else to do your bidding."

"This isn't finished yet," Adam said stiffly, and Phineas turned to glare at him.

"When it is, and I've recovered from this little injury, I'm going to punch that superior expression off your face for good." Adam surprised him by grinning. "What's so damned funny?"

"You," Adam said. "I'm trying to imagine you married, and to Isobel Maitland, of all the women in England."

Clearly, Adam didn't know her, couldn't see her yet, the ravishing woman behind the dull mask she wore. But he would. "Let's go," Phineas growled. His hand was sticky with blood, and he used the lace handkerchief to wipe it off, then tossed the smuggler's token away. "This wound needs stitching. You can sew it for me on the way."

Adam winced. "My needlework is only slightly better than Marianne's."

"Marianne can't sew a straight line," Phineas said through gritted teeth.

"Nor can I. But my sailors say that ladies love a man with a scar."

In the darkest hour of the night, a cart rumbled up to the door of Maitland House. The horse's hooves were wrapped in rags to keep them silent on the cobbled streets.

"I've come to collect a lady," a hooded man told Finch at the door. The other servants hovered behind the butler, staring at the man's scarred face with wide eyes.

"This way, if you please," Sarah said, taking charge. "She's right in here, taking a nap." She led the way into the salon and pointed at the prone figure on the settee. Her face was pale, and there was a damp cloth draped over her forehead, blood blooming on it like a single red rose.

The visitor didn't ask any questions. He picked up Jane Kirk, put her into the cart, and drove away.

Chapter 45

"**I**sobel!" Honoria looked as if she were seeing a ghost when Isobel walked into the drawing room at Waterfield Abbey. Her bulbous eyes widened even further when she caught sight of Marianne. "And Countess Westlake as well. What an unexpected surprise."

"Where's Robin?" Isobel demanded, not bothering with explanations. Her stomach was tight with fear for her child, and fury.

Honoria didn't answer. Instead she crossed the room to settle herself on a settee like a queen, glaring at her visitors in stubborn silence.

Isobel raised the pistol Marianne had given her. Her grip was sweaty, her hands shaking. "Where is my son?" she asked again, her teeth clenched. For a moment her mother-in-law's eyes widened as she stared at the weapon. Then she laughed.

"Oh, do put that away, Isobel. You're too much of a mouse to shoot anyone." She slid a scornful glance over Marianne. "I did not expect *you* to honor us, Countess Westlake." She waved a hand around the dusty room. "As you can see, we've only just arrived, and we are not in a fit state to receive guests."

Isobel looked around the once-familiar room. It was faded and out of date, like an old woman in a threadbare shawl. The paintings she remembered, the porcelain figurines her mother had treasured, were gone. There was no sign of Robin or Charles.

"We're not visiting," Marianne said tartly. "We've come to fetch Lord Robin."

"Where is he?" Isobel demanded again, unable to think or say anything else. She cocked the trigger and took aim at the place Honoria's heart would be, if she'd had one.

Honoria got up and walked toward Isobel, her eyes cold. She plucked the gun out of her hand. "Calm yourself. I'm certainly not going to answer your questions while you're threatening me. Robin is fine. It was a long trip, and he's fast asleep upstairs. Charles promised to take him to the beach later if the weather is pleasant." She crossed the room and set the pistol on the tea table, well out of reach.

"To the beach?" Isobel echoed, fear blooming in her chest. "Like Mr. Hart?"

Honoria's broad face flushed scarlet. "What *are* you talking about? May I remind you that *I* am the child's guardian? You made yourself unfit to be his mother, not I. Is Blackwood with you, by the way?" She made a great show of looking past Isobel at the empty doorway. "I see he is not. A moment's pleasure—or perhaps it was a jest—and he's gone on to his next conquest." Isobel felt her skin heat, but she held her mother-in-law's eyes, refusing to feel ashamed.

"Lady Honoria, I must insist—" Marianne began sharply, but Honoria turned on her.

"This is a family concern, Countess, and no business of yours."

"If you intend to harm an innocent child, then it is most certainly my concern," Marianne said fiercely. "I understand there have been threats—"

"Threats?" Honoria warbled. "Against my beloved grandson? What tales have you been telling, Isobel?" She turned back to Marianne. "Isobel has disgraced herself, and I am within my rights to remove my grandson from her influence.

There has obviously been a misunderstanding. Isobel, did you not beg me to allow Robin to spend a few weeks by the sea?"

"Yes, but not like this," Isobel began, but Honoria waved an imperious hand. Out of long habit, Isobel fell silent at once.

"You see, Countess Westlake? I'm afraid Isobel is given to flights of fancy, just like her mother." Her eyes bored into Isobel's, the message clear. *Whore.*

Isobel cast a sidelong glance at Marianne, saw the doubt on her face. Anger rose, made her bold. Honoria had far blacker sins on her soul than she did. "I want to see Robin at once."

For a moment it appeared Honoria would refuse, but Isobel held her mother-in-law's gaze. For once Honoria looked away first, lowering her eyes to stare at the ruby ring on her hand before she shrugged and crossed to the door.

"Obviously, you won't be satisfied until you see for yourself that the boy is safe." She sighed, and looked at Marianne, an ugly parody of concern on her face. "I hate to wake him so early after such a long journey. Children need their sleep, but I suppose it can't be helped."

Marianne stepped aside to let Honoria lead the way out of the room. Her skirts left a trail on the dusty floor, and Isobel followed in her wake.

Honoria led the way upstairs, down familiar hallways. "You remember this room, don't you, Isobel?" she asked, pausing before a set of double doors. "It was your mother's chamber, I believe."

Isobel rushed past her and opened the doors.

"Robin?" The room was dark and shuttered. Marianne followed her. "Robbie?" The bed was empty, the furniture draped in Holland cloth, gray with dust. Robin wasn't here. The only creatures here were ghosts.

Isobel spun, but it was too late.

The door slammed behind them and the key scraped in the lock.

Chapter 46

Charles leapt to his feet in surprise as the door to the study burst open, knocking over the tumbler of brandy he was enjoying as a late breakfast.

Philip Renshaw, damn him, didn't even flinch. He merely glanced at Honoria as she invaded the room and tossed Charles a lace-edged handkerchief to mop the brandy off his breeches.

"Gentlemen, there's a problem."

"What's the matter, Lady Honoria?" Philip asked, his tone edged with annoyance.

"Isobel is here."

"What?" Charles gaped at his mother's mottled face in disbelief. "She's supposed to be dead in a ditch by now. How did she get here?"

Honoria leveled him with a quelling look, as if it was *his* fault. "I assume Marianne Westlake brought her, since she is here as well. Isobel had a pistol, and she demanded to see the boy."

Charles felt Philip's sharp eyes on him. "This wasn't supposed to happen," he said, trying to placate Philip.

"We cannot afford mistakes," Philip said flatly.

"What do you propose we do, Mother? King Louis will be here in a few hours!"

"Do not call the traitor 'king,' if you please," Philip said.

"The French have no king. We have an emperor." He fingered the diamond pin in his cravat, an N for Napoleon, but his eyes remained cold, boring into Charles's as he drew the same manicured finger across his throat. "Kill the women along with the child."

Charles felt nauseous. Once, they'd been friends, but Philip had ceased to be amusing. His quest for revenge now made him frightening. Knocking a man on the head and pushing him into the sea was one thing. Cutting a woman's throat, a child's?

"Impossible!" Honoria declared. "Lady Marianne is the granddaughter of a duke, the wife of an earl. We cannot just dispose of her and have it remain unnoticed."

Charles cringed inwardly as Philip turned to her. She wore that hateful, haughty expression he loathed. He half wished Philip would do him a favor and use the sharp little knife he'd been using to pare his fingernails and cut his mother's throat.

Instead, Philip smiled. "You lack imagination, Honoria." He waved his hand, and a diamond ring flashed in the sun straggling through the dirty windows. "We will simply arrange a carriage accident or some such misadventure."

"But there will be questions! What if Westlake comes here?"

"Or Blackwood," Charles muttered.

"Blackwood!" Honoria spat. "What has that fool to do with anything?"

"Marianne is his sister, Mother, and we know what he is to Isobel. What if Marianne told someone else about her journey? The woman never stops talking," Charles added imprudently, and could have bitten his tongue in two. Philip's eyes flicked over him like a serpent's tongue.

"Ah, Blackwood. Even in Paris they talk about him. I feared leaving my wife in London, but I assume Evelyn's virtue is quite safe if Isobel is his mistress."

"She is not!" Honoria said. "What would a man like Blackwood want with a dowd like her? Jane told me she saw them together, but I don't believe a word of it. I merely went along with the story as a convenient excuse to be rid of Isobel at last."

"In my experience, it is the quietest ladies who are the most daring. Are you sure Isobel knows nothing of our activities here? Something she might share with a friend . . ." Philip raised his brows and looked at Honoria. " . . . or a lover?"

Charles watched his mother's face pale. Had they underestimated Isobel? She wasn't as stupid as Mother liked to think, and she could very well have seen or heard something. She might even have told Marianne, or Evelyn or Lady Augusta. And if gossip fell on the wrong ears—Charles swallowed.

"But discovery would mean treason and disgrace and death!" Honoria gasped. "Charles? Have you said anything in front of Isobel, or Jane? You know how you get when you drink—"

"Of course not!" Charles snapped. Guilt prodded him to confess, but he clamped his jaw shut. He could hardly tell them now that he had been using Waterfield to bring in contraband, when he was supposed to be securing the place for this single purpose, could he? He'd needed the coin, and it had been a small thing to use the cove below the abbey. What harm could it have done? He mentally counted the men from here to London who knew him, could point him out as a smuggler, and his stomach churned.

"What if we were followed from the Bosun's Belle, or the innkeeper survived?" Honoria cried, wringing her hands. "The authorities could be on their way here even now. We can't go through with this. We must leave for France at once, while there's still time!" Her vast bosom shook as she gulped lungfuls of air and her eyes bulged. "Charles?"

He stared at his mother. It was the first time she had asked his advice instead of giving him orders. He had none to offer. Her terror made his own spine melt.

Philip took her arm and forced her into the nearest chair. "Sit, my lady, before you swoon. It is too late to change our plans, and you are being well paid for the risks you are taking. You will deal with the ladies, and the boy, and in a few days you will be taking coffee with the emperor in Paris."

Honoria's only reply was a whimper of fear. She was sweating and there were ugly stains on her expensive gown.

Philip's face twisted with disgust. He crossed to pour a tumbler of brandy, and pressed it into her hand. "Calm yourself, madam," he commanded.

"Yes, Mother. The French king—er, the former Duc d'Orleans—is already on his way here." He watched his mother sip the brandy, and his own mouth watered. Damn her. She'd ordered him not to drink, to keep a clear head. She set the glass down, barely touched. He licked his lips.

Philip's glare was vulpine and dangerous. "Charles is right. We must see to the final preparations. It will give us something to do. I assume your 'guests' are safely locked in somewhere?"

"Upstairs," Honoria croaked. She was trembling, a great shivering blancmange. Charles hated her.

Philip nodded. "Good. Then I suggest you leave everything else to me, so this mission is completed to the emperor's satisfaction. Now, I need a meal. Are there any servants in this place?"

Honoria nodded. "A cook and a maid, as you ordered. No others." Charles noted that she kept her head bowed humbly, cowed at last.

"Excellent. Our transport has been arranged, and there isn't much time."

Honoria got up slowly. "I will go and see to your meal."

"My lady?" Philip called, stopping her. She turned, her flaccid face grim.

Charles felt a twinge of fear as Philip crossed to his mother and put a finger under her uppermost chin, tipping her head up, forcing her to meet his eyes. Honoria's eyes widened, mesmerized by his reptilian glare. "Don't try to flee. Any more mistakes will come with a heavy price, which you will personally pay. Is that clear?" He drew his finger gently under her flesh, from one ear to the other, his meaning plain.

Honoria leapt back, clasping a hand to her throat. Charles swallowed reflexively.

"I am in charge now," Philip whispered.

Charles felt sick as his mother's eyes jerked toward his, pleading, but he had no pity for her. He grabbed the glass of brandy she'd left and swallowed it.

Chapter 47

I sobel tugged at the window shutters, ignoring the cloud of dust that filled Charlotte's bedchamber as she wrestled with the warped wood, but the salt-rusted hinges stuck fast.

Marianne gave up trying to force the lock on the door and turned. "Surely you aren't going to try to climb out this window, Isobel. We're in a tower!"

"I will if I have to," Isobel said, her teeth gritted in determination.

"But that's—" Marianne began, but Isobel stopped her with a fierce look.

"I *will* find my son!" Her fingernail tore, bled, but she hardly noticed. "He's still alive. He must be. I'd know if he were already—" She couldn't say it. "Even Charles couldn't do such a thing in broad daylight."

"Oh, Isobel," Marianne said, her eyes sympathetic.

Isobel turned back to the shutters. How long had it been since they were opened? It was fifteen years since her mother was last here.

Marianne added her strength and the ancient latches relented at last, swinging open with a squeal of protest.

"No!"

There *was* no window, only a narrow medieval slit in the abbey's thick stone wall, cross-shaped, designed to keep marauders out and nuns in. The morning sun emblazoned the crucifix on the stone floor, and the wind slipped through the crack, whistling a mocking tune as it stirred the dust.

Isobel put her eye to the narrow gap and peered out. Beyond the cliff the sea sparkled, and she could smell the fragrance of roses in the garden. On the right, the park stretched wide and empty toward the unseen road, more than a mile away. She clenched her fists against the whitewashed stone, but it remained solid and unmerciful, even in the face of a mother's distress.

"There has to be another way out," she muttered as she turned to prowl the edges of the room. Old abbeys always had secret doors and hidden passageways, didn't they? Or was that just in novels? She pressed her cheek to the wall and peered behind the armoire. Nothing.

"We'll have to wait," Marianne said.

"For what?"

"For Adam. And Phineas as well, of course."

"Marianne, they don't even know we're here!"

Marianne smiled. "Between the pair of them, I have every confidence that they'll find us, especially if we give them a little help." She crossed to the wardrobe and opened it.

Her reflection moved like a ghost in the dusty mirrored doors. "There must be something in here we could use to speed up our rescue. It's nearly time for luncheon, and I'm hungry. Oh, Isobel, look at these!"

She pulled the dust covers off the garments still hanging in the wardrobe and ran her hand over the shimmering gowns.

Charlotte's gowns.

Isobel felt her chest tighten.

Marianne pulled one out and hung it over the door, standing back to admire it with feminine delight. Isobel brushed her knuckles over the pale blue silk. Silver lace shimmered on the sleeves, and the bodice was a low-cut scandal.

It reminded her of the pink gown she'd worn to Marianne's masquerade, of Blackwood's arms around her, of his hands on her skin, his mouth— She turned away from the dress, and the wave of longing.

"Petticoats!" Marianne gushed. "Just what we need." She stood on tiptoe to reach the bundle on the top shelf. "My husband will be shocked, and that will bring him running all the faster." She giggled wickedly as she tugged at the ribbons that held the muslin bag closed.

They cascaded over her, a tidal wave of lace and silk and satin, splashing across the floor, flooding the room.

A painted wooden box fell off the shelf as well, and broke open with a crash, disgorging a cargo of yellowed letters. The musical works began to play a rusty, hesitant rendition of an old minuet.

Marianne chose a violet petticoat trimmed with pink roses. She carried it over and tied the ribbons to the hinges of the shutter before pushing the frothy lace out through the cross-shaped opening. They watched it flutter in the wind, shocking against the gray stone of the abbey, an absurd flag announcing that the countesses of Ashdown and Westlake were in residence at Waterfield Abbey.

Isobel glanced at the spilled letters and dismissed them. Most were addressed to her uncle in a feminine hand that slanted over thick vellum. They wouldn't help her escape this room or find Robin. She searched the cobwebbed ceiling above her. Thick wooden beams supported solid stone. The floor had no loose boards or trapdoors to aid her. The room felt like a crypt.

Marianne scooped the letters off the stone floor. "Look, here's one addressed to you, Isobel."

"My uncle never wrote to me," Isobel said impatiently. "Perhaps we could pry the hinges off the door," she mused, though they were thick slabs of ancient iron.

"We haven't any tools," Marianne murmured, and opened the letter herself. "There's no way out, so we'll have to content ourselves to wait until Adam finds a way in. At least we have something to read."   •

"I can't just *wait*," Isobel said, and crossed to check the wardrobe again, searching the drawers for hairpins or needles, or something *useful* that could knock holes in solid stone walls.

But there was nothing but dust, and scraps of lace, and a brush and mirror.

She hefted the heavy silver-backed brush. It might make a suitable weapon if Honoria returned. She bit her lip. If Honoria hadn't been afraid of a pistol, a hairbrush wasn't likely to stop her.

Panic rose. She had to get to Robin. She glanced at Marianne, sitting on the floor, oblivious to the dust, reading the letters. Marianne had a child too. Was she so confident that her husband would rescue her? Of course she was. *Westlake loved her.*

She shut her eyes and thought of Blackwood.

He'd proposed, hadn't he? Surely that meant he had some regard for her. If her note had reached him, would he have come to her rescue? She looked out the window slit, past the fluttering petticoat and across the empty park. Would he come for her now? Hope pushed at the dark edges of despair.

"Come and sit down, Isobel," Marianne coaxed. "Honoria will have to send someone to feed us. We can escape then." She held out a letter. "You really should read this."

Isobel took the letter, keeping one eye on the door, her ears pricked for the sound of footsteps or the rattle of keys, the hairbrush at the ready by her side.

Her eyes widened at what she read. Protestations of love and longing leapt at her from the page amid tearstains and the brown spots of age and mildew. She sank to her knees, finished the first letter and picked up another, then another.

Dear brother, I beg you to find a way to send my child to me . . . How I miss my dearest Isobel . . . Tell me my daughter is well . . . Does Isobel remember me at all? She does not write to me, though I have written to her every day . . . You tell me you have been unable to get my letters to her, surely there is a way . . . Now she is old enough, send her to me in Florence . . . How did Fraser find out I had sent a man to fetch Isobel? Now she is married, and it is too late . . .

Isobel was hardly aware she was crying until Marianne pressed a handkerchief into her hand.

Her mother hadn't abandoned her. She had wanted her to come to her, tried to enlist her uncle's help. Had Lord Denby been too afraid, or too uncaring, to do anything but save her letters and leave them here in hopes that she would find them someday?

Isobel shut her eyes, imagining all the letters her father must have intercepted and destroyed, letting her believe that her mother had forgotten her.

Then he'd married her off to Robert Maitland, forever putting her out of Charlotte's reach, and Honoria had likely taken over the task of destroying her mother's letters. It explained why her mother-in-law insisted on reading her mail before she did.

She looked at the cross the sun now slanted over her mother's bed. This room had been as much of a prison for Charlotte as it was for her now. How many nights had she paced the floor, trapped and unloved, while she slept in the nursery?

Isobel shut her eyes. Her mother had loved her after all, spent years trying to get her back. She looked at the blue satin gown, and her eyes filled with tears. In the mist, she saw her mother wearing it, looking at her child with love in her eyes. Charlotte had come back to her child at last. Isobel the invisible stepped into the light.

She folded the last letter and got to her feet. It was getting late. Now she had to get her own son back.

Chapter 48

"There are only four guards by my count," Phineas said, scanning the abbey's gray stone facade. He handed the telescope to Adam and eased his position on the straw that filled the loft of the small stable, trying to ignore the pain in his shoulder. "It should be easy enough to get inside and find Isobel and Marianne."

Adam squinted at the grounds and the other outbuildings before handing the glass back. "There's no way to know what's happening inside, and we don't even know if they're here. We'll wait for my men to arrive," he said stubbornly.

Phineas wiped the sweat from his forehead and squinted at his brother-in-law. Adam wasn't sweating, damn him. His wounded shoulder nagged, insisting he needed a decent meal and sleep.

But he couldn't drink or eat or sleep until Isobel was safe. "Don't you think we'd better get them out before the trouble starts?" he asked. "I assume that's what you're expecting?"

Adam's jaw tensed. "Marianne is probably at home, where she belongs, and Isobel is there with her."

"That would be a sensible assumption if we weren't talking about Marianne," Phineas said sarcastically. "I know my sister as well as you do. If the Maitlands took Robin, then this is exactly where Isobel will be, and Marianne will be right by her side. You said yourself my sister was nothing if not loyal."

Fear crossed Adam's face briefly, but he rubbed it away. "I can't afford to jeopardize this mission now, Phineas. Not even for Marianne." He turned away, scanned the building again. "If I charge in and she's not there, then we'll have lost months of work."

"Is it better to lose your wife?" Phineas asked. "My sister? Isobel and her son?"

Adam snapped the scope shut. "Prove to me they're here, Blackwood! This time, I'm not willing to trust a hunch."

Phineas felt his gut tighten. His hunches had always been enough for Adam before. He'd counted on them. "Then I'll go in, find proof, and see what's happening."

"You're in no condition to go anywhere. Can I even trust your judgment? You've changed in the past weeks, and you're bedding a woman who may yet turn out to be a traitor. Would you arrest her if you had to? Shoot her?"

"I will do what's necessary," Phineas said through clenched teeth.

"Then you will wait until we have enough men to do this properly," Adam said, making it an order.

Phineas lifted the telescope and scanned the face of the building again. There were no windows on the upper floors, just cross-shaped slits in the stone, a reminder that this had once been a convent where women lived a life of peace and contemplation until Henry VIII's men tore their world apart. He swallowed. Was history about to repeat itself? His grip tightened on the telescope until the leather bindings creaked under the pressure.

A flash of purple against the gray stone caught his eye, and he turned the glass toward it and stared.

"You wanted proof?" He passed the telescope to Adam, and waited while his brother-in-law looked at the petticoat fluttering from the narrow window.

Adam pursed his lips and shut the glass with a snap. "I

hope that's not the undergarment my wife is supposed to be wearing."

"Perhaps it belongs to Isobel," Phineas replied.

"Hardly. Isn't hers hanging out of your pocket?"

Phineas glanced at the trailing scrap of pink silk that peeped from the pocket of his coat. The idea of Isobel *not* wearing it was just as arousing as the thought of her in it. He tucked the silken garment away.

"So now we have proof. How do we get in?" Phineas asked. "Assuming you don't want to go to the front door and inquire if your wife is inside and properly dressed, of course."

Adam stared at the fluttering petticoat and stalled. "Old abbeys like Waterfield always have a warren of secret passages and priest holes," he mused. "There are probably tunnels leading to the beach, or out to the stables. I've studied a number of tales about it. For instance, the hall at Carbrooke Abbey collapsed during a country dance a few years ago, and the owner discovered a secret room below his house, filled with forbidden books and religious treasures hidden there over two centuries ago."

"So how do we find the tunnels?" Phineas asked, nudging him back to the present.

Adam blinked. "We don't. That could take days. Nor can we knock on the front door. There are probably French agents inside, ready to shoot anyone suspicious. In a few hours, possibly less, our forces will arrive with the French king's decoy. Then we'll have enough men to mount a rescue, but I can't risk it now."

"Your wife is in there," Phineas growled. With Isobel.

"If Marianne is healthy enough to wave indecent garments out of a window, I assume they've locked her up unharmed." He met Phineas's hard stare with one of his own. "Maitland wouldn't dare harm my wife."

"And Isobel and her son? Isobel's maid said they took the

child from his bed in the middle of the night. What about him? Charles cannot take the title while Robin Maitland lives."

Adam looked away. "An unfortunate circumstance, but he may be dead already. We have no way of knowing, and there are more pressing matters at hand."

"What if it was Jamie?" Phineas demanded.

"It isn't Jamie. My son is at home where he belongs. For his sake, I will get his mother out safely when the time is right, without any pointless heroics that could get either of us killed."

"Glad to hear you love my sister," Phineas growled, wondering if Adam was made of wood and metal like one of his blasted inventions.

"More than life," Westlake murmured. "Even so, I will not charge foolishly into danger and risk my life or hers. My son needs a father, and siblings. When the time comes, I will do whatever I have to do to get Marianne back, and Isobel and the boy if it's possible. Until then I expect you to obey my orders, Blackwood, and stop thinking with your—"

"Captain Lord Westlake?"

Phineas pulled his pistol and spun on the man behind them. The sailor put his hands up and glanced at Adam.

"Ah, Mr. Gibbs. It's about time you arrived." Adam rose, brushing the straw from his coat.

"Sorry for the delay, sir. We hit some wind off Margate."

"Looks like you have all the help you need out here," Phineas said. "I'm going inside."

Adam's lips thinned. "No."

"I wasn't asking for your permission, Westlake." He got to his feet and clenched his fist as Adam opened his mouth to argue. "I am going inside, but I'll fight you first if I have to."

Adam looked at his bandaged shoulder and bloody shirt

with cold appraisal. "Do you really think you can best me—or Maitland—in your condition?"

Phineas silently raised his eyebrows, letting Adam read the determination in his eyes. For England, and for the woman he loved, he would face any danger.

Adam relented. "Just be careful, Phin. Keep them safe if there's trouble."

"You can count on it, Westlake, same as always."

He left the stable and skirted the wall, heading for the little courtyard that lay between the kitchen and the main building. Long shadows filled the cloisters around an overgrown garden, and he scanned the open area for signs of trouble.

A sudden scream made him spin, but the danger was inches from his face and it was too late to shoot his attacker. With a grunt of pain, he dove for the gravel.

A gull swooped past his head, missing him by inches. Phineas watched the bird climb toward the tower, its raucous cries and clumsy wing beats loud in the little courtyard. Another gull dropped from the sky to join the first, followed by another and another, until the small garden was filled with the noise and flap of a dozen large seabirds. Bread was flying from one of the high window slits, and the birds fought a pitched battle for every scrap.

A memory twitched in Phineas's mind. Jamie and Robin pelting the ducks with bread crumbs in Hyde Park. He looked up. High above him a beam of dying sun glinted on red curls in the narrow window as more bread dropped. He grinned.

Robin Maitland was still alive.

Chapter 49

Marianne read each letter as Isobel dropped it. "Oh, Isobel! Is this why you won't marry my brother?" she asked, finishing the last one with tears in her eyes.

Isobel's eyes widened. "Blackwood told you?" she asked. "About *everything*?"

Delight kindled in Marianne's eyes, and she swiped at her own tears, smearing dust across her cheek. "Everything? What 'everything'? He told me you refused his proposal. I explained that you were unhappily married and had no wish to repeat the experience. That's why you said no, isn't it? Is there more to it?"

"I—" Isobel hesitated, besieged by the pert questions.

"Is it Phineas's reputation?" Marianne demanded.

Isobel looked at her in surprise. "Oh no, it's not that at all—"

"I've never seen him so besotted, and I've waited years for it to happen," Marianne gushed. "I can see he's in love, and you're the perfect match for him."

He loved her?

Isobel wanted to believe it. Butterflies dizzily circled in her chest.

"Do you love him?"

Yes, she loved him. "Of course not!" she said. She looked

at her fingers, rubbed at the dirt. "I have responsibilities, and duties, and people that need me to be—"

Marianne gave an unladylike snort. "You're a terrible liar, Isobel. I've seen the way you look at him. *Of course* you love him." She pointed. "You see—that blush gives your secret away, even under all that dust." She picked up a petticoat and began to clean her own face. "We really must make ourselves more presentable before they arrive."

Isobel shook her head. "It makes no difference, Marianne."

Marianne blinked at her over a single clean patch of skin on her cheek. "What doesn't, dirt or love?"

"Love." Isobel breathed the word. "I cannot marry anyone, no matter how much I love him. It's impossible."

"Why?" Marianne demanded.

Isobel hesitated. She had never admitted to anyone that her life was not her own, but Marianne's eyes remained fixed on her, waiting. "We have time, so you might as well tell me."

If nothing else, the truth would shock Marianne into silence, so she could have time to think, to plan a way to free herself and her son.

"Robert's will forbids me to remarry, or even form friendships without Honoria's permission. If I do, I will lose Robin. I *have* lost Robin, because I dared to—" She glanced at the blue gown again. She was just like Charlotte after all. She clenched her fists, determined she would not spend the rest of her life trying to get her child back.

She had refused Phineas. Robin was all she had left. He needed her. Without her, Charles would—

She swallowed the panic that rose to choke her. There had to be a way.

"Oh, Isobel. I had no idea," Marianne said, interrupting her thoughts. There wasn't the slightest hint of shock in her face, only sympathy. "Does Phineas know?"

Isobel shut her eyes. "It's too late. I refused his proposal."

If—when—she escaped this room and found Robin, she'd leave London, even England if she had to, to keep him safe from Charles and Honoria. She'd probably never see Blackwood again, but hope hung by a thread.

Marianne put a hand on her knee. "Of course it isn't too late! Look at these letters—your mother had a second chance, a chance to love and be loved, and she took it. She did the right thing, Isobel."

A shock of betrayal shot through Isobel, and she looked at Marianne in surprise. "But my son—" she began.

Marianne held up her hand. "Hear me out. Charlotte's only mistake was leaving without you, hoping you would join her later. She should have taken you with her. Your father kept you out of revenge, even married you off to Robert Maitland for hatred of Charlotte. No wonder you have such a poor opinion of marriage! It won't be like that with Phineas, Isobel. Adam will arrive and find Robin, and you will tell Phineas you love him, and marry him, and you will both be happy at last."

Isobel shook her head. "It's still not that simple. Robert took my son away from me. Honoria and Charles are his legal guardians. What court would overturn a father's will?"

Marianne laughed. "Oh, that's a trifling thing! We Archers are one of England's most powerful families. We have titles, money, and we're friends of the king. Charles Maitland is just a gentleman with a courtesy title. We'll convince him to give up his wardship of Robin."

"You mean to bribe him?" Isobel asked, her eyes widening.

Marianne shrugged. "Given that he's imprisoned the Countess of Westlake, and the Earl of Westlake is rather unforgiving about such things, I doubt money will enter into it, and Phineas tends to be a hard man when crossed as well. He's protective of the ones he loves, and I think he loves you desperately."

Was it really possible to have every happiness? Blackwood loved her, and for the first time in her life, hope filled her heart.

Marianne glanced at the window. "I can't imagine what's taking Adam so long. It's nearly dark." She picked up the hairbrush and mirror. "Oh well, at least we'll have time to comb our hair and tidy our faces before our brave knights come and rescue us."

Terror replaced hope in a heartbeat. Night offered cover for sinister deeds like smuggling and murder. If Robin lived, she had to reach him now. She couldn't wait for a rescue that might not come.

Isobel watched Marianne calmly tie up her hair and pinch her cheeks like a debutante preparing for a ball. Marianne had no idea, she thought, what Charles was capable of.

She snatched the mirror out of Marianne's hand. She couldn't wait for Blackwood, and she could not, would not, allow Charles to harm anyone else. She crossed to the door while it was still light enough to see. Shutting her eyes, she smashed the mirror against the wall, ignoring her friend's gasp. Marianne probably thought she was as mad as the rest of the Maitlands. She didn't have time to explain.

Picking up a shard of glass, Isobel began to scrape away the crumbling plaster that held the first hinge in place.

Chapter 50

It was so quiet inside the abbey that Phineas could hear the beating of his heart as he moved along the dark stone corridor. The pain in his shoulder dropped away as his senses sharpened, came alert, watching, listening for signs of trouble.

Ahead, light spilled from a wide archway, and he followed it.

The large room had likely once served the convent as a refectory, but it was empty. There were few clues to divulge the purpose the room was meant to serve now.

No carpets softened the stone floors, but the walls were draped in heavy red velvet. There was a dais at one end of the room, with a long oak table upon it. Pitch torches hung on the walls, reflecting red and gold on the polished surface.

Three carved chairs had been set behind the table, as ornate as ancient thrones, but they faced a plain wooden stool that crouched miserably in the middle of the floor.

In the corner farthest from the door, a bulky shape loomed tall and ghostly under a canvas drape emblazoned with an N surrounded by a crown of laurels.

Napoleon's crest.

His fingers froze at the ringing echo of boot heels on the stone floor of the corridor.

He had only seconds to slide behind the velvet drapes. He

clung to the wall, the cold seeping into his bones. He drew his pistol, cocked it, and waited. His eyes burned in the darkness.

"We'll take our places as soon as he is brought in." Phineas recognized Charles Maitland's voice. "I'm sure you will agree, my lord, that since the matter is a fait accompli, there is no point in drawing it out. Given the circumstances, I think it best we leave this place as soon as possible. You have a ship waiting, I assume?" he asked nervously.

"Of course. In the cove," Philip Renshaw replied. "That's why I chose Waterfield, for the easy escape it offers. But you already know that, don't you, since you use the cove for smuggling?"

"I—" Charles faltered, but didn't bother to deny Philip's charge.

Renshaw's tone grew darker, more dangerous. "That's why I had to change my plans and come back to England through London, risking discovery. I've had this place watched, you fool. On any given night a dozen men wait for your shipments to land in that cove. It's only when there's a full moon that they stay away. Like tonight. We won't have company, will we?"

Charles cleared his throat, the nervous sound loud in the stone room, and Phineas peered carefully around the edge of the curtain. Charles was pale in the torchlight, his eyes hollow. He shook his head soundlessly in response to the question.

"That is just one of a number of mistakes you've made," Renshaw went on. "There was also the shooting at the inn, instead of a quick and discreet departure. And now we have others to dispose of, people who may have already repeated what they know."

"But it will all be over tonight, and we'll be in France by morning, in Paris by dinner," Charles said, trying for a light tone, though his voice shook.

Phineas listened to the slow cadence of Philip's footsteps as he roamed the room.

"This room, at least, is right." Phineas watched him caress the carved back of one of the chairs, mere inches from his hiding place. It had been nearly a year since he'd last seen Philip. His face was harder, older than he remembered. Too old for a wife as young and pretty as Evelyn. The torchlight cast harsh shadows under the pouched eyes, the thin lips and heavy jowls sculpted by bitterness and hatred. Still, Renshaw exuded power and determination as he faced Charles.

"For your sake, I'm glad that you got something right, Charles. *L'empereur* is not a patient man. He detests mistakes, and the fools who make them. More so when those fools are English."

"But you're as English as I am!" Charles protested.

Philip sniffed. "Napoleon has made me Comte d'Elenoire. It was my grandfather's title. I have renounced my English heritage."

"But I will still be Earl of Ashdown, won't I?" Charles asked.

Philip laughed and clapped him on the shoulder. "Of course, my lord earl, but if everything goes well from this moment, you and I will go to Paris, present our prize to Napoleon, and you'll be rewarded far beyond a mere earldom."

Philip waited until Charles relaxed and smiled before he leaned forward again. "But there must be no more mistakes. We must be the only ones to leave this place alive. Do you understand?" The unspoken threat echoed off the hammer beam roof.

"What about my mother?" Charles asked tightly, but Philip mounted the dais again and ignored the question.

"Shall we go over everything?"

"Of course," Charles mumbled.

Philip paused behind the first chair. "As Earl of Ashdown,

you will take your place here," he said. "I will sit in the middle, and Lady Honoria will take the last chair."

He pointed to the stool at Charles's feet. "The pretender Louis will sit there."

He walked to the draped structure, eyes alight, like a man going eagerly to his lover. He touched the crest on the wrapping, his fingers reverent, his eyes loving as he gazed at the golden N for a moment before turning back to Charles.

"I trust you read the account of the trial of Louis XVI?"

"Yes," Charles replied. "Will we follow it?"

"To the letter. If the Duc d'Orleans wishes to pretend to be King of France, we will try him as his brother was tried. We will serve as his tribunal of judges, so history cannot accuse us of not following protocol."

He pulled hard on the canvas and it fell to the floor with a growl. Torchlight gleamed on a deadly blade set in polished wood. Phineas stared at the guillotine, Philip's intended revenge now obvious.

Renshaw ran his hand over the polished wood, tested the grinning blade with his thumb. "I," he said softly, licking the blood from his skin, "will be his executioner, for the glory of France, and in payment for his insult."

Charles coughed. "We're going to kill him here? In this very room?"

Philip turned, brows raised. "Of course! If we transport him back to France alive, there is always a danger that he could be rescued by royalists sympathetic to his cause." He picked up a small box, holding it up to Charles. "So much more efficient, don't you think, to merely take his head? There can be no doubt as to his identity, and no escape."

Charles was silent for a long moment. "And my mother?" he asked again.

"She would hardly fit in at the French court. You know that yourself."

Philip walked quickly toward the door, leaving no room for reply. "Come, Lord Ashdown, there's brandy in the library. Let's drink to our success."

Charles did not protest his mother's fate. He just stumbled after Philip in silence.

Phineas waited until their footsteps faded. He rubbed a hand over the gritty stubble on his jaw. Time was short. The French king could arrive at any moment. Duty demanded he find Adam and advise him of Renshaw's sinister plan.

But honor was another matter. The woman he loved was a prisoner, one of the "mistakes" Philip intended to eliminate if there was no one to stop him.

He had a decision to make, and whatever choice he made, someone was going to die.

Chapter 51

Honoria climbed the dark stone staircase with the knife clutched in her hand. She felt sick, and the bone handle of Philip's weapon was slick with sweat.

How had it come to this?

She'd expected Charles to put Philip in his place, but he'd stood silently by as Renshaw demanded that *she* explain how things had gone so terribly wrong, as if it were her fault.

Isobel.

Her name dripped like venom in Honoria's mind. If not for Isobel, damn her, and Charles's incompetence, she wouldn't be in this position. She shivered. Philip Renshaw's eyes had been cold, filled with disgust. She knew then that things had taken a deadly turn.

She felt nausea rise again, and bone deep terror made her stumble on the steep stairs. She put a hand on the wall and pulled it away, shocked at the coldness of the stones.

Philip had rudely insisted that *she* clean up the disastrous mess that Isobel, Robin, and Marianne represented.

She knew by the look in his eyes, and the dagger in his hand, that there was nothing to do but obey if she wished to make it to Paris alive. When she got there, she intended to tell the emperor every detail of this disgusting insult, and then she would watch Philip tremble.

Surely Napoleon Bonaparte of all people would understand. She had tried to raise her fortunes. That wasn't so terrible, was it?

Charles was as ambitious as she was, with far greater sins on his black soul, but *he* was still downstairs, drinking with Philip.

She was an innocent, really. She had merely *suggested* to Charles that if Robert was to have an accident, then Charles might advance the family and himself faster. Robert had grown lazy and complacent with a wife, a fortune, and a son to content him.

Honoria hadn't expected Charles to shoot his own brother. Poison would have been so much more discreet.

She'd been the one to avert disaster after that mistake. She had forged a new will after Robert's death, one that kept Isobel's fortune in Maitland hands. If she'd been allowed to claim her money and all those rich estates, then where would that have left her?

Penniless.

She turned at the landing, glancing up at a stone cross carved into the wall. Henry VIII's men had managed to only partially destroy the icon.

She was like that cross, she thought, battered but unbroken. She had endured a life of near-penury after her husband squandered the entire Maitland fortune at the tables. Gambling was an unfortunate proclivity Charles seemed to have inherited, and like his father, luck scorned him with every toss of the dice.

It had been essential—and easy—to take control of Isobel's wealth. All it took was holding Robin hostage to ensure the widow remained obedient, quiet and unsuspecting.

Honoria had seen another chance to rise when Philip Renshaw asked for her help, needing a partner in his plan to make the French king pay for snubbing him, someone with an estate on the seacoast. She had always known Philip was a dangerous man, but not like this. He'd once been a gentle-man, and merely ambitious, like herself.

How had it come to this? she asked herself again.

Isobel was smarter than they'd thought.

She still could not believe the Marquess of Blackwood, a man who could have any beauty in England, would want Isobel. She had turned Isobel into a dowd that no one would want, especially a magnificent specimen like Blackwood.

She sniffed in disbelief, and the candle she carried, her only bulwark against the terrifying darkness that ruled the upper halls of the old abbey, flickered, and pitched grotesque shadows on the rough stone walls.

She tried to imagine the vivacious Charlotte Fraser here, in a former convent. Charlotte had been as bold as Isobel was timid, as vibrantly beautiful as her daughter was dull. Honoria's mouth tightened. She saw Charlotte's lovely face every time she looked at Isobel.

How she'd hated Charlotte! The beauty had dominated London society for years, casting every other lady into the shadows. She had been delighted when the woman fled, her glitter tarnished forever by the scandal.

It was a simple matter for her to convince Lord Fraser that his wife's affair would rise like a vengeful specter to torment him anew if he put his tainted daughter on the marriage mart. He'd turned her over to the Maitlands gratefully, along with his fortune.

Honoria was breathless. Was it yet another penance for the nuns, climbing endless stairs to the dormitories under the eaves? The uppermost cells had been converted to a nursery, where Isobel had once played, and Robin now awaited his fate.

Honoria leaned against the wall to catch her breath. She went over the instructions Philip had insisted she follow to the letter.

The leather flask in her pocket was filled with laudanum. Philip had the cook lace it with sweet fruit juice so the boy would drink it without protest.

"Do not give the boy the laudanum too soon," he had told her. "Take him from the nursery and lead him to his mother. Outside her door, make him drink. See that he finishes all of it. Isobel will be pleased to see her child and will imagine he is sleepy because it is night."

"Will it kill him?" she had asked.

He'd smiled. A hard, dangerous smile that made her blood run cold in her veins. "What do you think?" he asked.

She shut her eyes now, steps from the nursery door. She could hear the boy inside, singing some childish song Isobel had taught him about counting ducks.

She glanced over her shoulder. The looming shadows were stalking her. She felt unseen eyes watching, ghostly hands reaching for her, brushing her skin, making her shiver. A moan escaped her lips, startling in the silence, echoing through the abbey.

"Charlotte?" she whispered. The stones clutched the name to their breast, passed it down the hall like a summons. Honoria hurried to open the nursery door with shaking fingers.

The singing stopped. Her grandchild—no, he was Charlotte's spawn—turned, the copper flame of his Fraser hair gleaming in the candlelight. He didn't speak, just stared at her with Charlotte's eyes, as if he knew. Her flesh crawled.

"It's time to go. Your mother is here." The false croak sounded too eager, but the boy's face lit.

"Mama?" he asked.

She touched the flask in her pocket, ensuring it was still there, and held out her hand.

"Come along."

The boy hesitated before touching her, then slipped his soft hand into hers. She was glad of his company in the dark corridor, a small, innocent shield against the ghosts that closed in, the accusing eyes that followed her.

Did Charlotte know what she was about to do? She shut her eyes, feeling the woman behind her, but not daring to look.

Sweat slithered down her cheek, and she swiped at it.

Once she had drugged the boy and turned him over to his mother, she would dismiss Marianne, tell her she was not welcome to stay, that her coach was waiting to take her back to London. Isobel would be too busy with Robin to object to her friend's departure. Marianne would be in a hurry to get back to London, to tell her husband everything.

She would never arrive, of course. Her coach was rigged for death. Honoria pictured the axle splintering as the coach took the road that ran along the top of the cliffs above the sea. How Marianne would scream as the coach careened over the edge. Honoria smirked. The woman talked too much anyway.

Sending Marianne to her death would be easy compared to what Philip had insisted she do next. She gasped now, and Robin glanced up at her. She could not meet his eyes.

Once the child was drugged and asleep, Philip wanted her to cut Isobel's throat.

"I cannot," she whimpered again, just as she had in the drawing room, and felt the boy staring at her, another ghost in this accursed place.

Philip laughed at her protest. He'd hooked his arm around her neck, pulling her back against his body. She recalled the flash of the knife as he raised it, the reflection of her own terrified eyes in the polished blade.

"Like this," he whispered in her ear, and drew the blade across her throat, a caress rather than a killing blow. She would have fainted, but he kept her upright, shoved the knife into her hand and pointed to the door.

"Don't fail, madam. Our guest will be arriving within

the hour, and nothing must distract us from our task here tonight."

Charles had said nothing, done nothing, to stop Philip or defend her honor. She was left with no choice but to pick up a candle and go, her heart pounding against her bosom, making her gown, her very skin, too tight to let her draw breath.

Now she felt the dagger between her breasts, resting there, waiting, and she tightened her grip on the boy's hand.

Chapter 52

"Isobel, someone's coming," Marianne whispered. She reached for Isobel's hand, and they listened to the footsteps in the hallway.

Isobel held her breath as the latch shook, holding her breath. The sounds on the other side of the door were more terrifying in the dark.

The door swung open at last, and the growl of the hinges announced their unseen visitors. Isobel tightened her grip on the slippery shard of glass in her hand as the sudden glare of lantern light invaded the room, leaving her blind.

She couldn't see who entered. She hoped it was Phineas, but feared it was Charles. Panic leapt like lightning along her limbs as Marianne flew past her with a cry and launched herself at a figure in the doorway.

She watched the Earl of Westlake enfold his wife in a powerful embrace. Over Marianne's shoulder, Isobel watched Adam De Courcey's eyes close, saw his face melt with relief.

The glass dropped from her bloodied fingers, and she looked at the figure in the doorway behind Westlake. A big man in rough clothing nodded to her, his face grim, but there was no one else there.

Bitter disappointment threatened to crush her. She clasped her hands together, holding herself upright for dignity and sanity's sake, standing against the flood of emotions.

"Where's Phineas?" Marianne voiced the question for her.

Adam De Courcey met Isobel's gaze briefly.

"I rather expected I'd find him here with you."

Isobel didn't move. Couldn't.

Marianne gasped. "Here? Oh, no, Adam, we've been alone all day, no one has come—"

"Later," Adam murmured, squeezing his wife's shoulder gently to silence her. "There isn't time to discuss it now. I have men waiting downstairs to see you and Isobel safely aboard the *Lady Marianne*."

He held out a hand to Isobel, but she ignored it. "I'm not leaving without my son." She met the pity in Marianne's eyes without flinching, as if she didn't care, hadn't really expected him to come for her.

Phineas who?

Tears stung behind her eyes, but she refused to let them fall. She retreated behind the mask of calm and wished they'd stop staring at her with such insipid pity. She raised her chin and started toward the door. Westlake caught her arm, and his man stepped in front of her, an extension of the stone walls.

"I must insist that you come with us, Countess," Westlake said crisply. "It isn't safe to remain here."

Marianne added her grip to Adam's. "Please, Isobel. Come with us. You need food and rest. Adam's men will find Phineas and bring Robbie to the ship when—" Her husband squeezed her again and she stopped and looked up at him. Isobel watched the hope ebb from Marianne's eyes, saw it replaced by sorrow as she read Westlake's face.

Isobel pulled free and went to retrieve the hairbrush. "My son is not dead, my lord," she said, facing Westlake with all the maternal ferocity she could muster. "I'd know if he was. He's upstairs in the old nursery, or in one of the other bedrooms, waiting for me."

"Countess, time is of the essence. I cannot allow you—" Adam began, but Marianne stepped forward.

"Isobel, let Mr. Gibbs do it. Let him bring Robin to you," she said, and Isobel read the same grim certainty in Marianne's eyes that clouded her husband's, though it was couched with the soft edge of compassion. The Westlakes were trying to save her from heartache and grief, she realized. But they couldn't. Only one man could do that, and he wasn't here. Desperation struck her, as wild and brutal as a hurricane. Had she lost both her child and the man she loved?

"Blackwood!" The whisper burst from her.

"I don't know where he is, Isobel," Adam De Courcey said carefully, as if she were mad, like Honoria and Jane. She wondered if she was. She ran a trembling hand over her face. This was not the time to give in to emotions she'd spent a lifetime hiding. When this was over, she'd cry over Blackwood, but now there was Robin to think of. She met Adam De Courcey's eyes, held his stare, letting him see that she was indeed sane and he would not stop her from finding her child.

"Adam," Marianne pleaded, trying to break the stalemate. He glanced at his wife, then turned to the sailor.

"Mr. Gibbs, Countess Isobel will tell you where the nursery is. You will go and fetch the Earl of Ashdown and bring him to her aboard the *Lady Marianne*."

"I'll show him," Isobel said.

The big man looked downright tender. "You need only tell me where to look and I'll fetch your lad, my lady, but I doubt Lady Marianne will leave willingly without ye, and it's safest if you both go with Captain Lord Westlake."

Marianne beamed at the sailor. "There, Isobel. Robin couldn't be in safer hands. Gibbs is Adam's best man, and I'd trust no one else if it were Jamie. Save for Phineas, of course." Her smile faltered a little.

Isobel gave the sailor directions, her voice wooden. She

offered him the hairbrush, but he grinned and pointed to the savage knife in his belt. Bess, he called her, and said she never failed him.

Isobel watched him go, her heart a painful knot in her breast. She listened until his soft footfalls were swallowed by the darkness.

Adam drew a pistol and cocked it. "Time to leave."

Isobel and Marianne followed him down the corridor, away from Charlotte's empty room. In the darkness behind them, Isobel heard the broken music box chirp a few rusty notes of a decades-old minuet before it fell silent.

Chapter 53

Phineas stood in the darkness outside the nursery door, listening to Robin Maitland sing. He debated the wisdom of breaking the lock with a hard kick, afraid he'd frighten the boy. He raised his hand to knock softly, bending to whisper through the keyhole.

An anguished moan echoed off the stone walls, and his fist froze above the wooden panel.

The hair on his neck rose.

He didn't believe in ghosts, but the sound of shuffling feet and heavy breathing was real enough, and so were the shadows dancing along the walls, inching closer.

He pressed himself into an alcove that once most likely contained a *prie dieu*, but now held only shadows and cobwebs. He held his breath and waited.

He'd gone looking for Adam before coming up here. He could not let his brother-in-law walk into disaster, and he had to get Isobel and Marianne and the boy out of the abbey before the trial began. He shook off the image of Isobel seated on the little stool as Renshaw pronounced her guilty and led her to the guillotine.

There'd been no sign of Adam or Gibbs in the stable. So he did the only thing he could. He pulled Isobel's nightgown out of his pocket and hung it on a nail by the door, a message for Adam that he had gone after the woman it belonged to.

Phineas had climbed the steps of the tower in the dark, since he didn't have a candle, heading toward the room where he'd seen Robin. He tripped a number of times, scraping and bruising his elbows and shins. He ran face first into a wall where the steps turned sharply, splitting his lip and grazing his cheek. His shoulder ached like the devil himself was gnawing on it. For Isobel, he told himself as he tripped again and pitched shoulder first into the unsympathetic stone wall, he would endure anything.

Now the shuffling shadow came closer, and Phineas hugged the dark and waited.

Behind the nursery door, Robin was still singing, unaware of the dread beast moving toward him. Phineas squinted at the candlelight as the creature came into sight at last.

Honoria.

Dragon indeed. She stood and stared at the door for a long moment, her rouged and powdered face a sinister mask in the light of the candle. Phineas watched as she tucked a knife into her bodice and turned the key in the lock.

When she led the boy away, he followed.

Honoria approached the door of Charlotte's room. It was time to take out the flask, make the child drink. He'd obey. He was afraid of her.

She felt the unseen eyes of spirits watching her, knowing what she was about to do. Dread made her heart pound.

Honoria stumbled to a halt. The door to Charlotte's chamber stood open.

"Isobel?" Her voice was a quivering warble. The whistle of the wind was the only reply.

Or was it?

She let go of the child and walked to the threshold. Something swooped past the window on rustling wings, and Honoria started. "Isobel?" This time it came out as a croak.

She spun, and the candlelight fell on someone standing behind her. A woman hovered above the ground, a gleam of pale satin.

"Charlotte!" Honoria cried. The woman's shade haunted this place, and she had come to wreak vengeance on her. Honoria set the candle down and fished for the knife in her bodice. She held it before her like a talisman, but her fingers shook, too sweaty to hold it. It tumbled from her grasp, and she heard it clatter on the fathomless black floor.

She backed away, defenseless. She did not deserve this fate. It was Lord Fraser who had wronged Isobel. Soft hands caught at her ankles, and the scent of rose perfume filled the room.

She was here.

Charlotte Fraser had come for her child at last.

Moaning, Honoria kicked free of the clinging hands and sent something skittering across the floor. She heard it crash, and the satin-clad figure shifted and shimmered as the first soft notes of a familiar minuet began to play.

Honoria remembered the tune. She had watched Charlotte circle the dance floor as the orchestra played it over and over, just for her.

In her addled mind, Charlotte appeared before her now, dancing. Then the music stopped as suddenly as it had begun. The wind whined a warning as Charlotte reached for her.

Honoria screamed. She had to get away from this evil place. It was full of death and sorrow and ghosts. She bolted down the stairs, heading for the front door. She pulled at the ancient iron latch, and felt cold night air on her overheated skin.

In a thoughtless panic, she raced down the steps. There was a coach at the bottom, and she leapt in. "Get me away from this place!" she screeched as the horses were whipped to a fast start. A lady's cashmere shawl lay draped across the seat, and Honoria's fingers dug into the soft fabric, picking it up. She frowned. It wasn't hers.

Too late, she realized that she was in Marianne De Courcey's crippled coach.

At Honoria's scream, Phineas lunged forward to grab Robin. He held him out of the way as Honoria ran down the hallway.

What the hell had Honoria seen? Phineas stared at the open door, his chest tightening.

The fragile candlelight beckoned, and Phineas pushed the door wider, holding Robin's slight weight against his chest. The child clung to him, his eyes huge, too frightened to cry. Phineas knew exactly how he felt. Dread crawled up his spine.

What if Isobel was here, dead? His heart began to pound.

He pressed the boy's face against his shoulder, not wanting him to see.

The room was empty. Relief flooded through him as he set Robin on his feet.

Outside the narrow window the petticoat still fluttered in the night wind. The floor was strewn with a wild froth of similar garments.

A satin gown hung from the door of the wardrobe, undulating in the wind that whistled through the window slit. The low, lace-trimmed bodice reminded him of the gown Isobel had worn to Marianne's masquerade, and a wave of longing swept over him.

"Where's my mother?" Robin asked, gazing around the room with wide eyes. Phineas bent to pick up the knife, still warm from Honoria's body. A snarling wolf with ruby eyes was carved into the handle. Napoleon's crest was etched into the sharp blade. Phineas gripped it in his fist, hating Renshaw and the Maitlands.

He turned to Robin, and saw Isobel's eyes. At least her son was safe. He'd done that much right. The boy loved Isobel as much as he did. It made them partners.

He looked at Robin soberly. "Let's go and find her."

Chapter 54

"**S**top where you are." The command rang out as they crossed the front hall. To Isobel's surprise, Adam turned and fired a pistol at Philip Renshaw. Marianne shrieked.

Adam's ball hit the wooden door frame near Philip's head in a spray of splinters. There was a second explosion, and Westlake dropped to the floor with a grunt.

"Adam!" Marianne dove for her husband.

The smell of powder filled the air, and the smoke rose in the candlelight in hazy coils. Isobel rushed toward her friend, but Renshaw grabbed her wrist, spun her hard against his body and dragged her away. His arm circled her chest, and the rude jab of a pistol chilled the flesh of her throat, ending her struggles at once.

Adam had a second pistol in his hand, but his face was a mask of pain and the weapon shook in his grip. Marianne was mopping at the blood pouring from his thigh.

"My next shot will go through Isobel's head. Put your pistol down," Philip ordered.

"Renshaw," Adam grunted, but he dropped the gun. He pushed his wife's hands away. "Marianne, stop. Go through the salon and out the French doors. Find one of my men," he instructed.

"I'm not leaving you!" Marianne insisted, her tears silver tracks on her flushed cheeks.

"She's right, Westlake. She is staying right where she is," Renshaw said. "I suggest you use your petticoat as a bandage, madam." He shrugged. He spoke calmly, as if they were chatting over tea in Evelyn's salon. "Not that it will make a difference in the end, but it will slow the bleeding. May I assume you found Lady Honoria upstairs and dispatched her? If so, I owe you a debt of gratitude. You have saved me from having to do it."

Isobel gasped. *Honoria, dead?* The pistol burrowed deeper into the skin under her ear. "Keep still, Isobel."

"We have not seen Lady Honoria all day," Marianne said tartly as she shimmied out of her petticoat. "But you can be sure I'll have plenty to say to her when we do."

"Marianne, for once in your life be quiet," Adam ordered through gritted teeth as she pressed on the wound.

Philip gripped Isobel's jaw and twisted her face so he could look into her eyes, his gaze sharp as a dagger, assessing her in a slow, terrifying glance.

"Well, well. Dowdy little Isobel. Who would have imagined you could cause so much trouble? Is it true that Blackwood's been bedding you? That's a terrible mistake, my dear. He'll only break your heart." Isobel tried to twist out of his grip, but he held her easily and laughed. "Ah, I've touched a nerve. He's already abandoned you, then."

"Mama!" At the sound of Robin's cry, Philip spun and pointed the pistol at her child. Isobel's heart skipped a beat, then stopped dead in her chest.

"Robin!" she screamed, and the sound echoed to the vaulted roof, but Phineas was there, holding her son, protecting him, keeping him from racing down the steps.

"I haven't abandoned anyone, Renshaw," Phineas drawled. "Unfortunately, Evelyn can hardly say the same." The barb struck home, and Philip's grip tightened painfully, but Isobel's heart started beating again.

Blackwood.

He'd come for her, for Robin.

She drank in the sight of him. He was filthy, bloody, and unshaven.

He took her breath away.

"Blackwood, get the boy out of here!" Westlake said, his voice thick with pain.

Marianne looked at her brother sharply. "Phin, Lord Renshaw shot Adam! What the devil is going on? Does this have something to do with Evelyn? I've heard gossip, but surely it isn't true!"

"Don't talk, Marianne," Phineas said tiredly.

Renshaw gripped Isobel by the hair, tugging her head back. "Ah, yes! The infamous Marquess of Blackwood. Look your last at him, Isobel. It will be a pleasure to be the one to put an end to you, old friend. Someone's husband must have a bounty on your head by now. When history remembers this moment, men will glorify *me* as they piss on your grave. I wonder how many women will truly mourn you?"

"I can't say for certain," Phineas said lightly, the rake once again, but Isobel saw the cold intent behind his smirk. "Shall we have a drink and discuss it?"

"I haven't the time, old friend, and you'll be dead in a few minutes," Philip replied. "I'll hear your last confession, though. Have you made my wife your whore?" he demanded. Isobel felt him tense in anticipation of the answer.

Blackwood and Evelyn?

Isobel searched his face, but his expression gave nothing away.

"I never confess, Philip. It would be dishonorable indeed to besmirch a lady's honor, don't you think, to abandon her and let idle gossips tear her to shreds for my misdeed? My secrets will go with me to the grave."

Philip laughed harshly and brought the pistol back to

Isobel's throat, stroking her skin with it, a sensuous, deadly caress. Goose bumps crept over her flesh. "Whether you've had Evelyn or not hardly matters now. She's unworthy of my notice. I've got your current mistress. Come down or I'll shoot her."

Isobel kept her eyes on Phineas, telling him wordlessly that she would be all right now that he was there. She let love shine naked, unmasked, in her eyes.

He began to descend the stairs, moving at an insouciant pace that suggested Philip's threat mattered little to him, but Isobel noted the tightness of his jaw. He held Robin's hand, keeping her son behind him, protecting him. Her heart swelled, and there wasn't the slightest doubt in her mind that he'd come to rescue her.

She wished he'd hurry.

"Drop the pistol," Philip said, his voice a growl in her ear. She winced at the pressure of Renshaw's weapon on her temple.

Phineas slid his gun across the floor, and it stopped next to Philip's foot.

"Excellent. Now send the boy over here."

"He stays with me," Phineas said calmly.

"I'll shoot him," Philip warned, and Isobel's breath caught in her throat.

Phineas smiled. "You only have one bullet, old friend. You can't shoot everyone."

Renshaw swore savagely and his arm tightened around Isobel's throat, cutting off her air. She gasped, tried to wriggle free, but his grip was too tight. She stared at Phineas as black spots danced before her eyes.

"There's more than one way to kill," Philip snarled. She tugged at his wrist with shaking fingers but his hold was unbreakable. She felt her knees weakening.

"Isobel!" The scream came from Marianne and buzzed in

her ears, but it was too late. The room wavered as her empty lungs clamored for air.

"That's enough!" Phineas roared, crossing the room, but Philip swung the pistol on him and Phineas stopped.

It *was* enough.

For an instant Renshaw's arm loosened. Isobel dragged air into her starving lungs.

"Let her go, Renshaw. I'll take her place. Would you kill a mother in front of her child?" he demanded.

Lord Philip, damn him, seemed to be considering it. Isobel dug her nails into his arm. He swatted her fingers away with the point of the gun.

"I think, my lord, that I will keep your lady," he said, his tone soft and deadly. "Let's go, Isobel." He began to drag her away.

The door from the kitchen hallway banged against the wall like a cannon shot. Philip jumped, and the gun jabbed painfully into her flesh.

Mr. Gibbs stood in the doorway holding Charles by the scruff of the neck. Charles was rumpled and bruised, his eyes wild.

"Renshaw! Do something," he whimpered.

"Is this him, sir?" the sailor asked Adam, shaking Charles like a wet kitten. "You sent me to find the Earl of Ashdown, and this chap says he's him. I thought he might be a little advanced in years to be the young lady's son, but I brought him anyway." Charles let out a pitiful mewl.

"Isobel," she heard Phineas whisper. "Move."

She let her body go limp in Philip's grip, throwing her captor off balance for an instant. She saw Blackwood's arm rise, saw the glint of the knife in his hand, watched it fly, end over end toward her. She shut her eyes, trusting him, refusing to be afraid.

Hot blood sprayed her face and Philip screamed. When

she opened her eyes, the knife stood straight out of his arm, inches from her face. She stared into the ruby eyes of a snarling wolf.

Renshaw's arm went slack and she tumbled to the floor, but Philip buried his fist in her hair, dragging her away. "Damn you, Blackwood, now I'll kill her in front of you, make you watch." He pressed his pistol to her temple, cocked it, but his hand shook, the knife still embedded in his arm.

"Isobel!" Phineas's shout seemed to come from far away. Robin was screaming too, and Marianne, but Isobel's knee managed to hit Phineas's pistol on the floor. She fought Renshaw's grip, struggling to reach it. Her outstretched fingers touched the cold metal, gripped it.

She twisted her body and fired.

The flash lit in Philip's eyes like the reflection of hell.

A moment later she was in Phineas's arms and he was prying the gun out of her hand, tossing it away. The roar of the shot echoed in her head and she couldn't hear him, couldn't feel his arms on her. She stared up at him, saw the fear in his eyes, the love. She let herself go limp, let him hold her, breathed in the male scent of his body, curled her fingers against his chest to feel his heart beating. She was safe at last. "I love you," she whispered, wondering if he could hear her. But Robin crowded in and she hugged him too, caressing his soft red curls.

"Blackwood, if Isobel isn't Lady M, explain where she learned to shoot like that," Adam demanded, his voice husky with pain, his eyes filled with grudging admiration.

"From me," Marianne said proudly. "I taught her. And who exactly is Lady M?"

Adam Westlake groaned.

Chapter 55

Isobel marveled that the sea glittered placidly in the moonlight as if nothing at all had happened that day.

Phineas stood close behind her on the deck of the *Lady Marianne,* his hands on her waist, protecting her now from nothing more sinister than the cold sea wind, but she leaned into him, not wanting to be anywhere else.

Four strong men lifted Adam aboard, and Marianne hovered anxiously, issuing orders like a bosun.

Mr. Gibbs had the true Earl of Ashdown at last, fast asleep on his shoulder, and Charles had been sent to London in the custody of His Majesty's Guards, who arrived after the shooting stopped and everyone was safe.

"Evening, Captain," the real bosun greeted Adam as the sailors set him carefully on the deck. His leg was wrapped in frilly strips of Marianne's petticoat. The wind blew her thin muslin skirt against her legs, and her husband scowled as his sailors gaped at the fetching sight.

"Fetch my wife a cloak, Mr. Jessop, and make your report, if you please," Adam growled at the bosun.

"Surely that can wait," Marianne fussed. "Get the surgeon, Mr. Jessop. His lordship is hurt."

"So is Blackwood, but I'll hear the report first if you please, wife. I am still master aboard this ship, despite her name."

Isobel glanced at Phineas in concern, but he shrugged off

the bullet wound in his shoulder with a devil-may-care smirk that quickly became a wince.

Marianne folded her arms over her chest and frowned. "You have two minutes, Adam."

The bosun spoke quickly. "Lord Renshaw's ship has sailed, my lord. We considered giving chase, but our orders were to stand to and wait for you. A boat came from the shore, loaded up, and they weighed anchor with full sail."

Phineas looked at Adam. "Despite being wounded, Renshaw got away. No one saw him go. I assume he used one of those tunnels you mentioned."

Poor Evelyn, Isobel thought. She would be forever branded as a traitor's wife.

"Oh, and sir?" The bosun actually blushed. "The lads found this in the stable near the house. They brought it just in case it belonged to—" He cast a sweet-eyed look at Marianne.

Isobel gasped. He was holding a silk nightgown, pink with red ribbons. With a cry, she grabbed the lacy garment.

"That's mine! However did it—" She glanced at the grinning sailors and crumpled it behind her back, feeling her face heat. She looked at Phineas. He gave her his most charming rogue's grin, and her heart tripped over itself and tumbled.

"I believe I'll let you handle that question, Blackwood," Adam said, and turned back to the bosun. "If that's all, Jessop, fetch the surgeon and make ready to sail."

"For Westlake, sir?"

Adam sighed. "For London first. There's business to see to before we go home."

Phineas lay on the bunk with Isobel beside him. The surgeon had dosed him with rum, stitched and bandaged his wounds, and he was feeling drunk and sleepy. Every inch of his body ached, but Isobel was in his arms, and she was kissing him, sliding her delicious body against his.

"You came for me," she murmured yet again.

"Isobel, stop kissing me," he begged. "It hurts."

"Oh." She pulled back, but he dragged her close again. Having her more than a few inches away was as unbearable as the pain.

"Well, perhaps kiss me here," he said, indicating his chin, one of the few unbattered parts of his anatomy. She leaned over him, her hair brushing his chest, her mouth gentle.

"And here?" she asked, letting her lips trail over his jaw, down his neck.

"Mmm," he growled. Her breasts pressed deliciously against his side.

"And here?" She nipped at his flat nipple.

Desire stirred, rose, became urgent.

"Isobel," he murmured, reaching for her. "I love you."

" I know," she said. "You came for me, for Robin."

"We need to talk."

"We've never been very good at talking." She slid her hand over every uninjured place she could find, making him wild. She was distracting him again, driving every rational thought out of his head.

He caught her roving fingers, kissed them. "Why is it that every time I want to discuss something serious with you, I forget what I want to say the instant I touch you?"

She smiled wickedly. "I don't have that problem."

He groaned. "There goes my reputation as a lover."

She gave him a slow, seductive vixen's grin that raised his lust and tied his tongue in a knot. He pulled her on top of him on the impossibly narrow bunk.

"Once we're married, I'm going to buy the biggest, softest bed in England, and I'm never going to let you out of it," he said as she settled onto the part of him that ached most, and all for her. Her eyes closed in rapture. She moved carefully, gingerly, trying to be gentle.

"What did you say?" she murmured, obviously beyond caring.

"You're going to marry me." He thrust into her, hard, showing her he didn't want her to be careful. He wanted all of her.

"Yes!" she screamed, and as he tumbled over the edge of his own forceful climax, he wondered if he was that good, or if she had accepted his proposal at last.

Isobel slipped back into the cabin and shut the door. It was still dark, and the ship rocked gently on the waves. Phineas stirred and opened his eyes. "I went to check on Robin," she explained. "He's fast asleep in Jamie's cabin."

"Come back to bed," he said, lifting the covers, and she curled in beside him. "Yasmina," he sighed.

She stiffened in his arms. "I'm just plain Isobel."

He tightened his hold on her. "You've never been plain anything. You're the most incredible woman I've ever met."

"I'm Robin's mother, Phineas. He needs me."

She lowered her eyes so he wouldn't see her fear. He stroked her cheek. "Robin's a fine lad. I hope he'll be my son too. I'd like to give him brothers and sisters."

She felt something wonderful bloom in her chest. "You truly want to marry me?" she asked. "Not Lady Amelia?"

"She wouldn't suit me. Too plain."

He looked at her with so much love it made her throat ache, and she felt beautiful, and loved, for the first time in her life. She wrapped her arms around him, but he held her off.

"Wait, sweetheart. I have something for you," he said.

"Can't it wait?" she asked.

"You need to see it now." He pointed at his ruined coat, hanging on a hook by the door. She crossed to fetch it. The garment was stiff with dried blood, and she wrinkled her nose as she handed it to him. He fished out a packet of papers and held them out to her.

"What's this? A special license to have the bosun marry us?" she asked.

"That can wait until tomorrow. Read it." His gray eyes were sober, his emotions shuttered.

She unfolded the two legal documents and scanned them. Her limbs grew heavy with shock, then hot with fury. She spread the pages out on the table, comparing them. She was muttering by the time she was halfway through, yelling by the time she'd finished.

Jessop knocked anxiously at the door, and she told him to go away. She tried to pace, but the tiny cabin wouldn't allow it.

"Isobel?" Phineas said gently.

Livid with rage, she turned to look at him, stabbing the crumpled pages with her finger.

"There are two wills here, Phineas! Honoria forged Robert's will!"

"I know," he said.

"Robert never wanted her to have custody of Robin. She took it. She took my dowry, my estates, *my freedom*!"

"What do you want to do, Isobel? Do you want that freedom now?"

She looked at his face, so carefully expressionless under the cuts and bruises, waiting for her answer. He'd let her go if that's what she wanted. He loved her that much. Her happiness mattered more to him than his own.

Her eyes filled with tears, and she dashed them away with the back of her hand.

"I want to be happy, Phineas, I want to marry you, have more children, grow old with you. I love you. What do you think of that?"

He held out his arms to her, relief clear in his eyes. "I think it's the best revenge in the world."

Chapter 56

Phineas stood in front of Carrington's desk with his hands behind his back like a schoolboy. Actually, it was *his* desk, and *his* study, but he wasn't going to quibble about details today. Carrington was glaring at him, waving a letter.

"Do you know what this is, Blackwood?" he demanded.

"No, Your Grace," Phineas said.

"It's a note from Welford. He wanted me to be the first to know that Lady Amelia is betrothed to Colonel Lord Hollister. The wedding will take place at St. George's church on the twenty-second of next month. What do you say to that?"

"I wish them both well," Phineas answered. Everyone should be as happy as he was. "I have news of my own, sir—"

But Carrington wasn't through. "If that's not bad enough, a young gentleman came to see me yesterday about Miranda. A fellow named Fiddler or Fisher or something."

"Fielding, Your Grace," Phineas supplied. Good for Gilbert. He might have made a good soldier after all, if he had the courage to face Carrington.

"His name hardly matters, since he hasn't got a title or so much as a farthing attached to it."

"Does he love Miranda?" Phineas asked.

Carrington frowned. "Yes, damn it! And Miranda says she loves him and will have no other. I shall have to permit the match."

Phineas hid a smile. He'd give Miranda an estate as a wedding present, and a whole stable full of pretty horses.

"And just this morning, Marianne announced she's expecting again," Carrington ranted on. "Can this day get any worse?"

Phineas cleared his throat. "I'm afraid so, Your Grace."

The old man looked at him in disbelief, his white brows crumpling together over his sharp eyes, his face reddening. He crushed Welford's letter in his fist.

"What have you done now, Blackwood? I swear I will leave everything that isn't entailed to young Jamie this time."

"I've taken a wife, Your Grace."

"Whose wife?" Carrington demanded.

"My own," Phineas said. Repeatedly. In lace, in silk, and stark naked. In a real bed. In fact, it had taken him three days to drag himself out of his marriage bed and come to see his grandfather. He grinned at the old man's stunned expression and crossed to open the door. Isobel entered and curtsied to the duke.

His wife looked particularly pretty today, wearing pink from head to toe, with a saucy feather in her ridiculously fashionable hat, pretty red curls framing her glowing cheeks.

"Hello," Carrington said, his eyes widening at her beauty. "Have we met, my dear?"

"May I present my wife, the Marchioness of Blackwood and the Countess of Ashdown, Lady Isobel Archer?" Phineas said proudly, and Isobel held out her gloved hand.

"Ashdown?" Carrington murmured, frowning again. "Ashdown? As in Maitland? Isn't Charles Maitland under arrest for treason?"

"He is, Your Grace," Isobel said lightly.

"And Lady Honoria Maitland was recently killed in a carriage accident, wasn't she?"

Isobel sobered. "Correct again, sir."

"And wasn't your mother . . ."

Isobel raised her chin and met the old man's eyes. "Lady Charlotte Fraser."

Phineas tensed, ready to grab Isobel's hand and get her out of harm's way if Carrington exploded.

"Charlotte Fraser was the prettiest woman in England," Carrington said at last, his eyes softening with memory. "I was a little in love with her myself. I can see where you get your extraordinary beauty, my dear."

He looked at his grandson, and for the first time in his life, Phineas read approval in his grandfather's eyes.

Phineas touched a hand to his pocket, checking for the letter of resignation he'd written to Adam. Westlake House was their next stop. He bowed to Carrington, who was staring besottedly at Isobel.

The rake was gone. So was Yasmina. There was no more need for subterfuge or masks. Phineas and Isobel had found home at last. It wasn't an estate by the sea or a fashionable town house in London. They lived in each other, and in those they loved, and that was a grander home than the finest palace on earth.

Next month, don't miss these exciting new love stories only from Avon Books

Midnight's Wild Passion   by Anna Campbell

Blinded by vengeance for the man who destroyed his sister, the Marquess of Ranelaw plans to repay his foe in kind by seducing the man's daughter. But when her companion, Miss Antonia Smith, steps in to thwart his plans, Antonia finds herself fighting off his relentless charm. And she's always had a weakness for rakes...

Ascension   by Sable Grace

When Kyana, half Vampyre, half Lychen, is entrusted by the Order of Ancients to find a key that will seal Hell forever and save the mortals she despises, she has no choice but to accept. But when she's assigned an escort, Ryker, a demigod who stirred her heart long ago, she knows that giving into temptation could mean the undoing of them both.

A Tale of Two Lovers   by Maya Rodale

Lord Simon Roxbury has a choice: wed or be penniless. Surely finding a suitable miss should be simple enough? But then gossip columnist Lady Julianna threatens his reputation and a public battle ensues, leaving both in tatters. To rescue her good name and his fortune, they unite in a marriage of convenience. Will it be too late to stop tongues wagging or will it be a love match after all?

When Tempting a Rogue   by Kathryn Smith

Gentleman club proprietress Vienne La Rieux has her eye on a prize that would make her England's richest woman when a former lover, the charming Lord Kane, disrupts her plans. Neither is prepared for the passion still between them, but with an enemy lurking in the shadows, any attempt to mix business with pleasure could have tragic consequences.

At Avon Books, we know your passion for romance—once you finish one of our novels, you find yourself wanting more.

May we tempt you with . . .

- **Excerpts** from our upcoming releases.

- Entertaining **extras**, including authors' personal photo albums and book lists.

- Behind-the-scenes **scoop** on your favorite characters and series.

- **Sweepstakes** for the chance to win free books, romantic getaways, and other fun prizes.

- Writing **tips** from our authors and editors.

- **Blog** with our authors and find out why they love to write romance.

- **Exclusive content** that's not contained within the pages of our novels.

Join us at
www.avonbooks.com

AVON   An Imprint of HarperCollins Publishers

3 1901 04967 1771